"You don't need to risk falling off the bed."

"Right," Colt said, then scooted himself slightly more toward the center.

"Thanks for staying," she said softly, her lids growing heavy.

"You're welcome, Jenna," he said.

How she did like the way her name sounded in his soft, deep voice.

Lightning crashed with a simultaneous boom of thunder, and the next thing Jenna knew, her arms were wrapped around Colt's neck, her legs entwined with his, and though it was dark, she was close enough to see his eyes as wide as saucers.

"Sorry!" she said.

But she wasn't letting go.

She didn't want to let go.

She *wanted* to be held by someone she trusted.

She *wanted* to kiss a man who made her feel safe.

God, she wanted *him*.

PRAISE FOR A.J. PINE

ONLY A COWBOY WILL DO

ALSO BY A.J. PINE

Meadow Valley

Cowboy to the Rescue (novella)

My One and Only Cowboy

Make Mine a Cowboy

Crossroads Ranch

Second Chance Cowboy

Saved by the Cowboy (novella)

Tough Luck Cowboy

Hard Loving Cowboy

ONLY A COWBOY
WILL DO

A Meadow Valley Novel

A.J. PINE

FOREVER

NEW YORK   BOSTON

Copyright © 2020 by A.J. Pine
Sealed with a Kiss copyright © 2017 by Melinda Curtis

Cover design by Daniela Medina
Cover photography © Rob Lang
Cover copyright © 2020 by Hachette Book Group, Inc.

Forever
Hachette Book Group
1290 Avenue of the Americas, New York, NY 10104
read-forever.com
twitter.com/readforeverpub

First Edition: March 2021

Forever is an imprint of Grand Central Publishing. The Forever name and logo are
trademarks of Hachette Book Group, Inc.

The publisher is not responsible for websites (or their content) that are not owned by the
publisher.

The Hachette Speakers Bureau provides a wide range of authors for speaking events. To find
out more, go to www.hachettespeakersbureau.com or call (866) 376-6591.

ISBNs: 978-1-5387-4986-9 (mass market), 978-1-5387-4985-2 (ebook)

Printed in the United States of America

CW

10 9 8 7 6 5 4 3 2 1

For anyone who needs a reminder that there is more than one way to HEA.

ACKNOWLEDGMENTS

Thank you, first and foremost, to my early readers who have been asking about Jenna's happily-ever-after since *Second Chance Cowboy*. I knew the second I "met" her in that very first book that she was going to capture my heart, and I'm so happy she captured yours (and Colt's) too! Thank you for being patient as you waited for her story. I'm so thrilled to finally share it with you!

Thank you, always, to my agent, Emily Sylvan Kim, for your constant support. I'm so grateful to have you in my corner, and look forward to many more books (with HEAs, of course) with you!

To my editor, Madeleine Colavita, thank you for putting up with my mixed-up timelines, my incessant need to sneak Marvel references into a story whenever I can, my apparent (who knew?) love of names that start with C, and for your magical way of always knowing what a story needs to make it shine.

Chanel, Jen, and Lea—I write this not knowing what the state of things will be when this book releases, only that it's thanks to you (and CLOY) that my mental health has survived this year so far. Love you all. I can't wait until we can pile in a hotel bed and eat popcorn again—but maybe not in my bed?

S and C, there is no one I'd rather be with every single day than you two—quarantine or no. I love you 3,000 x infinity.

ONLY A COWBOY WILL DO

CHAPTER ONE

Jenna Owens *loved* a good party. She could turn the small-est of celebrations—like her great-nephew, Owen, pitching a no-hitter—into the biggest deal. Ice cream (*always*), cake, a water balloon fight, you name it. If she could think of an excuse to get festive, she'd do so in a heartbeat. The only person she tended to forget to celebrate was herself.

Thanks to her family, that so was not the case now as she stood over a three-tiered double chocolate cake alight with *forty-one* candles—yes, she counted—the *one* being for good luck. Next to the blaze of firelight sat a tub of strawberry ice cream—her favorite—just waiting to be scooped on top of its first slice.

She held her blond hair back from her face as the rest of the roomful of people sang the final "Happy birthday to youuuuuu!"

She was surrounded by everyone she loved, but what made the occasion even more special was that it was planned by her three nephews—Jack, Luke, and Walker. Although she'd raised them through their teen years, they were grown men now, taking care of *her* on her special day, and her heart swelled to three times its size at the constant reminder of the amazing men they'd turned out to be.

A loud *squawk* came from the floor below, and Jenna laughed. She almost forgot her partner in crime—Lucy, her sometimes psychic chicken.

"Looks like someone thinks it's time to blow out the candles," Jack Everett—the eldest of her three nephews—said. "Does it count as psychic ability if she's warning you that the cake might catch fire when we can *all* see that the cake is about to catch fire?"

Jenna waved him off. "Can y'all just give me a second to think of the perfect wish? This is the big four-oh, after all," she chided. "Plus everybody knows Lucy's only psychic about matters of the heart. She's special, but she does have her limitations."

Lucy squawked again.

"All right, all right," Jenna said with mock irritation.

She glanced around the room that was filled with everyone she loved. Her heart felt full to bursting. She had everything she wanted, yet...

No. It was too silly to put all the magic of a wish into *that*. It was selfish. It was— Dammit, it was her fortieth birthday, and she was going to wish for whatever the hell she wanted.

Okay, birthday wish goddess or whoever you are...would a fairy-tale ending of my own be too much to ask?

The only problem was that Jenna didn't know what that meant for her. She didn't know how her story was supposed to go, only that since her early twenties it had veered onto a course she'd never expected to take, and now she was forty and still clueless. Her farm and selling her eggs were successful enough. Her family, albeit unconventional, was one she loved. Her nephews, though, were grown and had started their own families. After the better part of two decades, they could take care of themselves now. What was the rest of her life if it wasn't taking care of *them*?

But fairy-tale endings came in all shapes and sizes. She just wasn't sure which one would fit *her*. So she'd let the wish take care of it.

And with that, she sucked in a deep breath and saved the B&B from being engulfed in flames.

Happy birthday to me.

She pulled a candle from the cake and skimmed it, even though it was chocolate-covered, across the top of the ice cream tub until she had equal parts chocolate and strawberry. Then she grinned and licked the candle clean.

"What'd you wish for?" Jack's wife, Ava, asked, then immediately covered her mouth. "Wait! Don't answer that or it won't come true."

Jenna raised her brows. "Oh, I know the rules of wishin'," she said. "My lips are sealed."

Lucy flapped her wings, getting everyone's attention, and once again squawked.

Jenna rolled her eyes. "Not sure what's up with her tonight. She doesn't usually get her feathers ruffled about something so common as a birthday." Then she shrugged. "Oh well. Who wants cake?"

After one slice too many—not that she was apologizing for overdoing it on her birthday—Luke popped open another bottle of the Crossroads Ranch and Vineyard's most recent vintage.

"Wait, wait, wait," his fiancée, Lily, said before he poured his aunt another much-anticipated glass. "It's time for presents!"

Before Jenna could protest that the party was enough, Olivia began piling wrapped gifts onto the long wooden table in the bed-and-breakfast's common room. It wasn't a huge pile. After all, the party was intimate enough. But still, didn't they get it? She was blown away by the party as it was. Jenna wasn't used to so much attention, and she certainly didn't need it. All she needed was to be surrounded by the people she loved, and she had that in spades. Now there were gifts?

"Open mine first!" Owen said.

He was twelve now. How was that possible? It would mean she was...Jenna laughed.

She was forty. *Forty.* Yet she still didn't feel a day over twenty-one.

Forty was a grown-up. Forty meant she had life all figured out.

Forty was a big, fat lie. Happy? Sure. She was happy. Wizened with all the answers? Not even close.

But she had presents. And that wasn't so bad.

"Okay, nephew of mine," she said to Owen. "Yours first."

He handed her the small, square box covered in her favorite recycled wrapping paper from the gift shop in town. She could tell he'd probably wrapped it himself, and that made her heart swell all that much more.

"What could it be?" she asked, carefully peeling off the tape in the hope of maybe using the paper again.

She held the plain white box in her hand and gave it a little shake.

"Hey," Owen said. "That's cheating. Mom and Dad don't let me shake my gifts, which means you don't get to shake yours."

She laughed, and there it was again, that heart swell. Jack didn't even know Owen existed before his son turned nine, and now here the boy was, calling him *Dad* like he'd been doing it since day one.

Fairy-tale endings abounded in the small town of Oak Bluff, California, which meant her wish wasn't so off base. Was it?

She lifted the top flap of the box and pulled out a mildly scuffed baseball, one that bore a signature on the cleanest patch of white.

OWEN EVERETT.

"From my last no-hitter," Owen said, his cheeks turning pink. "Coach let me keep the game ball and...I mean, I know you're just being Aunt Jenna when you say I'm gonna be in the major leagues someday, but in case you're right, maybe this will be worth something, and you can sell it for buckets of money."

Ava, Owen's mom, swiped at a tear under her eye. She and Jack sure had raised one hell of a kid.

Jenna stood and wrapped her great-nephew into the biggest hug, marveling at how he was almost as tall as she was.

"Not even if it was worth a million dollars—or more," she said. "No way in the world I'd sell something as important as this. Consider it priceless."

Owen let out a nervous laugh when she released him from the hug. "Okay, Aunt Jenna," he said, the pink in his cheeks blooming to a full crimson. "Anyway. Happy birthday."

She opened the rest of the gifts with a full heart and belly but with just enough room for another glass of wine. When she had a stack of perfectly preserved wrapping paper, her youngest nephew, Walker, slapped a white business-sized envelope down on the table in front of her.

"What's this?" she asked.

Walker gave her a single nod, one that told her to *just open it already*. Even after all these years, he was still a man of few words, yet he could say so much with a simple look.

He crossed his arms and planted his feet next to his brother Luke, who stood to Jack's right. All three of them had their arms crossed over their chests. All stared at her with a strange gleam in their eyes, though she noted Luke had to push his overgrown blond hair—the same color as his brothers' yet desperately in need of a cut—out of the way so he could give her that mysterious look.

They were a heartbreakingly gorgeous trio, inside and out,

and Jenna liked to think she had a part in them turning out the way they did. So what were they up to now?

"Y'all are making me nervous staring like that," she finally said.

Jack raised his brows.

Luke shrugged.

And Walker maintained his stoic expression.

She lifted the envelope and gave it a little shake, not that she expected to hear anything inside.

"*Cheating*," Owen reminded her.

"Chea-ing!" his toddler sister, Clare, parroted from her booster seat on the other side of the table.

Jenna laughed. "Okay, okay." Then she tore at the envelope, careful not to rip whatever was inside, until she pulled out one single tri-folded piece of paper.

Her brows furrowed. "It's a reservation for a two-week stay at the Meadow Valley Guest Ranch. That's Sam and Ben's place up north, isn't it?"

The three men nodded in unison. Hell, they could be mistaken for triplets if you didn't know there were two years between each of them.

"For me?" she added.

This time Ava, Lily, Olivia, and Cash—Owen and Clare, too—nodded along with her nephews.

"I still don't get it," she said. "I can't leave the farm for two weeks. And—and this had to have cost y'all a fortune. I can't possibly—"

"You *can*," Walker said, interrupting her.

"We've got the farm covered," Lily said, snaking her arm through Luke's. "Between all of us here—including the sheriff—"

Cash grunted his agreement, though Jenna wasn't sure if he'd volunteered for the duty or gotten roped into it by Olivia. It didn't matter. They'd planned it all out, her wonderful unconventional family. Her pulse quickened, and her belly flip-flopped. When was the last time she'd taken time for only herself without worrying about anyone or anything else?

She couldn't remember. She couldn't *fathom* the idea of being carefree for even a day, let alone two weeks.

"But what about—" she started.

Jack cut her off. "Sam's fiancée, Delaney, has an animal shelter on the property. Lucy will be right at home with the menagerie I hear she has there already."

"But how will I...I mean, my truck isn't meant for distance driving," she said.

"Colt Morgan—Ben Callahan's buddy, who owns the other third of the ranch—he's in town for the weekend to see his sister," Luke told her. "He's picking you up at eight o'clock sharp tomorrow morning, which means you're spending the night with Jack and Ava at the ranch. He'll give you a lift up north. And we got you booked on a puddle jumper to come back home when your stay is done."

Jenna didn't know what to say. Her eyes were leaking something fierce, so she was at least conveying her gratitude even if she couldn't think of the words.

Jenna had taken over the family farm in her early adult years when she lost her parents and had never thought twice about it. In fact, she'd grown to love it. When her nephews needed her at the most difficult time in *their* lives, she'd stepped up to the challenge without batting an eye. Not once had she asked for anything in return. Family was *everything*, and you did what you had to do for the people you loved.

But now they were doing for *her*, and she'd never felt more loved in her entire life.

She stood and strode to her nephews, attempting to wrap them in a group hug, but they were too tall and too broad.

"Oh, for crying out loud," she said with something between a laugh and a cry. "Hug the hell out of me if I can't hug all of you."

The three men breathed a collective sigh and wrapped their strong arms around her.

"It's not even close to what we owe you for all you've done for us," Jack said, softly so that only the four of them could hear. "But it's a start."

He was wrong, though. They'd done as much for her as she'd done for them. Maybe even more. They'd brought love and connection into her life when she'd lost her parents and then her sister, Clare—their mother—as well.

But she couldn't get the words out for fear she'd start sobbing all over their shoulders. So she said what she could until she could compose herself better.

"Thank you."

And then she hugged them a little harder, hanging on to the moment for as long as they'd let her.

That night, when she crawled into bed, she found a wrapped rectangular box—the size of a large picture frame—waiting on her pillow.

She pulled the small card from its envelope and read.

Dear Jenna,

I found an old box in the attic a couple weeks ago—stuff that belonged to my mother and I guess you too. I hope it's okay I waited until now to give it to you. And I hope you enjoy the gift.

Love,
Jack

Jenna's throat tightened at the mere mention of her sister, Clare. It didn't matter how many years it had been since she'd passed. Grief was forever.

Her pulse quickened, and her heart thumped against her chest as she tore the wrapping from the box and lifted the lid. Staring back at her was her high school yearbook from senior year. Colored tabs stuck out from various pages, and she opened to the first one—a picture of Jenna in the front row of the Outdoor Adventure Club—a club *she'd* created simply so she and her friends could plan camping trips and have the school foot the bill.

She laughed and ran her finger over the image on the page, pausing when it landed on Thomas Clayton—the boy who'd been her first kiss. It was awkward and amazing all at the same time, not to mention under a star-studded California sky. She couldn't complain.

She turned to the next tab—International Club—and her throat tightened. The club hadn't involved much more than sampling cuisine from countries around the world or diving into travel websites planning the trips they'd all take someday, yet that someday still hadn't come for Jenna.

Which was okay. She was happy. She had *so* much.

But when she flipped to the next tab, she had to stifle a sob.

There stood seventeen-year-old Jenna, president of the Creative Writing Club, holding up the prizewinning story she wrote based on her hero, her sister Clare.

She pressed the open book to her chest and heaved out a shuddering breath. That was when she noticed the yearbook wasn't the only thing in the box. Beneath a layer of tissue paper she found a brown, leather-bound journal and a package of brightly colored gel pens—because of course that was exactly what she'd choose for herself *if* she was going to ever put pen to paper again.

A sticky note sat atop the journal.

Maybe it's time to get back some of what you lost.
—Jack

The tears fell freely now, a mingling of hope and grief.

Her nephews had already given more than she could have imagined, and now Jack had bestowed upon her the memories of what once was—and the idea of what these next two weeks could be.

She wiped the tears from under her eyes and tore open the pens. She wasn't yet ready to write a story or anything like that, but she could start with *something*.

A list.

Fourteen Wishes for Fourteen Days of Me:

Then she crossed out *Fourteen* because a wish a day? Way too optimistic.

When Jenna blew out the candles, she'd wished for her own happily-ever-after. But what if she just enjoyed this trip without worrying about what she might have lost or what came next?

Seven Wishes for a Happily-for-Now . . .

She could at least achieve a wish for every two days, right? She thought about the tabs Jack had left in her yearbook.

1. Sleep outside under the stars.
2. Eat food from a country I've always wanted to visit.
3. Eat the *best* ice cream in town.

Okay, she would have insisted on number three whether there was a list or not.

Her eyes went back to number one. She'd had her first kiss under the stars. What if, on this trip, she had her first . . . ?

4. Have a vacation fling. (And do not *fall* for said fling
    because...then it's not a fling, silly.)

There. She wrote it. She had to do it, right? She had to admit
the idea was far-fetched. After all, what were the odds of meeting someone in the span of two weeks, getting to know them,
and proposing a fling?

She laughed softly to herself.

*You don't need to get to know a fling, Jenna. That's what
makes it a fling. That's what makes it fun.*

Maybe that's what Jenna had been getting wrong in the relationship department all these years. She'd tried to make every
connection a *forever* connection. Perhaps it was time to simply
have fun.

5. Skinny-dip.

She giggled, and her cheeks flushed even though no one
else was around. How had she made it to forty without having
done this? Probably because while getting her school to sponsor
camping trips was a clear financial gain, it *did* make running
naked into a lake much more difficult to pull off. And because
she hadn't camped since...

6. Be the last one at the bar at closing time.

That one might sound silly to some, but for a woman
who'd been waking with the chickens for as long as she
could remember, staying out past 9:00 p.m. was a feat in and
of itself.

7. Write something more meaningful than a list.

There. She wrote it all down, which meant she had to do it—a binding contract with herself. She even signed her name at the bottom of the list.

Maybe it wasn't the happily-ever-after she'd wished for when she blew out forty-one candles, but it was a start. For years Jenna Owens had lived her life for everyone else—for those she loved—and she wouldn't have it any other way. But for two weeks she could be selfish. For two weeks she could worry about nothing other than having fun. For two weeks, Jenna would put *Jenna* first.

CHAPTER TWO

Colt Morgan hugged his sister tight and then held her an arm's length away, his hands still on her shoulders. He wasn't quite ready to walk out the door.

"When did you go and grow up on me?" he asked, the question only partly teasing.

She laughed, her brown eyes crinkling. The eyes were the only physical trait they shared, despite having the same birth parents. Where Colt's hair was sandy blond and his skin olive, Willow's hair was a warm chestnut, her skin fair. You had to look at the eyes to know.

"I've been touring for two years now," she said, referring to her fledgling singing career. "I'm a big girl, Colt. Have been for a long time."

His jaw tightened. "I just hate all the time we missed," he said, recalling the years they lived apart—Colt bouncing from one foster home to another while Willow's very first foster family adopted her. Five years her senior, he wasn't allowed to contact her until *she* was eighteen. And the wait had been agonizing—only for him to find out she'd lived one town away the whole time. They'd been back in each other's lives since then, but even though she was twenty-five and a grown woman, he still saw her as the six-year-old girl he'd lost all those years ago.

She shrugged. "You could join me next time I head out. A struggling artist always needs an extra roadie."

He raised a brow. "Or you could establish yourself as a local artist up in Meadow Valley, live at the ranch. Promise you wouldn't struggle for anything."

She crossed her arms. "That's *your* dream, brother. Putting down roots, filling a house with a brood of mini Colts. Me? I prefer the road."

She hugged him again, then nodded toward the door. "Go on now. You don't want to be late. And here." She grabbed a round blue tin off the table next to the front door of the small house she rented. "Baked these last night when I couldn't sleep. Figured you'd need some sustenance on the road."

He opened the tin and peered inside, then raised his brows. "You made me toffee shortbread cookies?" He grinned. No one could replicate their mother's recipe like Willow. And in addition to the cookies being his favorite, they were also a reminder that despite what happened all those years ago, he and sister had found their way back to each other and were a family once more.

She nodded. "Two dozen. And you better share with Jenna."

His smile faded. "Not if I hide them in my duffel."

She slapped him playfully on the shoulder. "Colt Morgan. That woman is going to be a guest at your ranch for *two* weeks. I suggest your hospitality begin the second she gets in your car."

He grabbed a cookie and tossed the whole thing straight into his mouth. The rich, buttery dough tasted like home, the decadent toffee awakening his taste buds, making him feel like he hadn't truly tasted food since—since the last time Willow had baked for him. Not that he'd ever admit such a thing to Luis, Meadow Valley Ranch's resident chef.

He closed his eyes and groaned.

"It's a twenty-minute drive to Crossroads Ranch," he said, his mouth still full. "There might not be anything left to share. And I'm as hospitable as they come, sis. You know that."

She reached for the tin, but he closed it quickly and pivoted away, like a child guarding his favorite toy.

"You're impossible," she said.

He swallowed, then kissed her on the cheek.

"I better see you up north soon," he said, his playful tone disappearing.

"Soon," she said, drawing out the word, which he knew meant the exact opposite. He decided not to call her out on it. He didn't want to ruin the moment. Besides, what reason could she have *not* to want to visit him?

"Love you, Wills," he finally said.

"Love you, big bro." And she kissed his cheek as well.

Then he was out the door, tossing his bag and the most precious cargo—his tin of cookies—into the trunk of his hybrid SUV.

He loved Meadow Valley and the ranch he both ran and had helped build. But every time he came back to Oak Bluff—and then left again—he left with an empty feeling in the pit of his stomach. Sure, he could fill the pit with toffee shortbread cookies and the memory of the time he spent with his sister, but how long would that last? Only about as long as the contents of the tin. Then he'd be back to searching for what he still couldn't find.

Connection. A family of his own. A chance to be the father he'd never had. Correction...He and Willow had *had* a father. He just decided parenting wasn't for him after Willow was born. And their mother?

He shook his head. He wasn't going down that road. Not when he was about to share a six-hour car ride with someone he barely knew who'd probably want him to talk or at least not brood for the entirety of the ride.

On second thought, it was *his* car, and he was giving her a free ride. Plus, Ben and Sam had given the Everett brothers the friends-and-family discount for their aunt's stay—not that Colt even knew there was such a discount.

He climbed into the vehicle and reminded himself that he wasn't a brooder. Those days were far behind him. Despite what he thought he lacked in his life, he was happy. Enlightened, even. Wasn't that what meditation was for? That was what he told himself, at least. And for the past few years he'd believed it.

He kept up the reminder, a silent mantra in his head, as he made his way toward the Crossroads Ranch and Winery. By the time he got there, he'd have bet top dollar that the smile plastered on his face looked genuine.

He'd never met the Everett brothers' aunt, but he figured the older woman deserved not only his respect but also some semblance of pleasantness. And he'd learned to be damned pleasant when the occasion called for it.

He was ready to ring the doorbell when he saw the note taped to the screen door.

Colt—

Door's unlocked. Come on in.

—Jack

He shrugged, kicked the dust off his boots as he pulled open the screen, and gave the handle of the main door a gentle turn.

The house was eerily silent for a residence occupied by Jack, Ava, their two children, and a dog.

He cleared his throat. "Hello?" he said at full volume while careful not to yell. "Everett?"

A woman rounded the corner from the kitchen and approached. Her blond hair was pulled into a ponytail, revealing a tan, crescent-moon-shaped birthmark on her neck. Her plain white T-shirt—the front of which was tucked into cutoff denim shorts—complemented her sun-bronzed skin, and he guessed she spent a good portion of her time outdoors.

She was—wow. For a second he wished *she* would be his road-trip partner rather than Jack's aunt. But then again, the safest way to drive was to keep his eyes on the road, and whoever this woman was would make that *really* difficult.

"You must be Colt," she said, holding out her hand.

He swore he heard the hint of a Southern twang in her first couple of words.

He shook her hand. "I am," he said, his brows furrowing. "I'm supposed to pick up Jack Everett's aunt."

Maybe this woman was her daughter? He didn't remember Jack and his brothers making a reservation for more than one guest. And all Sam had said was that he was picking up Jack's aunt. No mention of anyone else. Hell, Willow's cookies wouldn't last more than the six-hour ride if *three* of them went to town on the tin.

The woman laughed, her blue eyes crinkling at the corners.

"I'm Jenna," she said. "It's nice to meet you. Poor baby Clare woke with an ear infection in the middle of the night. Jack and Ava just got her down about an hour ago and fell back asleep themselves. Owen and the dog are sleeping in his room, so I promised we'd leave quietly. I just have to grab my bag from the kitchen and my chicken from the backyard."

She spun on the heel of her well-worn sneaker and strode back in the direction from which she'd come.

Colt blinked, letting the information sink in.

Jack's aunt was called Jenna.

Her name was Jenna.

She was grabbing her bag—to go with *him*.

And her *chicken*?

"I thought I was here to pick up Jack Everett's *aunt*," he called after her.

She reappeared and delivered a quick *shhh*! Then she pressed her palms together, laying her head on top of them to mime the act of sleeping.

Right. Sick baby. Whole house asleep.

Colt winced, then mouthed the word *sorry*. He glanced over his shoulder at the door and motioned for her to follow him out, and she nodded.

He let himself out of the house, careful not to let the door slam, then practically tiptoed back to the car as if everyone inside could hear his boots against the pavement.

He figured he was safer waiting out here than evoking the ire of a sleep-deprived family. Though if he was any sort of a gentleman—which he liked to think he was—he'd have offered to help her with her bag and her—chicken?

Whatever. It was too late now. If he barged back into the house, he'd only make things worse.

He leaned against the vehicle's hood and crossed his feet in front of him. Not two minutes later she strode out the front door, a backpack hanging from one shoulder and a live chicken trailing behind her.

He straightened and made his approach, intending to do the gentlemanly thing and grab her bag. But the animal—the chicken—sped around her feet squawking her head off as she pecked at Colt's boots.

"*Lu*-cy!" Jenna whisper-shouted. "He's our *ride*, not some sort of threat." She laughed nervously and picked the chicken up, holding her under her arm like a football. "Sorry about that," she said. "She usually has great intuition, but her abilities seem a little off kilter this morning."

Colt knew he should probably bite his tongue, that the answer to the question would likely leave him more confused than he already was, but he couldn't help himself.

"Abilities?" he asked.

She nodded with a grin that made his pulse race, especially with that lone dimple in her right cheek.

"Psychic abilities," Jenna said.

He snorted, and narrowed eyes along with a set jaw replaced her smile.

"If my nephew was awake," she said, "he'd confirm it. But right now I guess you're going to have to take my word for it. If there's one thing you should know about me, Colt Morgan, it's that I don't lie, and I take Lucy's intuition to heart. When she's onto something. But clearly she is off her game today."

The chicken squawked what sounded like disapproval. Great, now Colt was getting aboard with the whole psychic-chicken thing?

Jenna shushed Lucy again.

"That was two things, by the way," Colt said.

Her brows furrowed.

He raised his. "You said that if there's one thing I should know, it's that you don't lie and that you take Lucy's"—he waved a hand in the air—"I don't know…predictions? You take her predictions to heart. I was simply pointing out that you had just shared *two* things about yourself rather than one." He crossed his arms. Everything about this strange woman made him want to push her buttons, to figure her out. He needed to understand how he was face-to-face with this gorgeous, intriguing woman instead of someone more—*grandmotherly*? "Also, how in the hell are you the Everetts' *aunt*? Heard you raised the three of them, and I can't quite piece together how you're old enough to have done such a thing."

"Mister, where I come from, men don't speculate about a woman's age. Y'all can get yourselves in a heap of trouble if you do."

He opened his mouth, then closed it. She was right. Anything else he said right now would land him in a heap of trouble.

She crossed her arms, and he readied himself for a well-deserved talking-to, but instead the corner of her mouth curled into a crooked but decidedly wry grin.

"How old do you *think* I am, Mr. Morgan?"

He coughed. No, choked was more like it. Choked on any word or number that came to mind because it would be wrong or insulting... or wrong *and* insulting.

"Cookies!" he blurted, then silently cursed himself for giving up Willow's gift so easily.

She glanced over his shoulder toward the car.

"Are you trying to buy your way out of the corner you backed yourself into with baked goods?" she asked.

He finally reached for her bag—not without another protestation from Lucy, of course—and Jenna let him take it.

"Yes, ma'am," he said. "I mean miss. Dammit," he growled. No matter which way he sliced it, he was sure he'd either just insulted or demeaned her or both. Not to mention she had him babbling like an idiot, and Colt Morgan was as far from a babbler as you could get.

He spun toward the SUV, her pack slung over his shoulder, Lucy pecking at his heels as he made his way toward the trunk.

"You're a nervous one, aren't you?" Jenna called after him. "Jack didn't mention anything about you being the jumpy sort. You sure it's safe to drive in your condition?"

He ground his teeth together and opened the trunk, tossing her bag in and begrudgingly pulling his sister's cookie tin out. Here he thought he'd been pushing *her* buttons when instead she'd pushed every one of his in nothing short of a few minutes.

He ducked out of the trunk door's way and pivoted back in her direction, not realizing she'd followed him, and knocked his forehead right into hers.

She yelped.

For a second Colt saw stars, and then he saw her stumble backward and lose her footing. He dropped what he was holding and lunged for her, catching her around the waist and pulling her to him—as the cookie tin crashed open, the contents spilling all over the pavement.

In his head he heard himself roar a guttural *Noooo!* But out loud—to the slightly dazed, unquestionably beautiful, yet wholly maddening woman pressed tight against his chest—he whispered, "You okay?"

She blinked once, twice, then wrenched herself free from his grip.

"Lucy, *no*! You'll toss your lunch if you eat those!"

Jenna dropped to a squat and grabbed for the chicken, but Lucy scrambled away with a chunk of shortbread inside her beak. She growled and chased after the bird while Colt snatched up the tin in an attempt to salvage what was left—*three* cookies. Out of two dozen.

He sealed the tin and threw it back in the car. Then he rummaged through his trunk until he found a reusable tote bag, and with a hollow heart—and belly—he gathered the fallen shortbread.

Lucy strutted toward him with Jenna still chasing after her as he picked up the final crumbled bits. The chicken pecked at the crumbs that were too small to gather, and Jenna threw her arms in the air with exasperation.

"That's it!" she exclaimed. "Now you have to ride in the crate so you don't mess up Colt's nice car tossing that lunch all over the place."

Colt straightened and sighed, biting back a grin. Thanks to her, Willow's cookies were chicken feed now, but for some reason, he couldn't find his way to anger with this woman.

"Isn't it *toss your cookies* and *lose your lunch*?"

Jenna's eyes narrowed. "Is it? Huh. Like you just tossed *your* cookies?"

He couldn't help but laugh—at her mismatched idiom, her psychic chicken, and the fact that her observation was, in fact, spot on. He'd just tossed Willow's cookies all over the damned driveway.

"Twenty-eight," he said with a wince. "Figure you're not letting me off the hook until I put my foot all the way in my mouth, so there. I guessed. Can we go now?"

She stared at him for a long moment, eyes wide, like she was waiting for him to say something else. When he didn't, she walked right up to him, placed a palm on each of his cheeks—and kissed him.

Colt's stomach fell out from under him like he'd just gone over the top of a roller-coaster drop. What. Was. *Happening?* He was meant to pick up the Everetts' *elderly* aunt and drive her up to the ranch. Now he was locking lips with a stranger who was anything but—and he'd give the rest of Willow's toffee shortbread cookies to do it again.

"Yes," she said matter-of-factly, but her cheeks were flushed, which was probably nothing compared with his wide-eyed stare. "We can go now. Right after I do this." She pulled her phone out and said, "Say cheese!" then captured whatever his expression looked like and added it to her photo feed.

"That's not going up on any sort of social med—" But he was interrupted before he could finish his request.

Because Lucy paused her crumb scavenging and straightened, letting out a loud and definitive *squawk*.

A dog barked, and a toddler let out a wail as a light went on in the Everett house.

Jenna threw a hand over her mouth.

"Now!" he yelled as she grabbed Lucy into her arms.

And, laughing, they both ran toward the car.

CHAPTER THREE

In their mad dash to escape Oak Bluff before her nephew gave her a well-deserved earful, Jenna had had the forethought to grab Lucy's travel coop from where it had been waiting beside the house, so now Lucy was quiet-ish in the rear of the vehicle.

Jenna studied her road trip—partner? Accomplice?

Smooch buddy?

Holy hell. She'd *kissed* him. Just like that. And he'd kissed her back. It wasn't under the stars, so it didn't exactly check an item off her list, but it was as if putting the words to paper had unlocked Jenna's inhibitions in a way that made her think she might actually accomplish at *least* items one through six. Seven—seven would have to wait and see.

Colt's sandy hair had that rumpled, just-out-of-bed look she guessed was often covered with a Cattleman when he was out on the ranch. It suited him, though, this relaxed look that not all men could pull off.

"Sorry about your cookies," she finally said when they were a good hour from Jack and Ava's house. Jenna had suggested a more scenic route. After all, she had a full two weeks at the ranch. Why spend six hours on a boring highway when they could drive through vineyards and farms and enjoy the view?

Colt hadn't argued, but he also hadn't said much since she'd made the suggestion. They'd shared a laugh and the adrenaline rush of peeling out of the driveway before getting themselves in a heap of trouble with her nephew and family. She *did* feel bad about waking the baby up, but the thrill of the situation...It had been a long time since she'd felt so alive and in the moment. She'd thought Colt was on the same page, but as soon as they'd gotten on the road, he'd gone all but silent, letting whatever was playing on the radio fill the space between them.

His jaw tightened in response to her apology, and then he exhaled.

"They must have been pretty damned good to warrant that kind of reaction," she added. "A few survived, didn't they?"

He nodded. "Three. Three of my sister's *two dozen* toffee shortbread cookies survived. Your hen got the rest."

She winced. "If you hadn't turned around so fast—"

"If *you* hadn't sneaked up on me like you did," he interrupted.

She rubbed her forehead at the memory of their collision, and he finally glanced her way.

"Aaaand, I'm an ass for not double-checking if you're okay," he said. "Are you—okay?"

She waved him off. "A little bump on the head? It's nothin'. I've handled worse." As soon as the last sentence was out of her mouth, she wished she could take it back. What if he asked what she meant? The *worse* that she'd handled was behind her. The last thing they needed to do was start digging up painful pasts after having met less than two hours ago.

He smiled, and his shoulders relaxed.

"You're a strong woman," he said matter-of-factly. "I bet you can handle anything."

Her cheeks flushed, and she silently cursed herself for leaving her sunglasses in her backpack. But it was overcast, and she hadn't needed them until now when she wanted to hide her reaction from the man beside her.

She laughed nervously. "You don't even know me," she said.

He shrugged, keeping his eyes on the road. "Maybe not, but I'm pretty good at reading people. Kinda like Lucy, I guess."

Maybe he was making her blush, but at least he wasn't so bent out of shape about those cookies anymore.

"You're psychic?" she said.

He chuckled. "I like the way you say that word. With your accent. *SAH-kik.*"

This time the flush spread from her cheeks, down her neck, and all the way to her belly. Was he— Was Colt Morgan flirting with her?

They went on like this for at least another hour, maybe more. It was harmless at first, but the more Jenna got in her head about it, the more she convinced herself that all his compliments and niceties would fall by the wayside the second he knew the slightest truth about her.

Colt had just turned up the radio and started humming to a country tune—which only made her like him *more*. So she cracked.

"I'm forty!" she blurted, putting an end to any such thing before it began. "The stay at the ranch is a gift from my nephews for my birthday."

His brows rose, but other than that, he barely reacted.

"And I'm thirty," he said. "Glad we got the formalities out of the way." He glanced her way and winked, his lips parting in a heart-stopping grin. "Happy birthday, Jenna. We'll have to celebrate once we make our way up north."

As soon as the words left his mouth, lightning lit up the sky. In a matter of minutes their drive went from quiet and *almost* flirtatious to a torrential downpour, making it almost impossible for them to see out the windshield while Lucy screeched from the back of the SUV.

"Oh my God," Jenna said. "My weather app said nothing more than clouds for today. Where is this coming from?" Storms in California were few and far between. Storms like this? Jenna hadn't seen one like it since she was a kid in Texas.

Colt swore. "Tropical storm off the coast of Mexico!" he called out, his voice barely audible against the pounding rain. "Was supposed to miss us! I guess it changed its mind!"

Thunder seemed to shake the road in front of them, and for a second Jenna wondered if they were in the middle of some apocalyptic earthquake/tornado mash-up. They hadn't fallen into the earth's core. Not yet, at least. But the vehicle started to lean to the left, like it was toppling over.

Jenna yelped.

"It's okay," he said, and she could tell he was fighting to stay calm. "It's just a flat tire. I have a spare. But we need to pull over and wait out the storm before I can change it."

She watched the windshield wipers try and fail to keep up with the downpour.

"There!" She pointed, the flash of red ahead the only indication they might actually find shelter. "I think it's a farmhouse. If we can make it…" She didn't like the thought of them stranded on the side of the road in such a blinding storm.

He nodded, his knuckles white as they gripped the wheel.

Every rotation of the other three tires felt like it would be the one that finally knocked them over. She bit back another yelp. That wasn't what he needed right now. Then instinct took over as she leaned forward, straining to make out the entrance to the farmhouse's private drive. She placed a palm on his thigh and gave him a reassuring squeeze.

"I can see it!" she said, filled with that same adrenaline from when they'd first left Oak Bluff. "Slow down," she added with as much calm as she could muster. "It's on your left—there!"

Colt turned the steering wheel as the vehicle thumped and pitched and finally rolled past the entrance to the farm's property and off the country road. He let it go a few more feet before putting on the brakes and shifting into park.

"You did it!" Jenna squealed as another clap of thunder shook the ground. Without thinking, she undid her seat belt and wrapped her arms around his neck, squeezing him tight.

"*We* did it," he said softly, his warm lips so close—*too* close—to her ear.

She jumped back into her seat and cleared her throat, then held out her hand for a more appropriate shake.

"Well done, Mr. Morgan," she said, way more formal than necessary.

He laughed and obliged her by reciprocating the gesture. "Well done, Ms. Owens. Should we hole up here or see if anyone's home?" There was a glint of mischief in his eyes.

They definitely should *not* hole up alone and so close to one another in a disabled vehicle.

"I have to pee like you wouldn't believe!" she blurted. Because nothing said *Please, if you were flirting with me (which you probably weren't because as nice as you are, I'm a whole fifth grader older than you), let me clear any notions from your head about me being attractive by bringing up urination.*

Colt laughed. "Knocking on the door it is, then. I'll be right back."

With that he hopped out of the car and into the downpour, likely soaked before his feet hit the ground.

Oh *no* he wouldn't. There would be no chivalry here. Not if she had anything to say about it.

She opened her own door and took off after him, drenched by the time she caught up to him at the red farmhouse's front door.

He tried yelling something over the rain as his fist pounded against the door, but all she heard was something that sounded like *possum*.

Possum? Why in the world would he be talking about—

The door flew open, and an older couple stared at them.

"We have a flat!" Colt called over the downpour. "And I can't change it until—"

"Come in! Come in!" the woman said, ushering them inside.

But before Jenna was through the door, she gasped and spun back toward the car.

"Lucy! I can't just leave Lucy!" she cried.

"I'm on it," Colt said, and he raced back down the drive without giving Jenna a chance to protest.

Not cool, him being all chivalrous again when she was prepared to get her chicken herself. It made her like him more when she didn't want to *like* anyone. She wanted to have fun. She wanted a fling. Not a knight in shining armor saving her chicken from a storm.

The older woman before her placed a hand on Jenna's dripping forearm and urged her over the threshold and into the house.

"Who's Lucy?" the man asked, and now that water wasn't dripping incessantly down her face, she could see the tall, lanky farmer more clearly. He brushed a wisp of thinning gray hair off his forehead.

Jenna offered a nervous smile. "My chicken?" There was no question whether or not Lucy *was* her chicken; the question in her tone was more of the *Is-it-okay-if-I-bring-her-into-your-home-so-she-doesn't-die-in-an-abandoned-vehicle* type.

The woman smoothed her dark, only slightly graying hair behind her ears and smiled. "We don't have a coop of our own, but she's welcome in the garage with the tractor. We can get her some water and some fruit and veggies to eat if that works. I'm Maggie, by the way. And this is Robert," she added, nodding toward the man Jenna assumed was Maggie's husband.

Jenna let out a shaky breath and nodded, her arms wrapped around her torso trying to keep herself warm, the storm having brought an unseasonal temperature drop right along with it. "That would be wonderful. Thank you!" Then she stared downward, where a muddy puddle pooled around her feet on the kind couple's rustic wood floor. "I'm so sorry!" she said. "Y'all are being so nice to perfect strangers, and I seem to be ruining your floor. And I'm Jenna." She held out a dripping hand, then thought better of it when Maggie hesitated and went back to hugging herself—not that it was helping.

"Nonsense," the other woman said with a wave just as Colt burst through the door behind them.

Jenna spun to find Lucy's travel coop in his arms—and Colt covered in mud from head to boot. Her mouth fell open while Colt's seemed to be clamped shut—probably so he wouldn't swallow any of the mud on his lips.

She was too wet for her journal, which was still trapped in the car anyway. Also, it wasn't as if she was suddenly ready to put pen to paper, but when and if she was, the sight before her would be quite the fun inspiration for a story. She could see the title now: "California Mud Creature Strikes Again." Or something less ridiculous. What could she say? She was rusty as hell at this, but *thinking* about writing was a step in the right direction, wasn't it?

"Please forgive me for this," Jenna said, then pulled her phone from her pocket and snapped a couple of photos of him. His expression, the dark, dripping muck, and Lucy safe amid it all—it was a portrait like nothing she could have imagined.

"Oh no!" Maggie said. "Robert, get the chicken to the garage while I show Jenna and her—"

"Friend!" Jenna blurted. "I mean sort of. Colt and I only just met an hour or so ago, but we're driving to…" She trailed off, realizing her verbal vomit meant standing here wet and cold— and Colt standing there covered in mud—even longer. "Sorry," she said, wincing in Colt's direction. "Maggie, you sounded like maybe there was somewhere we could clean up?"

Maggie nodded, and Robert was already en route with Lucy.

"Stay here for a minute while I get you some towels. Maybe we can minimize the mess by having you towel off first. Then I'll show you to the guest room and bathroom. It's not much, but it's better than you two being out there." Maggie nodded over their shoulders. Then she stared at Jenna and Colt for a moment longer, her lips pursed. "I can see the SUV's flat, and you two and your chicken look safe enough…"

Jenna smiled and held up her right hand like she was taking a formal oath. "Y'all have nothing to worry about with us. We'll be out of your hair as soon as the storm lets up and Colt can change the tire. I'll even give you my driver's license once we get our stuff out of the car." Her eyes widened as recognition bloomed. It was clear by Colt's current state that it wasn't exactly safe to go back to the car yet again. "Our bags are sort of in the car."

Maggie gave her a warm smile. "I'm sure I have something you can borrow." She looked the silent Colt up and down. "You look about Robert's height. Broader for sure, but we'll find you some dry clothes too. Now," she said, "back in a second with some towels."

"Thank you!" Jenna called after her. Then she shivered and pivoted in her growing puddle to face Colt.

She bit her lip and tried to stifle her reaction. "Did you—fall?" she asked, the corner of her mouth twitching into a smile.

Colt's eyes narrowed, which only made him look more like a sinister swamp beast, and Jenna couldn't help herself. She burst into a fit of laughter, but it was cut short when her foot slipped in its own puddle and she pitched forward, wrapping her arms around Colt for purchase as she slammed against his muddy chest.

"How about that for karma?" he said, his deep voice tinged with self-satisfaction.

She found her footing and pulled away, her cheek and T-shirt following the rest of her body as they peeled away from the thick, wet mud.

Now he was grinning. It was the biggest smile she'd seen since she'd met him this morning.

"I could get all salty about this," she said with her brows raised. "But I like to see the positive side of things. Glass half full and all that." She itched to wipe the mud from her nose and cheek, but then it would just be on her hand, and what would she do after that?

"Do share," Colt said. "I'd love to hear your spin on the situation."

She shrugged. "Before *you* were salty, and I was the only one smiling. Now look at you. You might resemble a creature from a B-rated horror film, but you're smiling from ear to ear. You're welcome, by the way."

He opened his mouth to protest, but Maggie reappeared with a stack of dark green bath towels in her arms.

"All right," she said. "Let's see. Maybe if you take off your shoes and socks and wipe away as much as you can from what might drip along the way..." She handed them each a couple of towels. "Up the stairs and to the right, you'll find the guest room and bathroom where there are more towels, and I'll drop off some clothes you two can wear while we get yours clean and dry."

Jenna kicked off her sneakers while Colt struggled with his boots but somehow got them off without falling ass-over-elbow.

"Thank you," he said as Maggie handed him his towels. "And my apologies for being less than cordial when I walked in."

Maggie laughed softly. "Don't think twice about it," she said. "You remind me of our son, Jonathan. He got caught out in the hay field one time—I think he was about fourteen? By the time he made it back to the house, he looked a lot like you do right now. And he was a *lot* less cordial."

"Is Jonathan here?" Jenna asked as she wiped as much mud from her face, shirt, and legs as she could.

"He's going to be a senior at UC Santa Cruz," Robert said, returning from the garage without the chicken he'd left with. "Stayed there for the summer to do an internship at some beach resort. Grew up on a farm and decided hotel management was for him." Robert shrugged. "As long as he's happy. I just hope he doesn't end up working any farther away than he is right now."

"Okay, okay," Maggie said. "We're not going to get all weepy empty-nester on you two. We'll tell you all about Jonathan when you're cleaned up. For now, how about you toss those dirty towels on the floor and head on upstairs? You both must be freezing."

Jenna nodded. She wanted nothing more than to stand under the spray of a hot shower. She was chilled to the bone. But she supposed it was only fair to let Colt go first, seeing as how he was barely recognizable as human at this point.

"Thank you," they both said in unison. Then Colt gestured for Jenna to head up first.

"In case you fall again," he said with a wink. "Want to make sure I'm there to catch you."

Jenna tried to ignore the little flip in her belly at his words. He was teasing her. It didn't mean anything more than him wanting to muddy her up again.

Muddy her up again. Why did that sound—appealing?

She shook her head and laughed to herself as she made her way up the stairs, carefully so as not to fall.

Her attraction to Colt was undeniable, and *Have a vacation fling* was also undeniably on her list. But his flirting with her? It could be nothing more than the same stupid chivalry he'd shown when he went outside to rescue Lucy.

Colt Morgan was a good man—a gorgeous, *younger* good man. Men in Colt's shoes had the world at their feet. They wanted love. They wanted families. She *knew* men like him. Hell, she helped raise three of them. Why in the world would someone like him be in the market for a fling with an older woman who had nothing to offer him other than two weeks?

Nope. Nope. Nope. The muddied, chivalrous cowboy walking up the stairs behind her who was maybe, *possibly* checking out her rear end was *not* an option.

Jenna made a mental note to add another item to her list once she had her sketch pad in hand.

No more flirting with Colt.

CHAPTER FOUR

Colt wasn't sure a shower had ever felt better than the one he'd just taken. For several minutes the water had run gray as it washed away the mud that was caked on his lower arms, his neck, and his face—the rest matted in his hair. He was worried he might clog the drain, turning it into a veritable swamp. But soon the water ran clean, and the drain seemed no worse for the wear.

Now he stood with a towel wrapped around his waist and a fogged-up mirror staring back at him, his wallet, phone, and other contents from his pockets piled onto a corner of the counter.

Today was supposed to be simple—say good-bye to his sister, snack on some home-baked cookies, and give a guest a ride back up to Meadow Valley. Now he was stranded in the worst storm he'd seen in California since—ever—with a wholly unexpected woman who'd kissed him mere minutes after meeting him.

He ran a hand through his wet hair and laughed. Today had been a day, all right. And Jenna Owens was something else. First of all, she was *not* the elderly aunt of three grown men he'd expected her to be. Quite the opposite. Also, she nearly gave him a concussion sneaking up on him when he was loading the SUV. She was *definitely* the cause of him losing most of Willow's homemade cookies. And now she was, what...his roommate for the night? Because according to the forecast, this storm was supposed to keep at it until daybreak tomorrow.

He pushed through the door that connected the bathroom to the bedroom and was greeted with cool air that felt good after the time he'd spent in the heat.

"Oh!" Jenna said, her eyes wide where she sat gingerly at the edge of the bed, likely in an attempt to keep their sleeping area clean from the mud she'd picked up. "You're—naked."

He glanced down at his bare chest and the towel still secure around his waist.

"Technically," he said, "I *am* wearing the towel. It was either this or put my clothes back on, and that's not exactly an option."

Jenna patted a pile of clothes on the bed next to her and let out a nervous laugh.

"Right," she said, the word sounding more like *rahht* with her Texas lilt. "Maggie just brought all of this in for us. Guess I forgot you'd need to get dressed out here."

She stood and grabbed the pile that was meant for her.

"So I'll just head in and get cleaned up myself," Jenna said.

But she didn't move. And she hadn't taken her eyes off him. And he was enjoying it more than he should.

"See something you like?" he asked, and she gasped.

"I wasn't—" she stammered. "I mean I didn't—" She blew out a breath. "Colt Morgan, I swear. This day is nothing like I expected."

She gave him a playful whack on the side with the folded pile of clothes in her hands. And the towel that was holding firm a second ago decided it was relieved of its obligation and fell to the floor.

He crossed his arms. Because now she was *really* staring, eyes as wide as saucers and her chin almost hitting the floor.

"*Now* do you see something you like?"

Her mouth snapped shut. For a second he expected her to turn and run out the bedroom door, but instead she squinted and tilted her head toward his nether region.

"See what?" she asked with doe-eyed innocence. "Is there something there?"

Before he could answer—because this time *he* was the one mouth agape and speechless—she snorted with laughter and sauntered past him and into the bathroom, kicking the door shut behind her.

Did she just—? She didn't really think his—did she?

He tilted his head down to get a better look at what she saw and grinned proudly.

Nah. She's just messing with you, Morgan.

But something in their dynamic had shifted. They were flirting, weren't they? He shook his head and laughed. What would it matter if they were? She was on her way to spend two weeks at his ranch—*with* her hen, no less—and wasn't looking for any romantic entanglements. Or was she?

Was *he*?

It was almost six years ago that he'd thought he'd be off the market for good. Yet some days, that *almost* still felt like *only*. At the ripe old age of thirty, Colt had found both a family and a lifetime career running a ranch with Sam and Ben Callahan. All he was missing was someone to spend that lifetime with, someone with whom he could build a family of his own. He hadn't given up on that part of the dream, but the fear of losing it again had made him stop chasing it. Now it felt like his bubble of safety was bursting. After barely a few hours together, Jenna Owens was making him think things he hadn't thought in a long while.

He picked his towel up from where it sat pooled at his feet and laughed again. Then he grabbed his own stack of clothes from the bed and slid into a long-sleeved green Henley and a pair of jeans. He wondered if the clothes were Robert's or if Jonathan had left some stuff behind. The fit wasn't bad—the shirt a bit snug over his arms and the jeans a bit loose so they hung a little lower on his hips—but it still felt odd to be in a stranger's clothes, in a stranger's house, on a day that continued to prove pretty damned strange.

He pushed up his sleeves and shook his wet hair out like a dog before finger-combing it into what he hoped was some sort of presentable look, then he flopped down onto the bed, crossing one ankle over the other while he rested his damp head in his hands.

He could do this, a house on a nice piece of land. He'd never thought of farming as a livelihood, but sustainable living was high on his list—along with a house filled with kids and someone to share it all with. It wouldn't have to be far from the ranch. Sam and Delaney were doing it, and there were plenty of plots in Meadow Valley that were untouched.

He was still daydreaming when he heard the bathroom door click open and Jenna clearing her throat.

"Do we need to talk about sleeping arrangements?" she asked. "Because we're stuck here until tomorrow, aren't we?"

He nodded, his eyes closed and legs still outstretched. Now that he'd settled in after the flat tire, the mud, the shower, and his inadvertent striptease, his adrenaline gave way to exhaustion. He'd be fine if he didn't move another muscle until dawn.

"We sure are," he said groggily.

He and Willow had stayed up most of the night talking, catching up, because who knew when their paths would cross again? And he was always good at surviving on little sleep, but something about today—the adrenaline of making it off the road and out of the storm safely—suddenly hit him like a brick wall.

"Hey, birthday suit," she said softly, and he felt the side of the bed slightly dip.

He laughed and cracked an eye open to see her in some sort of flowy, floral top and her own pair of jeans, her wet blond hair tucked behind her ear.

She sure was a sight, one that made him force the other eye open to better appreciate the view.

"Guess what you claimed you couldn't see left an impression, huh?" he said with a grin.

She backhanded him softly on the shoulder. "Be serious for a second, will you?"

He furrowed his brows and forced his smile into a frown.

Jenna groaned. "I just wanted to say thank you. For getting us off the road, for going back out into that monster of a storm to get Lucy."

He raised his brows. "And here I thought me plastered head-to-toe in mud was strictly for your amusement."

She laughed. "It *was* pretty entertaining. But it was also real sweet of you to do all that, especially the Lucy thing."

"Would have been nice if that psychic chicken of yours could have predicted the storm," he said.

She gave his shoulder another playful tap. "How about you just say *you're welcome* when someone offers their gratitude?"

He sighed. It wasn't as if the guests at the ranch were anything less than cordial to him when he led them on a trail or organized a bonfire. He heard thank you all the time. But the *doing* for those folks, that was his job. And their thanking was all part of the ranch owner / guest arrangement. *Her* gratitude felt different. Then again, he wasn't usually attracted to the ranch guests like he was to Jenna Owens. Even if he was, Colt preferred to keep things professional between himself and paying customers. Although Jenna hadn't exactly paid for the trip *herself*...

Nope. He was so close to a much-needed nap. This was *not* the time to start thinking about other things he could do for her—*to* her?—to warrant her thanking him again.

"You're welcome, Texas," he said.

"How'd you know?" she asked, eyes wide.

"I'm psychic too," he teased, then added, "Plus, we had a family from Dallas a couple of weeks ago. They sounded a lot like you but not quite as sexy." He sat up on his elbows. "Not that I meant—I wasn't saying *you* were—" he stammered.

So much for keeping it professional.

Colt Morgan wasn't a stammerer. He was a tell-it-like-it-is-er. So that was what he did. "Aw hell," he said. "Your accent's sexy, Jenna Owens. Denying it would be like denying the earth is round or that gravity is what keeps us from flying off into space."

Her cheeks flushed pink. "Some folks do believe the earth is flat, you know."

"The earth is round and your accent is sexy. End of story," he said.

She pressed her lips together, and he could see the wheels turning, so he waited for whatever was coming, wondered if he'd crossed a line—but then remembered she'd recently seen him naked and had made a joke about the size of his Colt Jr. He figured the accent compliment was fairly safe.

"See, now," she started, "I don't know what to make of that. Or how to respond. Because while I do love that I kept some Texas with me all these years—and that a fine-looking young man like yourself finds it appealing—I...I mean you're..." She blew out an exasperated breath.

"Charming as hell?" he asked.

She rolled her eyes.

"Devilishly handsome?" he added. "Ruggedly sexy? Chivalrous as a knight? Or maybe just so damned fun to look at naked?"

She groaned. "Thirty! You're *thirty*, Colt. I've got an entire decade on you. When you were breastfeeding, I was trying on my first bra!"

He pulled himself up so he was sitting against the headboard now, his eyes level with hers. "I *could* point out how those two scenarios are related, but you've probably already made the connection. And how do you know I wasn't bottle-fed?"

"I'm trying to point out a very real truth with you and all your flirting, but you're being impossible."

He laughed. Hard. And she crossed her arms, defiant.

"Why is that funny?" she asked, her jaw set.

He shrugged. "Because that's exactly what I called you when I asked you to wait in the car, where it was *safe*, but you ran after me in the storm when there very well could have been no one home or Maggie and Robert could have turned us away."

"*Possum*," she said softly, like she'd just figured out the answer to a question he hadn't even known was being asked.

"What?"

She waved him off. "Nothing. You were on a roll. Wouldn't want to stop you."

He huffed out a breath. "Jenna Owens, you're—stubborn, and before you tell me that I'm the same, I'll be the first to admit that I'll dig my heels in when I think—or in this case *know*—I'm right. Ten years is nothing but time and space to me. It has nothing to do with whether I do or do not find you attractive, and I think we've already established it's the former."

He felt like she was testing him, and whatever the answer was, he wanted to get it right.

She stood up and smoothed out her shirt, then skimmed the

tips of her fingers through her still-wet hair, making sure it was secure behind her ears.

"I'm going downstairs to check on Lucy. I'll grab our muddy clothes from the bathroom and get to washing them too. And while I thank you for the compliment—and also admit that objectively speaking, you, Colt Morgan, are *very* attractive, both clothed and not so clothed—I think it's important to make clear that I don't date younger men. So while this flirting or whatever might be fun for *you*, it can't go further than that."

She turned on her heel and headed toward the bathroom.

"Jenna, wait," he said, sliding off the bed so he was standing now too.

She paused but didn't turn around.

There was something between them—the kiss, the banter, the flirting. He wasn't sure what he expected from it, especially with her at the ranch for only two weeks. He'd completely gone against his own principles of keeping things professional with ranch patrons, and where had it gotten him? He'd muddied things between them even more than the storm had.

"I'm sorry," he said. "I misread you." He sighed. "I overstepped. It won't happen again."

"Thank you," she said coolly. And then she was gone.

Colt was *way* off his game. Maybe having been in relationship hibernation for the past few years had dulled his instincts. Because he could have sworn there was something between them, some sort of connection. Not that he was looking for one, especially with a woman who lived seven hours away and clearly wanted nothing more to do with *him*. Getting his heart stomped once was plenty for one lifetime. Ever since he and Emma split, he swore that was it. No more relationships until he was sure the woman he wanted to be with wanted not only him but the same future he wanted too.

He wanted kids. A whole brood of them who wouldn't know

the foster system like he did, who wouldn't have to spend years wondering if a sibling would remember them once they made contact again.

It wasn't until he'd proposed that Emma had let the bomb drop. She didn't want children. As much as it had hurt, he respected her choice. His heart would have recovered in time. Except that she was now married with twins and a third on the way.

She hadn't wanted a family with *him*.

And here he was in his head, a place he tried to avoid as much as possible.

His stomach growled.

Yes. It all made sense now. He'd planned on snacking on a cookie or two on the drive to the ranch. He'd also planned on him and Jenna stopping for lunch to break up the ride, but the storm had done so instead.

Maybe his instincts hadn't gone to shit after all. Maybe if Maggie and Robert were kind enough to feed a couple of strangers, he'd get this whole Jenna attraction thing sorted and make sure he didn't say or do anything else that might cross the ranch owner / ranch guest line.

He padded downstairs in borrowed socks that were in the pile with his borrowed clothes. Once he had some food in him, he'd start thinking clearly again—instead of thinking how beautiful and funny and sexy his traveling companion was.

CHAPTER FIVE

J enna was spiralizing a handful of fresh zucchinis from Maggie and Robert's garden while Robert worked on his "world-famous" tomato sauce at the stove.

"And by *world-famous*, he means that Jonathan and I like it," Maggie said as she rolled out the dough from which she'd be making the noodles.

Robert shrugged as he continued stirring the contents of his pot. "Yours are the only opinions that really matter, so if you both approve, I call it a win."

"Y'all are so sweet," Jenna said, recalling the days when she and her sister, Clare, would help their own parents in the kitchen. She might be forty and all grown up now, but she still felt the pain of having lost them all too soon. Time could make life more bearable without the people she loved most, but it never erased the hurt. "Do you have any other family nearby?" she asked.

Maggie nodded. "If by *nearby* you mean a couple hours' drive, then yes. But we don't get to see extended family as often as we'd like. Such is the nature of farm life." She gave Jenna a bittersweet smile. "But having unexpected guests show up during a storm makes it a bit less lonely."

Jenna pierced another zucchini with the spiralizer and began cranking the vegetable into zoodles. "Do y'all do farm work?" she asked as she worked.

Maggie nodded. "I could have stayed and worked with my family, but Robert and I wanted to have our own place to start a family and raise our kids. We just ended up having a smaller family than we anticipated."

Jenna knew all about plans turning out differently than expected. She hadn't carried a child of her own or raised anyone from infancy to adulthood, but when her sister passed away and her brother-in-law took to the bottle to cope, she'd become a foster mother to her three teenage nephews. Raising them through the rest of their formative years after what they'd been through wasn't easy for her or them, but she loved those boys with every piece of her heart and was damned proud of the men they'd become.

"Do you have any children?" Maggie asked.

Jenna swallowed the small lump in her throat. "No. Raised my nephews, though. And they turned out pretty good, if I do say so myself."

"What can I do to help?" Colt asked, padding into the kitchen in his still-bare feet.

Now Jenna's throat was tight for an entirely different reason.

She shook her head and laughed softly to herself, pushing thoughts of an unexpectedly *naked* Colt out of her head. Though not really.

Why did he have to be so charming and sexy and—flirty? What bugged her more, though, was that she liked it. All of it.

She glanced up from her zoodle making in time to catch *him* glancing at her.

"Thought you might rest," she said coolly, remembering she'd done her best to shut down any further flirting between them.

Colt flashed her a grin, then seemed to think better of it, couching his expression like he'd just remembered their last interaction as well.

That seemed to be the problem for both of them. Jenna's first inclination upon seeing him was to smile, and his the same on seeing her.

"And miss all this fun?" he asked. "Also, I'm a little bit hangry. We missed lunch." He gave Maggie a sheepish grin, and she laughed.

"Dinner will be ready pretty early, but there's a bowl of fruit on the counter if you want to grab a snack," she said.

"You're a lifesaver, Maggie. Truly," Colt said, and he made a beeline for the fruit, inhaling a banana and then an apple while Jenna tried not to stare.

He was just so *himself*. Like he didn't care who was watching. And Jenna had put that open and honest man in his place just before because it was the easy thing to do. The *safe* thing to do.

As soon as Colt finished his snacks, he strolled up next to Robert to breathe in the garlicky aroma of his sauce, then behind Maggie where she fed her flattened dough through the pasta maker. "May I?" he asked. "My sister is a whiz in the kitchen. Taught me a thing or two about pasta."

Maggie stepped back, and Jenna couldn't peel her eyes away as Colt took over without missing a beat, turning flour and eggs into long strips of linguine.

"Wow," Maggie said, dusting off her hands. "You're hired."

Colt laughed, then looked at Jenna from across the butcher-block kitchen island only to notice her staring at him, mouth open in a small *O*.

"Surprised? Impressed? Or both?" he asked.

More like *turned on*, but she wasn't about to admit that.

"None of the above," she lied, then went back to her own meal preparation. Though she guessed needing to put her whole body into getting the spiralizer crank to turn was a little less sexy.

"To be honest," Colt said—she didn't know if he was speaking to her or the group but figured it was safer to keep her eyes on the squash—"I just about dozed off up there, but then I smelled Robert's sauce, and I couldn't have slept if I tried."

"See?" Robert said, covering the pot and leaving it to simmer. "World. Famous."

Maggie and Jenna laughed, and Colt's brows drew together.

Jenna liked that she was in on the joke but felt the urge to bring Colt into the fold too. She fought the urge, of course, just like she'd fought the urge to encourage his flirting and would continue to do so.

Her stay at Meadow Valley Ranch was going to be time to disengage, focus on herself, and figure out what came next in this new chapter of her life.

"Anyway," Colt said, breaking the short silence and dusting the flour off his hands. "I don't want to step on the pasta maker's toes. How else can I help?"

"How are you with dessert?" Maggie asked.

He shrugged. "Eating it or making it? Because I'm a champ at the former. Baking, though, that's all my sister. Willow makes this toffee shortbread. Had some for the trip up to Meadow Valley until Jenna and I had an unfortunate run-in behind my truck." He paused and looked at Jenna.

Jenna winced. "Accidents happen," she said with a nervous laugh.

Colt raised a brow. "And hens descend like vultures on fresh-baked goods."

Maggie smiled. "Sounds like quite the run-in," she said. "And that's a pretty name, Willow." Then Jenna saw something in the other woman's expression shift. "Colt, what did you say your last name was?"

A smile bigger than Jenna could have imagined spread across Colt's face. Seeing him that happy made it hard for her to breathe, so much so that she forced herself to look away even though she had no more zucchini left to spiral.

He was just—good *Lord* the man was beautiful to begin with, but the way he lit up when he thought about his sister? It made her pulse race and her palms sweat.

She dried them on her jeans, silently chastising herself for the little crush she was failing to shake.

"Morgan," he said. "Willow's legal last name is Hammond—for the family who adopted her after our mother passed. But she uses Morgan for professional purposes."

Jenna's head shot up, her eyes wide, forgetting all about her little crush because...

"Your sister is Willow Morgan?" she asked in unison with Maggie.

"Who's Willow Morgan?" Robert asked, and the two women scoffed, again at the same time like they were some sort of Greek chorus.

"She's an up-and-coming country singer," Maggie said. "Mainly local right now, but she's opened for a lot of big bands that came through the area."

Jenna nodded. "She played a short set at the state fair last summer. I drove all the way there just to see her." She turned her gaze to Colt. "I can't believe that's your *sister*. You never said anything."

Colt's smile faltered for a second, but it was enough for her to notice. "Didn't think we were doing the whole *tell-each-other-our-life-stories* kind of thing," he said.

She guessed they hadn't really had time for that. And after the way she'd shot him down upstairs, she suspected he wouldn't be sharing much more. Which was what she wanted, wasn't it?

Maggie squeezed his shoulder affectionately. "You must be

really proud of her. And I'm sorry for the loss of your parents," she said. "Sounds like you two might have spent some time apart, but I'm glad you found your way back to each other." She spun toward the white Shaker cabinets above the counter and pulled out a handful of ingredients. "Not as fancy as toffee shortbread, I imagine, but always a crowd pleaser."

She brandished a bag of Nestlé Toll House morsels and laughed.

"Thank you," he said to Maggie. "Next time she and I are both in the area, you and Robert will have to head on out to Oak Bluff to meet her."

Maggie's eyes lit up. "Oh, that would be wonderful!"

Colt grabbed the bag of chips with a smile. "And as for the cookies being a crowd pleaser, we'll see if you all feel the same after entrusting this job to me."

But he went to work reading the ingredients, squinting at the back of the chocolate chip package until he finally pulled a small case from his back pocket and withdrew a pair of reading glasses.

Do not be adorable in those glasses. Do not *be adorable in those glasses.*

He put the wire-rimmed spectacles on and was, of course, unquestionably adorable.

"Only ever needed 'em for reading," he said when he noticed Jenna staring.

Because of course she was staring at the handsome rancher who somehow managed to get more attractive every moment she was in his presence.

"I'm going to go peek in on Lucy," Jenna said, after scraping the last of the zoodles into a bowl. "Promise I'll be back when it's time to cook all the pasta."

She didn't wait for a response, deciding that removing herself from close proximity to Colt Morgan was the best course of action for now.

She strode toward the garage and let out a long breath when she was finally on the other side of the door, Lucy squawking with excitement to see her.

Jenna squatted down to greet her feathered friend, but instead of Lucy crawling onto Jenna's lap like she usually did, she pecked at Jenna's knees and her toes. Then she squawked, paced, and pecked again.

"I know," Jenna said. "You don't like sleeping in an unfamiliar place any more than I do, but Maggie and Robert are taking good care of us. By this time tomorrow, we'll have you at the ranch where you can stretch your wings a little more."

Lucy henpecked her way to the door that led back into the house, tapping her beak against the bottom of the two steps that led to the door.

Jenna sighed. "Sorry, girl. You'll have to sleep out here tonight."

Sure, Jenna let the animal into *her* home from time to time, but for the most part, Lucy preferred the outdoors. It wasn't cold in the garage. Not by any means. And Robert and Maggie had left her plenty to eat. So what in the world did she want in a strange house?

Lucy looked at Jenna, then at the door, then back at Jenna again.

Jenna's brows drew together. "You want me to leave?" she asked, incredulous.

Lucy squawked her approval, and Jenna shook her head and laughed.

"Fine. Have it your way. I'll see you in the morning."

Jenna made her way back to the door, and Lucy actually moved out of her way, staring her down with her beady chicken eyes until Jenna was up the stairs and back through the door.

So much for getting her head on straight before seeing Colt again.

Her stomach flipped and her throat tightened at the thought

of heading back into the kitchen, but her only other option was the storm.

She looked out the window at the downpour, considering the alternative for a millisecond, then groaned.

Lucy didn't think—she wasn't *forcing* Jenna to spend more time in the kitchen with Colt.

Was she?

"You really are off your game, girl," she whispered through the door. "Because as much as I want to make this fling thing happen, you've got the wrong guy for the job."

Then she sighed and strode back the way she came, hoping at the very least the guy had put those damned glasses back in his pocket.

CHAPTER SIX

Colt leaned back in his chair and rubbed a hand over his satisfied belly.

"Maggie...Robert...Everything was delicious. I can't begin to tell you how grateful we are for your hospitality," Colt said.

Then he second-guessed himself. Should he have referred to himself and Jenna as a *we*? They *were* traveling together, and for a hot second he thought they might have even been flirting.

Okay, he'd definitely been flirting, but he'd also definitely misread her. He'd thought they cleared that all up, but Jenna had barely made eye contact with him throughout the whole meal, which had been a feat because she was sitting right across from him.

"Yes. Delicious. Grateful for y'all taking us in," Jenna said, echoing his sentiment. "I'll clear everyone's plates!"

She sprang from her wooden chair before Maggie or Robert could protest and began busing the table like it was peak dining hours at the most popular restaurant in town.

"Wow," Maggie said, eyes wide as Jenna moved with remarkable speed and dexterity around the table. "I guess I'll put on the coffee and we can see how Colt did with the cookies."

Colt finished the last of the red wine in his glass and blew out a breath.

"I don't think I could eat another bite," he said with a tinge of regret. Those chocolate chip cookies smelled good. No, fantastic, if he did say so himself.

Robert folded his hands behind his head.

"I'm with him," the older man said. "Already unfastened the button on my jeans."

"Oh Robert," Maggie chastised, but Colt could see the hint of a smile. "Not in front of our guests."

Robert shrugged. "I mean no offense to Jenna and Colt, but when a man eats to his heart's content—and then some—the button's gotta go."

"Don't mind if I do," Colt said with a grin, then undid his own jeans as well. He sighed. Being here with Maggie and Robert—with Jenna—it felt like he'd known them all for years rather than hours. For someone who spent so long without a true family of his own, Colt could tell he was among three people who got it, who understood the importance of what he'd missed out on and what he was still trying so desperately to find.

People with whom—a *woman* with whom—he was comfortable enough to be completely himself.

By unbuttoning his pants when he was full.

Maggie threw her hands in the air and then laughed.

Dishes clanged in the sink, and they all looked at Jenna, who was staring straight back at them.

"Sorry!" she said. "I just—I wasn't expecting everyone to be undressing at the dinner table."

Maggie raised her brows. "*See?*" she said, narrowing her gaze at both men, victorious. Then she glanced back at Jenna. "Robert doesn't get out much," she teased. "I'm guessing neither does Mr. Morgan."

Colt leaned back and crossed his arms over his chest. "Not

many places to go in Meadow Valley other than the local inn or tavern. Guess I just feel very much at home with you and Robert."

Maggie laughed and stood from the table. "Should I even bother with the coffee, or are you men about to burst?"

"Burst," both of them said.

"You both must be exhausted after the drama that started out your day," Maggie called over her shoulder as she moved past Jenna to where the cookies sat on a cooling rack next to the oven. "How about I make you a plate of cookies and give you a bottle of fresh milk to bring upstairs. You can relax, snuggle into some pajamas..." She spun back to face the table where the two men were both still sitting. "Robert, can you grab them each something to wear to bed?"

Colt straightened in his chair. "No need for that, Maggie. Looks like there's a break in the rain. I'll run out to the car—carefully, of course—and grab our bags."

The last thing he wanted was to put Maggie and Robert out even further *or* to take another mud bath.

He watched as Jenna looked up from where she stood at the sink.

"Are you sure?" she asked him. "I would love my own stuff, especially my toothbrush—and my homemade face mask."

"Oh?" Maggie said, eyes wide. "I'd love to try it."

Jenna beamed, and Colt felt an odd sensation in his gut that had nothing to do with how much he'd glutted himself at dinner. This was a light, fluttering sort of feeling that happened in direct reaction to Jenna Owens smiling, even if she wasn't smiling at him.

"Come on, Colt," Robert said, and he stood and buttoned his jeans. "I'll help you with the bags. Then we can give these two a little face mask time while you tell me about your ranch."

"Deal," Colt said, following suit and doing up his own

jeans—which were Robert's jeans. It would feel good to have his own stuff as well. Only, he didn't exactly have pajamas. He wasn't sure he knew another thirty-year-old man who did, but maybe that was just the circles he ran in—the pajamaless circles.

He shrugged and followed Robert to the door and braced himself to tread through the mud once more, this time, he hoped, with far better success.

They made it back inside just as the rain started up again, a light drizzle for now, but a new storm front was supposed to show up in a couple of hours.

"We can finish the dishes," Robert said to Maggie and Jenna when they'd made it safely inside and removed their mud-caked boots. "You two can go do your face masks, and Colt and I can get to know each other a little better."

Maggie gave her husband a pointed look. "You're going to break into that bottle of bourbon Jonathan gave you for your birthday, aren't you?"

Colt looked back and forth between the couple, his brows raised. He liked bourbon. Though he guessed the kind a son gave his father for a gift was a little nicer than any Colt had tried before. Either way, he could make some room for bourbon.

Robert shrugged. "*You* don't like the stuff, and a man doesn't like to drink his bourbon alone. Plus, it makes doing the dishes a hell of a lot more fun."

Maggie grabbed the cookies she'd plated along with a quart of milk in a glass bottle she'd packed with ice inside a bucket, then kissed her husband on the cheek.

"You boys have fun," she said before sauntering out of the kitchen and toward the stairs.

"I can take those," Jenna said, nodding toward the bags on either side of Colt's feet.

"Oh," he said. "Right. Thanks. You sure? They're kind of heavy."

She hoisted one over each shoulder, and for a second he thought she might depart with the same gesture as Maggie and her husband. Which was ridiculous, because why would Jenna *kiss* him? Or maybe the better question was, why did he still want her to?

Instead, she pressed her lips into a firm smile and thanked him. And then she was gone, leaving a trail of her freshly showered scent mixed with the sweetness of the cookies in her wake.

"Hoo boy," Robert said from behind him, following his words a long whistle.

Colt spun to find him standing, bottle of bourbon already in his hand and two rocks glasses on the counter in front of him.

"What?" Colt asked.

Robert raised his brows. "I may not get out much, Mr. Morgan, but I can tell when a man has his eye on a woman. Don't forget, I raised a boy not quite a decade younger than you."

Robert filled the bottom of each glass with an ounce or so of the amber liquid. Neat, just the way Colt liked it.

"Guess I don't have much of a poker face, do I?" Colt asked, reaching for the offered glass. He had no problem admitting his crush on his road-trip partner. Colt didn't embarrass easily. It also didn't hurt that Robert had just compared Colt to his own son. By the time Colt was old enough for serious crushes, he didn't have a father to call him out or to sit him down and tell him about the birds and the bees.

Oh God. Robert wasn't about to have *the talk* with a thirty-year-old man, was he?

Nah. That would be ridiculous—but also hilarious.

Colt laughed softly to himself.

"But it's a one-sided sort of thing," he added. "So I'm just going to enjoy the view and leave it at that."

Robert nodded.

"You're a good man, Colt," he said. "I'm sorry if, for whatever reason, she doesn't see that in you. But when you find the right woman—like I did with Maggie—you'll know. She'll not only see the good that's already there, but she'll make you want to be better. Just for her."

Colt thought he'd had that once. With Emma. But she hadn't wanted the life he did. And while he respected that, it had made him gun-shy to put himself back out there again. Still, five years of gun-shy was finally taking its toll.

He wanted to feel something real again.

"To women who make us better men," Colt said, raising his glass and hoping they'd change the subject.

"Cheers," Robert said, tapping the bottom of his glass against Colt's.

Colt took his first sip. It was sweet and oaky, warm as it went down his throat.

"And now..." Robert added. "To finishing the dishes."

Colt grinned. That, at least, was a short-term goal he could attain. That woman who made him better, though...

It was a marathon, right? Not a sprint. After half a decade, though, he hoped he didn't have to run much farther.

When he finally made his way upstairs, Colt was two glasses of bourbon in. He was relaxed, the stress of the morning a thing of the past. And despite how full he was after dinner, he now had a hankering for a chocolate chip cookie or two.

The bedroom door was partially closed when he reached the top of the stairs, a sliver of light poking through. So he knocked lightly before entering, not wanting to wake Jenna if she was sleeping—and half hoping she *was* sleeping so he could avoid any more awkwardness between them. From here on out, she was a guest at the ranch and nothing more. He'd get over his attraction or whatever he was feeling once he was back in familiar territory tomorrow afternoon.

"Come in!" Jenna said, although the words weren't entirely intelligible.

He pushed the door open to see Jenna sitting cross-legged on the floor, leaning on the side of the bed, wearing a plain white T-shirt much like the one she'd had on this morning and a pair of soft gray shorts. Practical. No nonsense. Yet she wore it like it was somehow the height of fashion. Or maybe it was just that she was so damned beautiful that anything looked good on her. Her blond hair was piled on top of her had in a messy bun, her face free of any trace of makeup—or whatever homemade mask she and Maggie had been wearing.

Yep. He was still attracted to her. But also, she was eating all the cookies.

"Please tell me you saved me a few of those," he said, striding into the room and dropping down next to her.

She swallowed the cookie she'd just finished and then back-handed him lightly on the chest.

"I had *one*," she said. Then paused. "Okay, *three*, but you can't blame me. You make a damned good cookie."

She offered him the plate and then reached for the bottle of milk on the nightstand.

"Shoot," she said. "We forgot glasses."

Colt shrugged. "I'm good with sharing if you are. Otherwise I can head back down…"

But she'd already unscrewed the top and started chugging.

He gently elbowed her. "Hey there, thirsty. Sharing means you actually leave me some."

She lowered the bottle from her lips and laughed. "Hold your horses, cowboy. I was just taking a few sips." She laughed again. "It's funny 'cause it's a saying, but you really are a cowboy."

He shook his head, trying to ignore how adorable she was.

Cookies. Cookies were a perfectly reasonable short-term cure for her adorableness.

He popped a whole one in his mouth, then let out a small moan as his teeth sank into a just-crunchy-enough bottom before hitting the soft, gooey center.

"See?" she said, offering him the milk. "You make a damned good cookie."

He washed the damned good cookie down with the damned good fresh-from-the-cow milk and leaned his head back against the bed.

"Guess that means I'm good at following directions, huh?" he asked.

She knocked her knee against his, and he tilted his head up to look at her. Those blue eyes of hers could knock him on his ass if he wasn't already sitting. But he'd keep that observation to himself.

"Things aren't weird now, are they?" she asked. "I don't want them to be weird, especially if I'm spending two weeks at your ranch."

And another few hours in the car together tomorrow. And sleeping in this room tonight.

"Not weird," he said. He liked her. A lot, it seemed. But it didn't mean they couldn't be friends.

"Good," she said. "Because sometimes when one person sees another person naked..." Her cheeks turned pink, and he had to bite back a grin.

Had she liked what she'd seen? If she had, then maybe he wasn't imagining their chemistry, which at least softened the blow to his ego.

She cleared her throat. "I just mean that I didn't want you to feel bad or embarrassed by that."

He raised his brows. "*I'm* not embarrassed," he said. "But I understand if you are."

"I'm *not*," she blurted. "I mean, you have a very nice...Oh my God."

She grabbed another cookie and shoved it in her mouth, and Colt laughed.

"I'm going to wash up and get ready for bed," he said. "I should get out there pretty early to change the tire—providing the rain lets up. If you can spare a pillow and the top sheet, I'm good on the floor."

He handed her back the plate of cookies and the bottle of milk, then climbed to his feet, grabbed his bag from the floor, and made his way into the bathroom before she had time to say anything else.

For him washing up consisted of brushing his teeth and stripping down to his boxer briefs. For a moment, he hesitated doing the latter, not wanting to give Jenna the wrong idea. But all that was in his bag was another pair of jeans and a couple of already worn shirts he'd planned to toss in the wash when he got home. It was either just the boxers or *nothing*, his usual sleeping attire.

When he reentered the bedroom, Jenna was sitting on the bed, the top sheet in a pile on her lap and a pillow under her arm.

Her eyes widened, but just as quickly as they did, she couched her expression.

"I don't own pajamas," he said in explanation. "And I don't really have anything clean in my bag. I hope this is okay."

She swallowed and nodded. "Of course. Nothing I haven't seen before," she said with a nervous laugh. "I feel real guilty having you sleep on the hard, wooden floor," she continued. "There are three pillows. Why don't you at least take two? I don't need more than one."

He reached for the pillow and sheet.

"I'll be fine," he said. "One pillow is all I need. Always been big into camping. This is nothing." He dropped the pillow and then spread the sheet onto the floor so it was parallel to the bed, grateful that even though it looked as if the mattress was no bigger than a full, the sheet was clearly a queen and would be big enough for adequate under- and over-coverage. "Just promise you won't step on me if you wake up in the middle of the night to use the bathroom.

She pressed her lips into a smile. "Promise." Then she stood. "Guess I'll wash up too."

She brushed past him and closed herself into the bathroom, and, like before, he could smell the sugary sweetness of the cookies mingled with cherry almond scent of Maggie and Robert's shampoo. Damn if that weird flutter in his belly didn't happen again.

"No more cookies," he said aloud, then stretched himself out on the floor. Which was definitely cold and hard, but he was exhausted enough not to care.

The pillow was soft, and the bourbon had done its job. He barely had to close his eyes before sleep took him away—most likely to dream of a blond, cookie-eating beauty who wasn't the woman for him.

CHAPTER SEVEN

Jenna heard the sound before she was truly awake and thought it was something out of her dream. A drip, drip, dripping sound, like water hitting an unpeeled orange. Had she been washing fruit in this dream? Really, slowly washing fruit? Eyes still closed and feeling like she was halfway between conscious and not, she tried to concentrate on the noise.

Until she heard, "*Shit!*" in a whispered shout. It was a man's voice.

Her eyes flew open, and she found Colt standing, his body illuminated by flashes of lightning as he stared up at the ceiling while streams of water trailed down his chest.

If the storm hadn't kicked in again and the ceiling wasn't leaking, she might have been taken aback by the sight of him. She might have stared longer.

"Oh shit," she said, echoing Colt's words.

She sprang out of bed and, quickly remembering the bucket from the bottle of milk, grabbed it and ran to the bathroom to dump the water from the melted ice. She was back in seconds, kicking Colt's soaked pillow and sheet out of the way and placing the clear plastic bucket in their place. Then she flipped on the bedside lamp.

Splat. Splat. Splat. Splat. The drips came in such fast succession now that it was almost like a stream.

"What time is it?" she asked. "Should we wake Maggie and Robert?"

By tomorrow morning, this poor couple would probably be doing cartwheels after she and Colt finally left. Not that the leak in the ceiling was *their* fault.

Colt crossed his arms over his wet chest and surveyed the situation.

Stop thinking about his wet chest, Jenna. And stop looking at it too!

He shook his head. "Nothing they can do tonight other than what we've already done. Can't patch up a roof in the rain. I can offer to help in the morning," he said. "But that will get us on the road even later than changing the tire will." Colt grabbed his phone from where it was piled on top of his duffel. "And it's eleven thirty-seven," he added.

Jenna didn't care if they were stuck here all day tomorrow helping Maggie and Robert, not after the hospitality the couple had shown them. But she was also itching to get to Meadow Valley. Ever since it sank in that she had two weeks to herself—well, herself and Lucy—to soak in the summer sun atop a horse and roast marshmallows around a bonfire at night, she couldn't wait to get there. And to maybe put more space between herself and a young cowboy for whom she didn't want to feel the things she was feeling.

Like her pulse racing.

Or heat radiating through her every time she looked at him whether he was naked or fully dressed and wearing those sexy-as-hell reading glasses.

A different kind of warmth filling her heart when she watched him talk about his sister.

"So you obviously can't sleep on the floor," she said, trying to maintain her cool. Because she knew what the alternative was, and it was the complete opposite of putting space between the two of them.

Colt scratched the back of his neck. "I can head downstairs to the couch."

Her eyes widened. That was not the alternative she'd been considering.

"Don't be silly," she said, unable to stop herself from vomiting out the words that came next. "We can share the bed. I've got two pillows up here and a nice quilt. You don't even know if there's a blanket downstairs."

"I don't need—" he started.

She cut him off. "Plus, that bucket's going to need to be dumped at least a couple of times overnight if this storm doesn't let up, and if you think I want to sleep with one eye open and take care of that all by myself, well then, you've got another think coming, mister." She let out a nervous laugh. Then she slid back to the far side of the bed that nearly touched the window on the wall beside it. She patted the pillow next to hers. "There's plenty of room for two." If neither of them moved in their sleep. "I should have offered this in the first place, but..." *But I was nervous about you being so close. Not because I don't trust you, but because I don't trust me.*

"Are you *sure* about this?" he asked. Then he narrowed his eyes. "Wait, if I'm on the outside of the bed, that basically means *I* have to keep an eye on the bucket, doesn't it?"

She groaned. "I'll take the outside if that will prove my offer to be a genuine one." Lightning struck, and thunder shook the room.

Jenna gasped.

She'd been fine for years living on her own, but if there

was one thing she truly hated, it was being alone during a thunderstorm.

"Hey there," Colt said, a teasing lilt in his tone. He sat down on the edge of the bed. "You're not afraid of a little storm, are you?"

"*No*," she lied.

Another bolt of lightning was followed by another shake of the room.

This time she yelped and yanked the quilt over her head. "I mean, *yes*," she whispered, rolling her eyes at herself.

She felt the mattress dip and then Colt's strong hand rubbed her back over the blanket.

"It's okay," he said softly, and even though she knew he had no control over Mother Nature, Jenna believed him.

She peeked over the top of the blanket.

"So you'll stay?" she asked, feeling like a scared child simply posing as a forty-year-old woman.

He nodded. "I'll stay. And I'll even take the outside, but only on one condition."

She let out a shaky breath, her shoulders relaxing.

"Name your terms, cowboy," she said.

He tugged at the quilt that was basically piled in its entirety on top of her. "No hogging the blanket. If I'm getting the chance to upgrade from a cold, wet sheet to the real deal, I want the whole package." He raised his brows, and she laughed.

"Sorry," she said. "That's what happens when you live alone in a place that rarely gets the rain it needs. When it finally storms real good, it scares the pants off me. Figuratively speaking, of course," she said, feeling her cheeks grow warm. "My shorts and panties are still right where they're supposed to be."

He chuckled and gave the quilt another light tug, and she realized she still hadn't loosened her grip.

"Right," she said, finally relinquishing Colt's share. "No blanket hogging."

He threw the quilt over his lower torso and legs, then reached behind him and turned off the lamp.

"I'll keep an ear out for the bucket," he said. "But we should try to get some sleep. Got a lot to do tomorrow before we get back on the road."

It was a full-sized bed, so there was room for two. Barely, but there was room. Judging by the huge gap between her and her bed partner, though, Jenna could tell that Colt was balancing on the edge.

"Colt?" she said.

"Jenna?"

"You don't need to risk falling off the bed."

"Right," he said, then scooted himself slightly more toward the center.

"Thanks for staying," she said softly, her lids growing heavy.

"You're welcome, Jenna," he said.

How she did like the way her name sounded in his soft, deep voice.

Lightning crashed with a simultaneous boom of thunder, and the next thing Jenna knew her arms were wrapped around Colt's neck, her legs entwined with his, and though it was dark, she was close enough to see his eyes as wide as saucers.

"Sorry!" she said.

But she wasn't letting go.

She didn't want to let go.

She *wanted* to be held by someone she trusted.

She *wanted* to kiss a man who made her feel safe.

Have a vacation fling.

She *wanted* to not lead him on if *he* wanted anything more than tonight.

But God, she wanted *him*. Tonight. And hoped he still wanted her.

"I don't date younger men," she said softly but loud enough for him to hear it over the rain.

"I know," he answered, and she noticed he hadn't pulled away, but he hadn't actually embraced her either.

"But I like you," she added. "And against my better judgment I find myself wanting to kiss you." She worried her bottom lip between her teeth. "I've found myself wanting to kiss you quite a bit today, actually—and quite a bit more tonight."

He sighed, their breath mingling in the small space between them, and Jenna wasn't sure she could breathe anymore after that.

She shouldn't kiss him.

He shouldn't let her.

They shouldn't still be touching.

But they were, his chest pressed against hers, and she could feel his heart beating just as fast as hers.

Kiss me. Good Lord, just kiss me.

"Jenna?" he said slowly, carefully.

"Colt?" she answered, unable to hide her earnestness. Her hope.

"Are you sure about this? Because there is nothing I want more—nothing I've wanted more since the moment I saw you in the Everett house—than to kiss you until the sun comes up. But I don't want you to regret doing so in the morning."

She nodded. "Will you regret it?" she asked. "If I meant what I said—that I can't date you—but tonight I just really, *really* need to kiss you?" She cleared her throat. "Before you answer, I want to tell you something else—something about what this trip means for me."

"Okay," he said softly.

Her heart hammered in her chest, but this time it had nothing to do with thunder or lightning.

"Last night I made a list of things I want to do on this trip—a *Happily-for-Now* list."

"Okay," he said again, this time drawing out the second syllable.

"While I don't regret anything that's happened in my life up until now..." she continued, "...I think I realized last night that there are certain things I never got to do because I had to grow up a little sooner than expected. And, well, one of those things..." She swallowed, her throat going dry. "You know, this is really hard to ask you when we're all tangled up like this." She let out a nervous laugh.

He sighed, and she felt his breath warm on her cheek, which only made it harder for her to keep from smooching him right there on the spot. But she wouldn't do that again, not without his permission—not without him signing on for what she was proposing.

"You can tell me anything, Jenna. You don't have to be afraid."

Her stomach tightened, not so much with need but because he was right. She barely knew him, yet she believed everything he'd just said. She *felt* it in her bones.

"I want to have a fling—while I'm at the ranch. I've never done anything like this before. No strings attached, just two people enjoying each other for the time they have, and..." She blew out a long breath. "I would like it to be with you."

She squeezed her eyes shut, not wanting to see his immediate reaction because no matter what he said next, she was totally mortified for having even asked.

For a long moment he didn't move or speak, and Jenna was sure she'd just set herself up for two weeks of awkward at the Meadow Valley Ranch. But then his leg slid up between hers, and one arm wrapped around her waist while he gently slid the other between her pillow and cheek, cradling her head in his very capable palm.

"So what you're saying is that if I kiss you right here, right now, I'm signing myself up for getting to do it again and again over the next two weeks? No questions asked?" he said.

She opened her eyes and stared at him—stared at the nervous smile on his face.

"Have you—ever done anything like this before?"

He shook his head. "But the last time I tried the real thing, I got my heart trampled. Big time. Maybe..." He paused and licked his lips. "Maybe this is exactly what I need to ease myself back into the game. Two weeks with a beautiful woman with the guarantee that neither of us gets hurt? What could be better than that?" Then he pulled her closer and whispered in her ear. "And now you'll know that whenever you find yourself alone in your room at the ranch and wanting to kiss me again, I won't be too far away."

She sucked in a breath, but before she could say another word, his lips were on hers, and she knew the second it happened that she'd made the right choice in Colt Morgan. The only question was how two weeks of something this delicious would be enough.

She couldn't worry about that now, not when he was grabbing her thigh and pulling it over his hip. Not when she parted her lips and he slipped his tongue inside, letting her taste the need that matched her own. Not when he was pulling her shirt over her head so they were chest-to-chest, skin-to-skin, and she thought being with him, like this, until the sun came up might actually be better than breathing.

Not when she woke in the morning to a ray of bright sun streaking across Colt's empty pillow, a warm imprint of his body in the sheet the only evidence that he'd been there with her all night, that she'd slept wrapped in his arms, safe from the storm and from any painful memories of the past or worry of a future the two of them could never have.

"Oh no," she said out loud. Lucy—that damned psychic chicken of hers—was right yet at the same time so very, very wrong.

This was nothing more than a fling. She would *not* fall for him, even if she knew she could.

CHAPTER EIGHT

They'd gotten on the road earlier than Colt had expected, Maggie and Robert insisting they didn't need help with the roof after feeding him and Jenna a generous breakfast of fresh eggs, toast made from home-baked bread, and fresh-squeezed juice. They'd even sent them off with coffee in insulated mugs.

"Just means you both have to come back," Maggie had said before wrapping them both into warm hugs.

"You can count on it," Colt told her. "And I'll bring Willow next time too."

Yesterday—last night—it felt like it had happened in some sort of alternate universe. Strangers had taken them in like they were family, had treated Jenna and Colt like they were their own children. And then Jenna...

He'd almost lost a finger changing the SUV's tire because he was thinking about Jenna Owens's lips instead of making sure the jack was secure.

Even now, two hours into their drive while Jenna dozed with her head against the window and Lucy scuffled around in her travel coop in the back, he couldn't think about anything else.

All she wanted was a fling, and he'd agreed to it, but she'd kissed him like she needed his lips more than air in her lungs, and he'd been more than okay with that. What he wasn't okay with was how much he wanted to do it again knowing that they were already on borrowed time.

Maybe her hang-up about letting things go any further than her stay at the ranch wasn't that he was younger. The distance between thirty and forty wasn't *that* big. Maybe it was the *physical* distance between them. But he was back and forth between Meadow Valley and the Oak Bluff area as much as he could be, whenever Willow was in town. So if that was what was holding her back, it wasn't an issue.

But if that was what held her back, Jenna could have just said it. She hadn't.

Good Lord, he was overthinking one spectacular night with one hell of a spectacular woman whom he'd only just met *yesterday*.

Get a grip, Morgan. You've got two weeks with her still. This is your chance to get out of the woods, to prep yourself for the real thing, which you will *find someday.*

She stirred in the passenger seat, and Colt held his breath as if that could keep her from waking up. Other than superficial pleasantries—*Good morning. Need any help loading the bags. I'll go get Lucy*—they hadn't said a word about the night before, and he was beginning to wonder if she was having second thoughts—if they even *had* those two weeks after all.

They truly had kissed and touched and everything they could think of other than sleeping together until close to dawn. They'd doze and wake and start kissing again, and it was quite possibly the most intimate experience he'd had in years.

Colt never spent the night in a woman's bed and never brought one home to sleep in his. He always had the ranch as an excuse to put his pants on and get back home. Not that he was proud of one-night stands, but they were always consensual. And he always knew, in the back of his mind, protecting his heart had been the reason behind that excuse.

But Jenna Owens... He'd signed on for two weeks, no questions asked, convincing himself it would be enough, yet here he was silently agonizing over the thought of her changing her mind.

She sighed and stretched, interrupting his thoughts.

She was still wearing the white T-shirt she'd slept in with the cutoff denim shorts that, yesterday, were caked with mud. But thanks to Maggie and Robert, they were now no worse for the wear.

He itched to reach over and tuck her hair behind her ear, but he held fast to the steering wheel.

"Mmm," she hummed, her eyes fluttering open beneath her sunglasses. "The sun and the rhythm of the ride just lull me right off to sleep. You must be bored out of your mind—or happy as hell I'm not awake to bug you."

He shook his head. "Neither," he said coolly, hoping nothing about his tone or demeanor gave away that he'd been thinking about kissing her for every minute she'd been asleep. "You getting hungry? We can stop for a quick lunch in another hour or so. I know this great diner in Yuba City. Best club sandwich you ever had. And if you like milkshakes..."

Jenna turned to him and slid her glasses down to the tip of her nose so that when he glanced in her direction, he could see her wide-open bright blue eyes focused right on him.

"I *wasn't* hungry at all, but then you said the magic word. Now all I'll think about until we get to Yuba City is whether I'm in the mood for a strawberry shake, a chocolate shake, or *both*. Do you think they'll do a half and half? Or maybe two half-sized shakes? Or maybe—"

He chuckled, and she straightened in her seat, crossing her arms over her chest.

"I didn't realize my love of all things ice cream was so amusin'," she said.

He loved the way her accent dropped the *g* from *amusing*.

He shook his head. "It's not your love of ice cream," he mused. "It's the way you love ice cream, or home-baked cookies, or your unconventional pet back there..." He nodded toward the back of the vehicle. "Or, I'm guessing, *everything*. It's so—*big*."

He guessed by the generous gift her nephews gave her—two weeks at the ranch—that she was the same with her family, and that only made him like her more, which wasn't what he was looking to do.

Her shoulders relaxed, and she was smiling again.

"I love what I love," she said with a shrug. "And you're right. When I do love something, I'm all in. I love with my whole damned heart. I don't see the point in doing it any other way, do you?" She gasped.

"What's wrong?" he asked.

"Nothing!" She grinned. "It's just—my list! One of the items on my list is to eat the best ice cream in town. Since we're hitting Yuba City *before* Meadow Valley, that means I get to check it off my list *twice*." She cleared her throat. "That is— assuming there's spectacular ice cream in your neck of the woods as well."

Colt nodded. "Sure is. I'll see to it you don't leave town without getting that second checkmark."

He blew out a breath and kept his eyes on the road. Okay. *She* brought up the list. That meant he could check in, right? Make sure she still wanted to do what she said she wanted to do? Because he wasn't going to last the rest of the way to Yuba City if he didn't address the elephant in the room. And considering the room was the front seat of an SUV, that elephant was taking up a hell of a lot of space.

"I should have waited until you were awake before leaving the room this morning," he said.

Her body shifted so she was staring straight ahead as well.

"It's all right," she said matter-of-factly. "We laid everything on the table last night. Wasn't like there was anything to discuss."

"So you still want to do this," he said, motioning between them. "The—uh—fling? Because if you changed your mind..."

Jenna sat silent for a long moment, and he braced himself for her reaction. If she wanted to forget the whole thing—to chalk it up to the storm and the forced proximity of sharing the bed—he'd let things be. He wouldn't enjoy it, but he'd respect her wishes.

She let out a nervous laugh. "I thought *you'd* changed your mind, which is why *I* wasn't saying anything. Because if you have, that's okay."

He laughed too. "Clearly we are both clueless here, so let me be the first to say that in the not-so-cold light of day, I couldn't think of a better way to spend the next two weeks than being able to kiss you again whenever I feel like it—with your permission, of course."

"Of course," she said. "That's how flings work. We enjoy each other physically and leave all the emotional stuff at the door."

Colt's jaw tightened. "So—I don't get to know you, even a little bit?" He wasn't expecting her to reveal the most intimate details of her life, but a fling involved more than just the bedroom, didn't it?

"You know I love ice cream and that it's part of my list. Heck, you know about the list. I didn't even tell my nephews about that. Then again, I didn't make the list until the party was over and everyone was in bed, but that's beside the point."

She pivoted to face him, and he could see her arms cross again. He realized they were her safety barrier. A wall she could put between them.

But Colt was crafty. He could climb walls.

"Jenna...I'm not sure you and I are on the same page with the whole fling definition," he said, keeping his voice even so as not to spook her into thinking he wanted too much more than what she was proposing. But talking like this—with him staring out the windshield and her staring at him—wasn't working.

He moved onto the shoulder of the road, slowing to a stop and then shifting the car to park. He undid his seat belt and shifted to face her.

"What are you doing?" she asked, pressing her body up against the passenger-side door, her hand on the handle. Her eyes were wide with what looked like terror. Not the terror of thunder crashing and making her jump into his arms but bone-chilling fear, like she was afraid of *him*.

He reached a hand toward her, and she flinched, shrinking back even further.

Then it clicked.

Colt survived the foster care system but not without getting placed with one family who never should have been allowed to foster in the first place. His only saving grace was that when his foster brother took a swing at him, Colt was big enough to swing back.

"Who hit you, Jenna?" he asked softly, though inside he was boiling with rage.

She didn't move for several seconds. She just watched him, watched his hand lower into his lap, watched him wait without pushing her to proceed. Not if she didn't want to.

Finally, she let out a long, shaky breath.

"The last guy I dated. When I told him something he didn't want to hear."

Shit. The only time Colt had ever raised his fist to another man was when that man raised his first. But right now he wanted to hunt down whoever dared lay a finger on Jenna Owens with anything other than love and care.

He shouldn't have pushed. He should have just taken what she was offering.

"Jenna," he said softly. Carefully. "I will never, *ever* hurt you. No matter what you say. No matter what you do. No matter what you want today, tomorrow, or ten years from now. I will *never* hurt you. Okay?"

She nodded, then swiped at a tear as it fell below the frame of her sunglasses.

"All I was going to propose was us getting to know each other a little better, but if that's too much for you, I'll back off. I don't think it's any secret, though, that I like you. And I think…" He raised his brows, and the corner of her mouth turned up. "I *think* you like me, too, or at least find me tolerable enough. We can leave the emotional baggage at the door, but I think it's okay to at least share things like loving ice cream."

She lifted her shoulder in a small shrug. "Or cookies?"

He nodded. "*Especially* cookies—toffee shortbread cookies to be precise. How about this?" he asked. "If you share the list with me, I'll help you check everything off. That way, when we're not enjoying each other—um—*physically*, we'll have something to fill our time without pushing the boundaries of emotional connection."

It would be a win-win, wouldn't it? Having specific tasks to conquer would keep them from getting too close or getting attached.

Jenna's posture relaxed, and she finally let go of the door handle.

"You'd be willing to do all that for me?" she asked, still sounding hesitant.

"Yep."

"Do you promise not to laugh at the list if I show it to you?"

"Yes, ma'am," he said. "That's exactly what I'm saying."

She pursed her lips and narrowed her eyes. Then she reached into the back seat where her backpack was and pulled something out. When she turned to face him again, she was holding a leather-bound journal of some sort.

"Swear on it—on the book containing the list," she said.

He chuckled, then placed his right hand on the journal and held up his left. "I, Colt Morgan, do hereby swear not only that I will help you check all the items off your list, but that I will refrain from laughing at the items *written* on said list as well."

She gave him a satisfied grin and yanked the journal away, pressing it against her chest.

"And now our agreement is binding," she said. "You're a smart man, Mr. Morgan. I assume you know there will be penalties should you break the rules and laugh at or mock my list in any way."

He raised a brow. "You didn't say anything about *mocking...*"

Her mouth fell open, and he laughed.

"Of *course* I wouldn't mock you, Jenna. I meant what I said, and not just about the list. I won't *hurt* you. You can be sure of that."

Jenna exhaled, and her shoulders relaxed. "It feels kind of like we're friends now," she said, holding out her right hand to shake.

He wrapped his palm around hers, ignoring the cartwheels going on in his gut.

"Friends, indeed," he said.

"Friends who fling," Jenna added with a wink.

"Right," he said. "Friends who fling."

She was wrong, though. He wasn't a smart man, at least not this very moment.

Smart would be to stop fooling himself that he could keep his feelings out of this when he already liked her more each minute she was in his presence.

Smart would be putting the vehicle back in drive, putting the pedal to the metal until they made it to Meadow Valley, and then keeping his distance as best he could for the next two weeks.

No, Colt wasn't feeling very smart at the moment.

She finally took off her glasses and smiled, and though her lashes were wet, her blue eyes were clear and sure.

"Then get over here and kiss me, cowboy. We've a busy two weeks ahead of us, and I don't want to waste another second of it."

Kiss me, cowboy. That was all he needed to hear.

He leaned over the center console and cupped both of her cheeks in his palms. Then he did what he'd been itching to do since the second he'd woken in bed with this woman in his arms.

He kissed her as she smiled against him, as he tasted the faint memory of coffee on her tongue, as he imagined the possibility of a future he'd thought for so long was out of his reach.

And then he took her to Yuba City for the best damned club sandwich she'd ever had—and *two* milkshakes. One strawberry, one chocolate, both with straws that were meant for sharing.

By the time they made it to Meadow Valley, Jenna's list had its first checkmark. Now he had two weeks to spend with the most amazing woman he never expected to meet—and not get attached.

I, Colt Morgan, do hereby swear that might be the hardest part of the bargain to keep.

CHAPTER NINE

Lucy the psychic chicken squawked as she henpecked her way across the grass in a fenced-off area behind the still-new Meadow Valley Rescue, an animal shelter for rescues that included everything from kittens to goats, and right now the shelter had three of each.

Lucy directed one of her higher-pitched squawks toward a fainting goat who thought the chicken feed was for him. It wasn't. And the goat—whom Delaney Harper, the proprietor of the ranch's rescue, had named Winston—fainted.

Jenna laughed, and the other woman rubbed a hand over the swollen belly beneath her red sundress and simply shook her head.

"He'll never learn," Delaney said. "It's been two days already, and he's been down for the count every single time you feed your hen."

"Why do they do that, anyway?" Jenna asked. She knew chickens like the back of her hand, but her goat knowledge was definitely lacking.

Delaney squinted from the unrelenting July sun. "It's a

genetic disorder. Myotonia congenita. When they get startled, their muscles lock up, and they're temporarily paralyzed. So it looks like they're fainting, but really they're just sort of stuck for a bit."

Jenna winced. "That's—unfortunate." When she glanced back down at the goat, she also noticed that Delaney's ankles were about as swollen as her pregnant belly.

"Water retention is normal in the final weeks," Delaney said, likely having noticed Jenna's change in focus. "But being out in this heat—the heat I thought I'd escape by moving here from Vegas—makes my ankles about the same circumference as my thighs." Delaney sighed. "At least it snows a handful of times in the winter, right? Gotta keep reminding myself of that—and then five weeks from now I get to trade all this in for a beautiful baby boy or girl."

Her eyes got all glassy, and a lock of strawberry-blond hair fell from the messy bun atop her head over her right eye. She let out something between a laugh and a sob.

"I'm just so *happy*," Delaney said, and now she was sobbing.

"Oh, sweetie," Jenna said, taking Delaney's hand. "How about we head inside for a cold drink? According to the agenda my nephews so lovingly booked for me, lunch should be starting soon, and I bet there's some nice lemonade or iced tea just calling your name."

Jack, Luke, and Walker had booked Jenna's first week so that she was busy from sunup to sundown. They'd left her the second week to book herself but wanted to make sure the first half of her stay was spent trying out all the ranch had to offer, from trail rides to swimming hole excursions to bonfires and everything in between. The only reason she'd even had a free second to come and check on Lucy was because she'd skipped her arena riding lesson in favor of hiding out in her room and reading a book. She already knew how to ride a horse and was hoping this time might give her a chance to catch up with a certain cowboy whose schedule had run completely opposite hers since the minute they'd pulled onto the ranch's property.

Delaney sniffled and laughed. "I really *am* happy," she insisted. "But I swear these hormone swings in the final weeks are going to be the end of me. Do you have kids?" she asked. "Does it get any easier once the baby's out, or am I going to be on an emotional roller coaster for the rest of my life?"

Jenna felt a pang in her gut, in the empty space where a baby of her own would never be or—*could* never be. She didn't get the pang too often these days. In fact, she couldn't remember the last time she had. Maybe it was the whole milestone birthday. But she reminded herself that she already had a family, a pretty amazing one. And her future was wide open.

"Can't speak for the pregnancy bit," Jenna said as she led Delaney through the fence gate and on toward the dining hall where cold drinks and a place for the other woman to rest her feet waited. "But I *can* assure you that the emotional roller coaster doesn't really end. My nephews—I raised them since they were teens—are grown now. Strong, capable men. Ranchers, even, all starting families of their own. And I still worry about them every day. The only good part of it is that now they're old enough to worry about me too. It's kind of nice, them wanting to take care of me and all."

She'd thought for a while that their care was all she needed, that Jack, Luke, and Walker giving back what she gave to them was enough.

But then she'd lain in a man's arms for the first time in more than a year. She'd felt wanted. Cared for. Safe.

And he was willing to take what she could give him for two weeks, no questions asked.

"Oh, good," Delaney said, her voice still a little shaky. "So Sam and I just have to worry on our own for about eighteen to twenty years before we get some payback." Then she laughed at her own joke, and Jenna laughed too.

They made it to the dining hall, and Delaney breathed out a sigh of relief as Jenna held the door open for her.

"Air-conditioning," she said with a childlike glee. "*Air-conditioning.* I'm never going outside again. Jenna, would you like to buy an animal rescue? It comes with a volunteer vet and everything."

Jenna laughed. "I thought your fiancé built that place especially for you."

Delaney waved her off. "That was when taking care of animals was my dream. My new dream is cold air and feet that don't look like pillows."

"There's my girl!" a tall, dark-haired cowboy called from across the room.

Delaney's smile broadened so much, Jenna thought it might leap off her face. The woman quite literally lit up when she saw Sam Callahan, and Jenna could have sworn Delaney left a trail of light in her wake as she strode on swollen feet toward her guy.

"Well, hey there, stranger," Jenna heard from behind, and even though it was hot as Hades outside, her skin turned to gooseflesh at the sound of Colt's voice.

Jenna let the door to the dining hall fall shut before taking advantage of the air-conditioning herself. Instead she spun to face the man who'd agreed to her proposal of a fling, who was now the man she hadn't seen in two very long days and nights.

Her breath caught when she saw him, straw cowboy hat tilted down over his eyes, his short-sleeved plaid shirt unbuttoned low enough so she could follow the trail of a lone bead of sweat as it traveled down the toned torso that hid beneath.

She swallowed, her throat dry. She could really use a glass of that lemonade or iced tea she'd promised was waiting inside for Delaney.

"Cat got your tongue?" he asked with a grin. "Or maybe one of Delaney's fainting goats?"

She cleared her throat. "What?" she asked, the word coming out like a croak. "I mean, no. No one has my tongue. My tongue is—" Oh God, why couldn't she stop saying *tongue*?

"Come here," Colt said, holding out his hand. "I need to show you something." When she grabbed it, he threaded his fingers through hers and gently tugged her off the porch and around the side of the dining hall to a spot that had no window.

"Do I lose the upper hand if I admit that I've been thinking about kissing you for two days straight?" he asked unapologetically.

Their friends-who-fling arrangement had gotten off to a rocky start once Jenna saw the itinerary her nephews had planned for her. She hadn't realized until now—Colt standing in front very nearly admitting to *missing* her—how good it felt to see him too. If she had any intention of hiding the joy of finally being face-to-face with her road-trip cowboy, that was out the window now. Her smile stretched from one ear to the other, and she couldn't suppress it if she tried.

Jenna wrapped her arms around Colt's neck and yanked him so close she smashed his nose into her forehead.

"Sorry!" she yelped. "Are you okay?"

Colt rubbed his nose and chuckled. When Jenna was sure there were no visible signs of damage, she burst out laughing. "I was trying to be all sexy and show you there was no such thing as an upper hand here, and I totally failed."

Colt shook his head, then dipped it so his lips were a breath away from hers.

"Jenna Owens, I don't care how hard you try. There is *no* way you could fail at sexy."

He wrapped his hands around her thighs and hooked them over his hips, pressing her body against the side of the building for purchase and his lips against hers because if he didn't, she was going to get all clumsy again until she got what she'd wanted for two straight days. Clumsy, though, didn't begin to describe being kissed up against a wall by a cowboy—by *this* cowboy. Nope. Not clumsy at all. Instead it was probably the hottest kiss she'd ever had in the history of kisses.

His stubble rubbed her skin raw, but she didn't care. Not when she could taste him. Not when she could feel the muscles in his shoulders flex and move beneath her palms. Not when—

A throat cleared.

Jenna hadn't done it, and she was fairly certain Colt hadn't, either, which meant the secret part of their reunion was over and they were simply out in the open.

"Anna!" a man called out as Colt's lips stopped moving over hers and he lowered Jenna to the ground. "They found our make-out spot!"

Colt stepped back and smoothed out his rumpled shirt as Jenna did the same with her yellow-and-white polka-dotted tank top that had very visibly ridden up her torso.

Luis, the ranch's cook whom she'd met the day she arrived, stood with his arms crossed over his apron and his brows raised. The woman next to him—whom Jenna guessed was Anna— arched her own brow beneath her dark bangs.

"That was our spot, Morgan," the woman said coolly.

"We could kiss there," Luis said.

"And argue without anyone hearing us," Anna added, elbowing his arm.

"We don't *argue*," Luis protested, turning away from Jenna and Colt to face Anna. "We just—communicate. Passionately."

Anna placed her hands on her hips and narrowed her eyes at Luis.

"All we *do* is argue," she said. "Because you think you know produce better than me. Every time I bring you something new, something that will work better in your salad or your soup or even your famous strawberry tart that was *so* much better when you added my rhubarb…" She blew out a breath. "Every time, you make such a big deal about what I bring you—"

"Because it's not what I ordered!" Luis threw his hands in the air. "For once, why can't you just bring me what I ordered? Today I wanted fresh cilantro for my gazpacho, and what did I get?"

"Fresh basil," Anna said matter-of-factly. "Not everyone likes cilantro, and gazpacho is so much better with basil."

"Who doesn't like cilantro?" Luis bellowed, and even from several feet away, Jenna could see a vein bulge in his forehead.

"I don't," Jenna called out instinctively, raising her hand. They both froze and stared in her direction, and she immediately regretted butting in when clearly Luis was asking a rhetorical question. "It's—genetic," she continued, since their eyes were still fixed on her. "A super-small percentage of the population is actually predisposed to taste soap when they eat cilantro. I'm one of them."

Anna crossed her arms and grinned, triumphant.

Luis turned red. "You don't respect me," he said.

"You don't respect my suggestions," Anna countered.

Then Luis's hands were flying again as he continued in a flurry of Spanish while Anna simply waited, tapping her foot in the grass, until he finished.

"Should we leave them alone?" Jenna asked softly.

Colt wrapped an arm around her waist and pulled her close so they were hip-to-hip.

She'd thought that maybe he'd pulled her around the side of the building because he *had* wanted the whole him-and-her situation to be a secret.

But they were just standing here watching one couple apparently implode after being discovered as—well, as a couple in their own right.

Okay. They weren't a *real* couple. This was simply fun. Kissing Colt was fun. The *f* in *fling* stood for *fun*.

Yet she hadn't been able to forget what happened on the side of the road outside Yuba City.

I will never hurt you, Colt said.

Jenna believed him. She trusted him.

For the remainder of her two weeks, he might just be her first birthday wish come true.

"Nah," Colt said, bringing her back to the present. "This won't last too long. Either they'll make up or Anna will storm off. If it's the former, I'd love to introduce you. If it's the latter, she'll be back tomorrow, and the cycle will continue." He laughed.

"Wow," Jenna said as both Anna and Luis gesticulated wildly. "They go at it like this a lot? We're not, like, peepin' Toms on a couple about to break up, are we? I'd hate to see *that* happen."

Colt shook his head.

"Not even close," he said. "This is what it's been like since day one with them. Seems to just be their way."

And in fact, it was. Because before Colt had even finished speaking, Anna had Luis's back up against the building, the two of them kissing as wildly as they'd shouted at each other, hands groping instead of gesturing, voices silenced by one mouth covering the other.

"Okay," Colt said under his breath. "*Now* we're peeping Toms."

Jenna giggled as she slipped her hand into his.

"They said gazpacho. Without cilantro. And I'm melting. Do you think there might be some sort of frozen dessert?" she asked earnestly as she led Colt back toward the front of the building.

Colt laughed. "If there's not, I know a place in town that makes a certain frozen dessert from scratch. We can head there later if you want. That's on your list, isn't it? Taste the best ice cream in town?"

He raised a brow, and she nodded.

"I still get to *see* the list, don't I? If I'm going to help you check all the items off, I might need to know what I'm getting myself into."

She cleared her throat. "Right," she said. "The list. You can see it...As long as we're starting with ice cream."

He winked at her. "Ice cream part two."

She laughed. "Be careful. It's in your best interest to keep me inside the town limits. Otherwise you may be tasked with finding me yet another award-winning frozen treat establishment."

Colt shook his head and grinned. "You *do* like your ice cream, don't you?"

She shrugged. "It's my love language." Her eyes grew wide, and she slapped a hand over her mouth. "I didn't mean—" she stammered. "I wasn't saying that *we*..."

He leaned over and kissed her on the nose.

"You're sexy when you're embarrassed," he said. "But don't worry. I'm not going to use ice cream as a means to make you fall in love with me. I know the rules."

She swallowed.

The right woman wouldn't need to be bribed with ice cream to fall for a man like Colt Morgan. Jenna simply wasn't the right woman. Right now she was a lucky woman, though. A woman who was scheduled to the hilt for the rest of the afternoon and didn't have to worry about the combination of a sexy cowboy and the town's best ice cream and mention of rules.

"I would love to eat some frozen dessert with you later," she said, now afraid of even saying the words *ice* and *cream*. "But," she continued, "I'm supposed to go on this swimming excursion after lunch. Horseback ride through the woods to some hidden swimming hole or something. I'd skip it if I didn't know all the trouble my nephews went to in order to put this together—and if I didn't already bail on my riding lesson this morning."

"You know how to ride?" Colt asked.

"Sure do," she said. "Can't raise three rancher nephews without ever sitting on top of a horse."

He shrugged. "Then you didn't need that lesson. The swimming excursion, though. I don't recommend skipping that one. Heard good things about the rancher heading up that very same trail ride."

Jenna's insides did a little cartwheel. After two days, their schedules were about to intersect.

She thought about one of the items on her list. *Go skinnydipping.*

Her stomach tightened. They couldn't do *that* on a ranch excursion. And the list didn't exactly say she was supposed to do it with Colt—or anyone for that matter.

But he wanted to help her check those items *off* the list, which meant...

"Let's eat," he said before she blurted out something to the effect that skinny-dipping was her love language too.

They stepped through the door and were greeted not only by the refreshingly cool air but also by the cacophony of guests talking and silverware clanking against dishware.

"It's like a high school cafeteria," Jenna said with a laugh, more to herself than Colt. Because now it really was as if she'd stepped through some portal to a parallel universe where she *was* another Jenna.

"What's that?" he asked, placing his palm on the small of her back as they took their place in the short line for the gourmet-yet-serve-yourself-style lunch.

"Nothing," she lied. She was just having lunch with the cutest guy in school and then planned to sneak off with him on their upcoming *field trip* for a little more of what they'd been doing outside before Luis and Anna found them.

He smiled and nodded toward a table where Sam and Delaney sat with an older woman Jenna hadn't met yet.

"Looks like Clan Callahan saved us a couple of seats," he said.

They piled their wooden trays with gazpacho, salad, and hunks of rustic bread Jenna guessed was home-baked by Luis himself.

She followed Colt to the table and took the seat next to Delaney, who had her swollen feet propped up on an extra chair, a bowl of gazpacho balanced on her pregnant belly.

"Don't look at me like that," Delaney teased.

Jenna held her hands up in surrender. "I wasn't judging," she said with a laugh. "In fact, I think I was the one who suggested we get you off your feet. If that also means using your abdomen as a table, so be it. As long as you're comfortable."

Delaney lifted the bowl so it was under her chin, and Sam—even though he was saying something to the woman on his other side—seemed to instinctively place his hand in the spot the gazpacho had vacated.

The simple gesture made Jenna's throat grow tight.

She tamped down the silly urge to cry. After all, it wasn't Delaney's pregnancy that had her choked up. She saw pregnant women all the time and was perfectly content knowing her child-bearing years were behind her.

It was the connection between the two of them and Jenna realizing she'd never had that before.

And wanted it. For a fraction of a second she thought about adding it to her list but then remembered she wasn't in Meadow Valley for a happily-ever-after—only a happily-for-*now*.

"Barbara Ann," Colt said, and the other woman smiled softly at him. "I'm not sure if you've had a chance to meet Jenna Owens yet. She's the Everett brothers' aunt."

Jenna shook away the thought and forced a smile. Barbara Ann reached a hand across the table to shake Jenna's.

"It's so nice to have you, Jenna. My boys grew up with the Everetts until they were sent to live with you. I remember when they lost their mama. Your sister?"

Jenna nodded.

"The missing them? It never goes away, does it?"

Jenna shook her head this time. She knew Sam lost his father only months ago.

"I'm—" Jenna started.

The other woman cut her off. "No apologies, honey," Barbara Ann said, her voice warm and reassuring. "Loss is a kinship of sorts, isn't it? Those of us who know also understand that all the apologizing in the world can't change what's done. But just knowing you understand me and that I understand you—it's more than enough."

Jenna swallowed and nodded once more. Barbara Ann Callahan put her at a loss for words.

"We're going to be fast friends, Jenna. I can feel it," she said.

"*Hey*," Delaney complained as she held a perspiring glass of iced tea against her forehead. "I found her first."

Barbara Ann waved her off. "You can share. Besides, another few weeks and you'll be so sleep-deprived, you won't remember your own name let alone whether or not I stole your new friend."

Sam laughed, but then his face grew serious—and possibly a little green.

"Oh my God," he said. "In another few weeks, I'm going to be a *father*."

"And *I'm* going to be a grandmother," Barbara Ann said with much more confidence than her son. "Uncle Ben and Charlotte are going to visit from New York for the holidays. Even Delaney's sister and folks are flying in."

Delaney nodded. "It'll be a Christmas miracle, my parents leaving their little Vegas hotel in the hands of their new manager. They've never actually taken a vacation together for more than two days."

"The whole family will be in one place to celebrate what's going to be the most spoiled little baby in the history of babies," Barbara Ann added.

"And we'll get married in the snow," Delaney said, beaming.

Colt shook his head and laughed. "Still don't get how you're going to pull that one off," he said. "It could snow one day and be gone the next."

Sam shrugged. "That's why our online ordained officiant is going to be ready to go at a moment's notice during the two weeks Ben and Charlotte are here. Our officiant will be ordained by then, won't he?" he asked, brow raised.

"Yeah, yeah," Colt said with a good-natured groan, and it all clicked into place.

"You're marrying them?" Jenna asked but didn't wait for him to answer. "That's about the sweetest thing I ever heard."

Colt raised a brow and slid his arm across the back of Jenna's chair. "Guess I'm just full of surprises."

Goose bumps prickled Jenna's flesh, and she felt the heat rush to her cheeks.

Yes. Colt Morgan *was* full of surprises—surprises that caught her off guard and made her wonder what it might be like to have a man like him in her life for *real* someday.

Delaney, still grinning, nodded. "He's about the sweetest guy you'll ever meet. Next to Sam, of course. But in case you hadn't noticed, Sam's taken." She laughed as she rubbed a hand over her rounded abdomen; then she narrowed her eyes, her gaze darting from Jenna to Colt and back to Jenna. "You two are a *thing*! How am I just realizing this? I'm usually so good at spotting this kind of chemistry from a mile away." She straightened in her chair as best she could. "Spill, you two. There's nothing I like better than a happily-ever-after."

There were those words again. *Happily-ever-after.*

And again Jenna reminded herself that it wasn't why she was here.

"I mean..." Jenna started, then conveniently took a sip of her iced tea. "We only just met, but..." Why couldn't she say it? *It's nothing. Just a fling.* But all eyes were on her like she was seventeen and she'd just announced she lost her virginity. Good Lord, this really *was* like a high school cafeteria.

"We're enjoying ourselves while Jenna's in town," Colt said. "Nothing more. Right, Jenna?"

He stared at her, a smile painted across his face, but it didn't quite meet his eyes.

She got it. At least, she thought she did. Being around Sam and Delaney for only a few minutes had Jenna thinking and wanting things that weren't possible, not right now. What was it like for Colt to be around it every day?

"Right," Jenna said, forcing a smile of her own. "Just fun."

Delaney pouted. "But you two look so good together." She turned to Sam. "And I want to keep *her.* Can't we keep her?"

Sam laughed. "Jenna's not a stray goat, and I'm pretty sure she's happy back in Oak Bluff."

Jenna cleared her throat. "I am," she said. "Happy, I mean."

But why did it feel like only a half-truth?

Her farm was there.

Her family was there.

Her *life* was there.

Who was she to look a gift horse in the mouth? She'd been given so much.

"But I'm flattered at the thought," she added, and Delaney's shoulders sagged.

"Fine," the other woman said. "But even when I'm sleep-deprived and don't remember how much I like you, I hope you'll come back and visit after the baby comes."

Jenna opened her mouth to make a promise she wasn't sure she'd keep, but Colt slid his chair from the table and stood abruptly.

"I lost track of time. Gotta make sure the horses are ready to go."

"How many you got?" Sam asked.

"Riding?" Colt began. "Four plus Jenna, but there's another five that wanted to hike it and were getting a head start. Figured we'll pick up the rear and catch anyone who might have veered off trail." He turned to Jenna. "You need to head back to your room to change?"

His jaw was tight, and Jenna wondered if him having to clarify their arrangement in front of everyone else had pushed a button she didn't realize was there.

She shook her head. "Got my suit on underneath." Then she slid her chair back to show him she had her cowboy boots on with her cutoffs. "Figure I'll dry off on the ride back, so I don't need a towel."

She knew something was bothering him, but the mere mention of a towel made her gut tighten. Because she remembered Colt in a towel a few nights ago—and then that towel falling to the ground. And now she was picturing what was under that towel and ohmyGod she was at a table of people who were watching her picturing a naked Colt in her mind's eye, and for a second she wondered if they could *see*.

"So we should go!" Jenna blurted, sliding her chair out from the table and standing so she could avoid anyone's direct eye contact. "Sorry it was such a quick visit, but I'll see y'all for dinner or later this week, I'm sure."

Colt stood and nodded—clueless, she hoped, as to what was playing out in her head.

"You're on for the bonfire tonight, right?" he asked Sam.

Sam nodded.

"I'd stand to hug you good-bye," Delaney said. "But I'm not standing again, ever. So I'm just going to wave from here."

"Jenna..." Barbara Ann said, and Jenna *had* to look the woman in the eye. Dirty thoughts or no, she couldn't be rude.

"Yes, ma'am?" Jenna replied, acting like she was a child who'd gotten caught with her hand in the cookie jar.

"What does your schedule look like on Saturday?"

Jenna breathed a sigh of relief. Sam's mother *wasn't* reading her thoughts. Looked like that talent still belonged to Lucy alone. And thankfully, her hen's abilities didn't extend so far as to read Jenna's innermost thoughts. At least, she assumed they didn't. But what did Jenna truly know about a chicken's brain, especially a *psychic* chicken's brain?

She laughed softly and shook her head.

"It's open," she said. "The first day, actually, where I don't have anything booked."

"Good!" the other woman said, clapping her hands together. "You're coming with me and Delaney to Reno."

"Reno?" Jenna said.

"Reno?" Colt echoed.

"Yeah. Reno," Sam said with a laugh.

"Barbara Ann is taking me to this baby boutique to pick out some final touches for the nursery," Delaney said. "Please come with us! I mean, the ranch is fun and all, but doesn't a girls' day with shopping and lunch and an air-conditioned car ride to Reno sound like an absolute dream?"

Sam leaned over and kissed his fiancée on the cheek. "Sometimes I think you might leave me for a rancher in Alaska if the opportunity were to ever present itself."

"Never," Delaney scoffed, waving him off. "You gave me my first snow, and no other man can top that."

As hot as it was outside, Jenna suddenly needed some air. She liked Delaney. And Sam. And everyone she'd met so far. But she'd come here—according to her nephews—for some *her* time, and right now she wanted that time to be spent on the back of a horse and not thinking about relationships. She just wanted to *be*.

"Of course," she finally said, accepting Barbara Ann and Delaney's invitation. "Some girl time sounds wonderful." Then she turned to Colt. "I'll meet you at the stable," she said. "Just want to go tell Lucy I'll be gone for a while."

She waved to everyone at the table and then pivoted toward the door, not waiting to see if Colt was close behind.

The truth was, she needed a minute to collect her thoughts and remind herself that she was here to have fun—like Colt just said—not to fall for the town or the people, and certainly not a cowboy whose naked form still flickered in her mind's eye.

She was simply confusing her connection to Delaney and the warm welcome everyone had given her with feelings she couldn't possibly have after only being in town a few days. Jenna hadn't taken time for herself in years. *That* was what she was falling for.

Freedom from worry.

Freedom to simply enjoy herself.

Fun, she thought again, then repeated the word aloud over and over as she strode toward the rescue shelter on the far end of the stable.

But there was still the little voice in the back of her mind, warning her that she hadn't thought so much about any man—naked or not—since, maybe, ever.

"Hush, you," she said aloud as she let herself in to say a quick hello to Lucy, who greeted her with her most accusatory squawk.

Jenna squatted down to let the hen jump into her lap.

"I know, girl," Jenna said. "He's a good man. But this is only temporary."

Lucy might be intuitive when it came to sensing chemistry between a man and a woman, but she didn't exactly understand the finer details of it all.

She was a chicken. Of *course* she didn't understand. But it didn't stop her from squawking, and it didn't stop Jenna from thinking about what it might mean when the fun came to an end.

CHAPTER TEN

It hadn't been an easy ride to the hidden swimming hole. Sure, Colt knew the trail like the back of his hand. And Loki, the stallion he'd ridden countless times before, was—as always—steady and able beneath his saddle. What he'd forgotten, though, was that one of the ranch's horses was out of commission with a mild case of colic. He was being treated by Eli Murphy, their local veterinarian, which meant Colt had to share his horse with Jenna.

Which meant the whole ride to the swimming hole was spent with her chest pressed against his back and her arms wrapped around his torso.

This shouldn't have been a big deal. This was part of their agreement—him and Jenna being in close proximity. But Delaney at lunch, with all that talk of *keeping* Jenna, had made it hard to breathe.

If Delaney was already mourning the loss of Jenna going back home after a few days of knowing her, what did that mean for the guy who got to spend the next several days kissing her—or riding horses with her wrapped around him?

He could do this. He could detach and enjoy himself with the same woman for several days. He just had to keep reminding himself that was all this was. His physical attraction to her, though...*That* was another story. When she was this close, it made it awfully hard for him to concentrate on the fact that *he* was the professional, in charge of the safety and amusement of the whole lot of folks joining him on this excursion when all he wanted was Jenna Owens to take charge of *his* amusement in whatever way she deemed appropriate. *Or* inappropriate. Colt wasn't a picky guy.

When they finally made it to the clearing, where the hikers had set out their towels and packs and were waiting patiently for the riders, Colt's shirt was plastered to his torso with sweat, and the heat from Jenna's palms seared his skin even more.

He slowed Loki to a stop and then cleared his throat before twisting his head over his shoulder.

"You okay to dismount?" he asked. And although he couldn't see her, he felt Jenna's breath warm on his cheek. As if they needed any more heat between them.

"Yeah," she said, her voice hoarse. "I'm good."

She let go of him and deftly swung her right leg over Loki's back, bracing herself with one hand on the saddle just behind Colt's ass and the other likely on the edge of the saddle before she hopped down. Her phone was out and pointing at him in a matter of seconds.

She smiled at him and shrugged. "That's a keeper," she said.

He wasn't even thinking about the picture. He was thinking about Jenna's arms having been wrapped around him and that they were no longer there. It didn't matter how hot it was outside or how much hotter it had been riding double in the California heat. Colt felt the absence of her behind him in his gut.

He laughed softly to himself.

His physical desire for her was getting the best of him.

He hopped off Loki after Jenna was safely on the ground, then tied the horse off to a nearby tree and helped the other riders do the same.

"Thanks for waiting, everyone," he said to the hikers, who'd been instructed not to swim until Colt—a trained lifeguard—arrived. "The water doesn't go deeper than five feet, so there is no diving. And while most of us are taller than the water is deep, let's all enjoy ourselves while still exercising safety, especially for our younger swimmers." There were only two kids among the whole group, but everyone could always use some good old friendly reminders of how *not* to be an idiot in the water. So he went through the rest of his spiel, slowly and methodically, and finally ended with, "All right, folks. Pool's open!"

His announcement was met with whoops and hollers followed by all of the hikers and riders stripping down to their swimsuits before splashing into what he hoped was cool water. Well, all but *one* headed straight for the water. Jenna Owens was waiting about five feet away from where he stood, dressed in what would have been a simple white one-piece bathing suit had it not been for side cutouts that revealed most of her torso—a torso he had touched but not truly seen. What happened in the bed they shared the other night happened under cover of darkness save for the flashes of lightning that illuminated the room in short bursts of white light.

"You're staring," she said, the corners of her mouth quirking into a grin.

"You're damned right I am," he said unapologetically. "Wishing I was the one snapping photos now. But I'll wait until you give me permission to do so." He winked at her, and her mouth fell open.

"I've only ever taken pictures of you fully clothed. Candid shots that need to be captured to remember what was happening in that very moment. If it makes you uncomfortable, I can stop..."

He shook his head. "I admit I was a little worried about the one after I face-planted in the mud, but I'm trusting you're not posting said photo anywhere public without the subject's permission."

She laughed. "You know? I hadn't even thought of that. Probably because I don't do the social media thing. So no, Mr. Morgan. All photos are just for me."

Well then, that worked for him. In fact—not that he'd admit it aloud—he kind of liked her wanting to commemorate their shared experiences so far.

He dropped his hat onto the grass and kicked off his boots. Then he pulled his shirt over his head as he walked toward her.

"And the longer you stand there, the longer I'm going to keep on staring," he said when he was close enough to touch her but couldn't. If he did, he'd forget the other guests, which would completely negate his whole safety talk considering *he* was the one in charge of everyone's safety.

She looked him up and down as he unbuttoned the top of his jeans and slid them down his legs so he was in nothing but his swim trunks.

Jenna's eyes widened, and then she—giggled.

He crossed his arms and narrowed his gaze at her. "If you're going to make a joke again at Colt Jr.'s expense, I might have to renege on my promise to take you out for that homemade ice cream I told you about."

She shook her head, still laughing. "No, no. It's not—wait, did you say *Colt Jr.*? Okay, we'll talk about that later because first we need to discuss the adorable little blue turtles on your trunks. I guess they're not what I expected to see on a cowboy."

He glanced down at the light blue swim shorts patterned with dark blue turtles and then shrugged.

"Did you expect horseshoes or something?" he teased. "Maybe a bronc riding pattern instead?"

She crossed her arms. "I guess I never expected to see a cowboy in any sort of swim trunks, let alone cute turtle ones."

He raised his brows. "If you play your cards right, Ms. Owens, you may get to see *this* cowboy without any sort of swim trunks." Then he remembered she already had and added, "*Again.*"

She clasped her hands in front of her chest, like she was about to say a prayer.

"Please, oh *please*," she said, squeezing her eyes shut. "Let me play my cards right so I can catch another glimpse of *the* Colt Jr."

She opened her eyes and snorted, but she wasn't the only one who could tease.

He knew he'd pay the price of wanting her even more, but he had to win the round even if, eventually, she was likely to win the game. So he brushed his fingertips along the exposed skin on her torso, tracing a soft trail from her abdominals to her hip.

She sucked in a breath, and he grinned at the sound.

"That's all I needed to hear," he said softly. "I'm going to go cool off."

Then he strolled past her, his fingertips tingling at the memory of her skin on his. He kept walking until he was chest-deep in the water, and then he lowered himself under, washing away the heat from the ride—and from being near enough to kiss Jenna Owens but not letting himself lose focus on the reason why they were here in the first place. His job. The care and safety of his guests. And with Jenna being one of those guests, it was part of his *job* to ensure that she did, in fact, play her cards right.

What she didn't know, of course, was that there was nothing she could possibly do to play them wrong. They were on the same team, after all. And Colt Morgan wanted nothing more than for Jenna to succeed.

Colt Jr. was sort of rooting for her too.

He swam as deep as he could go, as far as the oxygen he had

left could take him, until he was finally forced to plant his feet back on the ground.

His torso emerged from the water, and he filled his lungs with air. And there she was, in the shallower part, having already made friends with the two young girls who'd hiked the trail with their parents. One was on Jenna's back while the other danced around her, splashing and chanting, "My turn! My turn! My turn!"

Forget what she looked like in that bathing suit…Okay, fine, he'd never forget *that*, but seeing her with those girls, the way they took to her after only just meeting her? Jenna was a natural with kids. He got that she'd raised her nephews and that maybe the one thing the decade between them had on her was that she was at a different place in her life. Still, he couldn't wipe the grin from his face as he watched her.

He swam toward them. Jenna was outnumbered, and he guessed she could use some help.

She laughed when she saw him, one girl still hanging from around her neck while the other waited impatiently for her piggyback ride.

"We all ran into the water together," she said as he approached. "And the girls and I just started splashing. I told their mom and dad to go take a quick swim while they had the chance."

Colt surveyed the situation, then knelt down in the shallower water.

"And what's your name?" he asked the girl standing in wait, whose smile had turned into a pout. Dark wet ringlets that matched her sister's framed her face.

"Melody," she said, the corners of her mouth still turned down.

"Hi, Melody. I'm Colt. It's a pleasure to meet you."

He held out his hand, and she placed her small palm against his.

"Martha gets to do *all* the fun things because she's younger. I *always* have to wait."

Colt's brows drew together. "I hear you, sweetheart," he said. "Waiting is *not* easy. You know what? I have a younger sister too."

Melody's eyes widened. "You do?"

He nodded. "And she used to get all the attention when we were younger, and it was hard for me too. But you know what else?"

"What?" she asked.

"Now that we're grown up, I don't get to see her very much because she lives far away. I miss her a whole bunch. So how about this?" he asked. "I'll give *you* a piggyback ride if you promise that during some of those times when you feel a little left out waiting for your turn, you remember how much you like your baby sister and how much fun you two have together."

Melody's frown began to fade. "But I don't *like* Martha, Mr. Colt. I love her."

Martha bounced on Jenna's back and held her hands out toward her big sister. "Huggies, Mel Mel!" she yelled.

So Colt hoisted Melody onto his back so she could give her little sister a *huggie*, and Colt was pretty damned sure this, right here, would be the highlight of his day.

"Wow," Jenna said as she and Colt were forced cheek-to-cheek as the girls embraced. "That might be the cutest thing I've ever seen. You're just one big softy, aren't you?"

That was the thing. If you'd have asked Sam, Ben, or Willow— the only three people who really *knew* him—if he was a softy, their first reaction would probably be doubling over in a fit of laughter. Maybe not Willow. She was the only one with whom he let his guard down, but that had been a recent development in his adult years. It took him a while to realize that once he'd found his sister, he wasn't going to lose her again. Only then did he dare to let the slightest bit of vulnerability seep through.

"I wasn't always," he finally said. "Guess you bring it out

of me," he admitted. "But you want to know what I'm not soft about?" There was a bit of mischief in his tone.

She must have sensed it, because she raised a brow. "What's that?" she asked warily.

"Winning!" He pointed to where Melody and Martha's parents were approaching from the deeper end. "Race you to Mom and Dad!"

He'd already started running before he finished the sentence, but Jenna was on the move only a second later. Melody and Martha squealed with laughter as he and Jenna pushed through the water trying to win the impromptu race.

Colt's legs were longer. And he *had* cheated. A little. But there was no rule book, so there wasn't much Jenna could do when he did, in fact, win.

"Thank you for giving us a few minutes to ourselves!" the girls' mom exclaimed as Martha jumped into her arms and Melody into her dad's.

"It was our pleasure," Colt said. "I hope you'll let me know if there's anything else we can do to make the rest of your stay any better."

The other man gave Colt a firm handshake.

"Thanks again. The girls can't wait to head back and play with all the animals at the shelter after this."

And then Melody and Martha raced back to shore on their parents' backs, their peals of laughter trailing in their wake.

"*Softy.*" Jenna poked him in the belly under the water. "Okay, so those abs are hard as a rock, but *behind* them is an ooey-gooey center." She shrugged. "Sorry. But you can't hide it."

And she couldn't hide how beautiful she looked, even with a clump of wet hair stuck to her cheek. It wasn't just *her*, though. It was seeing her take to those two little girls. It was him and Jenna *playing* like they were the girls' guardians, if only for a few minutes. They were so in sync. It felt so natural and right.

He freed the lock of hair from her face and hooked it behind her ear. "I *really* want to kiss you right now," he admitted.

Her cheeks turned pink. "I really want you to kiss me right now. But I understand you're on duty and all. Wouldn't want to look unprofessional in front of your guests."

"Or put anyone in danger by not paying attention to who is in the water," he added.

She nodded. "So, I guess we're going to have to wait, then."

He gritted his teeth. "I hate waiting."

Jenna laughed. "What about that sweet little chat you had with Melody about being patient?"

He skimmed his fingers up the exposed skin on her side, stopping when his thumb rested just below her breast.

She sucked in a breath.

"I guess I'm good at bullshitting a seven-year-old," he said. "Because right now I sure as hell don't want to practice what I preach." He rubbed his thumb back and forth across her skin.

He watched her throat bob as she swallowed.

"Colt?" she said with a nervous laugh.

"Jenna?"

"Everyone's in the shallow end or sitting on the banks."

He glanced the short distance toward the shore and saw that she was right. Guests were either sitting in practically zero depth of water or were making themselves comfortable on their towels.

"Guess all anyone needed was a quick dip," Jenna added. "And there's this little spot over here in the water behind a tree. Also, I think I should mention that another item on my list is to go skinny-dipping..." She trailed off, and her teeth skimmed over her bottom lip. Colt felt her hook a finger inside his swim trunks. *And* then he felt himself react to her finger inside his trunks—inside his trunks.

Well, what was a little spot behind the cover of trees for if not for kissing the woman he'd been thinking about nonstop for the past two days? But stripping down to nothing when all of those folks on the bank were under his care?

He shouldn't.

He *couldn't*.

But holy hell he wanted to.

"Let me..." He hesitated. The air was charged between them, and he felt like he was losing control. All he knew was that even if he kissed her now, it wouldn't be enough. He wanted more—needed more. "Go out with me tonight," he said. "Just you and me. Not just for ice cream but on a real date. Will you?" he asked before relenting to his own selfish needs.

She nodded slowly, then grazed her teeth over her bottom lip. "Are you gonna let me have my way with you behind this tree?" she asked. "Because I sure do hate waiting too."

And that was it. He was a goner. A goner who let her lead him into a tiny nook of privacy so she could clasp her hands around his neck and hook her legs around his waist. He didn't need the wall of a building for purchase this time, not when the water buoyed her in his arms.

Her lips crashed against his, and their tongues tangled in a frenzy, knowing they were on borrowed time.

"We can't let two days go by again without doing more of this," he said as they both gasped for air.

She shook her head and cradled his cheeks in her palms.

"I'm going to write a terrible review of the Meadow Valley Ranch on all the travel sites if you do," she said with a wicked grin.

He laughed. "I love my job more than almost anything in the world. But I wish to hell I didn't have to go back out there right now."

She squeezed her legs around him, propping herself higher to kiss him again.

"I'll make it easier for you," she said against him, then tugged at his bottom lip with her teeth.

Good God, he was not going to survive the next five minutes let alone the rest of the day before he was alone with her again.

"I'm going to hike back," she added. "Take a shower. A really cold one." She laughed. "And you can pick me up in front of the guest quarters whenever you're ready."

"Six o'clock," he said. "And then you're mine until tomorrow morning. Bring the list."

She nodded. "You got yourself a deal, cowboy."

She slid down to her feet, and he groaned as she traveled over the part of him that would keep him in the water for several minutes after she made it to shore.

"Five fifty!" he called after her. "I'll pick you up at five fifty!" Because he wasn't wasting an extra minute after he was officially off the clock at five thirty. He could shower and be ready in less time than that if he really tried, but he already sounded way more eager for their date than he should let on.

Jenna raised her hand in the air as she sauntered out of the water, giving him a thumbs-up.

This was it. Tonight he'd show her all that Meadow Valley had to offer her beyond a two-week stay—all *he* had to offer the right woman who wouldn't obliterate his heart.

CHAPTER ELEVEN

S how me what you got, girl!" Delaney called from outside the bathroom.

This was ridiculous. Jenna was putting way too much thought into a date with a guy who'd already seen her in her pajamas post-egg-white-face-mask. Still, it was the first time in so long that she'd *wanted* to look special for *someone* special.

Was that what Colt was? Someone special?

She shook her head and laughed to herself. She'd just met the guy. He was ten years younger. This was a fling. This. Was. Crazy.

"You promise you'll tell me if it's too much?" Jenna called back from behind the door.

"Cross my heart," Delaney said.

So Jenna threw open the door and took a wobbly step forward on Delaney's espadrille wedges.

Delaney chuckled from where she sat on the edge of Jenna's bed, then thought better of it and covered her mouth.

Jenna groaned.

"See?" she said, throwing her arms in the air. "I cannot pull off your sexy Vegas wear. I just don't have that kind of...I don't know...What do you call it? Game?"

Delaney pushed herself off the edge of the bed, one hand under her belly as if she needed to keep the baby from simply falling out if she wasn't careful.

She took a step toward Jenna, tightened the bow where the red romper tied over her right shoulder. The other was bare. For all intents and purposes, it was a one-piece top and shorts, but for Jenna, it was the sexiest thing she'd ever worn. Only she felt like she was playing dress-up in someone else's clothes. Which was exactly what she was doing.

"You look unbelievable in red," Delaney said. "And this isn't *Vegas* wear," she added with a chuckle. "I got it at Ivy's shop right here in Meadow Valley. See that little floral embroidery on the back pocket? That's Ivy's signature for her originals."

Jenna pouted. "I should put my cutoffs back on, stop trying so hard. It's just a date."

"You're right," Delaney said. "Colt's not going to be able to take his eyes off you no matter what. But I think I know what will fix everything."

Delaney raised her brows and then nodded toward Jenna's well-worn boots on the floor in the corner of the room.

"Really?" Jenna asked.

Delaney nodded. "If you still think the look isn't you, feel free to change. A girl needs to feel like herself on a first date." She cradled her baby belly. "I was just hoping to live vicariously through someone who actually *can* fit into my old clothes." She sighed. "Don't get me wrong. I'm grateful for what my body is doing, and I will love whatever shape I am when this baby finally arrives...*If* I can make it another five weeks on this swollen ankles and shortness of breath and feeling like I need to pee *all* the time because this mammoth child is parked right on my bladder." She blew out a calming breath. "It's just fun," she added. "Watching two people get all sweet on each other. I got to see it with Sam's brother Ben and Charlotte. And now you and Colt."

Jenna kicked off the espadrilles and grabbed her boots. As soon as they were on her feet, she sighed.

"*This*," she said with a satisfied smile, "is *me*." Then Delaney's last words sank in. "But we're not *sweet on each other*. Me and Colt, I mean. We're just…" She sighed. "Can I show you something?"

Delaney's eyes brightened. "Yes! I don't even care what it is. It's something new—something other than me worrying about my swollen ankles. What is it? Let me have it!"

Jenna laughed. "I don't think it's gonna knock your socks off like you think, but…" She grabbed the leather-bound notebook from her bag—the one she hadn't written in since the night of her birthday party—and handed it to Delaney.

"Ooh!" Delaney said, eyes wide. "Are you letting me read your diary?"

"Ha," Jenna said. "Hardly."

Delaney lowered herself back onto the bed and patted the spot next to her. "Okay, then. What am I looking at?"

Jenna nodded toward the journal and sat down next to her new friend. "Open it. I've only written on the first page, but I want you to see it."

"*Seven Wishes for a Happily-for-Now…*" Delaney said, reading the title to the list. She scrunched up her nose. "What's a happily-for-now?"

Jenna shrugged. "You know how you and Sam are in love and having a baby and you *know* you have this wonderful shared future?"

Delaney sighed. "Yeah," she said wistfully.

"*You* have a happily-ever-after. And I…I have no idea what my happily-ever-after is. But my nephews, when they gave me this trip as a gift, made me promise not to worry about anything other than myself for my two weeks here. Then Jack found my old high school yearbook and gave me the journal and...There were a lot of things I loved when I was younger that I never got to pursue. So I want to try them again now. And then when I go back to reality, I'll at least know I took these two weeks just for me. Happily for now."

Delaney glanced down at the list and then back up at Jenna, brows furrowed.

"Having a fling was inspired by your high school yearbook? I promise I'm not judging, but—"

Jenna burst out laughing. "Oh gosh. *No.* I mean, sort of. Most of the list is getting back to something I used to love. But high school was also a reminder of a lot of firsts. I guess I wanted to try something I'd never done before." She skimmed her teeth over her bottom lip. "Sounds silly, doesn't it?"

Delaney scoffed. "Not one little bit. Jenna, if everything on this list is going to bring you joy, then you better check off each and every item."

Jenna wrapped an arm over Delaney's shoulder and pulled her in for an awkward but well-meaning side hug. "Thank you!" she said.

"Are you *sure* I can't keep you?" Delaney responded.

Jenna blew out a shaky breath. "How about I fold you up and put you in my bag on the way home?"

Delaney snorted. "Is your luggage the size of a large walk-in closet? Otherwise I think we have a problem."

They were both laughing now, but Jenna's heart still squeezed. She'd somehow found a kindred spirit in this woman, and she already knew it would hurt to say good-bye to her.

To Colt too. But worrying beyond her time at Meadow Valley was against the rules, and she had to focus on what was right here, right now.

Jenna stood and smoothed out the material of the romper over her torso and caught a glimpse of herself in the full-length mirror on the outside of the bathroom door.

"Wow," she said, more to herself than to the other woman in the room, but she could see Delaney smile behind her.

"See?" she said. "You've got game—and legs, by the way—for days."

Jenna laughed.

"Whatever arrangement you and Colt have, you should probably know that Meadow Valley has a mind of its own. Call it a spell or enchantment or however you want to explain it, but when you fall for someone in this town, it lasts far beyond the here and now." Delaney raised her brows.

Jenna turned to face her. "You sound like me insisting my Lucy is psychic when it comes to matters of the heart." She was half joking and half terrified she was already under such an enchantment, one that had a lot less to do with the town than with a certain cowboy living *in* it.

"And do you truly believe Lucy is psychic?" Delaney asked.

Jenna shook her head. "I know it. She's never been wrong so far. Not with my nephews. Not with the sheriff and Olivia..." She trailed off because she already knew Lucy had been acting strangely since Colt came into the picture.

Delaney shrugged. "And I know this town is magic, so there you go." Then she gasped.

"Are you okay?" Jenna asked, eyes wide, and Delaney began to laugh.

She grabbed Jenna's hand and placed it on her belly. "The baby's kicking. *Hard.* If I didn't love it so much I'd be giving this child a talking-to right about now because *Ow.*"

Jenna was the one to gasp when she felt a tiny hand or foot press against her palm and move along the expanse of Delaney's swollen belly.

Her throat and chest both tightened, and she had to fight back tears.

"*That*," Jenna admitted, "was magic. Your little fairy-tale town, though..." She raised her brows. "It doesn't have anything my home doesn't have," she said coolly.

Delaney laughed. "Except for a strapping young rancher named Colt Morgan. I'm just sayin'."

Jenna walked Delaney to the lobby at five forty-five, sure she had another ten minutes at least to prepare herself for Colt's arrival. Not that anything was left to do. Her outfit, according to Delaney, was *on point*, whatever that meant. She'd let her hair air-dry, so it hung in loose waves just above her shoulders, and other than her lip balm, she'd been good to go until Delaney had pulled a small pink bottle out of her bag before they'd left her room.

"May I?" she'd asked. And though Jenna hadn't known what Delaney was asking permission to do, she trusted her new friend enough to nod.

"My little sister got me hooked on this stuff," Delaney continued. "She wears it on stage and off. She's a dancer. *Any*way, it'll give you that subtle dewy glow and..." She dabbed the dropper on her palm, then used a finger to brush a tiny bit of the shimmery liquid onto the apples of Jenna's cheeks.

And once again, Jenna was looking at herself in the mirror and mouthing *Wow*.

Now, as she was about to open the door for Delaney, Jenna had to ask for reassurance just *one* more time. "Okay," she started. "Y'all are a decade younger than me. Can I really pull this off?" She motioned from her glowing cheeks on down to where the shorts part of the jumper hit her mid-thigh.

Delaney laughed. Hard. "I don't think there's a look you *can't* pull off, Jenna. And I don't see this decade you're talking about.

In fact, the only thing I see between us is my watermelon of a belly." She leaned over in an attempt to give Jenna a hug, but her baby bump kept her from being able to truly wrap her arms around Jenna's shoulders.

Delaney groaned. "Tell me about the swimming hole so I can live vicariously through you. I'm dying to go for a dip, but the only way over the trail is via horseback or on foot, and both of those are a big fat *no* for me right now."

Jenna opened her mouth to tell her how great the swim was even though she felt terrible Delaney couldn't get there herself, but before she was able to utter a word, Delaney's eyes grew wide as she looked over Jenna's shoulder and toward the lobby door.

She started to follow Delaney's gaze, but Delaney shook her head.

"Wait!" she whispered. "From this angle he can't see you yet, but I can see him. He's checking his hair in the glass of the window in the door. Smoothing out his short-sleeved black button-up. Oh my God, this man is adorably nervous to see you!"

Jenna's stomach did a cartwheel.

"He's five minutes early," she told Delaney.

Delaney cleared her throat. "I have never seen that man bat an eyelash about anything, whether it be climbing onto the roof of the rescue shelter to clear away a wasp nest—I'm *deadly* allergic, and he got stung three times—or sitting on the back of a bucking horse after it got spooked by a squirrel. Yet there he is, making sure he's pretty enough for *you*."

Jenna couldn't take it anymore; she had to turn around. She peeked around the corner, staying close to the wall that stopped just before the door, and there he was, a man who needed *zero* help prettying himself up. Ever. And he was checking the time on his phone as he paced in front of the door.

"Oh my," Jenna said.

"And you were saying—about Meadow Valley not being magic?" Delaney said. "I think that's my cue to head on home and put my feet up. But I expect a full report in the morning!"

"Uh-huh," Jenna said, her gaze still transfixed on the nervous—albeit gorgeous—rancher just outside the door. "I mean, thank you. For the outfit. And the company."

Delaney blew her a kiss because they both knew the hug wasn't happening.

"If I don't see you before Saturday," the other woman said, "don't forget it's our girls' trip to Reno!"

Jenna nodded. "Reno. Right. Saturday. Good-bye." It wasn't until Delaney opened the door that Colt stopped his pacing to greet her, which was *Jenna's* cue to stop acting like the worst secret agent ever and make herself visible to her cowboy suitor.

She straightened—only after realizing she'd been crouching—and squared her shoulders. Then she followed Delaney through the door. Only Delaney was already in her car, backing out of the gravel drive.

"For someone who claims to be slower on her feet than usual, she sure makes a quick getaway, doesn't she?" Jenna said with a nervous laugh.

He held up a finger, then stared at her unabashedly.

"Wow," Colt finally said, giving his head a shake. "Just—wow."

Jenna fidgeted with the bow on her one covered shoulder. Sure, that had been her own reaction to seeing herself in the mirror just a few minutes ago, but the way he said that one word made her feel like he could see more than simply what she was wearing. It was as if he could see the tornado of thoughts swimming through her brain.

What am I doing? What if Delaney was right about Meadow

Valley and its magic? What if Lucy knows something about Colt I don't? What if I'm making too big a deal out of all this in the first place when I'm supposed to be having fun?

"I knew it," she finally said. "It's too much. I'm trying too hard. I should have just gone with my shorts and my cami and—"

Colt reached for her fidgeting fingers, resting his strong palm over them until they stopped moving.

"Can you keep a secret?" he asked.

Jenna nodded.

If you keep your skin on mine, I'll commit murder for you, cowboy. Okay, maybe not murder but I'd consider tax fraud or petty theft.

Oh good God. She was now incapable of coherent thought simply because he was touching her.

Then his hand slid off her shoulder, and she could think clearly again.

He scrubbed his palm across his clean-shaven face, and she noticed two nicks along his jawline. "My secret," he said softly, "is that I was so damned eager for this date I have tonight that after I showered, I rushed through the whole shaving routine and was this close"—he held his thumb and forefinger an inch apart—"to landing myself in the ER on account of blood loss. Now don't tell her, this date of mine, that *I* was trying so hard, or she might know I'm hoping to impress her."

Jenna's cheeks warmed, and she bit her bottom lip. "Are y'all for real, or is this somehow part of the package my nephews booked for me? Because in my experience, men like you don't exist in real life."

His sandy-colored brows drew together. "Men like me?" he asked. "How so?"

"Strong yet sweet," she said. "Confident *and* honest. And vulnerable enough to show up five minutes early and not give a flying you-know-what about what anyone thinks."

He chuckled. "You're right," he said. "At least about the last bit. But it's not a quality I'm particularly proud of. Got me in a lot of hot water when I was younger, but that's a story for another time. For now let's just leave it at this, Ms. Owens. Whether it's muddy, rain-soaked clothes, a bathing suit, or whatever you call the contraption you're wearing right now, my reaction upon first seeing you is always going to be *Wow*."

Her breath hitched. Then *she* said, "Wow."

"Exactly," Colt replied. "Now, do you think this eager cowboy who showed up five minutes early might get some sort of reward for his promptness?"

Jenna laughed and pressed her palms to his cheeks. "Like, maybe, a remedy for your wounds?" She rose onto her toes and pressed two soft kisses over the nicks on his jaw, and he let out a sigh.

"Something like that," he said, his deep voice barely more than a whisper.

She lowered herself onto her heels. "And for future reference, just so you don't bleed out next time—I have no objection to a little scruff. Though this…" She brushed her palm over his smooth cheek. "This feels pretty nice."

She imagined that cheek brushing against hers as he kissed her neck or maybe nipped at her lobe. She began to imagine a lot of things but was interrupted by an audible growl emanating from her abdominal region.

She gasped.

Colt laughed. "Hungry?" he asked.

She winced. "Famished, actually."

He winked. "Great. Now, how do you feel about dessert first?"

CHAPTER TWELVE

She hadn't balked at Colt's suggestion of checking off the typical date bullet points out of order. He hadn't seen *the list* yet but knew at the very least that this item was on it and that Jenna was counting on checking it off—again.

"Is it the homemade ice cream place?" she'd asked, but all he'd done was shrug and open the passenger door of his car for her. He wanted tonight to be different from any other date she'd been on. Part of that was keeping her on her toes, drumming up the anticipation—and hoping what he had planned delivered.

"What if I don't like surprises?" she asked as he made his way off the Meadow Valley Ranch property and onto the road toward town.

"What if I do?" he countered with a grin.

She raised her brows and crossed her arms, defiant, though he could tell even in his peripheral vision that she was fighting a smile of her own.

"Maybe you should blindfold me, then," she said.

"Check the center console."

She gasped and opened the console, where he knew she'd

find nothing more than a pair of aviators and a stack of napkins from various coffee stops he'd made on drives to and from Oak Bluff to visit his sister.

He laughed and Jenna groaned.

"You must think I'm pretty gullible, huh?" she accused, but she was laughing too.

"I *didn't*..." Colt said, already pulling onto First Street, Meadow Valley's main thoroughfare.

"Oooh!" Jenna said, turning to look over her shoulder. "Look at that beautiful town hall. And that courthouse!" She whipped her head back so she was facing the windshield. "Oh wow. *That*'s the Meadow Valley Inn?" She stared out her window at the historic building with its grand front porch where a young woman sat on the porch swing reading a book to two young boys, one on either side of her. "It's beautiful," she added. Then she pulled her phone out of her pocket—that outfit had pockets?— and lowered her window so she could lean out of it.

He slowed, almost to a stop, and let her snap her photo.

"Thanks," he said. "I mean, I didn't build the place, but Sam, Ben, and I helped with a few cosmetic restorations to the facade."

She turned to face him, her ocean-blue eyes wide. "Wait," she said. "I knew Sam and Ben did a lot of contracting work back in Oak Bluff and that y'all built the ranch from the ground up, but I guess I just figured you were along for the ride."

He laughed, and his brows drew together. "Um...Thanks?"

She backhanded him on the shoulder. "That's not what I meant. Well, okay, I guess I couldn't have meant it any other way. I just wasn't expecting you to be so multitalented." She shook her head and laughed. "That came out all wrong too. I swear I did not mean any offense. I'm simply getting to know you better, and seeing as how you like surprises, I guess I'm sometimes caught a little off guard."

Colt made a U-turn and parallel-parked right in front of their destination, not that Jenna knew *which* establishment had their so-called first course waiting for them.

"No offense taken," he said. "The truth is, Ben and Sam are good at the building. *Really* good. But it was always a means to an end for them, a way to take care of their late father and to get to where we are now with the ranch. Me? I like making something from nothing. Or even better, repurposing what others might consider useless or trash. When I finally build a place of my own, it's gonna be filled with trash and scraps and heaps of junk, though you'll never know it." He nodded back toward the Meadow Valley Inn. "That porch swing?" he said. "Made it from wine barrels. And the pillows are covered with the material from some old curtains Pearl, the inn's owner, was going to get rid of."

"You *made* the swing," she said, a statement rather than a question, but he could still hear the hint of disbelief. "And you sew?"

He laughed. "No. I've tried. And failed. Ivy made the pillow covers. But I'll take credit for the swing. Got to admit I was a little jealous you wanted to take a photo of something other than *me*, but since it was something I built, I'll let it slide."

"Can we go see it later?" she asked.

Colt tried not to swell too much with pride. It was just a swing. But he'd be lying if he said he wasn't trying to impress her with it.

"Sure thing," he said, doing his best to make it seem like it didn't matter either way.

Jenna beamed. "My nephew Walker makes furniture as his sort of side passion. I always thought it was good that he had something just for him, you know? I never found that."

Colt put the car in park and turned the engine off so he could undo his seat belt and face her.

"You mean eggs and farming aren't your passion?" he asked, trying to make a joke before noticing the longing in her eyes. "Okay, I'm an ass. Forget I said that."

She shook her head. "No, it's okay. I didn't mean to get all melancholy. Raising my nephews was sort of my thing when I wasn't expecting it to be, and I guess in a way it sort of still is." She laughed. "They'd never admit it, but I think them sending me here for two weeks was as much about getting me out of their hair for a bit as it was about giving me time to myself."

Colt placed his palm on her cheek. "I don't believe that for a second," he said. "The part about them wanting you out of their hair. But maybe they did want to give you this time to figure out what *you* want out of the rest of your life rather than having your choices revolve around them."

She pressed her lips into a smile. "That's a real sweet take on the whole situation. But I'm not sure I'm going to find my *thing* during a two-week stay at a guest ranch. I mean, I love the whole ranch experience and all, but I'm pretty solid on the fact that whatever my thing is, it's got nothing to do with stables and trail rides. Though I would not object to another trip to that swimming hole—maybe with less of a crowd, though."

He felt her cheek warm in his palm, which matched the heat growing from his insides to his fingertips. "The list," he said. "That about finding your *thing*?"

She shook her head. "It's more about getting back a thing or two I might have missed out on when I was younger." She closed her eyes. "Like skinny-dipping at a swimming hole," she said softly.

She needed to stop saying *skinny-dipping*. Just the thought of such an activity elicited a reaction behind the button and zipper of his jeans—one he was grateful she couldn't see.

He licked his lips. "Why are you closing your eyes?" he whispered.

She gave him a nervous smile, eyes still shut.

"It's like making a wish on my birthday candles. You close your eyes for the magic to happen—and so as not to embarrass yourself in front of a handsome cowboy who already knows too much."

"But you already told me about that wish. Truth be told, though—you should be careful what you wish for, Jenna Owens," he said. "Because I have the power to make that wish come true. And I just might do it."

The only problem was that if she asked him to grant *any* wish of hers—list or not—he couldn't imagine saying anything other than *yes*.

She opened her eyes. "I'm counting on it." Then she cleared her throat. "Now, about this dessert and doing-things-out-of-order tonight. I'm a little curious on what you have planned for my good-night kiss. Do you think I might be able to get a little preview?"

His pulse quickened, and he heard a little hitch in her breath as he leaned closer to her, his lips *almost* on hers but not quite as he said, "If I did that, beautiful, what would you have to look forward to?"

It took everything in his power to pull away without letting his lips touch hers, but he did it.

She drew in a sharp breath, her eyes going wide. "Colt Morgan, how *dare* you tease me like that."

Uh-oh. He had a feeling Jenna was prepared to match his teasing and likely raise the stakes even higher.

He looked forward to it.

"We're here," he said. "We should go inside."

"I'm confused," Jenna said, standing in front of the painted green door of the bookshop known as Storyland. "You asked if I wanted dessert first."

Colt nodded. "That I did."

"But this is a bookstore," she added, stating the obvious.

And because he could answer obvious with obvious, Colt said, "That it is."

She crossed her arms and gave him a pointed look.

"So," she said. "A man who likes to tease and who is full of riddles, huh? Well, we'll see how the shoe fits when *I'm* wearing it."

His brows drew together, and he tried not to laugh.

She groaned. "It's a metaphor. The shoe is our next date and me wearing it means *me* planning it, and you're not going to be too happy when that happens, mister."

This made him smile, which only seemed to infuriate her more, even if that fury was a bit of an act.

"Mr. Morgan, what has got you grinning at me like the cat that ate the canary when I am *clearly* indignant?" she asked, but he could see her fighting a smile of her own.

He shrugged. "You said *next date*, which means no matter what happens tonight, you already *want* there to be a date number two."

She pursed her lips and narrowed her eyes. "Isn't that how flings work?"

He shrugged. "That they do. But what if I fail miserably tonight? Who's to say you won't realize you've chosen the wrong guy for the job once I fall flat on my face planning an evening for you. *But* since you're so confident in my abilities..."

She swallowed, and he hoped that had something to do not only with his date-planning abilities but also certain abilities he'd displayed their first night together and again outside the ranch's dining hall. He raised his brows. "Maybe you're a little indignant about my teasing, but you're also *so* damned fond of me, you're already planning our second date."

He pulled the door open, and a small bell above the door frame rang as he did.

"After you, second date," he teased.

Jenna blew out an exasperated breath. "Possum," she spouted at him, then strode through the opened door.

All indignation faded away as she spun to face him, a smile spread from ear to ear. She kept spinning in a slow circle, taking in the light wood floors lined with dark cherrywood shelves; the purple-painted walls and exposed beams along the ceiling; the bay-window reading nook piled with pillows and a short staircase leading to the second level where each stair was painted to look like the spine of a book.

Jenna stood at the base of the staircase reading each spine aloud.

"*The Handmaid's Tale, On Beauty, Beloved, Little Women, The Joy Luck Club*..." She turned to face him. "They're all books by female authors." If it was possible for her smile to have grown exponentially, it had.

"My store, my design," a woman's voice said from over Colt's shoulder. "No one has to love the same books I do, but they sure as hell have to read their spines every time they want to use the restroom or visit the café."

He stepped aside so that he and Jenna were now standing in a half circle with a woman whose long gray braid hung over her left shoulder. Under her right arm she held a small-ish beagle like a football.

"Jenna Owens, meet Trudy Davis. This is her shop. And this"—Colt moved to Trudy's opposite side so he could scratch the dog behind his ears—"is Frederick."

Jenna reached out her hand to shake, but Trudy waved her off.

"Nonsense, sweetie. As long as you're in town, you're family. And don't worry, Frederick doesn't bite. He can't. Had to have most of his teeth pulled on account of his age. He might gum ya, though. Just a fair warning."

She pulled Jenna in for a one-armed hug, and Frederick let loose a soft howl.

"Don't mind him," Trudy said as she backed away. "He's always been a little anxious, but ever since the fire last summer he's been downright insufferable. Glued to my side day in and day out. And because his arthritis outranks mine, I carry him up and down the stairs. Were you two coming up to the café to start? Churned a fresh batch of strawberry this morning just for you, Colt."

Jenna blinked and looked back and forth between Colt and Trudy.

"Fire?" she asked. "Fresh batch of strawberry? Does that mean ice cream? A bookstore that makes its own ice cream? I have *so* many questions."

Trudy laughed. "Come on upstairs, honey. The café's empty, so we've got the whole place to ourselves. I've got stories upon stories to answer anything you want to ask." She turned her attention to Colt. "Why don't you go and grab a pile of books you think she'll like while we get to chatting. Then we'll see how well this night is going to go."

Trudy put her free arm over Jenna's shoulder and began leading her up the book-spine stairs.

"Wait a second," Colt called after them. "You're kicking me out of my own date? You're the bookstore owner. Aren't *you* supposed to find us a pile of books and try to sell them to us?"

But Trudy and Jenna kept on up the stairs, already lost in conversation like they'd been friends for years.

Great. He'd known Jenna for a handful of days. How did he know what she liked to read or if she was a reader at all? He'd brought her here for the ice cream. *That* was his surprise. Now he was tasked with picking the right books to impress her or show that he knew her? *That*, he knew, was well outside the confines of fling requirements. He'd rather spend the rest of the evening refinishing the shop's wood floors. At least *that* he knew he'd get right.

He snapped out of his *poor-Colt* thoughts when he saw Jenna and Trudy reach the second floor, and Jenna dropped to a squat as Trudy put Frederick on the floor, and then—as if he'd known her all his anxious life—the dog crawled between her knees and curled up on her feet.

It wasn't just that Jenna had raised her nephews through their teen years; she radiated a nurturing vibe that was undeniable. He saw it in the way Robert and Maggie took to her, saw it again with Delaney and Barbara Ann, with Melody and Martha at the swimming hole.

Maybe...

He scrubbed his hand across his jaw, then remembered Jenna kissing him there, where he'd nicked himself twice on her behalf. But before his mind could go too far elsewhere—like imagining her lips on him again and when or *if* that might happen tonight after his less-than-amiable move in the car—he saw it.

The children's section.

Colt wasn't a big reader in his own right, but as more families with younger children started booking stays at the ranch, he—with the help of parent suggestions and Trudy's expertise—started building up a small library in the lobby of the guest quarters.

One of the last memories he had of his own family was his mom reading to him and Willow when they were young.

He tucked a copy of *Where the Wild Things Are* under his arm. He had his own copy back in his room at the ranch, but that didn't matter right now. He wanted to share one of his favorites with Jenna—a book he hoped to read to his own children someday—and see if she loved it as much as he did. It would also force him to share something he should have told her on their way up from Oak Bluff. It wasn't a *pile* of books like Trudy suggested, but it was an important book. To him that was enough.

He made his way back to the book-spine stairs and up to the second level. Both Trudy and Jenna were sitting cross-legged in the café's upstairs window seat—because Trudy loved her window seats—with Frederick now curled up in Jenna's lap. Both women were laughing as they spoke with animated gestures, and Colt couldn't help but feel a little jealous. He wasn't sure if it was aimed at the dog or Trudy or both.

At least they hadn't started dessert without him.

He set the book facedown on an empty café table and nonchalantly strolled behind the counter.

"Will you be joining us, Trudy?" he called over to the two women.

She waved him off. "Don't be silly. I'm not going to intrude on a first date."

He laughed as he opened the small freezer under the counter and pulled out the tub of strawberry ice cream.

"Really?" he called back to her. "Because it looks like you and your dog are hitting it off pretty well with *my* date."

He pulled two chocolate-dipped waffle cone bowls from the Lucite cabinet, dropped them into two glass bowls, and then scooped both himself and Jenna a generous serving of the home-made frozen dessert Trudy made just for them. Colt wasn't one for calling in favors, but when Trudy told him the only flavors she had today were vanilla and mint chocolate chip, he asked what he could do to get her to find room in the freezer for Jenna's favorite. He hadn't expected her response.

"Take care of my little furballs over the weekend?" Trudy had asked. "Delaney said she could watch my animals at the shelter, but they'd all be so much happier in their own home. Especially Frederick. I'm going to see my sister in Santa Barbara, and it would be such a load off not to have to worry about all my critters."

And even though he'd never had a pet in his life and the only animals he truly understood were horses, he'd said yes.

For strawberry ice cream and the woman who was only his for two weeks.

When he'd finished preparing their first course, Colt set one bowl on the counter opposite him in front of an empty stool and kept the other—his—right in front of him.

"That's my cue to go check on my *paying* customers," Trudy said as she stood from the window seat.

"Hey now," Colt said with brows raised. "When have I ever skipped out on a tab? Plus, I know better than to mess with one of my all-time favorite people, Ms. Trudy. That you would accuse me of such a thing? Well, it just hits me right here." He beat his palm against his chest and gave her his best puppy-dog eyes.

Trudy scooped Frederick into her arms and laughed. "Young man, you *are* a flirt, aren't you? Well, keep it coming. If you end up with any books, I'll go ahead and charge you for those. But the ice cream is on the house. You're paying me back tenfold by taking care of all my fur babies this weekend."

Jenna's eyes widened, and she stood along with Trudy and Frederick. "Babysitting fur babies?"

Trudy gave Jenna another one-armed hug. "I'll let Mr. Morgan tell you all about our little arrangement." Then she turned her attention to Colt. "Just give a holler if any other patrons wander into the café. The place is usually pretty quiet until about eight o'clock, so you should have the place to yourselves until then."

She leaned over the counter and gave Colt a sweet kiss on the cheek.

"Slow and steady, sweetheart, okay?" she whispered. "She seems a little gun-shy. Let her fall for you *and* the town, and you're home free."

She straightened, and Colt did his best to couch his expression. He couldn't respond, not with Jenna sitting within earshot. For some reason, he didn't want to tell Trudy that she had it all wrong, that the thing between him and Jenna was only a two-week arrangement.

Saying it out loud to Sam, Delaney, and Barbara Ann had left a bad taste in Colt's mouth. He didn't want that tinge of bitterness on his tongue, not tonight. It was fruitless to like Jenna as much as he did already. He got that. But it didn't mean he had to taint the night with the truth when the truth wouldn't matter for well over a week.

"Thanks for the advice," he finally said and left it at that.

Then Trudy and Frederick sauntered back down the stairs, leaving Colt to try to figure out why he was growing more reluctant to admit the truth to anyone outside his and Jenna's arrangement.

"Hungry?" he said, his eyes meeting Jenna's.

She nodded, a smile slowly spreading across her face.

God, that *smile*. How had any guy let it go unappreciated, un*worshipped* even, let alone even dared to hurt the woman behind it?

He wondered at Trudy sensing Jenna's trepidation. Or had Jenna flat-out told the other woman about her less-than-romantic past?

He could still take Trudy's advice. Slow and steady was as much about protecting himself as it was about showing her that no matter what came of their time together, he was someone she could trust to keep her safe.

Jenna strode toward him, and had he mentioned her smile? How about her smile in combination with that outfit?

"Stop," he said, before she'd made it to the stool. "I mean, wait for just a second. Please." He pulled his phone out of his pocket and held it up, brows raised in question. "May I?" he asked.

Her cheeks flushed pink and she shook her head.

"Not like this, at least," she said. "It has to be candid, when I don't know that you're going to do it. That's the only way to capture everything a person is thinking and feeling. The only way to catch the true meaning of the moment."

He set his phone on the counter.

"So what you're saying is that I have permission to take your picture but only when you don't *know* I'm taking your picture, and that when I do I will understand all the thoughts and emotions swirling around in that head of yours?"

She climbed onto the stool and grinned. "Exactly."

If only it was that easy to read her thoughts.

"Now," she said, glancing down at her bowl of ice cream and then back up at him. "Tell me about this favor you're doing for Trudy and why we get to eat our dessert for free."

Did he want to show his cards this early in the game? Who was he kidding? He'd been an open book from the get-go. Why stop now?

"I knew strawberry was your favorite, but when I talked to Trudy earlier today, she said she wasn't going to have any until Thursday. So I asked her what I could do to change her schedule and have her whip some up for tonight." He shrugged. "And now I'm animal-sitting."

Jenna sucked in a breath, then bit her bottom lip as she tried to stifle her smile.

That was when he grabbed his phone, quickly opened up the camera app, and snapped her portrait. After glancing at his handiwork, he spun the phone so the Jenna-filled screen was facing her.

"Let me see if I got it right," he said. "You're thinking, *That Colt Morgan is the sweetest, most selfless, and sexiest man to do such a thing for me*. And you're feeling like you could skip the ice cream altogether and just while away the evening kissing me like there's no tomorrow."

Her expression quickly morphed into one of mild disdain, her big blue eyes now narrowed into slits.

"It *was* a sweet gesture, but you don't know me at all if you think I'm going to toss this bowl of heaven to the curb just for a man who prefers to *tease* me with that kind of kissing only to withhold at the very last second. No, thank you. Ice cream I can count on. Ice cream I can depend on. Ice cream I can—"

Before she could finish setting him straight, he scooped a spoonful of said dependable dessert onto his spoon and brought it to her mouth.

She wrapped her lips around the spoon, and her eyes fluttered shut as he pulled it clean from her mouth and she swallowed that first bite.

"That Colt Morgan," she began, eyes still closed, "is the sweetest, most selfless, and sexiest man to do such a thing for me." She blinked her eyes open. "Now you know. Ice cream is my truth serum, and I'm afraid if I finish this bowl—which I have no choice but to do—I'm going to tell you *all* my deepest, darkest, scariest secrets."

He leaned across the counter, dipped the tip of his finger in her ice cream, and spread it onto her bottom lip. She licked it clean away, her eyes turning glassy as he licked his own finger clean.

"I must confess," he said softly. "You do scare the hell out of me, Jenna Owens."

"See?" she said, almost whispering. "Truth serum. It's working on you too."

They were definitely close enough to kiss for the second time since the night began. But for the second time, he held back. Because say what she would about the effect Trudy's concoction had on *her*, if Colt kissed her now, he'd blow it, the whole slow-and-steady part of the evening itself.

He wanted to build the anticipation.

If he kissed her now—because holy hell, he wanted nothing more—all that expectant energy would be lost. And he wanted the kiss at the end of this night to knock the air out of her lungs.

Also, he wasn't really sure what came next. The ice cream was his grand plan. He wanted to leave the rest of the night to her—and he wanted to see what else was on her list.

So instead of kissing her, for several seconds he let their breath mingle in the small space between his mouth and hers. Finally, he said, "If you don't eat that ice cream of yours, I'll do it for you."

His bottom lip accidentally brushed hers—or maybe it was no accident at all.

She sucked in a sharp breath, and he pulled away, every part of him silently growling as he did.

"You're going to send me to an early grave, Colt Morgan," she said, and he watched as heat visibly spread up her neck, wondering if she could see the same thing happening to him.

"Don't worry," he said, hoping to hell and back that he was right. "It'll be worth it."

CHAPTER THIRTEEN

Trudy was right. The café was empty until just before eight o'clock, which was when she and Frederick showed up to take over behind the counter.

Jenna and Colt had eaten their ice cream across the counter from each other. Other than teasing her *twice* (she was keeping count) with almost-but-not-quite kisses, it was like Colt was keeping the counter between them as a safety barrier.

He'd kept the conversation safe as well, steering clear of anything that would suggest she should reveal those deep, dark secrets of hers. *Not* that she hadn't told him the darkest one already—about that last guy she dated and what he'd done. But once they got to talking, it started to feel like Colt was somehow retreating.

"Favorite color?" he'd asked her.

"Rainbow after a storm," she'd said. "Look." Then she showed him the photo she took of the rainbow over Maggie and Robert's farmhouse the morning they left and finally made their trip to Meadow Valley.

Once they made their way back outside for a slow stroll down First Street, the conversation veered into other innocuous territory like first time riding a horse and small-town life versus city life.

They walked side by side. Jenna had initially worried about whether or not they were supposed to hold hands—and why she wanted to—but Colt conveniently held the small Storyland bag in the hand next to hers, taking the question off the table.

So Jenna crossed her arms as she went on.

"I remember when I was little and Clare, my sister, was practically a grown-up . . . I was a surprise if you're wondering about the age difference. But there was this one time our mama and daddy took us to Dallas for Christmas dinner at this fancy hotel, and then we walked around to look at all the beautiful lights, and I swear it was the prettiest thing I ever saw. Swore I'd live there one day."

"What happened?" Colt had asked.

She shrugged. "We ended up in California eventually, and even though I could have gone back, we'd been successful with our small farm—which became *my* farm. Wouldn't know what to do with Lucy and her sisters in the city. It's been farm and small-town life ever since."

Now that she thought about it, Colt had let her go on and on about *her* life. He'd asked questions, and she'd happily answered. With verbosity. But not once had he shared anything even close to intimate about himself. It was as if he was now putting roadblocks in place to keep things between them from getting too intimate.

Colt stopped short and turned to face her. Here it was. He was going to kiss her. *Finally.* Maybe this was his way of returning the intimacy she hadn't expected to want from him. She tried to tell herself she didn't want this as badly as she did, but holy hell, he had better lay one on her already.

"Should I—feed you dinner?" he asked, brows furrowed.

Jenna's mouth fell open, then closed.

He winced. "I messed up already, didn't I? I played the ace

up my sleeve, and now you're hoping for more. I guess I was hoping—"

"No!" she blurted, cutting him off, trying to wipe the disappointment from her face. "Honestly," she added. "I think that bowl of ice cream *was* dinner. I mean, we even ate the bowls." It was true. She hadn't left a bite. She'd even eaten the last chunk of *his* chocolate-dipped waffle bowl when he'd claimed he was too stuffed to finish it. "Plus, you still haven't revealed your book picks. I'm quite curious to see how well you did."

"Or if I failed miserably?" he asked, grin back on his face.

She let out a nervous laugh. "Hardly."

He stepped closer to her and dipped his head.

Jenna sucked in a breath. Here it was. *Now* he was going to kiss her.

She closed her eyes and waited, felt his warm breath hit her lips.

"I'll show you mine if you show me yours," he said softly.

"What?" she asked, eyes still closed, mouth still ready to receive a long-awaited smooch.

"The list, Jenna Owens. It's time I see the list."

Her eyes flew open, and Colt had already straightened to his full height, his brows raised in anticipation.

She groaned, her shoulders sagging. She wanted to show him. That was always the plan. But *why* couldn't he just kiss her and put her out of her misery?

"I left my bag in the car," she finally said.

So he escorted her back to where they'd parked, even opened her door like a perfect gentleman, but she still huffed out an indignant breath as she pulled out the leather-bound notebook and hugged it to her chest.

"You are beautiful when you're frustrated with me," he said as she turned to face him.

She narrowed her eyes, but Colt just laughed.

"Let's hear it," he said. "Lay it on me, all the wild and crazy stuff you want to do before going back home."

While he kept the smile plastered to his face, Jenna could have sworn his jaw tightened as he finished the sentence. Would Colt Morgan actually miss her when she was gone?

The thought made her stomach tighten, made her wonder how much *she* might miss *him*.

"Fine," she finally said, opening the journal to the only page with writing on it. "Here it is, in order of how they popped into my head, but I am not tied to completing them as such." She squared her shoulders and jutted out her chin.

"I think it's already clear you're not tied to any prescribed way of doing things. Anyone who's okay with dessert for dinner is a free thinker in my book."

Ugh. Why was he so damned charming? It made it so hard to be angry about him holding out on kissing her.

Her expression softened, and she couldn't help but smile back at him.

"Okay," she said. "Here it is. Number one, sleep outside under the stars. Two, eat food from a country I've always wanted to visit. Three, eat the *best* ice cream in town." She skimmed her teeth over her bottom lip and felt the heat rush to her cheeks. "You already made that happen. *Twice.* Though I have to say Trudy's is top of the top for me."

He nodded. "Had no doubt it would be."

"Number four," she continued, and now her cheeks burned. "Have a—um—vacation fling."

Colt bowed. "Happy to oblige, ma'am."

Okay, He *really* needed to stop being so adorable.

"Five, skinny-dip. Six, be the last one at a bar at closing time, and seven—" She tried to rush through to the end but couldn't bring herself to say the last one—*Write something more meaningful than a list*—out loud. Not yet.

Colt's brows drew together. "Seven?" he asked.

Jenna blew out a breath. "Can I save that one for now? It's one I have to do on my own, anyway."

He shrugged, but his smile faltered for a fraction of a second, and she wondered if he was disappointed in her keeping the last one to herself.

"So…that's it, I guess. Nothing earth shattering, I know, but it all means something to me."

"Come on," he said, reaching around her and dropping the book bag in the car before closing the door behind her. Then he threaded his fingers through hers and gave her a gentle squeeze.

Jenna's belly flipped and flopped at the simple yet intimate gesture.

"Where to?" she asked.

"To find a good seat at the bar for when we close the place down."

"I'm Casey," the pink-haired woman on the other side of the bar said, reaching a hand across to shake Jenna's.

"Jenna. Nice to meet you. And I love your hair."

The corners of Casey's mouth turned up. "A girl's gotta let her creative side show, right?"

Jenna swallowed, thinking about the one unmentioned item on her list. *She* had a creative side once upon a time. But she couldn't seem to access that part of herself yet and was beginning to wonder if it still existed.

"Just wait," Colt added. "It'll be purple next week. Maybe blue the next. I don't think there's a color that *doesn't* look good on Midtown Tavern's favorite bartender."

Casey rolled her eyes. "I already said the first round's on the house. Stop trying to butter me up when you are clearly on a date, Morgan."

Jenna laughed, her shoulders relaxing. "Right?" she said. "The charm's just dripping off this guy here." She nudged Colt's shoulder with hers. Then she caught a flash of color on the inside of Casey's wrist.

"Is that a tattoo?" Jenna asked, nodding in Casey's direction. "What's it mean?"

The other woman huffed out a bitter laugh before brandishing the body art, which was a blue infinity symbol.

"This," Casey said, "is what I like to call a mistake. And because I'm not shelling out hundreds of dollars to get it removed, I like to think of it as my infinite reminder *not* to make the same mistake again."

She dropped her hand, and Jenna could tell that was the most she was going to reveal about whatever the story was behind that tattoo.

"I'm going to serve some paying customers," Casey teased. "Let me know if you need anything."

She winked and spun back toward the bar, making her way to the next waiting patron.

"I *do* pay," Colt said when Jenna turned her attention back to him.

"Sure," she said. "With buckets of charm and being a big old tease?"

Colt's eyes widened. "Are we talking about me and my bar tab still?"

Jenna sighed, then took a sip from the pint glass in front her. The slight carbonation bubbled on her tongue, and the amber liquid—although ice cold—warmed her belly as it went down her throat.

"I know we have an arrangement," she admitted. "And that nothing in that arrangement requires you to reveal *anything* personal to me. But you let me babble on at Trudy's about my childhood and my farm and I can't help thinking that maybe you don't *want* me to know even your favorite color, which is fine, but then maybe we throw that all out on the table—boundaries, you know?" Her stomach tightened. "Okay, so I know we've already crossed a *bunch* of physical boundaries, which is the whole point of—you know—the fling, but I wouldn't mind getting to know you a bit."

He raised a brow. "Wouldn't *mind*?"

She groaned. "I *want* to know you, okay? Just because this is all fun and games doesn't mean I can turn off wanting to know who you are, what you like and dislike, your hopes and dreams…It's simply in my DNA, wanting to know people."

But wanting to know you *especially. Maybe that will help me understand why I get butterflies when you hold my hand or why I'm going out of my mind about whether or not you'll kiss me tonight.*

Though she sure as hell wasn't going to say any of *that*.

"My favorite color," Colt said, matter-of-factly. "Your stormy, baffled blue eyes when you look at me like you don't know what the hell I'm saying."

She promptly rolled said stormy, baffled blue eyes.

"Well, that was ridiculously sweet," she mumbled.

He barked out a laugh. "Thank you?"

"You're welcome," she said, begrudgingly.

"*But*," he added.

"There's *always* a but…"

He leaned over and glanced at *her* butt, then straightened and gave her a mischievous grin.

Jenna's mouth fell open.

"*Some* butts are better than others. *But* the one I was referring to verbally is that you already know a lot about me. You know I have a sister who's a country singer and can bake like no one else I know. You know we lost our parents and ended up getting separated in the foster system. And you know I grew up in Oak

Bluff but joined Sam and Ben in building and opening the ranch up here in Meadow Valley. Jenna, you know more about me in a matter of days than some people I've known all my life. The reason I hung back at Trudy's is because I want to know as much about *you* as you'll let me."

"Oh," she said softly. Because—wow. Jenna wasn't sure how to respond to that, so instead she brought her pint glass to her lips and slowly drank until it was empty.

Tonight was starting to feel more and more like a date—a *real* date. One she'd go on with a guy she might want to see again after their two weeks were up. But this *couldn't* be that, not when they had an arrangement. Not when she was so sure there was more than simply the obstacle of age and physical distance between them.

Wasn't there?

"Okay..." Colt said, drawing out the word. "I think we better pace ourselves if we're going to make it until closing. Also, I probably should have mentioned that Casey has a tendency to ignore the hours posted outside the door. Sometimes she closes when she says she's gonna close, and sometimes people want to keep buying drinks, and she wants to keep letting them."

Jenna responded with a belch—one that sneaked up on her without so much as a warning until it was out there, in the world, on this date that wasn't a date.

Colt's eyes widened, and Jenna threw both hands over her mouth. But then, as if on cue, *both* of them burst out laughing at the same time.

"Don't worry," Jenna said when she finally caught her breath. "My nephews run a winery. I can hold my own when it comes to a drink or two."

Her bar stool lurched toward Cole's, and Jenna yelped. Then she noticed his boot hooked under the wooden rod that acted as the stool's footrest.

"It's time," he said, leaning in close, his mouth a breath away from hers.

Her breath hitched. "For—for what?"

"I wholeheartedly believe in your ability to hold your liquor, Jenna Owens. But just in case, I don't want you to forget."

"Forget? I—I don't understand."

Great. Apparently she could only stammer when Colt was this close.

"Your good-night kiss," he said.

Finally, *finally*, Colt Morgan's lips were on hers.

They weren't in a guest room in a secluded farmhouse or in Luis and Anna's secret make-out spot outside the dining hall.

They were in a crowded tavern that—while dimly lit—still put them on display for all to see. Yet Colt kissed her like she was the only person in the room, in the *world* for that matter—his hands in her hair and her knees hooked over his thighs. He slipped his tongue past her lips, and Jenna thanked the stars that "Sin Wagon" by the Chicks was blasting through the tavern's sound system. It meant no one heard the soft moan escaping her lips—except Colt.

He smiled against her, letting her know *he* hadn't missed the audible reaction.

He nipped at her bottom lip and slowly pulled away, a self-satisfied grin spread across his maddeningly handsome face.

Jenna's heart raced. She touched her swollen lips with the tips of her fingers.

"You just did that in front of *everyone*," she said, stating the obvious.

Colt shrugged. "It was important and needed doin'. Plus, in case you hadn't noticed, I like doing things out of order." He winked and then lifted his own glass, clinking it lightly against her empty one, and downed the contents in three large gulps.

"There," he said. "Now we're on equal ground."

She let out a nervous laugh.

Jenna liked this man. A *lot*. Apparently she hadn't read the fling manual, because she was pretty sure it said something to the effect of it being mighty difficult to have a lengthy casual encounter with someone you liked this much.

Equal ground? *Right.*

Not. Even. Close.

It was one in the morning by the time Casey cashed out the last customer—the last one other than Jenna and Colt.

"All right, you two. Go find somewhere else to kiss and make eyes at each other," Casey said, shooing them away with her hands.

They weren't sitting at the bar anymore. Sometime after Jenna's third pint, she'd convinced Colt that even though it wasn't line-dancing night at the bar, *they* should get up and dance.

Now her arms were draped around his neck, her head resting sleepily on his shoulder as they slowly swayed back and forth even though an uptempo Zac Brown Band song was playing.

"We did it," Colt said softly in her ear, and Jenna mustered up the energy to smile, even if she didn't have any left to actually lift her head.

"Can I help you clean up?" she heard Colt ask as her eyes fell closed.

"Go home, ya charmer," Casey called back. "You have more important things to take care of, but I appreciate the offer."

All she remembered after that was Colt scooping her into his arms and eventually depositing her into his SUV and after that her bed.

And the kiss—the kiss he gave her at just the right time so she wouldn't forget.

Nope. She would *never* forget that kiss. She was, however, in danger of forgetting one of the most important rules of their arrangement, one that she'd actually written down.

Do not fall for your fling.

CHAPTER FOURTEEN

Jenna sipped her iced coffee and sighed as she stared out at the hill that led up to the Meadow Valley Ranch, the place where she was supposed to be enjoying a lesson in barrel jumping, one of the few activities the ranch offered for more advanced riders. But she'd canceled. As she'd canceled her other activities the past couple of days.

It wasn't that she hadn't wanted to participate in everything her nephews signed her up to do. It was just that, after the other night, she didn't know how to face Colt Morgan. So she'd taken to the empty pages in her journal, trying to figure out her own thoughts. She wouldn't count it as number seven on her list—writing something *other* than the list. But it was a way to put out into the world what she was feeling without having to admit it.

She stared down at the one sentence she'd written so far. It was the same sentence she'd started with yesterday and the day before when she'd woken after her perfect date with what she was slowly admitting might be the perfect man.

I have feelings for Colt Morgan.

She added another few words.

Big feelings. What the hell do I do about that?

"Are you sure it's not too hot for you out here?" she heard Delaney ask from behind.

Jenna startled and slammed the journal shut, but Delaney didn't seem to notice.

She stepped through the back door that led to the deck Sam had recently added to their new home. Her hair was pulled back into a low ponytail, any loose strands held in place by a floral scarf. Her sleeveless black maxi dress swished back and forth above her bare swollen feet.

Jenna pressed her perspiring glass to the side of her also perspiring neck but shook her head. "I love the view. Helps me think." It didn't, however, give her any answers.

"You ready to tell me why you've been hiding out the past few days?" Delaney asked. "Don't get me wrong. I *love* the company. But if you want to talk about it…"

She trailed off.

Jenna tapped her pen against her bottom lip.

She'd spent the last two days either holed up in her room, helping out with Lucy and the other animals at the rescue shelter when she was sure Colt was out on a trail ride, or here at Sam and Delaney's house, hanging out with her new friend and trying to figure out why her date with Colt had gotten to her so much.

Sorry I missed you again today, Colt had texted last night. Think our paths might cross again? We still have an item or two to check off that list.

Jenna: Of course. As soon as our schedules match up again.

Colt: Are we still good? If anything's changed, say the word, and I'll leave you be. I won't enjoy it, but I'll do it if that's what you want.

Jenna: We're good. I promise.

But Jenna Owens—who had never been so before—was a lying liar.

"Aren't you supposed to keep your feet up whenever possible?" Jenna asked, changing the subject.

Delaney narrowed her eyes at her and sighed. "You're not getting me off your case that easily. But yes. My feet should be up. Blah blah blah. But I'm *so* bored. And I swear if you tell me I better enjoy my free time now before this baby comes and steals it all away from me like everyone else does, I'm gonna scream."

Jenna set her drink down on the umbrella-covered table where she'd been working and held her hands up. "I will say no such thing. And I'm sorry. I'm supposed to keeping you company. Not doing the best job, am I?"

Delaney waved her off. "It's fine. Barbara Ann and I are stealing you away for the whole day tomorrow. I suppose I can survive inside on my own. Binging on Netflix and clementines with Butch Catsidy curled up on my lap."

Delaney did love her three-legged cat, but Jenna could tell her new friend was going a little stir-crazy.

Delaney held up a small orange that was hidden in her hand. "I maybe ate an orange once or twice a month before I was pregnant. Now that's *all* I want. I have a glass of juice in the morning. I eat at least four of these before lunch. Luis puts mandarin oranges in all my salads, even if they don't go with the other ingredients, but I can't get enough."

Jenna laughed. "I bet that drives Luis crazy."

Delaney nodded, then pulled out one of the empty chairs at the table, propping her feet up on another.

"It's not too bad in the shade," she said. "Mind if I hang out while you do whatever it is you're doing in that notebook of yours?"

"I have a better idea," Jenna said. "When's the last time you had those pretty toes of yours painted?" Expert deflection again, if she did say so herself.

Delaney snorted. "I can't even see my toes over this." She patted her belly. "Which means it's been a *long* time, but it's very sweet of you to call them pretty. I'm sure they are quite the opposite."

"Where's your polish?" Jenna asked.

Delaney's smile suddenly vanished, and she was wiping a tear off her cheek.

"Oh no, sweetie," Jenna said. "We don't have to if you don't want to. I just thought it would be nice to give you a little pampering when you've been so nice to me letting me use your sun deck and your home and—"

"It's not *that*," Delaney interrupted, sniffling as she peeled her clementine. "It's just—we've been so busy at the ranch, which is great. But this really *is* the last of my free time before the baby comes and steals it all away, and it's already stolen my ankles and my cute clothes and my ability to see past my boobs. And I really wish my morning orange juice could sometimes be a morning mimosa, you know? My boobs are ginormous, though. So I guess that's a bonus."

Both of them laughed at that.

"Am I the worst soon-to-be mama or what?" Delaney asked.

Jenna blew out a long breath, reminding herself that she was lucky to have been—and still be—the closest thing to a mother her nephews had when they needed one the most. She reminded herself that even though she'd never had a baby of her own, she was healthy and happy and had a whole new stage of her life ahead of her.

Still, an unexpected pang of envy made her throat tighten and her eyes burn.

She cleared her throat and dropped down into a squat next to her friend.

"Not even close," she said to Delaney. "Your whole life is about to change. For the better, mind you. But it's still a monumental change, and it's okay to mourn the loss of the parts of your life that will never be the same. Although I'm pretty sure you'll get your ankles back."

Delaney blew out a long breath.

"Thank you," she said. "I've been so scared to say any of that to Sam. He's so excited about the baby. I don't want him to think for a second that I'm not. Because I can't wait to meet our tiny new human."

"Yeah, well," Jenna started. "Sam's hormones and ankles aren't rebellin' against him, so he's got nothing to complain about. *Not* that you're complaining."

Delaney reached a hand toward Jenna and swiped a thumb across her cheek. Jenna sucked in a breath as she felt the wetness against her skin.

"Are you having sympathy tears for me? Or does this have something to do with what's been going on with you for the past couple of days? We don't have to talk about it, Jenna. But we can—if you want to."

Delaney dropped her hand, and Jenna straightened back to her full height. She wasn't ready to talk, not while she was still trying to reconcile what it was that had her hiding out in the first place.

"Thank you," she said. "I appreciate that. But I think right now, if it's okay with you, I just need the distraction of spending time with a new friend." Colt was right. Despite her feelings, she had a list to check off and a cowboy with whom she needed to be honest, and she had an idea that might just get her out of hiding after all.

Delaney beamed. "Manis and pedis it is, then!"

"Perfect," Jenna said. "Now tell me where that polish is, because it's time you get some pampering."

CHAPTER FIFTEEN

Colt was a sweaty mess by the time he'd made it to the door of his suite in the guesthouse. Sure, the dip in the swimming hole was refreshing, but the hike back—no riders today, which meant they'd all traveled on foot—had been brutal. Then he'd had to hightail it on over to Trudy Davis's house to let the dogs out, feed the dogs *and* cats, wait for the dogs to finish eating, and then let them out again, since they apparently needed to do their business as soon as they swallowed their last morsel of food—especially Frederick. Now his day was finally done. He was hungry. Thirsty. And exhausted. And needed to recharge so he could be on his game when he saw Jenna later this evening.

Jenna Owens. Just the thought of her put a bit more pep in his step and a grin on his face—until he threw open his door, kicked off his boots, and felt that something was very, very wrong.

For one thing, the place was spotless, and he *knew* the sink in the kitchenette had been piled with half-filled coffee mugs, and the counter had been lined with empty bottles of beer that needed to be taken down the hall to the recycling bin.

Then his bed was *made*.

Colt wasn't exactly a slob. He would certainly straighten up if he was expecting a guest, but he never brought guests home. This was his sanctuary. The one place that was only for him. He didn't even let Jessie, a probie firefighter who moonlighted at the ranch on her off days, inside to straighten like she did with all the other rooms.

His. Space.

And someone had been here.

Crash!

Something hit the tile in the bathroom.

"What the...?" he said under his breath. Great. Not only had Jessie been in here straightening up, but she'd left the door open, and now he was being robbed? None of it made any sense, but the fact remained that someone other than *him* was in the room.

He grabbed the first thing he could find, which was a table lamp, to use as a weapon in case he needed to, what—crack it over someone's head like some slapstick movie? He yanked the lamp's cord from the wall as he crept stealthily toward the closed bathroom door. It looked like the light was off, which meant whoever was hiding in there was, in fact, *hiding*.

He made sure not to make a sound as he placed one hand on the door handle while he held the lamp over his head with the other.

He shook his head and sighed. The last thing he wanted to do was deal with some yahoo who thought it might be fun to break into the ranch owner's room, but here he was.

He counted to three in his head, then threw open the door with a roar he knew would scare the pants off the yahoo.

And it certainly did.

Because the yahoo was Jenna Owens—a very *naked* Jenna Owens, who yelped and sprang up from the bubble-filled tub with a start. And then she faltered, her hand slamming against the tiled wall.

Without a second thought, Colt tossed the lamp and bolted toward her, catching her under her arms as her feet went out from beneath her.

She clasped her hands around his neck.

"What the hell, Jenna?" he asked, half laughing, half angry—not *at* her but at the countless ways this could have gone so much worse. "You could have killed yourself! Or I could have—"

"Thrown a lamp at me?" she interrupted. "And here you said you'd never hurt me."

He straightened when he could tell she was steady on her feet, but she gripped him tighter.

"Wait!" she said. "A towel first? Unlike you and"—she cleared her throat—"*Colt Jr.*, I'd rather not have this conversation in the buff."

He reached for the towel hanging on the rack to his left while still holding her against him with his right arm. He handed it to Jenna, and she cleverly slipped it between them and then around her torso, tucking it tight over her breasts.

Colt crossed his arms and raised his brows. "So breaking and entering is a thing with you now?"

Jenna rolled her eyes. "I didn't exactly break in. I might have borrowed Sam's master key." She gave him a nervous smile.

"Sam *gave* you his master key? That doesn't sound like him. He's all about privacy and safety of the guests *and* his business partner and..." He shook his head and laughed. "Delaney."

Jenna winced. "Please don't bust her. She meant well. I'm just going to get dressed and get out of your way because this was obviously a terrible idea. Seems like when I surprise you—whether by accident or intentionally—you either lose your cookies or I almost lose my life to an unfortunate bathing blunder. I think I'll leave the surprising to you from here on out."

Colt held up both his hands. "Wait just a second there, my naked little felon..."

Jenna groaned, and Colt finally took a moment to glance around the rest of the room.

The light was off, and the counter was lined with flickering candles. The whole space smelled fresh and soothing, like eucalyptus.

On the floor next to the tub was a box of condoms.

His pulse quickened.

"You did all this for *me*?" he asked, looking back at her.

She nodded, a soft smile on her face.

"And straightened the place up?" he added, brows furrowed.

She let out a nervous laugh. "I clean when I'm nervous. Helps clear my head. That was the sound you heard." She glanced toward the toilet. "I heard you come in and realized the bottle of tile cleaner was still sitting on the back of the toilet, so I reached for it, knocked it down, and it banged the toilet seat shut, which I'd also forgotten to close..." She winced.

Colt hadn't seen her for two days and was starting to think she was avoiding him. So this *was* highly unexpected.

"Do you want me to go?" Jenna asked when he still hadn't spoken. "Because it still feels like I should probably go."

He wanted to spend every free minute with her, but he knew if he said that, he'd scare her away. Jenna wanted no strings attached, and Colt had agreed to the arrangement. *No strings* had been his own MO for years now, so this should have been easy.

Except when Jenna wasn't around, she was on Colt's mind. And every time he saw her for the first time in the day, it felt like seeing her for the first time at Jack and Ava's place. Something vacant in his chest felt like it could fill itself up, simply by being near her.

"I want to know what *you* want, Jenna," he finally said. "Because if you want to stay, *I* want you to stay. If you want to drop that towel and sink back into the tub—after I get to take a good look at you—then that's what I want too. And if you want me to join you in what I'm hoping is a bubble bath meant for two, then hell *yes*. I want you to stay."

She stared at him for several long moments.

"I'm afraid," she finally said. "That after one week of knowing you, I think about you as much as I do. I'm afraid knowing that after one night of sleeping in your arms, I dream about doing it again. I'm afraid that after all you did for me the other night—the ice cream, the tavern, getting me home and in bed safe…and kissing me at just the right time so it would be the last thing I remembered when I fell asleep and the first thing I thought of when I woke up—it all scares the pants off me— literally…How's a girl supposed to say good-bye in a week after all that?"

He laughed, and she continued.

"I know what I said I wanted, Colt, and I haven't changed my mind. But it's important for you to know that this isn't just physical for me. I—I care about you. It's part of my makeup, and I can't seem to turn it off."

He nodded once. "You have more heart than anyone I know, Jenna Owens. Didn't take long to figure that out."

She blew out a shaky breath. "I just thought it was important for you to know that I don't take it lightly what we're doing here, what *you're* doing for me and my silly list, and that even after I'm gone, I'll still care because it's what I do."

"It's not a silly list," he said. Then he pulled his T-shirt over his head and tossed it on the floor. Next he unbuttoned and unzipped his jeans, losing his boxer briefs along with the denim until everything he'd been wearing seconds ago sat in a pile on the bathroom floor.

"You need to stop calling it Colt Jr.," she said, eyes wide.

He laughed. "Your turn," he said.

She nodded and swallowed. "I need to point out, though, that this does *not* count as skinny-dipping. That, my friend, is still on the list. I just figured—well, I didn't want that to be the *first* time you saw me—*really* saw me—like this." Then she unwrapped herself and handed the towel back to him.

God, she was beautiful. He'd concocted a vision of her in his head based on what he'd seen in flashes of light during the thunderstorm and later in the bathing suit she'd worn for the trail ride to the swimming hole.

None of it held a eucalyptus-scented candle to the woman who bared herself completely to him now.

"Trust me," he said. "I'm not letting you off the hook for skinny-dipping." His pulse quickened. "And I *see* you, Jenna," he added, this throat tight. He saw it all, everything from her enormous heart to the stunning vision before him.

He knew now that he'd be in too deep once this night was through, but he also knew he couldn't walk away. Maybe he'd kept himself safe these past five years—content, even—by keeping any woman who came into his life at arm's length. But it took meeting Jenna to realize he'd only been living half a life. It took meeting her to finally admit to himself that he was ready for more.

He wrapped his arms around her and pulled her to him, chest-to-chest and skin-on-skin.

"This just feels right, doesn't it?" he whispered. "I can't explain it, but you and me? We fit." Even after years with Emma, after proposing to her *and* worrying about that stupid future he wanted so badly, he'd never been as sure as he was standing right here, right now, with *this* amazing woman.

"We really do," she said with a nervous laugh. "It's terrifying."

He tilted his forehead against hers and cradled her cheeks in his palms. He'd been through the worst and come out of it all the better. This? Her? Piece of cake.

Physical distance and a slight difference in age were nothing compared with what he felt when her body was pressed against his. If she felt it, too, then they could make this work beyond two weeks. He was sure of it.

But they didn't need to worry about that now. Not when they had what he hoped was one of a thousand firsts for them to experience together.

"We got this," he said, then kissed her.

Together they lowered their bodies unto the warm, bubble-topped water. He stretched his legs the length of the tub and she stretched hers over his knees.

"Okay, maybe this *can* count as skinny-dipping," Jenna said. "Because I think I like this even better."

He wasn't sure if it was minutes or hours that they sat like that, kissing and tasting and touching. Time didn't matter when they had all night.

But…the temperature of the water did.

Jenna's teeth chattered, and her lips trembled against his.

"You're freezing," he said with a chuckle.

"I am n-n-*not*," she lied, and he tilted his head back so his eyes met hers.

He rubbed his hands over her shoulders. "You are *covered* in goose bumps."

She groaned, teeth clattering together. "I th-thought this would be romantic. Just m-more proof that I am the *worst* at being the surpris-*er* and m-m-m-much better at being the surprise-*ee*."

He stood without warning, then held a hand out for her.

"Wh-what are y-you *doing*?"

"Being the surprise-*er*," he said. "Come on."

She grabbed his wrist and let him pull her up, wrap her in a towel, and then lead her out of the tub and back into his room.

He held up a finger, then reached down to where a small device hung from a cord over the edge of his bed. He threw the quilt and top sheet to the side and patted the mattress.

Jenna crawled onto the bed and sucked in a sharp breath.

"It's—*heated*," she said.

Colt grinned. "Surprise..."

Despite the plethora of supplies she had waiting for them in the bathroom, he opened his nightstand drawer and pulled out a condom of his own.

"Is this still what you want?" he asked, his heart in his goddamn throat. Because he'd never wanted anything more.

She nodded and opened up her towel, pulling it out from under her and tossing it on the floor.

His head swam. How the hell had she been a stranger only a week before?

He tore the small square package open and rolled the condom down the length of his erection.

He ached for her.

He *needed* her.

And when he crawled over her and sank between her legs, hearing her cry out as he buried himself inside her, Colt knew.

He was falling for her, and there was no turning back now.

Later they lay blissfully spent on Colt's bed, Jenna's hair still wet and his likely a crazy mess from having dried while they were—otherwise engaged.

Jenna's stomach growled, and it was loud enough to wake the dead.

She gasped, and Colt burst out laughing.

"Sorry, darlin', but I'm unprepared," he said when the laughter finally subsided. "Had I known you were breaking in..."

"I didn't *break* in," she said, pushing him on the shoulder.

"Uh-huh," he said, grabbing her hand before she could pull it away and kissing her palm. "Anyway," he continued, "if I'd known you'd be *breaking in*, I'd have come home with some sort of frozen treat for you. Instead, all I have to offer is the last cookie from Willow's almost trashed batch."

Jenna raised herself up onto her elbow and stared at him, eyes wide and mouth agape.

"I don't know what shocks me more," she said. "That you would share such a treasure with me—or that you already ate the rest and probably never would have offered if I hadn't busted in and rocked your world."

He laughed. "That's an admittance of guilt right there, Owens. And *your* chicken ate the rest of my treasure. There were only three left after that. The fact I'm even offering to share with you should be evidence enough of my good faith."

Hell, he'd give her anything she wanted right about now. All she had to do was ask. But he wouldn't put that kind of pressure on her. Maybe they were doing this all out of order, but Colt didn't care. He could still take things slow and steady to give her heart time to catch up to his. But for now, he could at the very least give her some food.

He slid his arm out from under her and rolled out of the bed, naked as the day was long. He grabbed the almost empty cookie tin from the kitchen and brought it back to bed.

He lay back down under the sheet, next to the still-naked woman, and pried the lid off the tin.

"Jenna Owens..." he started. "Will you have my last cookie?"

She placed a hand over her heart and gasped dramatically. "Oh, Colt," she said with even more theatrics. "I thought you'd never ask." Then she grabbed the cookie from the tin and brought it to her lips with a grin, opened her mouth, and—

"Whoa! Hold up!" he blurted.

She stopped mid-bite, mouth still open and teeth seemingly ready to chomp.

"Were you about to pop that whole thing into your mouth at once? Without sharing? Without *savoring*?"

She moved the cookie away from her lips, but instead of lowering it back toward the tin, she held it high and out of his reach. She smiled at him, wickedly, which made him want to kiss her and forget all about the damned cookie.

Or maybe he could kiss her to distract her and steal it *back*.

He went for it, dipping his head toward hers, but she retaliated by rolling onto her back and palming his face to keep it away.

Colt fell onto *his* back, and they both exploded into peals of laughter.

"Here," she finally said, slapping the pastry onto his chest. "You never wanted me to have it anyway, you overgrown child," she teased.

He pushed himself up to sitting, his pillow resting against the wooden headboard. Jenna did the same.

He broke the lone cookie in half, offering one portion to her and saving the other for himself.

"You're only half right," he admitted. "I never wanted you to have the *whole* thing."

She narrowed her eyes at him, and her stomach made another audible protest over having been ignored for too long. "Can I eat it now?"

He laughed. "*Yes*. But don't come crying to me wanting more when you've got Kentucky Fried Lucy to thank for that."

She gasped, this time for real, and then popped her entire half into her mouth without another second of hesitation.

He waited for what came next. Because he *knew*.

"Oh. My. God," she said and stopped chewing. "Why did you let me eat it all at once?" She held her mouth closed after that, unmoving.

He shrugged. "I did warn you."

She swallowed, her look so forlorn he almost offered up his half to her.

Almost.

As if she could read his mind, she batted her lashes at him and tickled his shoulder.

"Please?" she asked so sweetly that he almost handed it right over.

Almost.

Instead, he held the half-moon of buttery, toffee-speckled shortbread between his teeth, with two-thirds of it extending from his lips.

"You're going to have to *Lady and the Tramp* me for it," he said, hoping she could understand his half-formed words.

She was straddling him in a nanosecond, her teeth clamping down gently on the cookie's outer edge until she bit off the tiniest piece. Then she slid the rest from between his teeth, holding it between her fingers.

The little *thief.* But she was *his* little thief.

"Go ahead, Texas," he said. "You earned it after surprising me like you did today."

Her eyes widened. Though considering she wasn't wearing any clothes, his line of sight dipped a bit lower.

She broke his half in half, popped her portion into her mouth, and then fed him the other, letting her thumb linger on his bottom lip.

"I was always going to share, California. You should have more faith in me than that."

She braced her hands behind him on the headboard and grinned.

"You called me Colt before," he said softly. "When you were going all melodrama on my baked-good proposal."

Her brows drew together. "Is that simply an observation, or are you asking me a question?"

He placed his hands on her thighs and stroked her soft skin until he reached her behind. She sucked in a breath, and he smiled.

"No one calls me that," he said. "It's always been Morgan.

Especially with me and Willow. A reminder that we're family. That she's my *only* family."

"Oh," Jenna said. "I'm sorry. I won't—"

"No," he interrupted. "I meant I liked it. My name on your lips. Like it's something only for you."

"*Oh*," she said again. Then she leaned forward so her lips were almost touching his. "*Colt*," she said, her voice soft and sweet. "Like that?"

He nodded.

"Colt," she whispered, then brushed her lips over his.

"Like that too," he whispered back.

"Colt," she said one more time, barely audible, and then *really* kissed him.

And because he was a giver of more than just cookies, he *really* kissed her too.

Later, when Jenna lay tangled in his sheet, softly and sweetly snoring, he slipped into a clean pair of jeans and a T-shirt and slipped out the door and on over to the dining hall. Now that he and Jenna had finished the last of Willow's cookies, he was going to need some provisions for when she woke up.

What time was it? Eight, maybe? Nine? All he knew was that when he got there, the guest area was dark, but the kitchen light was still on.

He braced himself for either a Luis-and-Anna Armageddon-type argument or the makeup making out that usually followed. Instead he found Sam Callahan standing against the counter, his arm elbow-deep inside a tub of ice cream.

Sam froze when he saw Colt, and Colt had *no* idea how to react to his friend and business partner hiding out in the ranch kitchen going to town on what was left of the night's dessert rations.

"It's not what it looks like," Sam said, pulling out a spoonful of what looked like the salted caramel Luis had served that night with his summer apple crumble.

Colt scratched the back of his head and felt his hair sticking out at various angles. He realized he wasn't one to judge, but he was going to call it like he saw it.

"It looks like you're stress-eating a two-gallon tub of ice cream," he said.

Sam sighed. "Okay. Then it's exactly what it looks like." He plunged the spoon into his mouth and licked it clean in one go.

"I thought you were doing the bonfire tonight," Colt said.

Sam got himself another spoonful and shook his head. "Barbara Ann took it. Said I looked like I needed some time to myself to clear my head." He shrugged. "Figured this was as good as anything else."

Colt knew this had nothing to do with the ranch or he'd have known about whatever this issue was.

"So I have this meditation app," he started.

Sam shook his head. "*This* is my meditation."

Colt couldn't help it. He laughed.

He strode toward Sam and gave him a reassuring squeeze on the shoulder.

"You're the one who always has it together," Colt said. "No matter what's going on. Whether it's falling for the woman who's trying to take your land, your brother leaving…" He paused. "Losing Nolan? You've been unshakable, friend. So what's got you all shook?"

Sam gave himself another heaping spoonful, swallowed, and sighed. "Delaney had contractions this afternoon."

Colt's eyes widened. "And she's…?"

"At the hospital still. Turns out it's preterm labor, but they're hoping they can stop it with this medication that is making her so nauseous she can't even look at me without vomiting." He let out a bitter laugh. "I make my own fiancée vomit. Good news is if she makes it twenty-four hours without having the baby a month early, we should be out of the woods."

Sam dug his spoon back into the tub.

Colt crossed his arms and took a step back. "Buddy, I'm guessing it's the meds that are making her sick and not you."

Sam hugged the tub against his torso. "What if something happens to the baby?" he said, all humor gone from his voice.

"It won't," Colt said.

Sam's jaw tightened. "What if something happens to Delaney? This is all getting too damned real. There's nothing I want more than to build a family and a future with her, but none of this was part of the plan. If anything happens to either of them…" He gritted his teeth and shook his head.

Colt had never seen this. Even at his darkest, Sam Callahan never faltered.

Colt had no medical training whatsoever, but he knew one thing was true. "*Nothing* is going to happen to Delaney or the baby. You want to know why?"

"Why?" Sam asked. "What kind of bullshit wisdom do you have that I don't?"

Colt grabbed the tub of ice cream, but Sam held it tight.

"I can't talk to you like this," Colt said with a soft chuckle. "If you want me to impart my bullshit wisdom on you, it has to be without the ice cream tub."

"Fine," Sam said, the word short and clipped. But he relinquished his edible emotions, and Colt set it on the counter.

"Nothing is going to happen to Delaney, to your baby, to you…I mean, hell, you and Ben both got a second chance at a real future. Whether you believe something or someone is out there pulling the strings or not, what it tells me is that the odds are you didn't get that second chance just to lose it. And that kid of yours is lucky as hell. You and Delaney will spend the rest of your lives making sure your child has the best possible chance at a future so that one day *they* can stress-eat their own gallon or two of ice cream worrying about their own kid."

Sam swallowed. "You just pep-talked me into being a grandfather."

Colt laughed. "You're welcome. Now go get back to Delaney and keep on planning that future."

Sam clapped Colt on the shoulder. "Thanks," he said. "I needed that. You're going to kill it in the dad department someday. You know that, right?"

Colt's throat tightened, so he simply nodded.

Someday he'd get back everything he lost when the universe was a lot less than kind to him.

Someday.

CHAPTER SIXTEEN

Jenna knocked softly on the almost closed hospital door.

"Come in!" Delaney called out, and Jenna let out a long breath.

She pushed open the door and cupped her small gift close to her chest. She saw Sam first, pacing back and forth at the far end of the room in front of the window. Barbara Ann, Sam's mother, was standing over Delaney, adjusting her pillows while Delaney spoke.

"I'm fine. Really. You two should get back to the ranch. Poor Colt is all by himself."

Poor Colt hadn't even woken Jenna when he'd left early to tend to ranch activities. She'd passed out in his bed the night before after her surprise that had almost gone horribly wrong but ended up going ever so right. When she woke this morning, instead of finding Colt's warm body next to hers, she'd found a hastily scribbled note alerting her to Delaney's premature labor and adding that he had to leave early to take care of the ranch activities for the day and likely wouldn't make it back before ten that night.

"If I'm interrupting…" Jenna said.

Delaney met her eyes, shaking her head. "Thank goodness," she said, her smile brightening the whole room despite the nervous expressions both Sam and his mother wore. "See?" she added, turning her attention to the aforementioned nervous Nellies. "I won't be alone. Jenna's here, and look! She brought a plant!" She breathed in deep through her nose and closed her eyes. "Mmm, what is that? I love it!"

Jenna smiled. "I stopped by that adorable little flower shop in town and was so thrilled to find she had these mint plants."

Delaney held her hands out for the small white pot, and Jenna handed it over.

Again Delaney inhaled, the leaves right under her nose, and sighed. "This is so thoughtful, Jenna. Who knew I'd love a mint plant so much?"

Jenna laughed. "Peppermint is great for digestion when you drink it as a tea, but it's also really useful for just brightening your mood and giving a sense of calm and well-being. I figured you might need a little of both."

"I think we all could use a little of that," Barbara Ann said. She wrapped Jenna into a warm hug. "Can you stay for a bit?" she asked. "If I don't get Sam out of here for at least an hour, he's going to burn a hole right through the floor."

"I heard that, Mom," Sam called from behind her.

Barbara Ann turned over her shoulder. "I was hoping you would. Let me take you back to the ranch so you can shower and check in on things. I bet Scout needs to be let out."

Sam scrubbed his hand over his very stubbled jaw. "Doc Murphy is hanging at the shelter for the day, so I left Scout there. She'll be fine. And Colt's got Jessie and Carter helping him out at the ranch along with the new ranch hands we hired for the summer. They don't need me." He strode toward the bed. "But Delaney and the baby do."

"Sam," Delaney said. "I love you. So much. But look." She

pointed to her blood pressure monitor. "Your pacing isn't help-ing. I haven't had a contraction in a few hours now. If things continue like they are, I'll be out of here tonight. So please, go home for a bit and take care of you."

Sam's mom squeezed his shoulder gently. "She's right, sweet-heart. You haven't eaten. You haven't slept. That's not doing anyone any favors."

After taking one more sniff of the mint plant, Delaney set it on the table next to her bed and held her hand out for Sam. He took it, kissed it, and then pressed it to his chest.

"Please," Delaney said. "*I* slept. *I* ate. And I need you to do those things, too, okay?"

A muscle ticked in his jaw, but he nodded. "Okay," he said. "I'm coming right back, though." He leaned over to kiss her, once on the forehead and once on the lips.

"I know," Delaney said as he rested his forehead against hers.

He straightened and for the first time set his eyes on Jenna, as if he was just noticing she was there.

"Thank you," he said. "I'm glad she's not alone."

"Of course," Jenna responded. "I can stay as long as you need me. We were all going to be together in Reno today anyway. I have no other plans."

And with that, Sam finally let his mother lead him out of the room.

Barbara Ann clicked the door shut behind her, and Delaney released a long breath.

"It's called bed *rest*," she said. "Not bed *watch-your-fiancé-freak-out*." She winced. "Do I sound horrible and ungrateful for the amazing man who's going to be an even more amazing father?"

Jenna sat in the chair that someone had pulled up close to Delaney's bed.

"It doesn't sound ungrateful," she said, squeezing Delaney's hand. "It just sounds like it's not easy for either of you to relax, which is pretty understandable. Are you scared?"

Delaney nodded. But before she could speak, they were interrupted by a loud whirring sound.

Jenna's eyes widened and Delaney laughed.

"What *is* that?" Jenna asked.

"Lift the blanket off my legs," Delaney said.

Jenna leaned toward the far end of the bed but then looked back at Delaney. "Should I be scared?" she asked.

"Nah," Delaney said. "The only thing frightening under there are my swollen feet and ankles, and you've seen those already."

"Okay," Jenna said hesitantly. "Here goes nothing."

She lifted the blanket, and there were Delaney's swollen feet. But her ankles and calves were covered with what looked like long black sleeves that were filling with air.

"Compression pumps," Delaney said while Jenna was still investigating the contraptions. "They're to keep the blood flowing so I don't clot since I can't get out of bed. *Not* that I've been laid up for that long, but I guess it's standard procedure for patients stuck in bed."

Jenna's brows drew together as she turned her attention back to Delaney.

White wires protruded from the neck of her green hospital gown, from her neck where the IV was inserted, and from her feet where the pumps connected to their machine.

"On a scale of one to ten," Jenna said, "how uncomfortable *is* bed rest?"

"It's the worst," she admitted. "And if we make it to the twenty-four-hour mark without labor starting up again, I get to go home—and stay on bed rest for the last weeks of the pregnancy. But I'll do whatever I have to do for this baby to make it to full term or as close to full term as she can get."

Jenna gasped.

"What?" Delaney asked.

"Um... You just said *she*."

This time Delaney gasped. "Oh God! Don't tell Sam. We weren't supposed to find out. But last night when he ran home to get my stuff and it was just me and the doctor... I don't know. I was so scared. Was the baby okay? If the baby was born last night, what would the risks be? What would possible complications be? How long would the baby be in the NICU without me being able to hold it or nurse it or..." She forced a smile, but Jenna could tell she was holding back tears. "I just needed to know *something* for certain, something that made me feel like I was in control." She shrugged. "I wanted something to make me feel more connected to her." She let out a tearful laugh. "Connected to *her*. Can you believe it? We're having a little girl! And if I have to stay parked on my butt with compression cuffs on my legs to make sure we get to take her home with us when we leave the hospital after she's born, then so be it."

Jenna stood and hugged Delaney tight, careful not to tug one of her many wire accessories. "Congratulations, Mama!" she said. "Your secret is safe with me."

As happy and relieved as she was for Delaney and Sam, Jenna felt the pang of what she'd never have—a flesh-and-blood baby of her own. It made no sense. When Jack and Ava had Clare and had even named her after Jack's mom and Jenna's sister, Jenna hadn't felt anything but pure joy for her nephew and the woman he loved finding their way back to each other after so many years.

Her throat tightened as she understood the difference between then and now.

Colt. Colt Morgan was the difference. She was falling for him, which meant she was also mourning a future she'd never be able to have with him.

"Jenna, honey, are you okay?" Delaney asked.

The women were still embracing, but not until Delaney asked did Jenna realize she was crying.

Jenna loosened her grip and slid back into her chair, wiping her tears away and trying to laugh them off. The only problem was that nothing about the situation was funny.

"It's nothing," Jenna said. "You need to rest. Why don't we see what's on TV?"

Delaney crossed her arms as best she could over her pregnant belly and gave Jenna a pointed look. "As long as I'm focusing on something other than whether or not I'm going to have this baby today or four weeks from today, consider me resting. Plus, it will give me a chance to be half as good a friend as you've been to me this week." Her brows drew together. "Has it really only been a week? I feel like I've known you my whole life. See?" she said with a smile. "The magic of Meadow Valley. Now please, tell me what's wrong so I can fix it with some of that magic."

Jenna forced a smile. "I can't have children," she said. "And no magic in the world can change that."

She thought she'd made her peace with this reality, but then she'd never met a man like Colt Morgan—a man who made her want what she'd already lost.

Delaney's hand flew over her mouth, and her eyes glossed over. Her blood pressure monitor beeped a few times but then went silent again.

"See?" Jenna said. "I've upset you when you're supposed to be taking it easy. I'm so sorry. I shouldn't have said anything."

Delaney shook her head and rubbed a palm over her belly. "It wasn't you," she said. "Little girl just gave me a good kick in the side. No contractions, though. So we're both okay. But you've been here all week with me and my in-your-face pregnancy, and oh, Jenna... I had no idea."

Delaney reached for Jenna as far as she could without tugging her IV, and Jenna grabbed the other woman's hand.

"There's no way you could have known, and I've been fine with all of this for years. At least, I thought I was. I raised my nephews from teens to adults. I watched Jack, my oldest, become a father twice, and nothing has made me happier than seeing him and his brothers start lives of their own. And after they were independent and out of my care—and I felt like I was lucky to have had the opportunity to be *their* mother—I made the decision to prioritize my health over the *What if?* of having a family."

Delaney swiped at a tear from under her eye. "You tested positive for the BRCA gene," she said. It wasn't a question.

Jenna nodded. "My sister, Clare—Jack, Luke, and Walker's mama..." She swallowed the lump in her throat. It didn't matter how many years it had been. It never got easier talking about losing her favorite person in the world. "It was ovarian cancer. She got tested before she passed, and when she found out she was a carrier she made me promise I'd get tested too—that I'd learn my options, that I'd take care of myself." She blew out a shaky breath. "It was like she knew somehow that her dying would ruin Jack Sr., that the boys were going to need me someday."

She pulled her hand back from Delaney's, needing both to wipe her face clean from tears. "It was hard. *So* hard. I was barely done being a kid myself when I was suddenly the mother of three teens, all of whom were in such a bad place in the years following Clare's death. When we somehow came out the other side of it and I was in my early thirties I had a complete hysterectomy. And I've never regretted it. Not once."

It was finally time for tissues, and luckily there was a box on the bedside table. Jenna pulled three to start, keeping two for herself and handing one to Delaney.

"Until Colt," Delaney said after blotting her eyes dry.

Jenna nodded slowly. "Until *Colt*," she finally admitted out loud. "But that's ridiculous, right? I've only known him for a week." But it had been the best week in recent memory. No. That was a lie. It had been the best week she'd ever had. And she didn't want that to change. Still, she tried to logic her way out of the predicament of falling for him. "We both agreed this was just a fling," she added. But last night, something had shifted between them. She was pretty sure he felt it, too, which meant logic was out the window.

Delaney's circulation cuffs sounded, breaking the momentary silence and giving both women the excuse to laugh instead of cry.

"When in doubt..." Delaney said. "You can always count on my cankles to lighten the mood."

Jenna sniffled and laughed some more. "Your ankles are beautiful," she said. "They're a testament to what a woman's body can endure to do the most magical thing."

Delaney cradled the baby girl inside her stomach. "I know," she said. "You're right. About the magical part, at least. But wait until you see me at the wedding in December. I'm going to be wearing the most amazing strappy heels even if it's snowing...And it *better* be snowing."

Jenna's eyes widened. "I'll be back home by then, in Los Olivos." An hour away from her nephews' ranch in Oak Bluff—and five times that distance from Meadow Valley, the town that grew on her each and every day, not to mention the people here she was growing to care for by the minute. People like Delaney—and Colt. She cleared her throat and continued. "But I will count on you to send me lots of pictures. I'll leave you my email or you can text or—"

"Jenna Owens," Delaney said, her voice stern. "Did you not just hear me informally invite you to my wedding? We can start pricing flights now. Sam and I can even cover some of the cost, and of course you can stay at the ranch for free, but you *have* to be here. Please say you'll think about it."

Jenna's heart tugged at the thought of Delaney wanting her there five months from now.

"But if things with Colt end badly..." Jenna started. Because even though he might be falling for her, too, he wouldn't truly want to pursue a woman ten years his senior who couldn't have a family.

Delaney scoffed and tried to slide further up the inclined half of her hospital bed. "Why in the world would you assume something like that? That man is crazy about you. I've never seen him like this. And you forget where you are... *Magic* Valley." She winked at Jenna.

"I'm scared to tell him," Jenna admitted. "The last guy I was with—and it's been a long time—when I told him I didn't want to have children, that *that* part of my life was behind me, he, um, he hit me. And when I made the mistake of giving him a second chance and I tried to tell him the whole truth, that I *couldn't* have kids, he told me I was lying, and he hit me again." Jenna knew her choice to put her health first didn't make her any less of who she was. But the experience had scared her enough to keep men at arm's length ever since.

"Oh God, Jenna. Oh my God. I'm so sorry. Shit. You sure have been through your share of hell, haven't you?" Delaney patted the side of her bed and scooted as much as she could to her right. "Come here. Please." She held her IV'd arm out to her side so Jenna could slide in under it.

Jenna did as Delaney asked, shimmying herself as close to Delaney as possible so she didn't fall off the bed. Delaney held her close. She felt safe in her new friend's arms. She felt *safe* in Meadow Valley. If Lucy her chicken was psychic—which she certainly was—then maybe a town could be magic. And maybe that magic might just lead her to a happiness she didn't know she'd been looking for.

"Look," Delaney said. "I know I might be a few years younger than you, but I'm a really good big sister. I can give you a reference letter from Beth if you want."

Jenna laughed. "I don't need a letter. I believe you."

In a lot of ways, Delaney reminded Jenna of Clare—warm and nurturing and not afraid of the truth. As uncomfortable as it was trying to fit on the hospital bed along with her and as precariously as Jenna was perched, she felt protected. The only other person who'd made her feel like that was Colt.

"I told Colt I didn't date younger men," she said. "It's not because I think I'm old. I know I'm not. But I also know that he may want something I can't give him. So how can I admit I'm having feelings for him I didn't plan on having when doing so might only complicate things further?"

She rested her head on Delaney's shoulder.

Delaney huffed out a small laugh. "Honey, I think you already know the answer to that question. You *can* tell him how you feel because it's obvious he feels the same. And because we both already know Colt Morgan is about as good as they get—aside from Sam, of course—then we also know that he'll treat the situation with the same honesty and care he does everything else. He's not like the last guy."

Jenna sighed. "He is different, isn't he?" Different from any man she'd ever met before.

"They don't make many like him," Delaney said. "Or *you* for that matter, Jenna. If I've fallen this hard for you in one week, just imagine how Colt must be feeling."

"I'll tell him," Jenna said. "Before I go home next week. Then I'll see where we stand and if we're going to take this any further." She was happy Delaney couldn't see her poor excuse for a poker face. Because without even realizing it, Jenna had already given herself away. Colt Morgan had a piece of her heart she'd never get back.

"He'll make the right choice," Delaney assured her. "Which is *you*, of course."

Jenna's phone buzzed in her pocket, and she slid off the bed so she could grab it.

"Speak of the devil," she said, her voice still a little shaky.

It was a text from Colt.

I can't make it to Trudy's until later tonight. Any chance you can feed / let the animals out? She has a great backyard if you want to hang there and relax until I'm done here. I could meet you there around ten?

"Everything okay?" Delaney asked.

Jenna nodded. "Just one more second," she said, then fired off her response.

No problem. But I should warn you that you're in stiff competition with Frederick for my favor. Plus, he fits in my lap.

Colt replied with a winky-face emoji, and Jenna smiled as she saw the three dots that indicated he was typing something more.

You're the best. I promise to reward you for your service. I miss seeing your smiling face. Is that okay to say?

Jenna laughed.

I will hold you to that. Now go saddle up a horse or something, mister. And yeah, it's okay to say. I miss seeing your smiling face too.

He replied with the cowboy emoji, and Jenna's heart squeezed in her chest. She was pretty sure she'd just given him another small piece of it to keep.

She closed out of the texting app and opened up her phone's camera.

"How about we find a feel-good romance on one of the hospital channels?" Delaney asked. "I think we could both use a vicarious happily-ever-after."

The two women laughed, and Jenna handed Delaney the television remote.

Jenna had found an unconventional big sister in Delaney, and maybe something a lot like the L-word in her growing relationship with Colt. Maybe some of that Meadow Valley magic *was* making its way on over to her after all.

CHAPTER SEVENTEEN

Colt took a quick shower in the hope he'd no longer smell like a bonfire, but the scent usually stuck with him regardless.

He threw on a clean T-shirt and jeans, ran his fingers through his hair, and said to hell with it as far as shaving. Sixteen-hour days at the ranch weren't the norm, but they happened from time to time. He wasn't usually in a rush to head anywhere afterward other than his bed, but tonight he had someone waiting for him.

All animals fed, walked, and pretty much out cold for the night. Meet me out back at Trudy's. I've got wine, beer, and a sky full of stars.

Jenna's text kept him from flopping face-first onto his bed and instead had him out of the shower and in his car in mere minutes. And when he pulled into Trudy's driveway, he couldn't get out the driver's-side door fast enough.

Slow your roll, Morgan, he told himself. *She's not going anywhere. Remember what happened the last time you went full throttle into planning a future with someone.*

Not that he was planning a future with Jenna. He'd promised her that the here and now was all that mattered, and he'd meant that. It was just that the here and now was pretty damned good, and he couldn't help but think of all the ways it could get better.

He bypassed the front door and instead let himself into the backyard from the fence gate. He thought he'd discover her at the table enjoying a glass of wine, maybe reading one of Trudy's books in the gazebo. Instead he found her sprawled on her back on top of a blanket in the grass, hand under her head so that her pink T-shirt rode up and he could see the patch of soft skin between the hem of her shirt and the top of her long floral skirt.

She was lit by nothing but the moon and the stars. He wasn't sure he'd ever seen anything more beautiful.

"Evening, miss," he said as if he'd happened upon a stargazing stranger.

Jenna pushed herself up onto her elbows and met his gaze with a sweet smile.

"Evening yourself, Mr. . . . Morgan, is it?" she said, playing along.

He strode closer and saw two unopened bottles of beer perched next to her in the grass. Looked like he hadn't been completely off base on what she'd been doing while she waited for him.

Funny how he seemed to know her so well after such a short time.

"Mind if I join you?" he asked when he reached the edge of the blanket.

She stood up and brushed off her skirt. For a second he lamented losing sight of the skin on her torso he so longed to touch, but then she moved closer, and he could smell the scent of fresh-cut grass mixed with something sweet, like she'd just walked out of a bakery.

He wanted to kiss her and take a bite out of her all at the same time.

"I'd love the company," she said softly. "But I'm expecting

my guy any minute, and if he finds you here, I'm not sure what will happen."

She snaked her arms around his neck, and his stomach tightened.

My guy. He was hers, if only for another week. But she'd staked her claim, and he wasn't about to argue.

This woman.

"I could tell you what would happen," he said, his voice a low rumble against the chirping crickets hiding in the grass. "He'd lose his damned mind thinking about you with anyone else."

He could see her cheeks flush in the moonlight.

"Would he do something foolish?" she asked, and he set his hands on her hips, pressed his fingers into the soft skin that lay beneath the thin fabric of her skirt.

He nodded. "Probably."

She batted her lashes at him, and he was pretty much a goner.

"Start a fight, maybe?" she asked. "Defend my honor?"

She was kidding. He knew. But he also knew it was partly a test. She was still apprehensive about trusting him, and he didn't blame her. Not after the way the last guy had treated her. And even though he'd never raised a fist after an incident with his foster brother when he was a teen, if there was anyone he'd want to pummel, it would be the man who dared to hurt Jenna. But he wasn't going to be that guy.

"No. Not a fight," he said. "Something more civil. Like maybe a dance-off."

Jenna kept it together for maybe a millisecond after that before totally and completely losing it.

She doubled over, laughing hysterically, her hands pressed against her belly.

Colt crossed his arms and narrowed his eyes.

"What?" she asked when she finally straightened and collected herself.

"You don't think I could win a dance-off?" he asked, kidding, of course. But his ego still wanted the win.

She set her hands on her hips and looked him up and down. "I have no doubt you could cut a rug or two," she said. "But you have to admit it's a pretty funny thought, you dancing to win my favor."

He shrugged. "If that's what it took…"

She laughed again, but at least this time she wasn't doubled over in hysterics.

"I'll tell you what," she said. "Can I make a request—just in case it ever comes to that?"

Okay, now he was getting a little nervous. He could hold his own when Casey had line-dancing nights at Midtown. It *was* an excellent way to meet tourists who might want to meet a cowboy. But a request?

"Where, exactly, is this going?" he asked.

"Have you ever seen the movie *Ten Things I Hate About You*?"

He shook his head, and she rolled her eyes and groaned. "Of course not, because it's more than twenty years old, and you were a *child* when it came out. Well, if you ever need to win my favor via song and dance—"

"Wait," he said. "Now I'm *singing*?" Some lines he didn't cross, and that sure as hell was one of them.

"If you want to win my *favor*…" she continued. "Then you'll do so just like Patrick does in the scene where Kat's at soccer practice and he sings 'Can't Take My Eyes Off of You' to her *while* dancing in the bleachers."

His mouth fell open.

"With the school band," she added.

He hooked his index finger into the elastic waist of her skirt and sighed.

"So it's settled," he said. "To avoid any need for a battle to win your favor, I better not mess this up."

He grinned, but his stomach was tied in knots. They were

suddenly talking like this wasn't a fling anymore. Colt knew without a doubt he felt something for Jenna—something bigger than he could wrap his head around at the moment.

Did she?

She shook her head, and he had to remind himself that she couldn't read his thoughts, that she was simply answering his question. For a second her smile faltered. But she pasted it back on as quickly as it had disappeared.

"Can we—" she started.

"Open those beers and pretend this day never happened?" he said, finishing her sentence. He could tell she was fighting some sort of battle in her head, and he wanted to give her time to think. "Because I'll drink to that. Thank you, by the way, for spending time with Delaney so Sam could get some rest. I heard she got to go home this evening."

Jenna grabbed the beers and unscrewed one, handing it to him before popping the top off of hers and taking a long swig.

"Spending time with Delaney is as much to my benefit as it is to hers. Probably more so. She's amazing," Jenna said. "So strong. And so caring. I swear I feel like I've known her all my life."

Colt nodded. "Sam's a lucky man. He got the whole package with her."

There it was again, something like a wince in Jenna's expression, but again it vanished before he was sure it was even there.

"Is everything okay?" he asked, not sure if he was imagining things or not.

She nodded. "Other than you not having kissed me yet."

He laughed. She was right. The something-that-wasn't-right about this scenario was that his lips still hadn't touched hers.

"Well, Ms. Owens. Where *are* my manners?" he asked, wrapping one arm around her waist and the one that held the bottle of beer around her neck.

She followed suit, hooking both of hers over his hips, and he tugged her close.

"My apologies," he said.

"Forgiven," she responded, then rose onto her toes and pressed her lips to his.

Gone was the stress of his sixteen-hour day, of him worrying—not that he'd have told the already stressed Sam—about Delaney and the baby, of him wondering if this thing with Jenna was as real as it was starting to feel. When he kissed her, *tasted* her, felt her in his arms, everything else just fell into place. This *was* real. For him, at least.

"I baked," she said against his lips, and he could feel her smile.

He tilted his head back to meet her eyes. "You *what*? When? *Where?*" Although that would explain why she smelled good enough to eat.

She winced again, but this time it was for real.

"Tonight. Here. I *maybe* found your sister on Facebook and sent her a direct message asking her for her toffee shortbread recipe. I wanted to surprise you after a long day, but I'm just now realizing how I might have overstepped or violated your privacy. I mean, if you'd have contacted *my* family... Although I guess you already have since you know Jack. What I mean is maybe I should have waited, asked you first, and—"

He shut down her second-guessing with another kiss.

"Are you telling me there are toffee shortbread cookies in that kitchen?" he asked, glancing back toward Trudy's house.

Jenna nodded.

"And that you and Willow connected?"

She nodded again. "She actually has a gig in Sacramento on Wednesday night. Some other event—a play or something—canceled and they needed to fill the time slot. Anyway, it's a free show, and it's your sister. Plus Sacramento is only a few hours away."

"I know," he said with a grin. "She texted me today so I could make sure I had that night off. As long as Delaney is home safe, I think I can swing it—if you want to go together."

She smiled back at him, big and beautiful and knocking the air right out of his lungs.

"Are you asking me on a date, Colt? To meet your sister? One that includes a road trip? Because we've been on a road trip before..." she teased.

What was it about the way she said his name that drove him mad—in the best possible way? Maybe it was the way her accent made it sound like she was singing it. Or maybe it was that it felt as new and unexpected as she did.

Or maybe it was simply *her*.

"Yes," he said. "To all of those things. Jenna Owens, will you take another road trip with me?"

An hour later, there were four empty beer bottles on the blanket along with a plate containing nothing more than cookie crumbs.

She'd nailed Willow's recipe.

"I'm really going to have to feed you a proper meal one of these days," he said. "And as good as Luis is, something from the dining hall doesn't exactly count. That's included in your stay no matter what."

They both lay on their backs staring up at the sky.

"Why?" she asked, burrowing into the nook between his neck and shoulder. "I'm perfectly happy on a diet of cookies and ice cream from here on out."

He laughed. "In Sacramento," he said. "I'm buying you *real* food in Sacramento. Something that will check an item off your list—eating food from a country you've always wanted to visit."

Her cheeks turned pink again.

"You remember everything on the list?"

He shrugged. "I remember everything that's important."

Her cheeks turned pink again. There. He'd all but said *she* was important, and she wasn't running for the hills.

He rubbed his hand up and down her shoulder, feeling goose bumps pebbling her skin.

"You're cold," he said, stating the obvious, though it was still balmy outside, even without the sun.

"Not exactly," Jenna said, and she rolled on her side to face him. "It's more like you. Us. This place. Falling in love with the magic of Meadow Valley just like Delaney said I would."

"I'm falling . . ." he started but then caught himself. Jesus, he'd almost said he was falling in love with her, too, until her words clicked halfway through his *almost* admission.

"What?" Jenna asked.

"Huh?" he said, playing dumb.

She raised her brows. "I just told you I was in love with this town. And you started to say something but stopped."

He focused his gaze on a star that was so bright he wondered if it was a nearby planet. He half wished he were there, a world away where he hadn't almost just told her he was falling in love with her.

Think, Morgan.

He cleared his throat. "I'm falling asleep," he finally said. "Sorry. Long day."

He was an ass for not simply telling her the truth. But it had been ingrained in his memory for far too long that the truth often hurt, and it was too soon to risk putting himself out there like that.

"Oh," Jenna said, sitting up. "Right. Sorry. I should let you go. I didn't mean to keep you out so late after the day you've had."

He wanted to ask her about her day, about Delaney and Willow and taking care of Trudy's animals, but instead he'd just backed himself into a corner because he was a first-rate a-hole. He already felt like he owed her that dance and serenade. His only saving grace was that she had no clue.

He sat up, too, brushed her hair behind her ear, and tilted his forehead against hers.

Then it clicked.

"Want to sleep outside under the stars?" he asked. "It *is* on the list, and I'm sure Trudy has some blankets or sleeping bags we can borrow for the night."

She sucked in a breath, and the biggest, most beautiful grin lit up her face.

"I'd love to. But I have a barrel jumping lesson with Barbara Ann first thing in the morning, so I might have to sneak away before you wake up. Did you know she used to compete when she was a kid?"

"I didn't have a clue," he said. "We just let her teach those lessons and hope she doesn't hurt herself or any of the guests."

Jenna pushed his shoulder, and he caught her wrist in his hand and her lips with his own.

He kissed her long and slow, taking his fill because as much as he'd been saving face before, he knew that once they made up their outdoor bed, he'd lose consciousness the second his head hit the pillow.

And with every brush of his lips against hers, he fell a little faster. And *deeper*. And he realized he might not ever get his fill of Jenna Owens.

She wasn't kidding when she'd said *first thing in the morning*. Colt woke shortly after eight o'clock, and she'd been long gone. But the imprint of her body on the picnic blanket—next to her neatly rolled-up sleeping bag—was all the evidence he needed to know last night had been real.

He cleaned up the rest of their mess and headed back to his room at the ranch. As soon as he walked in the door, he headed toward the kitchen where he smelled fresh-brewed coffee. Next to an insulated carafe—that she'd likely borrowed from Luis—on the counter was a note that said, *Look in the fridge*.

He opened the refrigerator to find a glass container of fresh fruit next to another of what he guessed was yogurt. On the shelf in the fridge was another note.

Now look in the microwave.

He laughed, spun back to the counter, and opened the microwave door. Inside was a plate filled with breakfast potatoes and what he recognized as Luis's breakfast frittata. And of course attached to the plate was yet another note.

Something more than sweets. Luis said no more than forty-five seconds or the eggs will turn to rubber. Now go check the mirror in the bathroom. Last one. Promise.

He grabbed a cold potato and tossed it into his mouth, the savory taste making his mouth water for more.

Then he made his way to the bathroom, where the final note was posted on the mirror.

Sam's on duty tonight, so I offered to spend the night with Delaney since she's stuck either in bed or on the couch. Meet you back here at around 10:30 or 11?

She'd drawn an arrow pointing toward the left. He laughed out loud when he followed the arrow to find not only his bathtub, which he knew would be there, but the box of condoms she'd brought over the other night sitting right in the middle of said bathtub.

She'd broken into his place *again*—and taken care of him like he mattered as much to her as she did to him.

That was it. She couldn't ever leave Meadow Valley, not for good. Whatever was happening here was the real deal, and he would be one hell of a fool to let her go home without telling her as much.

Sacramento. The road trip. It would be perfect. It was how they'd met, so it should be how he told her that he was all in, ready to risk his heart on the woman he knew couldn't possibly stomp it to dust.

CHAPTER EIGHTEEN

Jenna sat with a goat in her lap and watched Lucy peck her way across the lawn.

"She really loves it here," a man said from behind her.

She twisted to see Dr. Eli Murphy, the local vet who volunteered his time at Delaney's rescue shelter a couple of times a week. A shock of his dark brown, almost black hair flopped onto his forehead and he pushed it out of the way.

"Yeah," Jenna said. "Lucy's really taken to the goats." The one in her lap—she wasn't sure if it was Billy or William, as Delaney had named them—took off after the chicken, only for Lucy to stop mid-henpeck, turn around, and squawk at her pursuer, who then fell paralyzed onto his side.

She laughed and stood up, brushing grass from the backs of her thighs.

"I thought Delaney was coming by today," Jenna said. The doctor had okayed her to spend time at the shelter provided it was from the seat of a wheelchair with her legs elevated. Sam was supposed to drive her over this morning before Jenna and Colt left for Sacramento.

Eli blinked, his blue-green eyes looking concerned. "Just got off the phone with Sam," he said. "She's not feeling up to it. Said she wants to stay home and rest."

Jenna's heart sank.

"It's not labor," Eli said, reading her mind. "At least, it doesn't sound like it. Just some heartburn and some uncomfortable swelling in the feet and ankles."

Jenna winced. "Must be worse than usual." At least she had those weird cuff thingies to keep the blood flowing while she had her feet up. "Sad to miss her but happy she's okay."

Eli nodded toward Lucy, who was circling the seemingly dead goat. Poor guy. As soon as he was able to stand back up, she'd probably squawk and paralyze him again.

"She still laying eggs?" he asked.

"Lucy?" Jenna said. "No. She's just a pet now. Though most of the time I'm pretty sure I belong to her more than the other way around."

She figured that might get a laugh from Dr. Murphy, but no such luck. He was a bit of a brooder, which was understandable with the man having lost his wife barely two years ago after a horseback riding accident. Still, Jenna tried to get a smile out of him, hoping that somewhere he still found things to smile about.

"I see," he said. "Not sure if Delaney told you, but I run the clinic off a small sustainable farm. Been thinking of a way to repurpose the stable now that the horses are gone, and I was thinking about hens. Hate to admit that as much as I know about caring for animals, I don't know much about the egg production time line and such. Think you could take a look at the place and let me know if it's feasible?"

Jenna's eyes brightened. "I'd love to. Can Lucy come too? There's no better judge of a space befitting a hen than a hen herself."

The corner of his mouth twitched. Still not exactly a smile, but Jenna would take it as a small win.

"What day is good for you?" he asked.

She pursed her lips. "Colt and I are leaving for Sacramento after lunch." Then she gasped when she realized she only had two days left in Meadow Valley. "Oh wow," she added. "I fly back home on Saturday morning. How about Friday? How far is the drive?"

He shrugged. "It's just a few minutes outside town. Do you think Colt could bring you?"

She nodded. "Or Sam. Or Barbara Ann. I'm sure I can get a ride. How about ten?" she asked.

"Perfect," he said. "The farm—that part was all Tess. She'd wanted hens, so..." He trailed off.

"Then we'll get you ready for some hens," Jenna said. "I'm happy to help. Before you know it, you'll be more than sustaining. You could turn a small profit at local farmers markets and such."

He nodded absently, and she figured she'd lost him to thoughts of his late wife. She couldn't imagine that kind of loss. Her brother-in-law had experienced it when Clare died and had slowly killed himself drinking because of it. Eli was still going through the motions of everyday life, but it didn't seem like he'd exactly made it back to the land of the living. Jenna was happy to help with what might be the next step.

How quickly she'd become attached not just to the ranch but to everyone she seemed to meet in this town. And she'd barely scratched the surface.

"I should go shower the goat off me before lunch," she said with a laugh. "Are you going to be okay on your own without Delaney?"

"Of course," Eli said. "I actually kind of enjoy it when it's just me and the animals. No offense," he added.

Jenna laughed. "None taken." She got it. Sometimes it was

easier being with company who couldn't talk back. "I'll see you on Friday. Ten o'clock."

"Ten o'clock," he said, and that was that.

Jenna had opted for denim shorts and a green tank top for the concert, with a hoodie tied around her waist in case it cooled off at night. She doubted it would, especially being three hours south.

She entered the dining hall to find the place buzzing with guests. But amid the melee she found her cowboy, sitting with the two little girls they'd met at the swimming hole, along with their parents. He waved when he saw her, then stood and started walking in her direction.

She paused to enjoy the view, the way his well-worn jeans hugged his hips and how his snug white T-shirt left so little to the imagination. Beneath the cotton lay a lean muscled abdomen she'd kissed up and down a time or two, and would again tonight. She pulled out her phone and asked her question with raised brows.

Fine, he mouthed, then shook his head with a laugh as she snapped a candid photo of the sexy cowboy that was all hers for the rest of the day and night.

When they were finally face-to-face, she could see his hair was damp, just like hers.

"Fresh out of the shower, huh?" she asked.

He nodded with a grin, but then his brows drew together as he realized her hair was still wet as well.

"I'm seeing a real missed opportunity here," he said.

She laughed. "True. But then we likely would have missed lunch. Or gotten on the road late. And we wouldn't want to miss any of Willow's set."

Or meeting her beforehand.

Jenna's stomach did a somersault at the thought. Willow was Colt's only family. And he *wanted* the two of them to meet.

He leaned down to kiss her, and Jenna held her breath. The anticipation of this kiss felt different. *Today* felt different. It hadn't when she'd woken up this morning, and it hadn't when she'd visited Lucy at the shelter. But the second she stepped foot in the dining hall and saw Colt, something shifted.

His lips brushed over hers. The kiss was quick and chaste. They did have an audience after all, but Jenna still felt like she'd been socked in the gut—in a really good but really terrifying way.

"Hey there, Texas," he said before pulling away.

His warm breath on her cheek and that soft, deep voice of his made the fine hairs on the back of her neck stand on end.

"Hey there," she said back, her voice coming out hoarse. She cleared her throat and tried again. "Hey there, cowboy Colt."

He beamed at her, which made her smile.

"You hungry?" he asked.

"Always," Jenna said.

"Good. Because Luis's BLT grilled cheese is probably the best thing you'll ever taste."

She raised her brows. "No dessert for lunch, Mr. Morgan? This doesn't seem right."

He laughed. "I told you, what Luis makes doesn't count. Even if it's fantastic. Tonight. Sacramento. I'm making good on my promise to feed you *real* food."

Jenna pouted. "Does that mean no ice cream?"

He slipped his fingers through hers and led her toward an empty table. "For you, Jenna, there will *always* be ice cream."

It was two o'clock by the time they packed up Colt's car with small necessities like snacks and emergency overnight bags. They weren't planning on staying the night, especially since Colt was working the stable the following morning, but based on what happened the first time they took a road trip together, they weren't taking any chances.

But there was nothing but blue skies and open road ahead of them, so when they finally hit the highway, Jenna plugged her phone into Colt's radio and insisted she be the DJ for the duration of the trip.

"So," she said, when she had her music library opened and ready to go. "What do you like to listen to?"

He didn't say anything for several seconds, but she could see the wheels turning as his eyes stayed focused on the road.

"You mean other than Willow Morgan originals?" he asked with a grin.

"I've got some of Willow's songs in here," she assured him. "But she's pretty new on the scene. What did you listen to growing up? What kind of music was the backdrop for your life? Like, if you were putting together a slideshow of *my* life, the music would be all over the place. My teen years were filled with a mix of No Doubt, New Kids on the Block, and the Cyrus that came long before Miley." Jenna laughed. "Awkward, thirteen-year-old Jenna had a really big thing for Billy Ray."

Colt glanced her way, and even though his eyes were covered by his aviator sunglasses, she could tell they were narrowed at her.

"Didn't Billy Ray Cyrus have a monster mullet?" he asked.

"I like to refer to it as *spectacular*," she said. "But yes. Total and complete mullet, and it worked for him. And for me. Billy Ray Cyrus was my first crush."

Colt ran a hand across the back of his neck. "There's not a lot I wouldn't do if you asked," he said. "But never ask me to grow a mullet."

She rumpled his sandy hair with her palm. "Wouldn't dream of you doing any such thing to this already sexy 'do' you got going on here."

This made him smile. "You start talking like that, and I'm going to have to pull over at the first rest stop I can find and let you *really* mess up my *sexy 'do'*."

She backhanded him on the shoulder.

"You just stay focused on the road. We need to make it by five thirty if we want to spend some time with Willow before her show," Jenna said. "So give me a song or a band or *something* so I don't play 'Achy Breaky Heart' on repeat for the next few hours." She didn't want to be the rational one here, because the thought of what they could accomplish at a rest stop in the back seat of his car had her squirming in place. This was why they needed to get a playlist going: so they could carpool-karaoke their way to Sacramento and keep their minds from wandering into inconvenient territory.

Colt sighed. "You promise you won't judge?" he asked.

Ooh, this was going to be interesting. "I just admitted I crushed on a man with a mullet. What could possibly be worse than that?"

"It's not worse. It just says a lot about my frame of mind during *my* teen years. While you were crushing on mullet man, I was listening to *The Black Parade*...My Chemical Romance...pretty much on repeat."

Jenna's heart sank. She hadn't considered what period in his life she was forcing him to recall. Jenna was lucky. Despite the tragedy in her life, she'd had a loving family—especially her mom and her sister—for much of it, especially her formative years.

"Yep," he said when she still hadn't responded. "I was emo as hell behind closed doors and angry as hell in front of them."

Jenna hesitantly placed a hand on his thigh, and he covered it with his own.

"I should probably tell you something about—about my time in foster care."

"Colt, you don't—" she started, but he squeezed her hand and shook his head, his eyes still focused on the road ahead.

"No," he said. "I do. I need to get this off my chest before we meet Willow—and before I tell you any of the other million things I want to tell you before you leave."

Her throat tightened, and she nodded.

"The book I bought you at Trudy's...it's in the bag on the floor behind my seat if you want to grab it. It's—um—part of the story."

Jenna hadn't forgotten that night, but she *had* forgotten the book. She reached for it now with nervous hands but smiled as she pulled it from the bag.

"*Where the Wild Things Are*?" she said. "I don't understand."

She watched his throat bob as he swallowed. "*Where the Wild Things Are* is the last book I remember my mom reading to me when I was a kid and Willow was a baby. When I had a family." A muscle in his jaw ticked. "I have my own copy hidden away in my room at the ranch."

Her heart squeezed, and she wanted to wrap him in her arms. "And you wanted me to have a copy of a book that means so much to you?"

He blew out a breath. "Yes, but—I also wanted to explain where *my* copy came from."

"Okay," she said, her pulse quickening.

"Back when I was sixteen and in my first week at what was—let's see—the fourth high school I'd attended in three years, I got into it with my foster parents' son."

Jenna held her breath. She knew what *got into it* meant. It meant violence. When she didn't say anything, he went on.

"My foster brother, apparently, was not too happy about having a new sibling who seemed to hit it off with his ex-girlfriend. One day after school he came at me before we were off school grounds and threw the first punch. Split my lip. I told him I wasn't going to fight him. I couldn't, not after some minor run-ins I'd had before. I *knew* if this went south I wasn't getting off with just a warning. If I messed up again, it meant I might not be around to find Willow once I turned eighteen.

"So I ducked a few times, pivoted out of his reach once or twice. Then he decided to throw some choice words my way about why my birth parents didn't want me—not even knowing my father *had* left or that we lost our mom in a car accident—which caught me off guard, and the next time he swung, I just stood there. He broke my nose, and that was it. I swung back. Once. Knocked him out cold and broke his jaw."

Jenna pulled her trembling hand from his thigh, the reminder of what a man could do with his fists making every muscle in her body tense.

"If you want me to pull over or take you back to Meadow Valley, Jenna, just say the word. I won't blame you and I won't chase after you because the last thing in the world I want to do is scare you. But if you trust me...If you trust what I told you, that I would *never* raise my hand to you, then I'll tell you the rest."

She pressed the copy of *Where the Wild Things Are* to her chest and crossed her arms over it, like it was somehow the life preserver that would keep her head above the river of fear that was suddenly coursing through her.

She reminded herself of her nephew Jack, of the terrible incident that happened between him and another boy at a graduation party the summer of his eighteenth year. Despite the justification for his actions, Jack had put that boy in the hospital and had almost gone to jail for it. She reminded herself that even though Jack had lived for years as a victim of his father's abuse, that *one* incident when he was a teen hadn't defined him. He broke the cycle so many were unable to break, and Jenna realized the man next to her wasn't the boy he used to be either.

"I'm still here," she said, not even trying to hide the tremor in her voice.

She watched the rise and fall of Colt's chest as he inhaled and exhaled before continuing.

"Didn't matter that I was a bloody mess. Didn't matter that I had an audience full of witnesses. I was expelled from the school," he finally said. "And spent six months in a juvenile detention center. And the book? *Where the Wild Things Are*? I stole it."

He let out a long breath, though Jenna felt like she was still holding hers.

"My foster family had it on this massive shelf of books they all pretty much ignored for the short time I was living with them—so I took it with me for my *trip*, and I never gave it back. Ended up reading it every night while I was away. I didn't care that it was a kids' book because it reminded me of Willow and my mom and what I wanted for myself one day—a house full of kids of my own who felt loved and safe. Always." He shrugged. "When some foster family in Oak Bluff took a chance on me, I decided not to mess up my last chance. Met Ben Callahan at school, and give or take a few years, here I am."

For several long moments, neither of them said another word. Jenna simply breathed as Colt continued to drive.

"I've never raised my hand to another person since then," he finally said. "Hell, Sam works out in the boxing ring at the fire station, and I won't even spar with him no matter how many times he asks." Then he laughed softly. "But be sure you ask Delaney about the time she did and almost laid him out cold. By accident."

This made her laugh, too, and she sat up straight and shifted so she could face him, the tension in her shoulders relaxing.

His mouth was curled into a sweet smile, but it didn't reach his dark brown eyes. For a man who'd seemed so comfortable in his own skin—especially when that was all he was wearing—since the day she'd met him, he looked so unsure.

"I'm not afraid of you," she finally said.

He let out a shaky breath.

"And I'm glad you told me," she added, realizing tonight was the night they both were putting it all on the table. She could tell him right now about not being able to have kids, but something he said sank in.

A house full of kids of my own who felt loved and safe.

She swallowed. If she told him now, that would be it. They'd be done before the night began. So Jenna tucked it away, deciding to make the most of what she now realized would be their last great night together—before she told him she loved him but couldn't give him the future he wanted.

"I'm not that pissed-off kid anymore," Colt added.

"I know you're not." He was the man she was falling for, and even if he felt the same, how could that be enough? She wanted him to have *everything* he'd missed out on, just like he was helping her experience everything she thought she'd missed when she was younger.

"Hey," he said. "You were trying to do the music thing for fun, and I feel like I've sort of killed the vibe here. So...sorry about that."

Jenna scrolled through her list of artists with one hand, keeping the other on Colt's thigh.

"No worries at all," she said. "No My Chemical Romance on my list, so we don't have to go there."

"But you have Billy Ray?" he asked, the corner of his mouth turning up. "And New Kids on the Block in their *first* iteration?"

Jenna scoffed and backhanded him on the shoulder, thankful for the levity even if her stomach was tied in knots. "Did you just make the first-ever joke about our age difference? Because if so, it is *on*, mister."

He laughed. "I didn't mean it like that. I swear." He crossed his finger over his heart. "It's just that I've only ever known the band since their comeback a decade or so ago."

She lowered her own sunglasses so he could clearly see her pointed look. "You're still *doing* it. And by the way, you existed on this earth when NKOTB was first a thing. Maybe you were too young to care or realize their greatness, but that doesn't change the fact that you're not *that* young."

"Ouch," he said, then laughed again, and she decided that it was time to school her younger man on a little bit of musical history.

"We'll start with one of my favorites." She queued up a classic and hit PLAY. And then, because she couldn't help it, she sang along to every word of "Please Don't Go Girl" while Colt shook his head and laughed the whole way through.

And that was how the boy band of her youth became the soundtrack to their ride. Only when they were just outside of Sacramento did she run out of songs, so she just put her entire list on shuffle.

The first song to pop up was "Achy Breaky Heart," and she skipped it as soon as it started. "I've put you through enough," she teased. "Even though I still love that song." Before he could respond, the opening to the Garth Brooks version of "To Make You Feel My Love" started. "I can just skip over this one too," she said. "I'm guessing country maybe isn't your thing altogether."

He placed a palm over her wrist and shook his head.

"I like this one," he said. "Willow always covers it at the end of a set. You know it was originally a Bob Dylan song, right?"

Jenna nodded. "Yeah. But this is my favorite version."

"Mine too," he said. And then somehow her hand flipped so it was palm up, and her fingers slipped between his.

And as if she'd timed the perfect all-New-Kids-on-the-Block playlist—save for one song—they rolled into downtown Sacramento just as Garth crooned the final line of the song.

"I mapped it out ahead of time," he said. "There's a parking garage on Tenth Street. Then it's just a couple of minutes to the park, which Willow said will be lined with gourmet food trucks—or we can find a sit-down place nearby."

Jenna's whole body thrummed with nervous energy. She didn't want things to end. She didn't want to lose Colt. If tonight went as well as it felt like it could, maybe it would soften the blow of what she had to tell him. She'd never ask him to give up the future he wanted, but she didn't want to be a painful reminder of his past.

Tonight simply had to go off without a hitch, and what better way to start than by exploring a new city with a man who meant more to her than she possibly could have imagined less than two weeks ago.

"If we do the food truck thing, does that mean we can walk and eat? I've never been to any sizable city other than Houston. I'd love to see some of Sacramento before we head to the park."

"Deal," he said as they quickly found the garage and headed in. Once parked, Colt texted his sister. "Okay. Food trucks in ten minutes. Willow can hang with us for a bit before having to set up for sound check. And then it's showtime. It only goes until nine, and Willow and her band need to get right back on the road for another gig, so I should have you back to the ranch by midnight or soon after."

She raised her brows. "In case I turn back into a pumpkin or something?"

"Or in case you want to spend the night. I have an early morning, but that doesn't mean we can't find a thing or two to do before our heads hit the pillow." He turned off the car and undid his seat belt so he could turn to face her. "Not sure if you can tell, but that was one hell of a long ride, and I'm sort of dying to kiss you."

Jenna unfastened her own seat belt and scooted as close to the left edge of her seat as she could without sitting on the center console. "Not sure if *you* can tell, but I'm sort of dying to do the same."

He slid his seat back as far as it would go, which wasn't much from where it initially was. But he'd made just enough room between himself and the steering wheel.

"Come here," he said, patting his thigh, and Jenna willingly complied, scooting *over* the console and onto his lap so her back was flush against the driver's-side window.

He ran a rough palm up her bare thigh, and she sucked in a breath.

"Colt...Darlin'..." she said.

"Jenna? *Darlin'*," he said in response, then teased her by sliding a finger underneath the folded cuff of her shorts until it brushed the spot where her underwear met the crease of her thigh.

This time she gasped and squirmed on his lap.

"We can't," she said. "We need to meet Willow. We're going to be late."

With his free hand, he slid his fingers into her hair and urged her head toward his. Then he kissed her, hard and deep, which was nothing at all like the greeting she'd received in the dining hall.

"I know," he said. "Just want to make sure you know what's in store for you when we get back to my place tonight."

He rubbed his thumb once over her center and slid his terrible teasing fingers back into view.

Jenna whimpered.

"Colt *Morgan*," she said. "There is nothing, and I mean *nothing* cute about a man who teases a woman like that."

Sexy as hell and making her want more, more, *more*? Sure. But not cute.

"Willow's never on time," he said, his voice a low rumble she felt in the pit of her stomach.

She nodded, and this time he unbuttoned the top of her shorts and slid them, with her panties *and* Jenna's help, down to her knees.

"For the record," he said. "I wasn't trying to be cute."

Twenty minutes later they were speed walking out of the garage and onto the bright and busy sidewalks of downtown Sacramento, which wasn't easy when your legs felt like Jell-O. And Jenna Owens's legs were barely holding her upright after her few minutes on Colt's lap.

Even *that*, which he'd done for her plenty of times before, felt different. Better somehow, which was saying a lot since they'd been cramped in the driver's seat of his car.

She wanted to take in the sights as they made their way toward the park, but all she could do was stare at the man next to her, at the square line of his jaw and the golden stubble she hoped, come winter, turned into a golden beard. Or would he be clean-shaven for Sam and Delaney's wedding? Either way, she was picturing him there, decked out in a fancy suit, bearded or not—and for the first time, she pictured herself there with him.

She could picture a small office where she would maybe, *possibly*, write if she ever got past this block. There were her hens, still. Of course. And Lucy ruling the roost. But she thought bigger now than simply the status quo. She wanted and deserved more, and she wished it could be with the man by her side.

Maybe her future was back home. Or maybe it wasn't. All she knew was that she'd wished on forty-one silly little candles, and now here she was. With Colt. And everything was different.

This was *real*.

They were real. Which was why she knew he wouldn't bolt when she told him her truth—just like she hadn't run when he'd told her his.

CHAPTER NINETEEN

Big bro!"

Colt heard his sister before he saw her. But then there she was, like a desert mirage. For him, family was better than water or cool air.

She stood on the sidewalk in front of a shawarma truck waving with both hands. She was unassuming in her Rolling Stones T-shirt—the one with the big red lips—jeans, a pair of Chuck Taylor tennis shoes, and her warm brown hair in loose waves on her shoulders. She looked like anyone else walking the city streets—until she got on stage and it was clear she was something bigger and bolder than anyone could have imagined.

Colt picked up his pace, as did she. She was remarkably fast for her petite stature, her legs significantly shorter than his. When they met, she threw her arms around him in a warm hug, and his throat tightened.

He knew it had only been a couple of weeks since he'd seen her, but every time they met, he was reminded of the years they lost.

"Willow Morgan," he said, when they separated. "This is—"

"Jenna!" Willow exclaimed, then hugged the other woman

even tighter than she'd hugged him. "I'm so thrilled to *officially* meet you! When you reached out and asked for my cookie recipe—which I *never* share—I was skeptical at first."

"What convinced you?" Colt asked, eyes narrowed.

Willow shrugged. "She told me what happened to the batch I made and how you shared the very last cookie with her." She shook her head. "You are as generous as they come, big bro. But *not* with coveted baked goods. I realized Jenna must be pretty special for you to do that—and for her to want to right such a wrong. Seeing you together now...I'm pretty sure I made the right choice." She raised her brows and gave them each a look. "You're both toast, aren't you? Come on. Let's eat. I'm always famished before a show. Do you like shawarma, Jenna? Because this truck is my favorite."

She spun and headed back toward the food truck, and Jenna stared at him, her cheeks flushed.

"She gets a little amped before a show," Colt said with a laugh. "It's the adrenaline. It's like she has to be *on* even if she's not performing. You know? After a set, though, she's as chill as can be."

Jenna grinned and they watched as people did double takes, not sure if they were recognizing the up-and-coming artist or mistaking her for someone else.

Finally, a young girl and her mom approached and asked for an autograph, to which Willow warmly obliged.

"See?" he said. "I don't know how she does it. I like the quiet. I like my privacy. I like my small circle of people I have to interact with, and that's that."

"She's fearless," Jenna said as she watched the interaction between Willow and the little girl who was clearly starstruck. Willow dropped to a squat to take a picture with her, then hugged her before straightening to her full height, which was only five foot four.

"Maybe," Colt said. "Or maybe she just channels her fears better than the rest of us."

"Sorry about that," Willow said after her admirers went on their way. "It doesn't happen much, but it's kind of cool that it does, right?" She beamed.

"Hell yeah, it's kind of cool," Jenna said. "You do *not* need to apologize for being a badass superstar."

Willow hooked her arm in Jenna's and glanced at her brother. "I like her," she said.

Before he could comment, the two women strode ahead, arm in arm, as they got in line for the shawarma truck. The conversation between them never ceased as Colt stood behind them and listened to Jenna brag about her nephews and even mention her vacation *list* while Willow halfheartedly complained about sleeping on the tour bus. Colt knew she actually loved it.

The same held true as they moved from shawarma to the taco truck, where Jenna opted for fish tacos.

"It's on my list," she insisted. "Eating food from a country I've never been to. I've never been anywhere but here, actually."

"You better not let Luis know you tried out the competition," Colt warned. "He considers himself taco royalty. Also, you *do* realize the proprietors of said food truck are Sacramento hipsters, so it's not quite the authentic experience you're making it out to be."

Jenna laughed as she bit into her second of three tacos. "My lips are sealed as far as Luis is concerned," she said. "But holy wow these are good." She held up a finger indicating she wasn't done, so he waited for her to swallow. "And I'm changing that item on the list because—well—it's my list and I can. I want to travel. I want to see the world beyond my home. I'm not settling for just the food, even though I *love* a good meal. I want more," she said.

There was a sureness and a finality to her words that made Colt wonder—that made him *hope*—the *more* had something to do with him as well.

"Then you should have more," he told her.

I want to give you more.

Jenna stared at him for a long moment before Willow whisked her away again.

They walked up and down the streets near the park, but he wasn't sure any of them were paying one bit of attention to the city, especially the two women, who'd been in constant conversation about everything from their shared love of ice cream to Jenna's admission of having attended the last Lilith Fair tour and Willow's lamentation that she was barely out of diapers by then let alone old enough to go. Colt had all but lost his date to his sister and his sister to his date, and he couldn't remember the last time anything had made him smile so much.

He'd spent years focusing on work, on convincing himself he was content with the status quo. But meeting Jenna Owens made him realize what he'd been missing. He thought agreeing to this fling would be the first step to getting out of his own way. Emma hurting him might have been the catalyst, but *Colt* was the one who put up his walls, who thought safety and contentment were a substitute for happiness.

Well, he'd done it. He'd let Jenna past the barrier. Only instead of letting their arrangement be practice for the real thing, he'd let her straight into his heart.

"That's it," Willow said as they stopped conveniently right outside a frozen yogurt storefront. "I'm in love with her, big bro. Don't mess this up."

Colt laughed, and his long-dormant heart felt like it grew to twice its size in a matter of minutes.

Also, it wasn't fair that Willow got to throw those words around so easily and that Jenna didn't run for the hills when his sister said them. Women were like that—able to become fast friends and think nothing of it. But admit to a woman that you were falling for her after barely two weeks—a woman who made it clear that she was hesitant to date in the first place—and he was likely to spook her all the way back to Los Olivos.

But Jenna had said it. She wanted *more*. Maybe she was no longer spooked.

"What do you think, Texas? Willow's pretty stubborn about getting what she wants, and if we're being honest, I'm a little afraid to argue with her," he said.

Jenna blushed, and he hoped that part of it was for his round-about admission that he wouldn't mind at all if his sister got her way with this one.

She crumpled the papers that once held her tacos and dropped them in the trash bin behind her. "I think..." she started. "That we need to top this meal off with some froyo."

"Definitely," Willow said. And once again she and Jenna were arm in arm, heading into the store, while Colt stood by and watched the two women he cared about most in the world light up each other's night like they lit up his whole damned life.

"I am in love with that woman," he said to no one in particular.

To hell with spooking her. She was heading home in two days, and he wasn't going to let her go without telling her that she was worth a whole lot more than the six-hour drive between his home and hers.

He'd put his heart on hold for five years after Emma pulled the rug out from under him. But Jenna was different. He knew without a doubt that she couldn't do the same.

He watched the two women go back and forth between the self-serve machines, smiling and laughing as they piled their frozen treats with topping after topping, and he found himself standing there laughing too.

All he'd ever wanted was the family he'd lost, to make up for the years that he'd drifted from house to house without ever truly having a home, a place where you knew that once you walked through that door, you were loved and safe. He wanted what he'd lost with Jenna.

Colt pushed through the door and pulled his wallet out of his back pocket as Jenna and Willow added chocolate syrup to their mile-high sundaes as the finishing touch.

The teen girl behind the counter grinned when she saw him.

"Welcome to Frosties," she said. "Our flavor of the day is chocolate hazelnut."

"None for me, thanks," he said. "I'm just here to treat these two sugar addicts to desserts they're probably going to regret in an hour a two."

Willow gasped dramatically. "*Never*," she said. "Just means I'll have more energy to burn on stage. By the time my set's over, I'll be ready for seconds!"

Jenna shrugged. "I've never met a dessert I regretted, and I'm sure as hell not starting tonight."

Colt narrowed his eyes at the dish in her hands. "Are those—gummy worms?"

Jenna raised a brow. "When you said you wouldn't judge my list, I took that to mean you wouldn't judge my choices. Period."

Willow dipped her finger into her own dish and swiped it onto the tip of his nose. "You heard the woman," she said. "No judging."

Colt rolled his eyes and grabbed a napkin to clean himself off, but he knew better than to retaliate, verbally or otherwise. He was outnumbered.

He held his hands up in defeat and then handed his debit card to the girl behind the counter.

"Can you add three bottles of water, too?" he asked. Despite the sun being on its way down, it was still a scorcher out there, and they were going to need it.

They made it back to the park in time for Willow to get to her sound check and for Colt and Jenna to grab a spot right up front before the show began.

Soon the rest of the crowd started filing in, and Colt couldn't help but be impressed at the turnout.

"She's something, isn't she?" Jenna asked as she watched him watch everyone else who was there to see his kid sister.

"Every time I see her perform, it's a bigger venue with an even bigger crowd. Did Eli tell you she's opening for Ash at his next show? That'll be her biggest crowd yet."

Jenna's brows furrowed. "Why would Dr. Murphy..." But then her eyes widened with recognition, and she grabbed Colt's arm. "Shut the front door. Ashton Murphy is Eli Murphy's brother?"

Colt laughed. "And Boone Murphy too. He owns the Meadow Valley auto body shop. I don't think you've met him yet. They grew up on their family's ranch but kind of went their separate ways after high school."

She shook her head. "That's great. But can we get back to your sister opening for one of country music's most scandalous stars? Hasn't he been arrested for trashing hotel rooms and bar brawls and stuff like that? Like...multiple times? How have I been here two weeks and not heard a *word* of this?"

Colt shrugged. "Everyone in Meadow Valley's known him since he was a kid. Guess he's not such a big deal at home— especially with all the stuff you just described. The town's pretty quiet about him in general, but I figured Eli at least might have said something."

She shook her head. "Eli doesn't say much at all, actually. Only what needs saying."

Colt sighed. "No. I guess he doesn't. Not sure if that was always his way or if it's because of losing Tess. It's been a couple of years now since it happened, but you can't put a cutoff date on grief."

"He's so young," Jenna said. "I hope he finds someone to make him happy someday. When the time is right." Then she raised her brows. "Still can't get over him having a famous brother, though. Where I come from, small towns are all about gossip. You'd think in almost two weeks that I would have heard *some*thing from *some*one."

He hooked a finger inside one of the belt loops of her shorts and tugged her close. "We're not without our share of gossip, but from what I can tell, when it comes to Ash Murphy, the town's either pretty damned protective of him—" He hesitated. "Or ashamed. Not really sure. All I know is he hasn't been home in years. Guess Eli doesn't really talk about him either."

Jenna's smile fell. "I feel like I'm only just figuring Meadow Valley out, and now I have to leave."

Colt dipped his head closer to hers. "You don't *have* to do anything, Jenna. Not if you don't want to."

He kissed her before she could question his indirect invitation for her to stay.

"Good evening, Sacramento!" Willow's voice boomed over the mic.

The crowd cheered while Colt and Jenna continued to kiss. There'd be no way they could discuss what he'd just said now, not until the concert was over, so he decided to simply enjoy the night with the amazing woman in his arms.

As predicted, Willow and her band ended her set of originals with her own rendition of "To Make You Feel My Love." He stood behind Jenna, his arms wrapped around her midsection as they swayed slowly from side to side, her back pressed to his chest.

He leaned down to kiss her cheek, and her skin was warm to the touch, warmer than usual.

"You okay?" he asked. "The heat getting to you?"

She turned to face him, and her forehead was beaded with sweat.

"Maybe a little," she said. "It was hotter than I thought it would be tonight."

He nodded even though he thought the temperature had gone down a bit along with the sun.

"We'll get you in the cool car soon. I just want to say good-bye to Willow after she wraps up. That okay with you?"

"Yeah," she said. "Of course." But then she swayed where she stood—and *not* the dancing kind of sway.

He caught her before she toppled over, sliding his arm beneath hers.

As if she knew, Willow caught his eye right as it happened, and he mouthed *We need to go. Sorry.*

She blew them both a kiss, and he made a mental note to call her later and fill her in. But first he had to get Jenna out of the heat and into the car.

"Hey," he said, and Jenna tilted her gaze to meet his. "Are you sure you're okay? Can you walk? I'll catch up with Willow later. We're going to head out behind the stage. That's the quickest way to the car." Willow had introduced them to the security crew on the way in, so it wouldn't be a problem to sneak out an unofficial exit.

She scoffed. "I'm *fine*. Just a little hot. That's all. See?" She pushed away from him and strode haughtily in the direction he'd pointed, so he shrugged and followed her.

Maybe she'd just been momentarily light-headed. Either way, it was best to get her cooled off and start heading home.

Since they'd long finished the water from the frozen yogurt shop, Colt grabbed a bottle from one of the food trucks that was still hanging around on the outskirts of the park. It was only a few minutes until they made it to the parking garage and then the car, but Jenna already looked worse as she leaned against the door, her cheeks flushed and her lips pale.

Colt unlocked the door and helped her inside, fastened her seatbelt, and then handed her the cold bottle of water.

"Drink this," he said. "It'll help." At least he hoped it would.

In his line of work, Colt was well aware of the symptoms

of heatstroke, and Jenna's added up, all except for the sweating. The hot skin and *lack* of perspiration were the surefire signs.

He hopped into the driver's seat, which was still pushed all the way back from their earlier *activities*. What a difference a few hours made.

He got the car running and turned on the air before adjusting his seat.

"Mmm," she hummed as the air blew out from vents. It wasn't yet cool, but at least it was something. "That feels nice."

She'd barely sipped the water and was instead holding it against her neck while she closed her eyes and rested her head against the back of the seat.

"Jenna," he said. "You're kind of worrying me. Maybe I should get you to a doctor."

She shook her head. "I'm fine. Really." She rubbed her hand up and down his thigh. "I just need to cool off and maybe take a little nap if that's okay. You can play my music if you want," she said groggily. "I've got that song, the one from the movie I was telling you about…"

She sighed and trailed off, leaning her head against the window.

Sleep was probably a good idea. Colt wasn't a doctor, but everyone felt better after a little rest.

"You got it, Texas," he said softly. "If there's anything you need, though, you'll let me know, right?"

She nodded and patted his knee before pulling her hand back to her own lap.

"Righty-o, cowboy," she said and then drifted off.

Colt opted for no music at all during the ride but instead kept an ear out for Jenna, now and then pressing his palm to her cheek to see if she was still burning up.

She was.

They were twenty minutes outside Meadow Valley when she bolted upright in her seat.

"Pull over!" she cried. "OhmyGod Colt pull over, please!"

His heart rate sped up as he veered onto the shoulder of the highway and pretty much slammed on the brakes once they were free and clear from being rear-ended.

The car had barely come to a stop when Jenna threw open her door and flew out.

He wasn't far behind when he found her squatting in the grass, her back to him and one hand held up in his direction as if for him to halt.

"I don't want you to see me like this!" she called out, but then he heard her retch.

He couldn't just leave her be. So he didn't.

In seconds he was holding her hair and rubbing her back as she did what she needed to do.

"This isn't from—you know—the gummy worms, is it?" he asked when she seemed to have emptied herself completely. He was only half kidding, because obviously something wasn't sitting right.

She shook her head. "Food poisoning," she said, her voice weak. "I had it once before. And if it's anything like the last time, this is just the beginning."

"But we all ate . . ." He stopped. "Willow and I had shawarma. *You* had fish tacos." So much for him finally taking her out for some real food.

She responded with something between a whimper and a laugh. "Guess Luis doesn't have any competition after all."

She still wouldn't turn to face him, but he pressed a palm to her cheek.

"Jesus, Jenna. You're on fire. I think we need to go to the ER. You're going to need fluids."

She nodded. "Can you get me a napkin or something? Please? And maybe the water?"

"Yeah. Of course." Colt ran back to the car and grabbed

what she needed. He waited a few paces back while she cleaned herself up, then helped her back into the car.

"I'm sorry," she said weakly. "We didn't even get to say good-bye to Willow."

"It's okay," he said, getting the vehicle back on the road and grabbing her hand with his. "All that matters is you right now, okay?"

She nodded, and he put the pedal to the metal. The hospital was only two exits from where they were, and all he could think about was how much he hated seeing her suffer and what he wouldn't do to fix it. What he wouldn't do for this woman. Period.

They barely made it into the waiting room before Jenna was sick again, this time in a hospital version of those lovely bags you find on airplanes the woman behind the registration desk had handed her.

"Can you fill out her paperwork, sir?" she asked Colt, and he nodded. "Good. We have an open exam room we can take her to right now, and you can do it there."

He followed nervously as a health care assistant pushed Jenna in a wheelchair to the designated room. Once there, he began scribbling on the forms at breakneck speed, as if filling it out faster meant she'd be better faster.

"Middle name?" he asked as she lay with her eyes squeezed shut on the exam table.

"Beatrice," she said with a small groan. "It was my grand-mother's name."

Her reaction made him smile. His Jenna was still there, regardless of the pain she was in.

"Insurance?" he asked.

"In my purse," she said, pointing to where it still hung across her torso.

He filled in the pertinent information and then got to the medical history.

"Any allergies to medication?" he asked.

"No."

"To latex?" he added, and she shook her head.

"Up to date on vaccinations?"

"I think," she said. "Maybe. I don't know. Say yes."

She bolted up, hand on her stomach, but then blew out a relieved breath.

"False alarm," she said, lying back down and closing her eyes again. "But my head is throbbing and my stomach is churning, and I'd really like to get off this ride."

"Soon, Texas. I promise," he said. "Date of your last menstrual period? Wow. Can't remember the last time I asked a woman that." He laughed and waited for her to remember the date, ready to write it down.

"Don't get it anymore," she said. "Full hysterectomy. Six years ago. And if there's a part about past surgeries, you can add my tonsils when I was a kid."

His hand froze with the pen still resting above the box that read *No*, and something—no, *everything*—inside him sank as low as it could possibly go.

A second later, Jenna's eyes flew open, and she pushed herself up to sitting.

"Colt…" was all she said because she must have seen it in his eyes. In one stupid hospital intake questionnaire, he'd gone from man in love to man who'd gotten the rug pulled out from under him. Again.

And then the doctor walked in, followed by a nurse rolling an IV over to the side of Jenna's bed, blocking her from his view.

CHAPTER TWENTY

Jenna woke with a start in a strange bed in an equally strange room. It took her several seconds to get her bearings, but the tube in her arm and the man sleeping in the chair next to her bed gave her the clues she needed to piece it all together.

Willow's concert.

Fish tacos.

Food poisoning.

Colt finding out before she had a chance to properly tell him.

He was still here, though. That meant something, right?

Last night her fever had spiked to 104 degrees before finally breaking sometime around 3 a.m. The time between the ER and being admitted was a haze. This morning, even though she felt like a train had hit her, backed up, and hit her again for good measure, she still felt a million times better than when they'd arrived the night before.

"Hey," she whispered, her voice hoarse. "Are you awake?"

His long body looked anything but comfortable in the cramped chair, and when he shifted at her words, he did so with a groan. He blinked and straightened, then rolled his neck to either side.

His stubble now looked like the start of a beard, and dark circles rimmed his usually vibrant brown eyes.

"I'm not sure who looks worse," she said, attempting to make light of what she knew would soon be a heavy, *heavy* situation. "You or me."

"How do you feel?" he asked, his tone still full of warmth but also something else she didn't recognize.

"Both like hell *and* a hell of a lot better, if that makes any sense," she said.

He nodded once.

"My phone is dead," he said flatly. "I'll go check the time."

He rose from the chair with a quick, painful glance in her direction, rolled his neck one more time, and then strode out of the room. He was back a minute later with a cup full of ice chips.

"It's six in the morning," he said. "Nurse said you can try these, see if you can keep them down."

He handed her the cup.

"Thank you," she said. "Not just for this."

He moved past her bed and to the window that looked out onto the parking lot, and she popped an ice chip into her mouth. She couldn't remember anything ever tasting so good.

"Can we talk?" she asked. "About last night? About what I meant to tell you in a much better way than—"

"Not now, Jenna. Not here," he said, spinning to face her. The words weren't cruel or angry. They weren't *anything*, and somehow that scared her more than if he'd been mad.

"So, what? I get discharged, head back to the ranch, and we have a big blowout there?"

He ran his hand through his hair. He looked so tired, so defeated, and it clicked. It clicked so hard Jenna swore she actually heard something snap.

"This was only supposed to be a fling," she said, hating the words as they came out of her mouth. "We weren't supposed to—we agreed that..." She shook her head, realizing that *she* hadn't done anything wrong here. Neither of them had. The situation just—sucked. But they could get past it, couldn't they? "You know what? Screw what we decided," she said. "I know how I feel, and I'm pretty sure you feel the same, which means we should be able to figure this out."

"Jenna," he said, pinching the bridge of his nose. "Please. Not now. Not when you're—"

She swung her legs over the side of the bed and stood. Her head swam, but only for a couple of seconds, and then she felt like she was standing on solid ground. She made sure her gown was closed in the back then did her best to stand tall and unwavering—in front of the IV bag to which she was connected.

"There," she said. "We've both got equal footing here. No one has home-court advantage, so to speak. So out with it. You want a family, and I can't give you one, and that makes you angry."

"Please," he said again, and the pain in his voice gutted her.

"Admit it," she countered, still pushing because the only way out of this for either of them was through. "You're angry. You feel duped or misled or..."

"Jenna, I'm begging you. I don't want to do this here. Not before I know you're okay."

Because they weren't going to survive this. He wanted her to be okay before he ended what they never should have started.

"No," she said, her throat tight. "We're almost out of time as it is."

A muscle ticked in his jaw, and he pressed the heels of his hands to his eyes. "Fine," he said, starting to pace. "You want to know *everything*, Jenna? Here it is. I *lost* my family. I spent *years* of my life feeling like I was nothing more than a burden or a meal ticket to whoever took me in. I could have continued down the dark path I was on as a teen, but instead I found Ben and Sam. I found Willow again. And I found—" He shook his head and let out a bitter laugh. "I found a girl I thought was the love of my life—until she told me she didn't want to have kids. Turns out, though, that she just didn't want them with me."

His voice broke on the last word, and Colt cleared his throat, then inhaled deeply through his nose.

"Oh God, Colt," she said, her own voice shaking. "I'm so sorry. I didn't know."

"And I didn't know you couldn't..." He trailed off, unable to even say the words.

"Couldn't have a family of my own," she said flatly.

"I'm in *love* with you, Jenna. I know that wasn't the plan, but there it is. I fell for you, and maybe if I'd have known..."

Tears burned the corners of her eyes, and her cheeks suddenly flamed with anger. "It wasn't *yours* to know," she said. "I didn't *owe* you that information."

Colt flinched, his eyes wide. "Jenna...I didn't say...I didn't *mean*—"

But she was on fire now. She couldn't stop.

"If you'd have known when you met me that I couldn't have children, you'd have made *sure* you didn't fall for me, because someone like me couldn't possibly be enough, right?"

Her pulse raced, and the room started to spin, so she lowered herself onto the side of the bed.

Colt stopped in front of her and dropped to a squat, his hand on her knees.

She sucked in a breath, not prepared for how she'd still react to his touch.

"Jenna," he said softly. "I'm just trying to take this all in. Can you maybe cut me a little slack? It's a lot to realize you're in love with someone and—all *this* at the same time. I don't know what the right words are here."

The right words would be that *she* was enough. That despite all the possible directions her life could have gone when she was younger, everything she was today was *enough*.

But it wasn't fair to ask him for that. It wasn't fair to ask him to give up *his* future for her. So she'd sacrifice their hearts for *both* their good.

"You should go," she finally said. "I can call someone to pick me up." Her throat was tight and her chest ached and she just needed this to be done. There was no need to prolong the pain.

"Jenna, I'm not just going to leave you here."

She wrapped her hands around his, and then squeezed them, and gently pushed them off her knees.

"Please?" she said, unable to hide the tremor in her voice. "I think that would be easiest. For both of us."

He hung his head, shaking it from side to side.

"Colt," she said. "Now I'm begging *you*."

He rose to his full height and crossed his arms, and Jenna hated that even now she wished he was wrapping them around her instead.

"So that's it, then? I don't get to say anything else?" he asked.

"Are you going to say that you were just kidding? That you don't want someone who can give you the family you've always wanted? I'm not faulting you for that. But I can't stand the look in your eyes right now that tells me that even if you *do* love me, it's not enough." She'd already lost her heart to him, so there was nothing left to lose by putting it all out there, blunt and clear so there were no more misunderstandings.

"Jenna," he said, but he hesitated first. And that hesitation was all she needed.

"Good-bye, Colt." She swiped away the tears that were falling freely from both eyes.

He opened his mouth to say something but then closed it.

"Good-*bye*," she said again, barely holding it together.

He let out a long, shaky breath, and then strode out the door.

"I loved you too," she said out loud, not sure if he was still close enough to hear. But at least it was out there.

She dropped her head into her hands, alone in a hospital room in a town that had almost felt like it could one day be home, tears streaming down her cheeks.

Everything the past two weeks had been for what? To prove to herself that she could relive the life she'd lost?

Hanging on to the past was getting her nowhere.

She pulled the journal from Jack out of her bag and opened it to the one page she'd used, her list, and ripped it out.

Then she crumpled it up and tossed it onto the table next to her hospital bed.

Jenna was done looking backward. She was done thinking it was selfish of her to want more than she already had.

She *deserved* a happily ever after instead of just a happy for now.

It just wouldn't include Colt Morgan.

An hour later she was released, but before she could attempt a ride share so as not to bother anyone back at the ranch, Barbara Ann, Sam's mother, showed up at her hospital room.

"Knock knock," the other woman said from the open doorway while Jenna was sitting in the chair—fully clothed, finally—signing her release forms.

"What are *you* doing here?" Jenna asked. "Sorry if that sounded rude. I just wasn't expecting..."

"I don't know what happened," Barbara Ann said. "All I know is that Colt said you were here alone and that he didn't want you to be."

Her sunglasses were propped on top of her head, and she wore a denim shirt on top of a pair of khaki shorts and cowboy boots, which meant she'd probably been pulled from ranch duty to come and get Jenna.

"You didn't have to leave work for me," Jenna insisted. "I'd have figured out an Uber or Lyft or whatever y'all have up here." She forced a smile, but Barbara Ann gave her a pointed look.

"Honey," she said. "When you're at the ranch—or in our town for that matter—you're family. And family doesn't leave anyone alone in a hospital room. Period."

And that was all it took for the waterworks to start up again.

In a matter of seconds Barbara Ann was there, her arms wrapped around Jenna in the kind of warm, mama-bear hug she hadn't felt since—she couldn't remember when. For so long *Jenna* had been the mama bear. *Jenna* had been the one to give the hug when someone needed to cry in *her* arms. This? It was awful and wonderful all at the same time. She didn't *want* to be heartbroken, but oh how she needed this simple little hug that, right now, felt like the biggest thing in the world.

"It's okay, sweetheart," Barbara Ann whispered, even though they both knew it wasn't.

And then neither of them said anything, not for several minutes. Barbara Ann simply held her, and Jenna let herself be held.

Soon after that, they were in Sam's silver pickup and on the way back to the ranch.

"I could take you for some coffee? Something to eat?" Barbara Ann said. "The doctor said you should take it slow, but I'm betting you're pretty hungry."

Jenna's stomach growled in response, but she had some crackers back in her room. That was probably all she could handle right now, anyway. Plus, she was still wearing last night's clothes.

"Thanks," she said. "But I need a shower. And to regroup." She looked at Barbara Ann, who smiled even though her eyes were trained on the road. "Colt really didn't tell you anything?"

The other woman shook her head. "Just said you shouldn't be alone but that you didn't want him there. Whatever happened, sounds like he thinks it's your story to tell. I'm all ears if you want, but I understand if you're not up for rehashing what led him to knock on my door at seven thirty in the morning, red-eyed and looking like he'd been to hell and back."

Jenna's chest ached, for the hurt she'd caused him and the hurt he'd caused her right back.

And then, because it felt like she had an ally or at least a neutral third party, she told Barbara Ann everything. By the time she'd finished, they were parked in front of the Meadow Valley Ranch's guesthouse.

Barbara Ann turned to face Jenna, laying a palm over Jenna's hand. "Oh, honey. What the two of you have *both* been through and lost at such young ages? Those wounds are deep. They shape who you are and what you want out of life. Does he even know *why* you had the surgery?"

Jenna shook her head. "The *why* doesn't matter. It doesn't change that Colt wants a family and that I can't give that to him. I don't fault him for wanting it. He deserves *everything* in life that would make him happy. It's just not me."

Barbara Ann sighed. "I'm sorry. I wish I had an answer for you. But if there is one, it's for you and Colt to figure out."

But she would never ask Colt to give up the future he'd always wanted. He shouldn't have to settle for anything less than what would make him truly happy. And neither should she.

Jenna squeezed the other woman's hand. "Thank you, and I don't just mean for the ride."

Barbara Ann gave her a sad smile. "I know," was all she said. Then she gave Jenna one more of those mama-bear hugs that

Jenna would always remember before Jenna hopped out of the truck and back to her room.

It was hard for her to let go, not only from the embrace but from the sheer hope that she'd maybe, *finally*, found what she hadn't even known she was looking for.

CHAPTER TWENTY-ONE

Colt pulled onto the private road that led to Dr. Eli Murphy's farm and veterinary clinic. As he bumped over the gravel, William, his goat companion, bleated from the rear of the vehicle.

"Yeah, yeah," he said to his unconventional companion. "We're almost there."

He'd definitely had his share of animals this week, especially after watching over Trudy's brood, but the second he learned Delaney had a sick goat who needed a lift to the vet, he'd been the first to volunteer.

He couldn't count how many times in the day before that he'd brought Jenna's number up on his phone, pressed the green button to initiate the call, only for her to send him straight to voicemail.

"Hey. It's Jenna. Leave a message. Or a text. Or you can just call me again later. Bye, y'all."

The sound of her voice, the lilt of her accent—it kicked him in the gut every time he called.

He *loved* her. With every molecule in his body. But he'd stumbled over his words and said all the wrong things, so she pushed him away. Even if she had answered one of his calls, what would he have said? He wanted her, but he also wanted the future he envisioned, which meant he didn't have a clue how to make any of this right.

It was Emma all over again, except it wasn't. Only now, when he knew how much he loved Jenna, did he realize that with Emma it was the *idea* of them he loved—the future that marrying her represented—but not the woman herself. When he finally parked in front of the clinic, his heart sank like deadweight straight to his gut. Jenna had him out, but maybe it was for the best. He wanted a family. A future. With *her*. And it couldn't happen.

He'd risked contaminating his car with a pinkeyed goat because apparently goats were as susceptible to the eye infection as humans. *And* because if Colt wasn't at the ranch, he wouldn't have to risk running into Jenna on her last day in town not knowing how the hell to fix what felt like it couldn't be repaired.

He opened the trunk and grabbed the leash attached to William's collar. William bleated, then hopped out of the car.

The goat was surprisingly cooperative as Colt led him to the clinic, but when he opened the door, the receptionist desk was empty with a note taped to the front that said *In the stable. Back in ten.*

Colt shrugged.

"Okay, buddy," he said. "Guess we're going for a walk."

He and the goat headed back the way they came and crossed the parking lot to the small expanse of grass that separated Dr. Murphy's house and farm from the clinic.

He wondered what Eli was doing in the stable. There hadn't been a horse living on the property since Tess died. Other than the ranch, the only other horses in town were the couple that Mayor Cooper had at his restored horse farm. And if there was one thing everyone in Meadow Valley knew, it was that Eli

Murphy steered clear of horses unless they were in need of medical attention.

The stable door was open when they got there, so Colt walked right in. Before he had a chance to get his bearings, a chicken squawked and came barreling toward him and the goat. A second later William went stiff as a board and toppled over on his side.

Lucy.

Only when he realized *whose* chicken it was that had just paralyzed his goat did his eyes register the two people staring at him from a couple of stalls down—Eli and Jenna.

The two of them stared at him as he stared right back. He was sure Dr. Murphy was wearing something along the lines of a shirt and jeans, but all he could see was Jenna in her blue sundress, her blond hair in one of those messy buns on top of her head with loose wisps framing her beautiful face.

Colt's stomach tied in knots, and all the air escaped his lungs in one large *whoosh*, so that he felt light-headed. What did he expect, that after one day and one very serious truth bomb, Jenna Owens wouldn't still take his damned breath away?

Of course he didn't expect that, which was why he'd been trying to avoid this exact type of confrontation when he knew she didn't even want to talk to him.

He cleared his throat. "Delaney says William's got pinkeye? She came by to check on and feed all the animals this morning, but Sam's teaching a riding lesson, and Barbara Ann was on an errand...." He figured he knew how Jenna had gotten here now. "Anyway, she was hoping you could get him some drops, maybe keep him overnight so he doesn't pass it on to anyone else?"

Eli nodded. "Sorry no one was at the desk to greet you. My receptionist up and quit with only two days' notice. Can't seem to find anyone who actually enjoys the job and wants to stay.

Jenna, can you give me a few minutes to get William situated before we finish what we were talking about?"

"Sure," she said. "Unless you need a helping hand."

She was trying to get out of this confrontation too. At least they were both on the same page.

"It's probably best you tend to your hen," he said. "William's just coming out of his spell, and I'd rather not have to carry him back to the clinic."

Jenna let out a nervous laugh. "Right. Sorry about that." She dropped to a squat. "Lucinda Owens, you get over here right this second."

Amazingly, the hen behaved, and Eli was able to usher the goat out of the stable before he fainted again.

Jenna picked Lucy up and held her under her arm like a football. Then she closed the distance between them in a few long strides. Colt half expected her to walk right past him and out the door, but she stopped.

"Hey," she said, her voice sad but sweet.

"Hey," he said back, because right now that was all he could manage.

"*Squawk!*" Lucy said, pecking in the direction of Colt's chest, but luckily there was enough space between them that she couldn't actually hit her target.

"She doesn't like me much, does she?" he asked. "Guess she *is* psychic."

Jenna smiled, but it didn't reach her red-rimmed eyes. Had she been crying? As much as he was hurting, it gutted him to see her hurting too.

"Can't tell for sure," she said, bringing him back to the moment. "Lucy's been off her game this whole trip, from the second you picked me up at Jack's place."

Two weeks ago when the worst pain he'd felt in a long time was the loss of his tin of cookies. Now look where they were.

"Jenna, I'm—" he started right when she started to speak as well.

"Sorry," they both said. "You first."

"*You* first," he said again.

She nodded and blew out a breath. "I didn't mean to put this all on you," she said. "I was hurt. And maybe not thinking clearly on account of emptying my guts the night before and a fever that had me burning hotter than the underworld." Another forced smile. "I'm sorry for how you found out, but I'm not apologizing for waiting to tell you. I needed to be sure about my feelings for you—about yours for me—because we both know this wasn't part of the plan." She blew out a long breath. "You deserve everything you want out of your life, Colt, as much as I deserve what I want out of mine."

"I want *you*," he said.

Her eyes went glassy, and she shook her head.

His chest tightened. "That's the part that kills me, Jenna, that you would ever think that *you* weren't enough. That *I* would make you think that."

She pressed her lips together and nodded. "I'm not, though. Not for you. And that's okay." She sniffed, and a tear leaked out of the corner of one eye. "I mean it's not *okay*. *I'm* obviously not okay, but I will be. You will be. And you'll find someone who can give you everything."

Lucy squirmed in her arm, so Jenna put her back on the ground. The hen squawked again and pecked at Colt's boots.

"Enough of that, Lucy," Jenna said, shooing the bird away.

She gave Colt's boot one last peck and then took off down the aisle of stalls, probably hoping to find another goat to paralyze.

"Eli wants to turn part of the stable into a chicken coop," Jenna said. "He wants to turn the farm into more of a small business, hire some folks to run this and that." She let out a bitter laugh. "Even offered me a job overseeing the hens and the egg laying."

Though he knew it was ridiculous, hope surged through his veins. If she was staying, they could... They could... What could they do but still want each other while also wanting different futures?

"Did you accept?" he asked, trying not to give away every warring emotion that flooded through him.

She shook her head. "I wouldn't do that to you. *Or* to myself. You don't get over someone by parking your behind where you might run into them on a regular basis. This was..." She motioned between them. "We were... We had a fun couple of weeks, but that's all it's ever going to be. We messed it up real good, didn't we?"

"*Jenna...*" he said.

But she shrugged. "This was *always* where we were going to end up, Colt. Don't you think it's better we pulled back these past couple of days before it got too real?"

Too real? *Too* real? He'd flat-out told her he loved her, and maybe she thought he hadn't heard, but she'd said it too. She'd loved him right back. Maybe that was past tense now, but they'd traveled well beyond *too real*.

He opened his mouth to argue his point, to prove to her that this *was* real, even if it was ending.

But he stopped himself. Because it *was* ending. They were ending. By this time tomorrow, Jenna would be gone, and he'd be back to his regular day-to-day on the ranch, heart shattered more than he'd ever imagined possible.

"Sure," he finally said, even though he was lying through his teeth. "Better sooner than later."

"I'm not sorry we met," she said, but her voice was shaking. She held out her right hand, and he clenched his jaw so hard he was sure he'd grind his teeth to dust.

"You want me to shake your hand?" he asked, incredulous. "After everything?"

She pressed her lips together and nodded, and he could tell she was holding back more tears. But he had no intention of making this easy. For either of them. Because it *wasn't* easy.

"What else are we supposed to do?" she asked.

"Let me ask you something," he said. "You wouldn't answer any of my calls. If I hadn't run into you today, would I have even seen you again before you left?"

For several long seconds she said nothing, and then she slowly shook her head.

The air in the stable seemed to grow thinner. Colt could barely breathe.

He crossed his arms, and she dropped her hand.

"Sorry I messed up your plans," he said. "I'll just go check in with Dr. Murphy and make sure he's okay keeping the goat for the night. Good-bye, Jenna."

He turned to walk away but couldn't move. He wasn't cruel. He wasn't the kind of guy who punished others for hurting him. And he wasn't sure which was crueler, if he simply walked away or if he turned around and did what he wanted to do. What he *needed* to do so that Jenna Owens knew how truly real they'd let this get.

When he pivoted back to face her, she hadn't moved. And when he took the one step needed to close the gap between them, she didn't retreat.

And when he cupped her cheeks—wet with tears—in his hands, she clasped hers around his neck.

He said good-bye to her the only way he knew how, kissing her one last time with everything he had. She held him tight and kissed him with a fierceness he hadn't felt from her before. Because this was it.

When they broke apart, she pushed past him and out the stable door, not giving either of them a chance to say another word.

His phone buzzed with a text. It was Eli.

Treated William. He can stay the weekend just to make sure it's clear. I'll bring him back to the ranch on Monday.

Colt texted him back a Thank you. Then he got into his car and drove away from the woman who should have been his future but now would only ever be another painful piece of his past.

CHAPTER TWENTY-TWO

Are you sure you're comfortable on the couch?" Delaney asked, and Jenna nodded.

Delaney's three-legged black cat, Butch Catsidy, purred in Jenna's lap. It didn't fix what had happened between her and Colt, but it helped. A little. Lucy squawked away in the backyard, and as much as Jenna liked having her feathered friend near, the hen was lacking a bit in the snuggle category.

She couldn't stay at the ranch tonight. Not knowing Colt was in the same building as her. Not after that kiss that pretty much wrecked her. If only she could have made it to tomorrow and her flight home without running into him. He probably would have hated her for leaving like that. But wouldn't that have made things easier for him?

"Are *you* sure Barbara Ann doesn't mind driving me to the Reno airport in the morning? What if you go into labor? What if Sam's at the ranch and you need—I don't know—an orange or something?"

Delaney sat across from Jenna on a recliner love seat with her feet up in front of her. "I promise to have Sam leave me with a bowl of oranges right next to the remote." She sighed. "I wish I could come to see you off. At least you'll be back in December for my snowy winter wedding, right?" She winced because she knew what Jenna's response was going to be.

"You know how much I want to be there for you and Sam— and the baby," Jenna said.

"But...?" Delaney asked. In that one word Jenna could hear her sad resignation.

"But I don't know if that will be enough time for me to be around Colt and not—"

"Still love him?" Delaney winced again.

There was no use in lying, so Jenna nodded.

"I *really* want to be mad at him on your behalf," Delaney said. "But I can't fault him for wanting what he never had."

Jenna nodded again. Neither could she.

Delaney lowered her feet and pushed herself to the edge of her seat.

"It's late," she said. "You have an early morning, and I need to go toss and turn all night while this baby sits on my bladder and makes me feel like I have to constantly pee."

Jenna scooted to the edge of her couch bed so she could hug her friend good-bye.

"It's an open invitation," Delaney said. "For the wedding. I don't care if you wait until the day before to tell me if you're coming. There will always be room for you in Meadow Valley." Delaney pulled out of the embrace and sniffled.

Jenna sniffled right back at her.

"This was supposed to be two weeks of self-care," she said. "And now I feel like I'm leaving so much behind. Y'all will take good care of Colt, won't you?" she asked.

Delaney nodded, brushing tears off her cheeks. "Of course we will. But who's going to take care of you?"

Jenna shrugged. "I have my nephews and friends in Oak

Bluff." Though they were still an hour away from her farm. "I can spend more time with them…until things get easier."

"Do you think…?" Delaney started. "Do you think there's a chance you and Colt could work through this? Maybe if he knew the whole story—if he knew why you elected to have the surgery…"

Jenna shook her head. "It doesn't change that I can't give him what he wants." She squared her shoulders. "I made the right decision for *me*, and I don't regret that. And I don't fault Colt for knowing what will make him happy even if that doesn't include me. We just got in too deep, you know?"

Delaney nodded. "But I also know he loves you too."

Jenna swiped at an escaping tear. "I know I sound like every brokenhearted love song out there, but sometimes love isn't enough."

"Stupid brokenhearted love songs," Delaney said with a half-smile.

They hugged again, neither of them wanting to let go. So for a little while longer, they didn't.

When Jenna and Lucy—not too thrilled after the plane ride in her travel coop—made it out onto the sidewalk outside the small Santa Ynez airport, she breathed a sigh of relief when she saw her nephew's truck waiting for them. The familiar sight—the familiar *face* behind the wheel—was exactly what she needed right now.

Jack hopped out of the driver's-side door and strode toward her, arms already spread to enfold her into a hug.

"We really missed you," he said as he squeezed her tight. "Who the hell came up with the bright idea to send you away for two weeks anyway?" he asked with a laugh.

He grabbed her bag and Lucy and loaded them into the bed of the truck, and Jenna followed to make sure both were secure and safe, which, of course, they were. This was Jack Everett, father of two and head of the Crossroads Ranch and Winery. He did everything by the book.

"*You*, nephew of mine," she teased—or at least tried to tease. But everything about her, even her own voice, just felt heavy.

"Hey," he said, turning to face her and reaching for her door so he could open it. "Everything okay?"

His blue eyes stared at her with the kind of concern you'd expect from a big brother, not a nephew a decade her junior. But that was Jack. For all she did to take care of him when his life was flipped upside down, he repaid her tenfold now that he'd grown into the man she always knew he'd become.

"Yeah," she lied. "Just tired. Think I might need a vacation after my vacation, you know?"

He laughed. "What is this *vacation* you speak of? I don't think I remember what those are."

He opened her door, and she hopped into the truck, her shoulders relaxing at the familiarity of it all. She was safe here. Safe with the life she'd built for herself.

Jack rounded the car and hopped back into his seat, putting the key into the ignition and getting the air blowing in the already sun-heated vehicle.

"Would you trade it?" Jenna asked as they pulled away from the curb and onto the road. "Wife, kids, being a lawyer on top of a twenty-four-hour-a-day job at the ranch—for a real vacation?"

"No," he said without hesitation. "Not for a second. None of it's easy, but any life without Ava, Owen, and Clare—without any of the people I love..." He glanced at her and then set his eyes back on the road. "That includes you. Hell, even Luke and Walker." He laughed at his joke about his two younger brothers. "The life I have, Jenna...You know it's all thanks to you. Don't you?"

Her breath caught in her throat. "Jack, you don't have to say that."

He shrugged. "Why not? I don't think I say it enough. My parents were great when we were kids. I'm not discounting that. But losing Mom and what happened to Jack Sr. in the aftermath—we never would have survived the fallout without you." His brows drew together. "Are you sure everything's okay? Is this because—*dammit*," he said softly. "I forgot Delaney was pregnant. Jenna, Jesus, I'm sorry. I should have said something. I know it probably wasn't easy—"

"Jack, stop. Please." She rested a hand on his forearm. "My greatest joy . . . No, my greatest accomplishment in life is that not only did I *not* screw things up with you and your brothers, but I got to be a mother when y'all needed one most." She forced a laugh. "And I didn't even have to change any diapers."

Jack grinned as they neared the street where Jenna's house and farm stood, no doubt well taken care of while she was gone by those wonderful boys she raised.

"You can come over and change Clare *any*time you want. Although, I gotta admit, Owen's getting pretty good at it," he said.

They rolled down the small country road that led to her farm, and when they made it into the drive that brought them to her front door, it was all Jenna could do not to weep with joy at the safety and security that was home.

"Would *you* trade it?" Jack asked hesitantly. "The decision you made?" He put the truck in park and turned to face her.

She pressed her lips into a smile and shook her head. "I'm healthy," she said. "Which means a longer life with you and Luke and Walker. I'd *never* trade that." And she meant it. "But—and I know this sounds crazy because I had *no* idea what I was doing when y'all got thrust into my care—I miss it. I miss helping Walker with his geometry homework and reading your

English essays. I miss watching Luke put on his first suit for a school dance. Hell, I even miss the parent-teacher conferences." She laughed, but then her smile grew sad. "I loved getting to be your second mom, but it went by so fast."

Jack leaned over and kissed her on the forehead, then looked at her with a grin.

"You could do it again," he said.

She opened her mouth to argue the *very* obvious, but he shook his head.

"I mean the later stuff—the homework, the dances. One of my buddies from law school works in adoption. He's always telling me about the older kids in foster care who bounce from family to family, but no one wants to adopt them."

Kids like Colt, she thought. Kids like Jack, Luke, and Walker if she hadn't been there for them.

"They'd really benefit from being cared for by someone like you. It's just a thought," he concluded with a shrug, as if what he'd said was part of their normal, everyday conversation.

Jenna sat there for a long moment, worrying her bottom lip between her teeth.

"How did you know what you were *meant* to do with your life?" she finally asked with a nervous laugh. "I feel like I should know this by now. I feel like I should have known it before the three nephews I raised were grown with lives of their own. But I look at you, Luke, and Walker... You all seem to have figured out your purpose while I'm still sitting here so lost."

Jack blew out a long breath. "I overstepped with the year-book and the journal, didn't I? I'm sorry, Jenna. I wasn't trying to push. I guess I just saw all these things about you I never knew and wondered if you maybe regretted how things turned out because—" He cleared his throat. "Because you had to put everything aside for us."

Jenna shook her head without a second thought. "You're my

family, and there's nothing more important to me than that. Maybe my life didn't turn out the way I thought it would when I was eighteen, but that doesn't mean I'm not grateful for the direction it went. *Everything* that happened—from leaving Texas, to working my parents' farm, to losing the family I had and gaining a new one with you and your brothers—it all brought me here." It brought her to meeting Colt, and even if that meant coming home brokenhearted, it also meant learning how much she wanted that kind of love in her life—and how much she deserved it too. "There's nowhere else I'd rather be," she added.

Jack nodded. "Then maybe you have found your purpose. Just—think about what I said, okay? About my buddy who's an adoption attorney." He checked his watch. "I can help you get your stuff inside," he said. "But then I have to get going. Owen has a game in a few hours, and he wanted to practice some pitches at the house before we head to the field. You are under no obligation to come, because you need to get settled in, but you always have an open invitation."

She nodded, Jack's suggestion just now starting to sink in. "I'll be there," she said. "Wouldn't miss it for the world."

She made it inside the house and let Lucy out back where she could roam with the rest of *her* family. She opened her suitcase to toss her dirty laundry into the wash and stopped short when she saw a blue bookshop bag, with STORYLAND printed in a thick white font, resting on top of her clothes. Her breath caught in her throat as she slid the contents of the bag into her hand.

Where the Wild Things Are, by Maurice Sendak.

But it wasn't just the book. From between the pages, a wrinkled piece of paper stuck out like a bookmark, and Jenna tugged on it slowly, releasing it from the book.

It was her list.

Barbara Ann had found it in her hospital room when they

were packing Jenna up to be released, but Jenna had told the other woman it was garbage. Apparently she not only hadn't thrown it out but had passed it on—to Colt. Because underneath her last item, *Write something more meaningful than a list*, there was an addition, written in handwriting that most definitely wasn't her own.

> 8. Know that you are enough no matter how many lists you make, no matter how many items you check off or don't. I love you, Jenna. —Colt

She let loose a hiccuping sob.

When had he...? How had he...?

She pulled out her phone to see she had one missed call and a voicemail, and her heart jumped into her throat as she tapped the green phone icon to see who it was. When she saw it was Delaney, her shoulders slumped. Of course she was thrilled to see a message from her new friend, but it wasn't Colt. She'd pushed him too far, which meant the book and the list were nothing more than closure, their final good-bye.

Jenna released a trembling breath, pressed PLAY on the voicemail, and put the phone to her ear.

"Hey, Jenna. I just wanted to check that you made it home safely...and to make sure I didn't cross a line by doing one last favor for Colt. He stopped by our place before you came over and gave me the book. He told me not to open the bag but to just give it to you, and I swear I didn't peek even though I really wanted to. You were just so sad last night, and I didn't want to upset you more, so I stuck it in your suitcase after you fell asleep because—let's face it—I don't sleep anymore and from what I hear won't sleep much again for the next several years. Anyway, I hope whatever Colt left for you brings you some sort of peace, but if you need me to give him a stern talking-to, you just let me know. Miss you even more than I miss my ankles. Love you more than clementines. Call me after you get settled. Bye."

Jenna thumbed through the pages of the children's book that had been Colt's refuge during the darkest time in his life. She thought of him—nose broken and faith in the world shattered—as he spent night after night in a juvenile detention center with no one to love him, no one to keep him safe. She thought about how easily that could have been Jack, Luke, or Walker if she hadn't been there for her nephews. If she hadn't loved them and kept them safe even when they made mistakes, which they certainly did.

She held her breath and opened the photo app on her phone, thumbing through her pictures from Meadow Valley, almost all of them candid shots of Colt. He got a final chance to turn his life around with a foster family who actually cared for him, and look at how he turned out.

Colt Morgan had grown up to be a wonderful, caring man with a heart so big he wanted to share that love with a family who needed and deserved him. And even if it was only for a short time, Jenna got to feel what it was like to be on the receiving end of such a love, and it had changed her in ways she could never have imagined. It made her realize that she'd already found what she'd been meant to do. She'd just been too caught up in the past to see it.

You could do it again.

Jack's words played themselves back in her head, and it was as if lightning struck and shook her entire world. But then a crash trailed not too far behind, and Jenna realized it was *actual* lightning from an actual storm, which was followed by a text from Jack letting her know the storm had already hit Oak Bluff, which meant Owen's game would be rescheduled.

She yelped as a second thunderclap shook the room, then

laughed nervously as she powered up her laptop and opened her browser.

It didn't take long for her to research and find information about becoming a foster parent. She printed out literature she would read curled up on her couch later tonight. She printed forms she'd fill out and deliver in person on Monday so she could inquire about the training and having her home inspected. She wrote her cover letter—the story of Jenna Owens and why she would make an ideal foster parent—and realized she *had* ticked off the final item on her list. The letter—inspired not only by her nephews but by the love she had for a man she never expected to meet—was the most meaningful thing she'd ever write.

This was it. Her thing. She was all in.

CHAPTER TWENTY-THREE

This was ridiculous. Colt wasn't invited. He would likely get thrown out on his ass. Yet here he was, his SUV rolling slowly up Jenna Owens's driveway in the middle of the night in yet another ridiculous storm. He could feel the soft earth beneath his tires, which meant it wasn't exactly a *paved* driveway. Fantastic. What *was* it with rain and mud and this woman?

He turned the car off and sat there in the dark, listening to the rain hit his windshield and the roof of the car. If she got angry, he'd just blame it on Delaney. *She* gave him the address. *She* was the one who said she wouldn't confirm or deny his suspicions about *why* Jenna had the surgery all those years ago.

"She told me in confidence," Delaney had said. "And it's not my place to share her story with you. If you want to know, you need to ask her yourself."

The thing was, the *why* didn't matter. The only thing that mattered was Jenna and that they *could* have a future, maybe one that was a bit different than either had imagined, if she would hear him out. If he wasn't too late.

He could have called or texted or even emailed. There were countless ways he could have gotten in touch with Jenna without leaving Meadow Valley. But here was the thing...Colt didn't want to *be* in Meadow Valley anymore, not without Jenna there. He thought he'd known what he wanted. He thought he'd had it all figured out, especially after everything went to hell with Emma almost six years ago.

He let out a bitter laugh, realizing both his and Jenna's lives took a drastic turn at about the same time, before they even knew one another or that their paths would cross. But they had crossed. And everything had changed.

"What are you waiting for, Morgan?" he said out loud.

The rain wasn't going to die down. That would make this all too easy, and when it came to loving Jenna Owens, nothing about that was easy.

Good thing Colt didn't want easy. He wanted *her*. They could still have the future he dreamed of. It just might look a little different now, and he was an idiot for not thinking of it sooner. But that was the thing about love. It could tear you down as quickly as it could lift you up—and turn you into a temporary idiot who says *all* the wrong things. Emphasis on the temporary, because Colt was ready to get it right.

He grabbed his umbrella and his phone, cued up a song, and figuratively crossed all his fingers and toes.

When he stepped out into the cold, wet night, his boot sank into mud. Of *course* it did. But since when did he let a little mud get in his way?

When his other foot hit the ground, it didn't land as steadily as the first but instead slid out from under him. Colt hadn't even taken his first step, and he was already ass-first in what was slowly turning into a swamp. He'd let go of the umbrella in order to break his fall and save his phone, which meant he was drenched in seconds.

Getting up one-handed proved to be a comedy of errors. If his boot couldn't keep him steady, what good was his hand?

Good enough to flip him over and ensure he was mud-covered from the torso on down as well.

"*Shit*," he hissed. But he finally made it to his feet, phone still safe in his mud-free hand, umbrella abandoned on the ground, hoping his water-resistant phone case could resist for a minute or two longer.

He trudged carefully, his steps slow and deliberate, up to her covered front porch, where the outside light went on as soon as he was in front of it. Motion sensors, he guessed.

What time was it? Would he wake her? Scare her? Why the hell hadn't he thought this through?

He pressed a finger to her doorbell and realized it was one of those bells with a camera. She could see it was him before she even opened the door, which meant she might *not* open the door.

Yeah, he really hadn't thought this through. But there was no going back now. At the very least, he needed to wash and dry his clothes before he could get back in his car and head home.

He pressed the button and held his breath. Here went *everything*.

Seconds later, a light went on behind the door, and even through the rain, he could hear the tumbler of the dead bolt as it was unlocked. Then the door flew open, and there was Jenna Owens—blond hair piled on her head in her signature bun, a thin, white cotton tank covering her torso above a pair of pink shorts.

She blinked a few times, her blue eyes groggy with sleep.

"Colt?" she said, confused. Then she took in the sight of him. "Oh my God, *Colt*. Get inside. You'll catch your death out there."

He shook his head. "Not yet," he said. Then he lifted his phone where he had "Can't Take My Eyes Off of You" by Frankie Valli and the Four Seasons cued up. She'd made it clear to him that this was the only song worthy of winning her back, should he ever have to do so, and he *had* to. Right here. Right now.

"I'm sorry I don't have a marching band," was all he said before he hit PLAY and sang along, *terribly*, telling her how he loved her and needed her, that she most definitely was too good to be true.

She stood there staring at him with her hands over her mouth and her eyes brimming with tears, and God, he hoped that was a good sign. That they were happy tears.

He belted out every word from the chorus until the end of the song. There wasn't any room to dance like Heath Ledger had in the movie, but he hoped it was enough.

When the song ended, she was still in her open doorway, silently staring, mouth still covered so he couldn't see if she was hiding a smile or a frown.

"You told me you wanted me to find someone who could give me everything, Jenna. And what I should have told you right then and there was that the only definition of *everything* was the one that included *you*. I thought I knew exactly what I wanted out of my future, but that was before you existed in my life." He blew out a breath. "You lost your sister to cancer," he said. It wasn't a question.

Tears spilled from Jenna's eyes, and she dropped her hands from her mouth. "I never said..." She trailed off, but then she nodded.

"I was so tangled up in what the news about your surgery meant for us as a couple—for me and what I thought I wanted— that I didn't even ask why." He knew enough about the genetics of cancer, especially when it came to the strains of the disease that affected women, that when he'd finally had a minute to think straight, it all made sense. "You carry the gene, don't you?"

She nodded again.

"Jesus, Jenna. I was so damned selfish." he said. He wouldn't blame her if she never forgave him for walking away like he had that morning in the hospital. He should have fought to stay. Maybe it was too little too late, but he was fighting now. "But here's the thing. The *why* doesn't matter. What matters is that you're here. That you exist in the world and that if I'm not too late, you'll exist in *my* world too."

"I love you, Colt," she said. "But I can't ask you to give up being a father. Even if you know why I did it, it doesn't change what you want. It doesn't change that one day you might resent me for what you gave up. And I could never live with that."

"But—" he started. He wanted to tell her that he could still be a father. With *her*. That there were options he hadn't considered before because before—before, there was no Jenna.

She shook her head.

"Come inside. Please," she said. "It's cold and you're soaked and—I need to show you something."

Because he *was* soaked *and* starting to realize he was shivering, he obliged.

She closed the door behind him, and then left him standing there dripping on her rug. She ran to the coffee table that was in the living room just off the entrance and grabbed a stack of papers before pivoting and striding back to him, a scared yet expectant look on her face.

She laughed nervously. "Here." She handed him a sheaf of papers. "This is what I've been working on since the second I got home this morning."

He didn't need to see what was beyond the first page because on top of the pile was a cover letter she'd written to the state of California—to become a foster parent. He squinted without his glasses but was able to make out the rest.

Colt's stomach tied in knots and his throat tightened as

he read about her experience becoming a guardian to Jack, Luke, and Walker, as he read on to where she mentioned her latest inspiration for wanting to foster—a nameless boy who got knocked down by the system but was then given a second chance with a family who helped him become the amazing man he was today.

She'd made this decision in part because of *him*.

"I *do* want to be a mother," she said. "You and Delaney and my own nephews taught me that. I want to be a mother to kids who bounce from house to house because others deem them too old to adopt. I want to keep siblings from getting separated like you and Willow did. I want my house to be a home to kids—"

"Like *me*," he said, barely able to get the words out. He wanted a house filled with kids. He wanted a family so big that the house would never be empty. As foster parents, they could give safety and stability to as many children as they were able. They could give them a *home*. "This is it," he added. "*Our* definition of family. This is what I didn't want to tell you over the phone or text. This is why I *had* to come here, Jenna. I didn't think—I mean, I hoped..." He shook his head and exhaled a trembling breath.

She let out a hiccuping sob. "You want to do this *with* me?" she asked.

"God, *yes*, Jenna. I want to do everything with you. *Everything*." He took a step forward and cradled her cheeks in his hands. "You didn't let me finish before. What you did six years ago? It's likely because of that decision that you're here right now. That I got the chance to meet you. That I have the god-damned privilege to be the man who gets to love you. A world with *you* in it is what matters. A world where *we* get to have the family we're meant to have, the future we *both* want."

"But..." she said. "But it's only been two weeks. And...And I live here, and you live there, and..."

He grinned. "Okay. So maybe there's a certain chronology to all of this. But we were never good at doing things in order. We can figure it out each step of the way. Together."

She launched herself into his muddy arms, wrapping her arms around his neck and her legs around his waist.

"The forms!" he said.

"We'll print new ones," she said laughing. "But one thing about that *everything* before I kiss you something fierce."

"You name it, Texas."

She bit her lip. "Leave the singing to your sister?"

He threw back his head and laughed, then looked at the half-muddied woman in his arms, the woman he loved.

"And here I thought you didn't date younger men," he teased.

She dropped the papers onto the floor and placed her muddy palms on his cheeks.

"I don't," she said. "I fall in love with them."

He raised his brows. "*Them*?"

She laughed. "I guess we'll never know. Because I fell in love with the first one who came my way, and I'm a goner from here on out."

"That's more like it. Now…about that kissing me something fierce?"

She squeezed her legs around his waist, and even though he was cold and wet and covered from head to toe in mud—*again*—heat coursed through him when this woman was in his arms.

She dipped her head, her lips a breath away from his. "I'm going to do a whole lot more than kiss you, cowboy."

He let loose a soft growl. "Can we start that *whole lot more* in the shower? I seem to be covered in mud once again."

She nipped at his bottom lip. "Make a left at the kitchen. It's the first door on the right."

With her still in his arms, Colt managed to toe off his

boots without dropping her or sending them both tumbling to her ceramic-tiled floor. He was just that adept when he was ass-over-elbow in love.

He kissed her hard, and she writhed against him.

"Left at the kitchen," he said, repeating her words as he began to move.

"And first door on the right," she said, breathless.

He piloted her to what turned out to be her bedroom and then to the connected bathroom. She slapped at the wall until a light went on and he could see the small but cozy space—a rustic wooden vanity against gray shiplap walls, a black-and-white-patterned tile along the floor. The shower/bathtub combo boasted dual showerheads, one on each end of the tub.

He slid her down to her feet and took a moment to let his eyes simply drink her in.

Sure, her top was smeared with mud, as was the tip of her nose and her cheek. The whites of her eyes were now pink, hopefully from tears that were happy rather than sad because right here, right now, in *this* bathroom, Colt Morgan was the happiest he'd ever been.

"What?" she said, then she wiggled her nose. "Do I have something on my face?"

He laughed. She knew she was almost as much of a mess as he was.

"You're so beautiful," he said.

She rolled her eyes. "Have you seen me lately?"

He shrugged. "I don't need to see you to know. Don't you get it? Mud-splattered or squeaky-clean, you will forever have the power to knock the air clean from my lungs."

He lifted the hem of her tank and pulled it over her head. Then he kissed each of her free-from-mud breasts. Not that he would have refrained had the situation been otherwise.

She sucked in a breath as he lowered himself to his knees. He saw them now, the tiny scars above each hip, barely visible unless you knew they were there.

"You're staring," she said, a nervous tremor in her voice.

"Because they're as beautiful as you are," he said.

He brushed soft kisses over one and then the other, and he heard her breathing hitch. Then he looked up, his eyes locking on hers.

"Thank you," he said. "For doing what you had to do so you could be with me now, and tomorrow, and all the days you're willing to put up with me. I love you, Jenna."

She nodded, her expression breaking into a smile that lit up his entire world.

Then he lowered her shorts and panties in one swift move and properly worshipped the woman who saw fit to give him a second chance.

After that came a long, hot shower—together—and after *that*, Jenna showed him to her bed.

She knelt over him, her hands braced on either side of his head.

"There is one benefit to my—um—situation," she said, her wet hair curtaining her face.

He grinned at her. "You mean aside from you being healthy and alive, which is all the benefit I need?"

She raised her brows. "I can't get pregnant."

"I know," he said. "And I promise I'm okay with that, Jenna. You don't have to worry—"

"You're not listening," she interrupted, and her blue eyes locked on his, heavy with need. "I. Can't. Get. Pregnant." She dipped her hips toward him, letting him nudge her opening, and his eyes widened with recognition.

Then he nodded, and that was all the warning she gave him before sinking over him, burying him to the hilt, until he didn't know where he ended and she began.

"I love you, Colt Morgan," she whispered in his ear.

"Love you more, Texas."

The rain pounded, and lightning lit up the dark room from time to time, but neither of them seemed to notice. Maybe, subconsciously, Jenna knew. She didn't need to be afraid anymore because Colt would always be there for her. Loving her. Spending every single day reminding her of that very fact.

The storm let up before dawn, and Colt lay on his side with Jenna's head on her shoulder, her legs still entwined with his.

"Are you asleep?" Jenna asked groggily, her eyes closed.

"No," he admitted.

"Are you staring at me?" she asked, eyes still shut and a smile spreading across her face.

"Busted," he said with a grin.

"Go to *sleep*," she said, feigned admonishment in her voice.

But he was afraid that if he did actually take his eyes off her, he'd wake and find out it wasn't real. He'd spent far too long telling himself that this kind of happiness wasn't for him; convincing himself that he could survive just fine choosing contentment over the real deal. But now that he knew what the real deal was, he feared it could all go away as quickly as it had come to him.

She squeezed her body tightly around his and sighed, her eyes fluttering open.

"I'm not going anywhere," she said, as if she could read his thoughts. "And you're going to need your rest so you can come with me tomorrow to tell my nephews I'm going to sell the farm and take that job with Dr. Murphy in Meadow Valley." She let out a nervous laugh. "It will take some time for me to get everything in order here. So we may be commuting for a while. But I'm all in, cowboy. If that's what you want."

He kissed her forehead, then buried his face in her hair.

"Yes," he whispered.

They stayed like this for several long moments, the only sound that of their soft exhales and inhales. Then, somewhere outside the house, he heard a loud, satisfied squawk.

They both laughed.

"I guess Lucy wasn't off her game after all," Jenna said. "*I* was."

He kissed her, long and slow, until they'd both had their fill and his shoulders finally relaxed and his eyes grew heavy.

"I can't wait to get you home," he said softly.

"I can't wait to *be* home," Jenna said. "With you."

EPILOGUE

Jenna kicked the snow off her boots before opening the door to the coop. As soon as she stepped inside, she dropped to a squat in the hay waiting for Lucy to break free from the group to come and greet her. But after several seconds and *no* Lucy, she stepped gently through the bedding, which was framed by small hay bales, to her chicken—and the rest of Dr. Murphy's brood.

"I see how it is," she said, watching her golden-feathered Lucy play hide-and-seek with a snippet of bedding while Judith, a black-and-white Plymouth hen, chased after her to find it. But even though she'd been rebuffed by her longtime companion, Jenna couldn't help but smile. She'd worried most about Lucy adjusting to the move. Well, that and how Jack, Luke, and Walker would take her leaving.

"Are you kidding?" Jack had said when she'd told him first. "After all you've done for us, you think we'd be anything but supportive of you finally living your life for *you*? We'll miss the hell out of you, but it's just a six-hour drive."

"Or an hour in a *really* tiny airplane," she'd said. "Which, by the way, I'm never doing again."

They'd hugged each other hard, and there had been tears on both ends. But Jack was only half right. She hadn't been living her life only for her nephews. She loved her family more than anything, and taking care of them had been one of her greatest joys. It had simply been time for more joy, and that had come in the way of a certain *slightly* younger cowboy called Colt Morgan.

She freshened the hens' water and cleaned up the bedding just in time for her phone to ring. She grinned when she saw the name on the screen—COLT—accompanied by the photo she'd taken of him after falling in the mud at Maggie and Robert's house on the day they'd met.

"Hey handsome," she answered.

He laughed. "Almost," he said. "Just picked up my suit and stopping by Ivy's to grab your dress. What did you need me to ask her for again?"

Jenna shook her head with a grin. "She said she found you a pocket square that matches my clutch, which she also has. So don't forget to grab the dress, the clutch, *and* the pocket square."

"Remind me what a clutch is again?" he asked.

She was the one to laugh this time. "A small purse that you *clutch* in your hand."

"When you say *you* . . ."

"I mean the collective *you*, not that *you*, Colt Morgan, will be clutching my clutch tonight."

"This conversation—"

"Is turning into the *Who's on first?* of wedding prep," she said. "I'm just finishing up with the hens and I'll be home to shower before heading to the bride's room to get ready with the rest of the women."

"I love it when you call our suite at the guesthouse *home*," he said.

She loved it even more that he was working nights and weekends—and letting her help—building them a real home they would fill with *their* family. Come the first of the year, the house would most likely be done. Then all they had to do was wait for a call from the local foster care facility saying they were going to meet their first child.

"As long as you're there, it's home," she said.

"Should I wait for you to shower?" he asked, and she could hear the mischief in his voice. "I could help you reach all those hard-to-reach spots."

Heat coiled in her belly just thinking about the spots she'd love him to reach.

"I'll be there in twenty," she said. "You better be back from Ivy's, and you better be wearing a hell of a lot less clothes than you are right now."

"Love you. Bye," he said quicker than she'd ever heard him speak. And then he ended the call.

"*Squawk!*" Lucy said, finally acknowledging Jenna's presence.

"I see how it is, girl. Colt's your favorite now, huh?" She shrugged. "Can't say I blame you." He was her favorite too.

She finished up in the coop, then trudged through the fresh powder over to the veterinary clinic. Inside, Dr. Eli Murphy stood behind the front desk, bent over the phone. Jenna grinned when she saw her framed photo of Eli's farm on the wall in the waiting area, the first photo she'd snapped of the farm once it was part of her new home.

"I understand. Thank you. Look forward to hearing from you soon." He hung up the phone and groaned.

"Still no one to work the desk?" she asked.

He braced his hands on the desk and hung his head as he shook it. "That was the local community college. I just wanted to make sure they had the job posting up on their bulletin board as well as on the website because not one person has applied for it."

Jenna winced. "I can help..." she started, but she trailed off, already knowing what Eli's response would be.

"You have your hands full with the farm, and I know you and Colt are waiting on that call from the foster care organization. There's no way I'm letting you work more hours than you already do. But thank you. I'll figure it out eventually."

Jenna liked Eli. A lot. But even in the months she'd worked with him and gotten to know him, he was still a man on an island. Not letting anyone get too close, even if it was one friend offering another some extra help.

"Well, you know where to find me if you need me," she said. "See you in a couple of hours at the wedding?"

He looked up, then straightened to his full height.

"The wedding. Right. Of course. I'll be at the ceremony, but I'll probably head back here before the reception begins. I've got that Rex rabbit I just started on antibiotics yesterday. He'll need looking after tonight. To make sure treatment is going according to plan."

Jenna nodded. "Right. The rabbit." She hated the thought of Eli holed up alone at the clinic when everyone else in town would be at the reception. But it wasn't her place to pull him out of his comfort zone. Not if he still wasn't ready. "Well," she said. "I'll see you at the ranch for the ceremony then."

"Drive carefully back up the road," he said. "Looks like the snow is picking up again."

Jenna smiled.

Perfect.

The winter wedding everyone was hoping for.

Colt stood at one end of the arena, which, only hours ago, had been transformed into an outdoor wedding venue. Rows of white folding chairs lined each side of the snowy aisle. The fence was wound with twinkling white lights. A string quartet to Colt's right played Canon in D. And just about everyone they knew—even Jenna's nephews and their significant others who were also friends of the groom—sat patiently waiting for the bride to come down that aisle.

First it was Ben Callahan, Sam's brother in town from New York—the best man, of course, escorting Beth Spence, Delaney's sister and maid of honor. That was it for the bridal party. They'd wanted to keep it simple and quick so they could get to celebrating.

Next was Sam, dapper as hell in a tux. Colt had no qualms about admitting that.

"Nervous?" Colt whispered as his friend approached.

"Not even a little bit," Sam said without hesitation. "Of course, Nolan could have one of her signature diaper explosions at any second, but my mom is on diaper duty, so I'm going to pretend I didn't say that."

Both men glanced at the front row of the groom's side where Barbara Ann Callahan bounced Sam and Delaney's bundled and adorable four-month-old on her lap.

"And I'll pretend I didn't hear it," Colt said with a laugh.

And then, without warning, the music changed to "Ode to Joy" and both of their heads shot up, their gazes fixed back on the aisle.

There was Delaney, head covered by the ivory hood of the cape she wore over her gown.

Sam sucked in a breath, and Colt clapped him on the shoulder.

"She's beautiful," Colt said.

"I know," Sam answered.

And even though it was true, Colt couldn't help but try to get a look *behind* the bride, at the woman in the long-sleeved emerald-green dress who carried the bridal gown's train.

He fidgeted with the matching pocket square on his chest until Jenna came into view, and *he* was the one finding it hard to breathe.

I love you, she mouthed, and he pressed his palm to his heart, trying to maintain composure. After all, he was the officiant, not the groom. He needed to keep it together for Sam.

Someday, *soon*—if Colt had any say in the matter—Jenna Owens would be the woman in white, making her way to him. But tonight was about Sam and Delaney. Colt would say a few words and then let them read their vows to each other. Then they'd all head to the dining hall to celebrate for as long as anyone cared to stay. Jessie, the Meadow Valley firefighter who moonlighted at the ranch's guesthouse, was set to take baby Nolan home and put her to bed in a couple of hours.

"After that," Delaney had said, "sky's the limit. Jessie's spending the night so we can stay in the honeymoon suite at the Meadow Valley Inn." She'd laughed. "We'll probably be so excited for a full night of sleep that *we'll* be the first to leave."

But it turned out the limit was somewhere in the vicinity of three in the morning.

Colt and Jenna stumbled into their shared suite, a little tipsy and deliriously exhausted.

"I know this sounds ridiculous," Jenna said, kicking off her shoes and throwing her coat on the small love seat to the right of the door. "But I'm kind of hungry."

Colt laughed. "We're out of ice cream."

Jenna raised her brows. "But there are still cookies in the tin."

Colt's pulse quickened. He thought he had until tomorrow, but it looked like this was happening now.

He cleared his throat. "Okay," he said. "Grab 'em and bring them over here, but don't open the tin yet. I'm just going to check my voicemail. Looks like I missed a call."

He didn't recognize the caller and figured he was in for a robot-generated spam call, which would buy him a few seconds to collect his thoughts. But when he heard, "Hello, Mr. Morgan. This is Lydia from Plumas County Child and Family Services," he lost his footing and stumbled backward, catching himself against the wall.

When the message ended, he looked up to see Jenna standing in front of him, the opened tin of toffee shortbread cookies in one hand and the ring he'd laid on top of the waxed paper in the other.

"Colt…" she said, a slight tremble in her voice. "What is this?"

This was happening. *All* of it.

"You weren't supposed to open the tin yet," he said.

"I opened it," she answered.

He laughed, then dropped down to one knee.

"That was Plumas County on the phone," he said. "If we can finish the house by January thirty-first, they have a twelve-year-old boy and ten-year-old girl they want us to meet. Brother and sister. Their current foster family, for whatever reason, can't care for them any longer."

Tears pooled in her eyes. At least he thought they were tears, but his own vision was beginning to blur.

"Think they maybe want to help us plan a wedding?" he asked. "I thought we'd honeymoon out of the country and check another item off your list, but that may have to wait."

"Oh my God," Jenna said. "Forget the list! We're going to be parents?"

She was still holding the cookies and the ring.

Colt laughed. "Do you think you might also want to be my wife? Or should we just dive into the cookies and call it a night?"

He grabbed the cookie tin from her shaking hand and set it on the ground. Then he reached for the ring, and they held on to it together.

"Will you marry me, Jenna?"

He pressed PLAY on the song he'd kept queued on his phone for this very moment. Except this time, when Frankie Valli belted the chorus, Colt did *not* sing along.

Jenna covered her mouth with one hand, and with the other she stroked his hair. "I wished on a silly candle," she said with a sniffle. "Okay...forty-*one* silly candles. But I didn't believe— I didn't for one second think that wish could be *you*." She laughed. Or maybe she was crying. He couldn't tell. There were tears, but she was smiling.

He took her hand in his and kissed her palm. "Is that a yes? 'Cause I'm sort of on pins and needles here."

"Yes!" she said with a laugh. "Yes." And then she dropped to her knees as well, letting him slide the ring onto her finger. "*Yes*."

DON'T MISS THE FIRST BOOK
IN A.J. PINE'S
MEADOW VALLEY SERIES!

MY ONE AND ONLY COWBOY

AVAILABLE NOW

ABOUT THE AUTHOR

A librarian for teens by day and a romance writer by night, A.J. Pine can't seem to escape the world of fiction, and she wouldn't have it any other way. When she finds that twenty-fifth hour in the day, she might indulge in a tiny bit of TV when she nourishes her undying love of vampires, superheroes, and a certain high-functioning sociopathic detective. She hails from the far-off galaxy of the Chicago suburbs.

You can learn more at:
   AJPine.com
   Twitter @AJ_Pine
   Facebook.com/AJPineAuthor

KEEP READING FOR A SPECIAL
BONUS NOVEL FROM *USA TODAY*
BESTSELLING AUTHOR
MELINDA CURTIS:

SEALED WITH A KISS

For Kimmy Easley, showing up at her ex's wedding without
a date is unacceptable. She's got to find someone—and fast—
because she can't face going alone. Convincing her childhood
friend Booker Belmonte to go with her is easy, but that starts the
spread of gossip through Sunshine Valley quicker than wildfire.
Kimmy has never thought of Booker as anything more than a
friend, so it's funny how she never noticed how nicely he fills
out a tux...

Booker could never say no to Kimmy—he's had a secret
crush on her for years. Accompanying her to the wedding is a
no-brainer; not getting his hopes up that it might lead to more
than friendship is going to be more difficult. But now that the
matchmaking Widows Club has set their sights on Booker and
Kimmy, will they be next to walk down the aisle?

PROLOGUE

I'll see your two cents. And raise you two cents." Clarice Rogers tossed pennies into the pot in the middle of the card table. "Was I the only one who didn't get an invitation to Haywood and Ariana's wedding?"

It seemed like everyone in the town of Sunshine, Colorado, was going except Clarice. Rumor had it the reception had a Bohemian theme, and Clarice dearly loved anything Bohemian.

Clarice and her two closest friends were playing a high-stakes poker game at the cozy home of Mims Turner.

Bitsy Whitlock checked her cards and then tossed in additional pennies. "I'm not sure why I received an invitation." She adjusted the black bow in her bobbed blond hair. Her hair bows had a tendency to slip. Nothing else about Bitsy ever slipped. "I only met Haywood last Christmas."

"You helped Haywood pick out an engagement ring when you were having your jewelry cleaned." Mims Turner tossed in two cents. "Besides, everyone knows you give good gifts. I got an invite because Ariana's grandmother is my cousin. Call. Two pair." She snapped down her cards and tugged at the ends of her beige fishing vest. "Winner!"

Not waiting for Clarice, Bitsy fanned her cards gracefully on the table. "Two pair, kings high. Looks like I win again."

"Wrong! Full house!" Clarice tossed her cards down with such verve that her gray braids bounced. "The pot and game are mine." And as the winner, she was allowed to choose whom they applied their matchmaking expertise to next.

"Who should I choose?" she wondered aloud but it wasn't a rhetorical question. Clarice had been thinking about whom she'd select if she won ever since Haywood and Ariana first announced their engagement. Happiness swirled inside her chest like courting pigeons on a spring day. Weddings generated lots of events, many of which created pressure to bring a date. And the need for dates opened the door to matchmaking opportunities.

Clarice tapped her chin as if she was perplexed. She said again, "Who should I choose?"

Mims and Bitsy rolled their eyes.

The trio made up the board of the Sunshine Valley Widows Club, a group devoted to providing emotional support to those who had lost their spouses. Privately, they called themselves the Sunshine Valley Matchmakers Club, a group devoted to helping Cupid's arrow find its mark. They were more successful than those swiping dating apps.

"Just say it, Clarice," Mims grumped, gathering the cards. She was on a losing streak.

Clarice drew herself up, tossed a braid over her shoulder, and said, "I choose Booker Belmonte."

Mims stopped sweeping up cards. "Booker's not a widower."

"He's not even divorced." Bitsy gave Clarice a gentle frown. "You should know that's against the rules." The people they matched were on their second time around.

Rules. How Clarice loved them. As club secretary, she had the pleasure of reminding members what the rules were. But in this situation... "I present a special case. Booker is nearly thirty-two and on the brink of success. And you know what can happen to a man when he's trying to catch the success train."

"That's right." Mims nodded, grumpiness fading. "He loses life balance."

"And he waits too long to find love." Bitsy's tone implied that she found merit in Clarice's selection.

"It's like a public service." Since her friends were warming to the idea, Clarice spoke with more confidence. "And the timing couldn't be better. His best friend Haywood is getting married." The wedding Clarice wasn't invited to. "Booker will have marriage on his mind."

"He'd be a good fit with Wendy Adams," Mims suggested with a fluff of her round white curls. "She's so easygoing."

"Or Avery Blackstone." Bitsy nodded, black velvet bow slipping again. "She has a certain flair."

"All good options. But…" Clarice raised a hand and her voice, which made her realize she might have forgotten to put in her hearing aids again. "I was thinking more like Kimmy Easley. She and Booker hung out in the same crowd in high school. And I always thought there was a spark between them."

Mims and Bitsy both sat back, their mouths making small Os. The three widows had been together so long their brains often shared the same track.

"Kimmy worked at the Burger Shack for years," Bitsy said quietly. The restaurant was owned by Booker's family.

"Along with the groom and Booker." Mims raised her gaze to Clarice's. "Didn't she date Haywood once when he and Ariana took a break? That could be awkward."

"Indeedy. It could be." Clarice rubbed her hands together, so filled with glee that she would've gotten up to dance if she'd had a good pair of knees. "Oh, she'll be looking for a wedding date, all right. The perfect wedding date."

CHAPTER ONE

There was a line at the deli in Emory's Grocery.

Kimmy Easley took pride in the deli's popularity and hurried to move the lunch line along.

"What's the special today, Kimmy?" Clarice Rogers leaned on her hickory walking stick. The free-spirited former hippie had been slowing down lately and claimed to be holding out as long as possible before having her knees replaced.

"Garlic-butter Italian-sausage sandwich." Kimmy finished assembling a ham-and-cheese panini for Everett Bollinger and put it on the grill. "It's served on a crusty baguette with melted cheese on top. Can I make you one?"

"Yes. It sounds delicious, like something my Fritz would've liked." Clarice eyed the selection of salads, her long gray braids swinging against the orange paisley of her blouse. "And a side of the wedding salad." She chuckled. "I have weddings on my mind. Specifically, Haywood's." Her expression turned wistful. "Are you going?"

"Yes." Kimmy tried not to let talk of Haywood's marriage diminish her shine. She was happy for Hay but she had a little over a week to find a wedding date. She sliced open a baguette for Clarice and stuffed it with garlic-butter-soaked sausage.

Welcome to my thirties. The reality decade. Unmarried. No prospects. And light-years behind her peers in getting a career in place.

"I'm sure you have a date already." Kimmy could tell Clarice was trying not to seem like she was prying. But this was Sunshine. People pried. When Kimmy didn't immediately respond—what with being busy prepping the sandwich—the old woman added, "Not that an independent woman like you needs a date."

Oh, Kimmy needed a date, all right. She needed one like Batman needed his mask.

"I haven't thought that far ahead," Kimmy lied. She slid Clarice's sandwich into the toaster oven, checked Everett's panini, decided it needed more time, and dished out Clarice's wedding salad.

"Did you know the Widows Club is hosting a bachelorette auction Saturday night?" The reason for Clarice's visit became clear. "It's a great way to meet someone new and perhaps find a wedding date."

Kimmy hadn't signed up. She never signed up. She expected being on the auction block at Shaw's Bar & Grill on a Saturday night to be like showing up at her high school reunion in a sundress and forgetting to shave her legs. Mortifying.

But mortification was exactly what she was going to experience if she showed up at Haywood's wedding dateless.

If only it were the fall, which was when the Widows Club hosted its *bachelor* auction. Kimmy would rather be empowered to choose her own date, not wait for someone to bid on her.

Kimmy rang up Clarice's order and then sighed. "Do I have to give you an answer now?"

"No, dear." Clarice paid in cash, dollar bills plus exact change, which she counted out in pennies. Thirty-seven of them.

"You can sign up until the bidding begins." She smiled kindly. "Hope to see you there."

A few customers later and her boss, Emory, came behind the counter. He was old-school and wore a white button-down with short sleeves and a red bow tie. "I'm worried."

"I can handle the line," she reassured him, working on a sandwich for Paul Gregory, one of her regulars and the owner of the local exterminator business. "It moves quickly."

"I'm not concerned about you." Emory shook his grizzled head. "I'm worried about the Burger Shack. I hear Booker is back for the wedding."

She'd heard that too. The news had given her a warm, fuzzy feeling. She, Haywood, and Booker had been close in high school.

"You should be anxious, Kim." If the worried emoji had been based on a real face, it would've taken inspiration from Emory's. "Booker bought his parents out and plans to change the menu."

Kimmy couldn't worry about that. "It's about time." The Burger Shack menu hadn't been updated in forever.

"You don't understand." Emory shook his head once more, this time causing a lock of stringy gray hair to fall onto his forehead. "They're adding gourmet burgers."

A tremor of unease worked its way through Kimmy. "Gourmet?" Gourmet sandwiches were her thing. Emory's was the only place in town you could get gourmet anything.

Used to be the only place in town.

"Yes." Emory rubbed a hand behind his neck. "Fancy burgers." The unease turned into apprehension.

A tall man with thick black hair got into the end of the line. He stood next to Clarice's friend Mims Turner, chatting amicably.

Booker Belmonte. He'd been her rock throughout middle and

high school. Maybe he still was. Just looking at him settled her nerves and turned the inclination to frown into a smile.

"Speak of the devil." Kimmy nodded in Booker's direction.

"He's here to check you out." Emory, being in his seventies and a bit naive, didn't catch the double meaning of his words.

"My sandwiches, you mean," Kimmy said under her breath, because Booker was like family to her. She handed Paul his order. "Did you get new uniforms?" His shirt was lime green and printed with brown cockroaches, vaguely reminiscent of a Hawaiian shirt.

"Yes." Paul turned to show her the back, which was more of the same. "Do you like it? I got tired of boring blue."

"It's a bold choice." Kimmy gave him a thumbs-up.

"The American species is a bold creature." Paul tapped a cockroach on his shirt. "He takes what he wants. I've decided I should be more like him. And since I've been wearing these shirts, business is up."

"Please don't say the c-word." Scowling, Emory scrubbed the top of the deli case near Paul.

"Congratulations, Paul. See you next time." Kimmy gave Paul her patented customer-service smile and turned to the next customer before he could go in depth on the bugs he loved to terminate. They'd taken some classes together at the community college in Greeley so she knew Paul loved to talk about his work.

"Will there be a next time?" Emory muttered, wiping down the counter because he was a stress-cleaner. "Everyone's going to want to check out the sandwiches at the Burger Shack."

"Maybe a time or two." Kimmy gestured to Lola Williams that she was ready to take her order.

Kimmy looked upon the Burger Shack with nostalgia, having worked there for three years during high school. At the Shack, she'd been one of the guys, along with Booker Belmonte and Haywood Lawson, boys higher on the popularity ladder than

Kimmy. They'd taught her how to grill, and she'd taught them the importance of loyalty and keeping their word. Her father always said a kept promise was a true sign of character.

When it came to making promises, Booker and Haywood had balked at girlish pinkie swears. Instead, they'd given their word while holding a hand over a hot basket of French fries. Silly kids' stuff. But it had meant something to her, even if Booker's promises had often come with conditions.

"If our customers head to the Burger Shack for lunch more than a time or two," Emory said mournfully, "I'll have to cut staff hours, maybe even resort to layoffs." The old man spoke as if gourmet burgers at the Burger Shack were already trendier than gourmet sandwiches at Emory's Grocery.

Truthfully, at the words *cut* and *layoffs*, the bottom dropped out of Kimmy's little world. Six more paychecks and she could afford a new transmission for the food truck she and her dad were restoring. If she lost this job before the truck was ready...

She glanced at Booker. At broad shoulders and the face of reliability.

It wouldn't come to that. It couldn't come to that.

Still, it took her a moment to work up enough saliva to reply to her boss in an upbeat voice. "It'll be okay, Emory. Can you work the register for me?" Kimmy tried to take Lola's order, not to mention smile and not look like Emory had put her off her game. But she reached for jalapeños instead of green peppers for Lola's wrap, something her customer pointed out.

Somehow, Kimmy made it through four more specials, two wraps, and a chef's salad before Emory was called to the front of the store and Booker appeared before her.

With his jet-black hair, deep-brown eyes, and infectious smile, Booker had always been handsome. But the years had given him an air of hard-won confidence.

Confident enough to put the competition out of business?

No. Never.

But the seed of doubt had been planted. Gourmet sandwiches weren't just her thing; they were her future. She needed some confidence right now.

And a wedding date.

Not necessarily in that order.

Staring at Kimmy working behind the deli counter, Booker Belmonte was at a loss for words.

Which was unfortunate since he had a lot to say to her.

Doubly unfortunate since Mims Turner was filling the void during their wait in line with good-natured babble that kept him from collecting his thoughts. He slid his damp hands into the back pockets of his jeans.

Mims finally came to her point as they reached the front of the line. "Booker, it would be a pleasure to have you as a guest emcee for our bachelorette auction this Saturday."

The old woman had gray curls and a full-cheeked smile like Mrs. Claus. Unlike Mrs. C., however, Mims wasn't helping Santa make a list and check it twice. Nothing Mims and her Widows Club cronies did was ever that straightforward. Mims wasn't fishing for an emcee. She was out to make a love match.

Booker glanced at Kimmy, who was wiping down the counter.

"Say you'll accept the honor, Booker." Mims stared up at him as if she didn't expect to be rejected.

"I'm just the new owner of the Burger Shack." Booker tried to put Mims off, even as he smiled at Kimmy, ignoring the tension between his shoulder blades. "I'll take the special."

He hadn't seen Kimmy Easley in what seemed like forever. They kept up with the occasional tag on social media. He was happy to see she looked the same. Same vivid brown eyes. Same dark-brown hair contained in a neat braid. Same tug at his heart when he set eyes on her.

In high school, Kimmy hadn't liked making plain burgers, the Burger Shack's bread and butter. It wasn't unusual for her to take an order and suggest to a customer that they add garlic hummus, mushrooms, or aioli. After hours, she'd practiced her sandwich-grilling skills by feeding Booker and Haywood. So it was no surprise that she'd put her own stamp on things when Emory had hired her to work the deli counter.

What was surprising was her response to his order. "Sorry, Book. We're all out of specials." Her lively brown eyes were guarded.

Does she know?

"Darn it." Mims pouted, just a little. "I should have come earlier. But I got to talking to Booker, and...I suppose I'll have a grilled cheese."

"Shoot." Kimmy's gaze softened but only when she looked at Mims. "I'll make you a surprise special."

"And me? Your old friend?" He hoped they'd still be friends when he confessed what he'd done.

"I can scrounge a grilled cheese for a childhood friend, I suppose." Kimmy cut him no slack. "Plain and simple, like those burgers you serve."

He sensed it was time for damage control. "Let me apologize."

"For what?" Kimmy was still looking at him warily but her hands were moving—buttering bread, sprinkling seasoning.

Watching her work in the kitchen had always been mesmerizing. "I'm assuming you're going to tell me what to apologize for. You always do."

Kimmy scoffed, cheeks turning a soft pink, not an angry red.

Booker drew a deep, relieved breath.

"Are you going to participate in the bachelorette auction this Saturday?" Mims asked Kimmy.

"I'm thinking about it." Unhappily, if her expression was

any indication. "And don't"—she shook her knife in Booker's direction—"give me any grief about it."

"*Moi?*" Booker tried to look offended. "Make fun of you? I'd never." As teens, they'd joked that the Widows Club events were for the dateless and desperate.

"I'm not either of the things you're thinking of." But Kimmy looked grim. Datelessly grim.

What was wrong with the male population of Sunshine that they couldn't see the appeal of Kimmy Easley?

Booker leaned over the counter for a closer look at what Kimmy was using on Mims's sandwich. It looked like spicy guacamole, heavy on the garlic. Garlic being her obsession.

If he was honest, it was his too.

"So, I can count on you on Saturday, Kimmy?" Mims was nothing if not persistent. "All proceeds go to the Sunshine Valley Boys & Girls Club."

"I suppose." Kimmy relented. "Unless something comes up."

Booker frowned. What was going on here? Kimmy was pretty and clever and creative. She should have had guys dangling from a string, waiting for a chance to date her. When they'd been in school, she'd had Booker on a string, and she hadn't even known it.

"Thanks, Kimmy." Mims paid for her sandwich, hefted her yellow pleather purse onto her shoulder, and fixed Booker with a stern stare perfected from years of working in the school cafeteria. "You'll be our emcee, won't you, Booker? It'll give you a chance to talk about the Burger Shack's new menu."

Kimmy sighed but didn't glance up from her work.

Booker reluctantly nodded. "I suppose I'll have to agree if one of my best friends is helping raise money for a good cause." Although, judging by the look on Kimmy's face, he suddenly feared their friendship had fallen by the wayside. His shoulders knotted. Booker needed Kimmy to be his friend. Friends forgave each other's bad decisions and betrayals.

"Oh, I'm so happy you'll be our emcee, Booker." Mims hugged him. Her purse banged against his side with the weight of a brick—or a very large handgun, which Mims was rumored to carry.

With her mission accomplished, Mims took her sandwich and walked toward the exit.

No one was behind Booker in line. Earlier diners were busy eating what looked to be a darn good sandwich. Emory had disappeared somewhere. And Kimmy had her back turned to Booker, smashing his sandwich with a grill press.

"I have a break in five minutes," Kimmy said in a distant voice. "Meet me out back?"

"Sure." Relief skimmed through Booker, untying his knots.

Their history was flooded with work breaks taken together behind the Burger Shack, where they'd sit on a sturdy plastic picnic table and dream of leaving Sunshine and making their mark on the world. Kimmy by opening a specialty sandwich shop. Haywood by selling million-dollar homes. Booker by owning and managing a chain of high-end restaurants.

Only two of their trio had achieved anything close to their dreams—Haywood and Booker. Only one of them had left town.

Kimmy had unwittingly played a role in Booker's success.

And now Booker had to make up for it.

CHAPTER TWO

I haven't seen you in years and you show up with Mims?"
Kimmy pushed the back door of Emory's open and didn't
stop walking until she'd reached the employee picnic table on
the back patio near the receiving bay. She sat down across
from Booker with her sandwich and a bottle of water. "What's
happening here?"

Her gaze caught on him. On handsome him. And something
deep inside her stirred with interest.

I need to date more.

Who was she kidding? She needed to date. Period. Starting
this week.

"You made me lunch. That's what's happening." Booker held
up his grilled cheese sandwich. "Cheddar, Muenster, and Swiss.
But you spiced it up with…"

"Grainy Dijon mustard, walnuts, and super-thin apple slices."
Pride had her smiling back, despite a small voice in her head
whispering that Booker was the competition now. Her attractive
competition.

Stop. This is Booker.

The guy she'd studied geometry with and thrown French fries at. The guy who'd taken her to prom because neither of them had had dates, although that had turned out to be a disaster. He was her friend. He could still be her friend.

As long as he doesn't kill Emory's lunch business in the next six weeks.

She sighed. "It makes the cheese more interesting, doesn't it?"

"I've never done more than salt and pepper on a grilled cheese sandwich. Well done." Booker took another bite. "You know what would make this better? Two thick slabs of French toast."

"Heavens, no." Kimmy unwrapped a shredded-chicken sandwich she'd made for herself. "The imbalance of bread to cheese wouldn't work."

Booker's smile fell a little.

"Maybe it would work between waffles," she said kindly, intrigued by the flavor combinations.

Behind him in the loading dock, several teenage boys were doing tricks on skateboards.

"Isn't that your brother?" Kimmy pointed to a teen who was shorter and skinnier than the others. "Dante?"

Booker turned, scowling when his eyes lit on his kid brother. "Dante! Aren't you supposed to be in school?"

Dante skidded to a stop, flipping his board vertical so he could grab the front axle. "We had an assembly today. Short day at school."

"Then shouldn't you be at the Burger Shack?" There was no mistaking the command in Booker's voice.

Dante shrugged. Translated from teen speak that meant *Yes, but I'm not going.*

The other two teens—the Bodine twins—took off in the other direction.

"Gotta go." Dante waved and followed them.

"But..." Booker twisted back around in his seat to face Kimmy, his expression dark. "Aren't you glad you have an older brother? Because..." He gestured toward the escaping Dante.

"At this moment, yes." Looking into Booker's dark eyes, she nearly forgot why she'd come outside to join him. *Mental head thunk.* Her future. "I hear you're changing the menu at the Burger Shack." Might as well address the elephant in the room.

"My parents' business has been struggling, and they wanted to retire. And I've been playing with the menu in the store I opened in Denver." His voice dropped into that low, soothing range usually reserved for lawyers and ministers dealing with sensitive topics. "The restaurant in Denver is all mine, and it's exceeded my expectations."

"You're a success." And she was just the deli clerk at Emory's. *Only for the next six weeks.*

Kimmy bit into her sandwich, pausing to relish the blend of basil pesto, melted mozzarella, baked chicken, and olives. They could take away her job but they'd never take away her ability to make magic in a sandwich.

"It's not exactly the dream I talked about when we worked at the Burger Shack." He pulled what remained of his sandwich in half, stretching the cheese as he did so and then wrapping it around the bread before taking a bite. "But it's just what my family needs. I hope to have the staff trained before the wedding. I've got to get back to Denver soon afterward." He paused to smile but it was a tentative thing. "I want to show you the menu."

He wants my input?

Kimmy made a noncommittal noise and took another bite of sandwich, considering the cowlick at Booker's temple. The rest of his hair fell straight and in line. And that was Booker's life in a nutshell. He knew what he wanted and marched straight toward it, overcoming obstacles like a tank on a battlefield.

Her path to her dreams was slower paced and more circuitous. Not that she wanted to discuss her plans with Booker, owner of the Burger Shack. Or help with his menu.

She switched gears. "I need to find a wedding date." She set down her sandwich, thinking it could use a bit more garlic. "Maybe I am desperate. Can you imagine? Me up on the stage at Shaw's?" Gawked at and bid on. She shivered.

What did I get myself into?

"You'll earn the highest bid of the evening." That was Booker, ever the optimist.

Booker back in town. Kimmy needing a date. The Widows Club at her lunch counter. Suspicion worked its way into her thoughts.

"I'm just going to be frank here." She wiped her fingers clean with a napkin, wishing she could just as easily wipe away her promise to be auctioned off. "You walked up to my counter with the president of the Widows Club. Mims cornered you to emcee the event and maybe something more."

"It's not what you think." Booker held up his hands. "My mom brought her into the kitchen at the Burger Shack, and then she said she had something to talk about but wanted to get her steps in, and suddenly I was in your lunch line."

Kimmy picked up her sandwich and was about to take another bite when she hesitated. "You don't think they're targeting the two of us as..."

Booker looked stricken and released a strangled "*No.*"

He either believed that or was friend-zoning her.

The friend-zoning stung given how smitten she was by his good looks today.

It's a by-product of my need for a date.

"Yeah, you're right." She stuffed some chicken back between the bread. "If they were trying to match the two of us, Mims wouldn't have asked you to emcee. You can't bid as the host."

"Bullet dodged," Booker muttered, not meeting her gaze.

Was the richness of the sandwich getting to him? Or was this conversation turning him off?

A cool mountain breeze swirled around them.

"I can still get out of the auction if I find a wedding date." Kimmy took another bite of her sandwich and savored the flavors.

"But...you promised."

Kimmy lifted her chin. "I caveated my acquiescence."

"High school vocabulary words aren't going to get you out of this." He wasn't teasing. He was serious. "You always said—"

"That a promise isn't to be broken." She hung her head. "Yeah, yeah, yeah. I can show and get bought, and the schmo can buy me dinner. But forget about that guy being my wedding date." She'd heard stories about drunken cowboys bidding. "Who can I ask from our high school class?"

Booker smirked. "First off, you want someone to talk to about the food they serve."

It was calming the way he knew her so well. "Yes, there's that."

"And someone who's willing to put up with your extraordinary dance moves." Booker grinned.

What Kimmy didn't have in smooth moves she made up for in enthusiasm.

Booker was eyeing her sandwich the way her father's dog eyed a hot Shack burger. "How about Jason Petrie?"

"He's still Darcy's guy." When Jason came home from the rodeo circuit, which was almost never.

"Iggy King?" Booker watched her take another bite. "I hear he's running a legitimate business now."

Kimmy swallowed and frowned. Iggy would be a fun wedding date if she wanted to drink too much and wake up in the wrong bed the next morning. *Pass.* "I'd put him in my last-resort category."

Booker seemed relieved. "I'd offer Dante but that seems a little extreme."

His kid brother? "I'm no cradle robber." Dante was thirteen years younger than she was. She pushed the remains of her sandwich away.

Booker scooped it up and took a bite. "Oh, man," he said after he swallowed, "this is good." He took another bite before asking, "Why don't you go stag?"

"Oh, I don't know." Kimmy propped her chin on her fists and adopted a sarcastic tone. "Maybe because ten years ago I went on a date with Hay."

It had been wonderful. Dinner in Greeley, followed by a movie and then a drink at Shaw's. He'd brought her home and kissed her good night. She'd been melting in his arms—her childhood crush, a tender kiss, visions of wedding veils dancing in her head.

And then Hay had broken it off, rested his forehead on hers, and said, "That was weird, wasn't it? I'm sorry."

He'd turned and walked away so fast that Kimmy hadn't worked up the nerve to say, *That wasn't weird. It was wonderful, you idiot.*

And he'd driven off, apparently straight to Ariana's house. *And that, my friends, was the end of that.*

"You aren't still freaking out over that kiss, are you?" Booker rolled his eyes. "Hay told me it was like kissing his sister."

And Booker had made sure he'd told Kimmy that, more than once. "We don't have to rehash it."

"But you've been rehashing if you're thinking you need a date because of that one mistake a decade ago."

"Ariana still looks at me funny." Like she wasn't sure Kimmy could be trusted around her man. "I'll ask Avery if she's got a castoff I can use." Avery was an avid dater.

Booker pulled a face. "Man up and go alone."

"No. Jeez. Don't you get it? This is Ariana's big day. I don't want her to look at me and think, *That woman is in love with my husband.*"

"Do you love him?" Booker's dark brows lowered.

"No." Crushes weren't love. When Booker narrowed his eyes, she tried to clarify. "It's like … when you're young and you look at a famous actor—in your case, an actress—and you imagine what it would be like to be with them. But you know it's not going to happen." Although in her case it had, but not with the desired result.

"So you do still love him." There was an odd note to Booker's words that she couldn't place.

"No." Kimmy made a frustrated noise deep in her throat. "I love both of you but I'm not *in love* with either of you."

"Well then…" Booker was building a grin, along with his point. "Ariana's not going to be jealous of you."

Like I'm not someone to be jealous of?

"Way to make me feel good about myself, Book."

"Kim"—he shortened her name too—"you have mad kitchen skills. You should feel good about yourself and let the past stay in the past." Booker crumpled their sandwich wrappers together. "Now, about my menu…"

He didn't understand. "I don't have time to fawn over your menu." Kimmy stood, awash in disappointment. "My break's over."

"Right. Time constraints." He threw the balled wrappers into the trash, a gleam in his eye. "Speaking of, you should get yourself a wedding date quick, before the good ones are gone. Don't forget what happened at prom." When they'd both hesitated and ended up going together. "But first, tell me what you put in your sandwich besides garlic." He blessed her with a grin that tugged something in her chest.

"Spill my secrets?" Kimmy wasn't falling for Booker's charm that easily. "Help me get a wedding date, and maybe I will."

* * *

"Hello, parents. What are you doing here?" Booker stood in the back entrance to the Burger Shack, where he had half the staff practicing making gourmet sandwiches. He wanted to check on their progress and then find Mims. "Go home. You're supposed to be retired." The business was his now, and he planned to manage it from Denver.

His dad looked down his nose at a pimento-chicken sandwich with waffles in place of bread while his mom was poking a finger at a jalapeño- and meatball-stuffed ciabatta. Both his parents had dark hair threaded with gray and wore the Burger Shack black button-down and black slacks, along with grease-stained running shoes. They'd come prepared to work.

"I don't know, Booker." His dad pulled a face. The one he'd used when Booker came home after curfew. "The Burger Shack isn't known for sandwiches."

The tension that had sat between his shoulder blades while he'd stood in line for one of Kimmy's sandwiches and when she'd refused to look at his menu returned. "I've proved both concepts work together." With the restaurant he'd opened in Denver. "People want options."

"But these sandwiches..." His mom looked just as grave. "They're like what Emory's Grocery offers."

The sandwiches were exactly what Emory's offered, since they were the same sammies Kimmy had made while they were in high school.

Those were the sandwiches Booker knew how to make. He hadn't thought anything of his use of Kimmy's creations until his lawyer suggested he create fanciful names for items on his menu and trademark them. The process of legal protection had made him realize the sandwiches had never been his to begin with. He had to buy the rights from her.

The double knots threaded their way up his spine, tightening at the base of his neck.

Booker needed to come clean. But he'd been putting it off, putting out smaller fires instead, like saving the original Burger Shack from bankruptcy. And now he had no firebreak. The fire was upon him.

"Booker?" His mom rubbed his shoulder. "Are you reconsidering?"

"No," he blurted. He needed the higher income the sandwich line brought if he was going to put Dante through college and pay his parents retirement dividends. But...His stomach did a slow churn. It wasn't as if Kimmy didn't need the money too.

"Booker," his father said in that firm voice he used as a start to a lecture.

His trainees were looking like they didn't want to witness their current and former bosses arguing.

"Guys, these sandwiches sell well." Booker took each of his parents by the arm and walked them to the door. "They'll help fund your golden years. Now, why don't you go look at those travel brochures I gave you?"

His mom slipped a glance at his dad, a hopeful smile on her face. "I did like the river cruises."

"Maybe next year when I don't feel so useless." His dad took the sunglasses from the top of his head and slid them on. "We ran this business for more than forty years. It'll take me more than a month to stop worrying about it."

"I appreciate you allowing me to take your vision and make it succeed another forty years." Booker glanced back inside the restaurant. "Where's Dante?"

"He's at school." His mom beamed, naive as to her youngest's whereabouts. "He's at track practice, and afterward he's going to Theresa's to study for their chemistry test."

His dad had on his poker face, staring to the west and Saddle

Horn Mountain, which was still blanketed in snow despite the spring sunshine. He likely knew what Dante was up to.

"Uh-huh." Booker decided not to mention that skateboarding wasn't a track event. "I wanted Dante to come to the Shack today." He had a sneaking suspicion that Dante had a severe case of high school senioritis, not conducive to part-time employment. "He should be shadowing me, like I did with Dad. He's going to help me manage the business one day." A string of Burger Shacks.

"Don't be hard on him," his mom said in the nurturing voice she reserved for her youngest. "You know, we demanded too much of you, Booker. Let Dante be a kid awhile longer."

Dante was almost eighteen, almost an adult. At eighteen, Booker had been writing payroll checks and prepping the Burger Shack ledger for their accountant.

"Our little Dante is special." His mother laid a hand on Booker's cheek. Her eyes filled with tears. "You never know what the future might hold."

True that.

When Dante had been three, their mom had found a lump on his leg, just below the knee. It'd been cancerous. Booker was sixteen at the time and had to step up and run the Burger Shack while his parents shuttled Dante to and from treatments in Denver.

But Dante was tough. He'd beaten cancer and been clean ever since. And ever since, he'd been doted on by everyone in the family.

"Dante is special, Mom." Booker squeezed her hand, squeezing back the wish that someday his parents might see him as special too. "That's why I want to make sure he gets the best college education."

CHAPTER THREE

How's my baby?" Kimmy walked up her parents' driveway and knelt in front of a jacked-up food truck, still thinking about Booker's successes.

In ten years, he'd hustled, started his own business, and bought out his parents. Envy banged around her head, making her temples pound. By comparison, Kimmy was a slacker. And so was her business plan, at least if you looked only on the outside.

Her food truck was rusted, dented, and dinged, but it was all hers. And someday soon—hopefully in six weeks—she was going to quit Emory's Grocery and make her living catering and selling grilled sandwiches out of it.

Her dad rolled out from beneath the engine. He still wore his blue-stained coverall uniform from the tire shop but he didn't look weary. He was as excited about Kimmy's venture as she was. "The new muffler came in this afternoon. I was just making sure everything's ready to put it in."

"And the stove?" Kimmy opened the van's door and stepped inside, conducting a slow inventory, wondering what Booker would say when he saw this.

He'd tell her Sunshine didn't have a large enough population to support three sandwich options—Emory's, the Shack, and hers. He'd point out she'd need to move from Sunshine to make a decent living. He'd remind her how close she was to her family, how important they were to her, the same way his family was priority one to him. He'd ask her whether she was willing to leave Sunshine to make it big.

Kimmy rubbed her temples. This time it wasn't envy banging around her head. It was impending sadness.

Leave Sunshine?

She drew a deep breath. An industrial kitchen on wheels and all her own. Kimmy thought it was beautiful. She didn't care if it never made her rich.

She'd bought the truck from someone in Denver who'd set the kitchen on fire and was getting out of the business. New paneling covered newly installed fire-resistant insulation. On the passenger side, the external features hadn't been damaged. The metal awning over the customer-service window swung up, and there was a customer counter that folded down.

She set her purse on the floor and ran a hand over the stainless countertop. She'd installed red-checked linoleum on the floor. Elbow grease had scoured the sink, the fixtures, and the cabinets until they gleamed. All she needed now were appliances—a fridge, stove, chargrill, fryer, panini press, steam table, warmer, and microwave.

And a special-order transmission.

She'd committed to everything. She'd ordered everything. All she needed were a couple more paychecks, and she'd be debt-free.

"Hank said the stove *might* come in today." Her dad joined her inside, wiping his hands on a rag. His dark-brown hair was gray at the temples but nothing about his knowledge of vehicles was aging. "Too bad it didn't."

Five months of work. Kimmy couldn't have restored the food truck on her own. Her dad, her uncles, her cousins—everyone had chipped in.

"It's okay, Dad. It's so close to being finished." She was so close to fulfilling her childhood dream of opening a specialty sandwich shop. "I can already imagine cooking in here."

Her dad slung his arm over her shoulder and gave her an affectionate squeeze. "The Garlic Grill is almost ready for launch."

"Hey." Her mom joined them inside. She had a streak of dirt on her cheek, and her hands were red from using cleaning products all day. She ran a small maid service in town. "Are you free on Sunday, Kimmy? Haywood hired me to clean his bachelor pad. He's having family and friends over Monday night."

"Um…" Kimmy didn't mind cleaning her friend's home but Booker's achievements proved Kimmy needed to take a step toward her dream every day to make it come true. "I was hoping to work on this but…"

"But we won't have all her appliances in," Kimmy's dad finished for her. "Of course she can help you. That's what family is for."

"Of course," Kimmy echoed, swallowing back guilt and excuses. She didn't want to appear ungrateful, and there were lines of fatigue on her mother's face.

"Thanks, honey." Her mom's expression eased. "Dinner in thirty minutes." She left, heading toward the house.

Kimmy and her father took in the fruits of their labor in silence.

"If my stove had come in, I could have cooked in here," Kimmy said wistfully.

"When this is done, my baby will be flying on her own wings." Her dad squeezed her once more. "I couldn't be prouder."

"Oh, Daddy." Kimmy tried not to cry.

"Hey." Uncle Mateo bounded into the truck, taking the stairs as if he were a much younger man. He lived just a few houses down. "I have logo designs for you from Ian." He smoothed wrinkles out of long sheets of paper with colorful renderings of the Garlic Grill food truck on them. "My boss at the shop says I can paint this beauty just as soon as you get her running."

They spent nearly thirty minutes admiring her cousin's graphics. She couldn't stop herself from wondering which design Booker would advise her to choose. Certainly not the one with pink. She wasn't selling cupcakes.

But Kimmy gravitated toward it anyway. The design featured a bright, happy sun in the top left corner, radiating across the side. "The name is really easy to read." In big pink letters.

"I'll tell Ian." Uncle Mateo placed that design on top. "He promised me he'd come by for dinner tonight and bring my grandkids." He grinned. "I haven't seen them in three days. And they live right around the corner. Crazy, huh?"

That was what Kimmy loved about her large, generous, close-knit family. They all pulled together. Helping to fix each other's vehicles and homes. Celebrating life's milestones. Supporting each other's dreams. It helped that her family lived in a four-block radius on the south side of Sunshine.

Kimmy hugged Mateo. "Tell Ian I remembered my promise to make his family lunch every Saturday for the next month." She was lucky her family let her barter for services.

"Lunch every Saturday for a month," her dad said, chest puffed out in pride as he looked at Kimmy. "A kept promise is a true sign of character."

"And love," Kimmy murmured.

"I won't have to remind Ian." Uncle Mateo rubbed his stomach. "He knows how good your food is. We all do."

The front screen door screeched open. "Dinner!" her mom shouted, letting the door bang closed behind her.

Kimmy grabbed her purse. "I haven't even cleaned up." She ran out of the truck and up the stairs outside the garage.

Skippy, her three-legged cat, met her at the door. The small apartment felt larger now that her sister, Rosalie, had moved out.

"We're running late, Skippy." She scooped up the gray tabby and gave her a cuddle as she crossed the small living room to the bedroom.

The only thing going slow in her life was the food truck renovation. Everything else was coming at her fast—Hay's wedding, Booker's return.

What could possibly happen next?

"Mims." After sending his parents home, it had taken Booker three hours to find the Widows Club president. "Can we talk?"

Hair wrapped in big pink curlers, Mims sat under a hair dryer in the Sunshine Valley Retirement Home salon, sound asleep, arms crossed over her fishing vest.

"Shhh." Lola Williams was fixing Harriet Bloom's hair. "Her hair will be dry in five minutes. Then you can wake her." Lola sprayed Harriet's hair, teased it with a long comb, and then sprayed it once more for good measure until it looked like a gray helmet.

The salon was small and looked even smaller with one wall painted a dingy rose color. The liveliest thing in the room was a large black feathered headdress hanging from the wall. It looked like something a Vegas showgirl would wear.

"Lola, I wish you'd master the art of a comb-out, instead of wasting your time on shopping for frivolous clothes." Harriet pointed to Lola's legs. "Have you ever seen such unusual legs, Booker?"

"Uh…" Booker hedged.

"Hush. You're embarrassing the man," Lola said but it was the hairdresser who was blushing. She wore an elegant black dress and lug-soled black boots. But what had caught Harriet's attention was her white stockings with edgy black tattoo patterns on them. "There's a viewing for Brillo Bryson later." Lola also worked as a hairstylist and makeup artist for the mortuary. "He was a biker. He'd appreciate my choice. And even if he wouldn't, sometimes a girl has to make a statement."

Kimmy had made a statement. She wasn't interested in seeing Booker's menu. He had to get her buy-in before he began officially selling sandwiches in Sunshine, because his sandwiches were her sandwiches. He wanted to make Kimmy an outright offer for her recipes. Cash money. But it wasn't the kind of business transaction you just tossed at a person without discussion and the appearance of negotiation.

The appearance.

Inwardly, Booker cringed. Never in his wildest dreams had he imagined his financial position would hinge on the work of someone else. He had to set things right without losing his friendship with Kimmy.

Mims snored. The loud kind that should've woken her up. It didn't.

Booker checked the time on his phone. Three minutes to go before her hair would be dry.

"I hear you're the best man at Haywood's wedding." Harriet caught Booker's gaze in the mirror. "That's a big responsibility. You've gotta make sure the groom doesn't have second thoughts."

"He won't." Hay had loved Ariana since they were in the sixth grade, probably since the time Kimmy had been crushing on Hay and Booker had been crushing on Kimmy.

"But he could," Harriet continued, holding her sharp chin high while Lola swept hair from her neck with what looked like a large paintbrush. "Who's your backup?"

"The other groomsmen?" Not that he needed them.

"No." Harriet made a derisive noise that deteriorated into

thick coughs. It took her a moment to catch her breath. "I mean your wedding date. You need a date to keep you sane when Haywood's toes catch a chill."

"I…" He glanced at Mims, hoping she'd wake up and save him from this conversation. "I thought I was there to carry the rings."

"Nonsense." Harriet scoffed, turning her head to and fro to check out Lola's work. "You're there to have an escape plan in place for Haywood, if needed."

Lola laughed, heading toward a waiting walker. "Don't let her throw you off your game, Booker."

She already had.

"Have pity on me." Harriet inched her chair around with the toes of her white orthopedic shoes. "I don't get out much. Who's your wedding date?"

"I don't have one yet." He'd been hoping to ask Kimmy. But even though they'd discussed her options, she hadn't seen Booker as anything more than a man who appreciated her sandwiches.

She'll never know how much I appreciate those sandwiches.

That wasn't true. Booker planned to tell her. Of course, if he told her, it was a certainty that she wouldn't be his wedding date. Which was why he had to talk to Mims. He had a feeling the secrets he had to tell would send Kimmy running. He needed her to sit still and listen.

Lola rolled the walker to Harriet and helped her out of the chair.

"You could take Lola," Harriet said without any tact. "Her husband's dead."

"Only just." Grief flickered over Lola's features. "You'd try the patience of a saint, Harriet."

"Foolish girl." Harriet worked her way slowly toward the door. "Look at Booker. He's prime real estate. You need to strike while the iron is hot."

"Crotchety old woman," Lola countered, albeit good-naturedly, as if their arguments were common. "You owe me a nickel for whining about my work." She glanced at Booker and then gestured toward a shelf, where her whining jar was halfway full of nickels and pennies.

"I'll bring a dime next week." Harriet cackled. "Same day. Same time."

Lola turned off the standing hair dryer, startling Mims awake.

"Booker. What are you doing here?" Mims opened her eyes wide. "No one is supposed to know I'm here. Barb over at Prestige Salon cuts my hair but she's booked, and my grandchildren are coming to town. Not to mention there's the bachelorette auction this weekend. I don't want to look like an unkempt mountain woman."

"Nobody's going to tell Barbara." But Lola made time to close the salon door behind Harriet.

"Mims, we need to talk," Booker said firmly, prepared for an argument. "I can't emcee the bachelorette auction."

The old woman blinked at him. "Why not?"

"Does it matter?" He didn't want to tell her the truth. "I promise to show up and bid." If he won Kimmy, she'd be his for an hour. The bachelorette auction included an informal dinner at the bar immediately afterward.

"Ah, I see." Mims gave him a forgiving smile. "Bring lots of cash. We don't accept credit or checks. And I expect Kimmy to go for a high price."

"Kimmy?" This was why Booker avoided Widows Club events. They could read minds and weren't shy about butting in where they weren't wanted. "Who said anything about Kimmy?"

"Who indeed?" Mims chuckled as Lola began unrolling the big pink curlers.

"Please don't get any ideas." His words had as much chance of being respected as a snowball in the Sahara. "Kimmy's made it very clear on several occasions over the years that she just wants to be friends." Which made his attraction to her inconvenient. He valued Kimmy's friendship too much to attempt to date her. "But if I do buy her—for reasons that have nothing to do with romance—can you make sure she gets a wedding date?"

"My boy, I have the perfect man in mind for her." Mims's smile wasn't reassuring. There were plans springing in that head of hers.

"Great." Booker said his goodbyes and headed for the door. "As long as you're not talking about me."

Her laughter followed him out into the hallway.

CHAPTER FOUR

How do I look?" Kimmy smoothed her green lace sheath over her hips. "I was going for sexy and sophisticated but now that I'm here, I think I might look grandmotherly and dated."

"You look fabulous." Her friend Priscilla Taylor was quick to reassure her. "If my divorce was final, I'd put myself out there too."

Kimmy was glad Priscilla wasn't joining in the auction festivities. She'd always been the center of male attention, while Kimmy had always been the girl on the outskirts of the crowd, male or female.

And speaking of crowds, Shaw's Bar & Grill was packed. The local hangout had a big stage and a dance floor on one end, and on the other were padded booths and large wooden tables surrounding a well-used pool table. The center of Shaw's featured a long, narrow bar ringed with stools. There were license plates on the walls and saddles mounted on the rafters. And on Saturday nights, customers tossed shells from free peanuts onto the floor.

It being Saturday, Kimmy had to watch her step in heels.

"Look at all these women." Priscilla grabbed on to Kimmy's arm. "They're lined up like it's Black Friday and there's a great deal on Michael Kors handbags."

Kimmy stopped walking and took count. Fifteen women. That was a lot for Sunshine. "This is a mistake." But she couldn't back out. She'd promised.

"It's no mistake." Priscilla pointed toward the dance floor. "Look. Have you ever seen so many cowboys?"

Kimmy hadn't been looking at the men. But now she could see there were cleaned-up cowhands milling about the dance floor, as well as local men in all shapes, colors, and sizes. Paul Gregory was wearing a suit and elbowing his way to the front of the stage, holding what looked like a strawberry daiquiri.

"The good news is I don't see my brother." Priscilla dragged Kimmy toward the line of bachelorettes up for auction. Her older brother was the sheriff, and when it came to fun, Drew was something of a wet blanket.

"The bad news is he would've made a good wedding date." Kimmy wouldn't have had to worry about Drew drinking too much and making advances. Although he probably wouldn't have been able to talk intelligently about food. Or more accurately, he might have dozed off while she did so.

"You're here!" shouted Clarice. She checked something off the list on her clipboard and took Kimmy's other arm. "Right this way." She gave Priscilla a frosty stare. "It's against the rules for married women to participate."

"I guess I'll be at the bar." Priscilla grinned and headed toward the center of the room.

"I wrote an introduction for you." Clarice continued to use her outdoor voice. Who could blame her? The crowd noise was nearly deafening. "Do you want to read it?"

Kimmy shook her head.

Clarice made another check mark on her clipboard and

hobbled off without her walking stick, her purple tie-dyed muumuu swaying with each step.

Kimmy took her place behind Darcy Jones at the end of the line. If Darcy was up for auction, Jason Petrie was most likely in the audience. Since they were an item, Darcy's purchase was a sure thing. Kimmy, being last, wasn't such a sure thing. She wasn't showing as much leg, as much cleavage, or as much makeup as most of the young women in line. By the time it was her turn, most of the rowdy cowboys would have lost their enthusiasm for the sport or already purchased their date.

Confidence. She needed confidence.

Lacking some, Kimmy started to sweat.

Mims moved to center stage and turned on the microphone. For all Kimmy had made jokes about the Widows Club and events like this, Mims's poise was calming. She wore a blue dress and white sandals and looked as comfortable as if she were wearing her fishing vest and blue jeans. "Thanks for showing up to the Date Night Auction to benefit the Sunshine Valley Boys & Girls Club. The bachelorettes for auction tonight—"

The crowd erupted with applause, whistles, and hollers.

Mims made a settle-down gesture with her hands. "Our ladies will be available for prescreening for the next few minutes on and around the stage." Mims stared down at the crowd. "Gentlemen, as a reminder, bidding starts at one hundred dollars. This is a cash-only event. Any man who sets foot on the stage makes an immediate purchase. Winning bidders also pay for dinner and drinks afterward."

Paul Gregory sauntered along the line. He'd lost the straw for his daiquiri, the drinking of which had stained his upper lip, making him look as if he had a red mustache. He stopped by Kimmy and said, "You look pretty tonight without your apron."

"Thanks?" Kimmy murmured, not wanting to encourage him,

but he was a good customer and a good exterminator. And she did so hate bugs.

The cowboys who ambled by next checked out the women up for auction the way she imagined they checked out cattle for sale. Kimmy smiled, in case good teeth were important in their judgment.

More residents came by. Dr. Janney, who did her annual exam. Jay Parker, a plumber who still wore his work coveralls. Darnell Tucker, a mechanic at the local garage. All customers at the deli.

During a lull, Kimmy touched Darcy's shoulder. "I feel awkward." Like she was lined up in gym class to be put on a soccer team.

"You'll be fine," Darcy reassured her. "Just remember it's for a good cause, and these people are your friends. Except for some of the cowboys. In which case, just remember dinner only lasts an hour." She turned to speak to the woman in front of her.

"Right," Kimmy said under her breath. "Good cause. Good friends. One hour."

Iggy King walked by. He paused when he saw her. "Hey, Kimmy. I've never seen you on sale before."

On sale? Panic set in. She grabbed his arm. "Iggy, I'll give you free sandwiches for a week if you buy me."

Booker appeared at Iggy's shoulder, looking handsome in a suit and tie. "You look great, Kim."

Ditto. But she couldn't say it. He'd think she wanted him to buy her.

"Thanks?" she said instead.

Who was she kidding? She'd be thrilled if he did. Not that he would. He was more likely to bid on someone from his side of town. And even if he did, it wouldn't solve her wedding-date dilemma.

Kimmy tried to catch Iggy's wandering eye.

"I'll think about it, Kimmy." Iggy headed toward Priscilla and the bar. "Good luck."

Shoot. That sounded like Iggy had thought about it and made a negative decision.

"Hey." Booker leaned in close enough to be heard over the crowd. "Are you okay?"

"I'm at the end of the line." Kimmy's heels were beginning to pinch her toes. "I think Iggy is my last resort." Heaven help her.

Booker frowned. "If it's stressing you out, don't do this."

Easy enough for him to say. "I have to. Wedding date, remember?" She straightened her spine. "Plus I promised." An Easley always kept a promise.

"It's time to get this party started." Mims's voice raised the roof once more.

A few minutes later, the bidding began.

Mims was a skilled auctioneer. Paul bid often but lost every time. He ordered another daiquiri and continued to suck his drink down without a straw. His bright-red mustache deepened in color. Winning bidders escorted their dates to reserved tables. Iggy and Priscilla were yukking it up at the bar, which in hindsight was where Kimmy should have been.

And every few minutes, Kimmy took a few steps closer to the stage. When Darcy's name was about to be called, she turned to Kimmy and wished her luck. And then Darcy was walking out on stage. Sure enough, Jason was in the audience and bid on her. He outbid Paul, who must have been on his fourth daiquiri.

"And now..." Mims smiled at Kimmy and gestured for her to join her on the stage. "Our last bachelorette of the evening, Kimmy Easley."

There were weak whoops and a round of applause, nothing like the enthusiasm for Mims's opening remarks.

Mims read Clarice's introduction. "Kimmy is a Sunshine

girl. She creates gourmet sandwiches at Emory's Grocery. She likes long walks in the park, and in her spare time, she likes to garden."

Gah! She sounded boring.

"A hundred bucks." Paul swayed near Kimmy's feet.

Kimmy swallowed, seeking out Iggy in the crowd. He wasn't even looking at her!

"One twenty-five." That came from a cowboy with a friendly smile.

She hoped he loved long walks in the park and food, especially garlic.

"One fifty." That bid came from the back of the crowd. Kimmy couldn't see where.

"Two hundred," Paul said wearily.

Kimmy would've felt sorry for him if she weren't his last chance for a date. The whole purpose of this exercise was to find a man who might be a good wedding date, someone who'd talk about food, not bugs.

"Two and a quarter." The cowboy was still smiling. He was wearing a straw hat and a blue chambray shirt that looked soft to the touch. He probably loved grilled steak.

She made a mean T-bone.

"Two seventy-five." Whoever was bidding in the back must have been short or hidden behind several Stetsons beyond the stage lights. Kimmy still couldn't see him.

"Three fifty." Paul set his drink on the stage, placed his palms on either side of it, and hung his head as if he might be sick.

Mims and Kimmy exchanged a glance and backed up a step.

"Four hundred dollars!" came the bid from the back.

The crowd gasped. It was the highest bid of the night.

The cowboy made a cutting gesture across his throat.

Paul lifted his heavy head and tried to spot his rival. He wasn't the only one looking. Everyone up front was turning around.

"We have four hundred," Mims said into the microphone. "Going once. Going twice. Sold!"

The crowd was parting, cowboys moving out of the way as the lights came up.

And then a man approached. A well-dressed man. A solid man. Booker.

Buying Kimmy hadn't netted Booker the response he wanted—Kimmy's gratitude.

Yes, there was relief in her eyes, but only temporarily.

Added to that, Paul and the cowboy who'd bid against him were lingering nearby.

"My hero," Kimmy said to Booker when they were seated in a booth in the back with two glasses of champagne and a dinner order placed. Her gaze darted around Shaw's, around his competition. "But let's be clear. Although I appreciate the save, you need to circulate through the crowd and find me a wedding date. You promised."

Fat chance, honey.

Bidding on Kimmy against other men had stepped on a nerve, one connected to a proprietary feeling for her. She might never see him romantically but for the next hour, she was going to be his.

"Look, we're here." Booker raised his champagne glass. "Let's toast. Here's to old friends and new beginnings."

With a sigh, Kimmy clinked her glass against his. "Hear, hear."

"We should take this time to catch up." Booker had a lot of explaining to do, and his hour alone with Kimmy had begun. "We didn't get a chance to do that the other day. What's new?"

"What's new?" Kimmy smirked. "I put myself out there in the Widows Club bachelorette auction." She'd looked miserable up there, smiling on command. "And that's about it for me. You?"

"I want to increase Burger Shack profits and put Dante through school." Booker was proud that he'd be able to do it. That is, if he could increase earnings at the original Burger Shack. And to do so, he needed Kimmy to sign a contract.

Instead of regarding Booker with warmth and respect, Kimmy frowned. "Why do you want to give Dante a free ride when you never had one? From what I hear, Dante doesn't even work at the Burger Shack anymore."

"He can't work because he's on the track team." And before that he'd been on the basketball team. And in the fall, the football team. Although there was the matter of the skateboard that shed doubt on Dante's school activities. Regardless, Booker had to stay on point. "Have I told you how hard it was to work and go to college?"

They'd talked more in the four years he was in college than in the last four years.

"Are you complaining? Seriously?" Kimmy sipped her champagne and stared at him over the rim of her glass. Her mouth tipped up at the corners. "From the way you talked, you loved every minute of it."

He had but Booker denied it anyway. "I ran an underground grill from my dorm room. I could have been kicked out at any time."

Kimmy crossed her arms over her chest. "Again, you loved every minute of it."

"I was exhausted and stressed 24/7." It had been a continuous adrenaline rush. "It probably took ten years off my life. I don't want it to take ten years from Dante's. Or worse, make him sick again."

She rolled her eyes. "Is your mother here? I think I just heard her talking about Dante's life expectancy." Although Kimmy was fond of Dante, she'd never been fond of the way Booker always came last in the family. "Oh, no. It was you who was babying him."

"Here it comes." Booker cupped a hand behind one ear. "The work lecture."

Paul passed by. He'd had too much to drink and was strutting like a peacock, all despondency over being dateless gone.

Kimmy's gaze chilled. "Hard work builds character, Booker. You know this."

"Is your father here?" Booker refilled their glasses. "Doesn't he always say that?"

"Touché." Kimmy and her siblings had been told, not encouraged, to find jobs as soon as they were old enough to drive. "Would you take it back? All those years spent working with your family at the Shack? I wouldn't." She leaned forward as if what she had to say needed to be private, despite the fact that they had to talk loud enough to be heard over the bar's music. "Don't you love cooking? Wouldn't you rather be in the kitchen than anywhere else? I know I would."

Before Booker could answer, Clarice showed up at their table. "Sorry to interrupt," she shouted.

Mims was right behind her, pointing to her ear and a bright-red clip-on earring. "She forgot her hearing aids."

"I didn't forget." Clarice bristled. "I don't need them in here. Everybody is shouting."

Mims patted her friend's shoulder. "We just wanted to ask Kimmy if she'd participate in our bake sale next week. It benefits the Little League."

Kimmy sat back, her expression turning wary. "Isn't that competitive?"

"No, no, no," Mims reassured her. "I mean, Wendy Adams always sells out her Bundt cake first but it's all for a good cause."

Booker was trying hard not to smile. Kimmy had given the

Widows Club an inch, and they were trying to take their mile. She'd be a prime target for every fund-raiser they had from now on.

"Oh, Booker." Mims smiled down at him. At first glance, it was a benevolent smile. But upon closer inspection, it was a smile that meant business. "Did you ever find a wedding date?"

"No." It was Booker's turn to fall back against the seat.

"There's Wendy now," Clarice shouted. "She was late and just missed being up for auction."

Sure enough, Bitsy, another Widows Club board member, escorted Wendy toward their table as if Kimmy or Booker were in need of her.

As if I want Wendy to be my wedding date.

Booker's shoulders cramped, sending a sharp twinge up his neck.

"I have an idea," Mims said, still smiling. "Why don't you two team up for the bake sale?"

"Booker and me..." Kimmy's eyes narrowed. "We don't bake. We grill."

Clarice frowned at Mims and shouted, "I think there's a rule—"

"There is no rule, Clarice," Mims said at the same volume. The Widows Club president wasn't good at hiding the high sign. She made wild eyes at Clarice and drew a make-believe zipper across her mouth. And then she turned to Kimmy with a big smile. "You could grill dessert." She cleared her throat and turned to Booker. "Together."

"I was just talking to Iggy," Clarice shouted at Kimmy. "He loves fried food."

Kimmy paled.

Booker wanted to laugh. The Widows Club was trying to match Kimmy with Iggy. But it wasn't a laughing matter. They were trying to play Cupid with him and Wendy and eating into his time alone with Kimmy. The auction had promised an intimate date but Booker wasn't getting his money's worth.

Bitsy and Wendy paused at their table.

Wendy, the shiest, most withdrawn girl from their high school class.

Paul danced past, scooting through the crowd. He'd fastened his tie around his head like a sweatband, and he had his dress shirt open, revealing a stark white T-shirt.

"Hi," Wendy said to Booker in that meek voice of hers, one he had to strain to hear.

He and Kimmy were better at secret high signs than Mims and her widows. Booker pressed his lips together and stared at Kimmy, willing her to read his mind: *Red alert. We're being cornered.*

Paul danced back doing the "Look Alive" dance, drawing Kimmy's attention away from Booker. "I'll buy Wendy." The town exterminator didn't stop dancing. "Two hundred. *In cash.*"

Everyone blinked.

Paul planted his feet but his hips kept moving, as did his shoulders. And there was a side-to-side head bob. The cobra dance move. Despite being drunk, the man had moves. People around them were applauding his skill.

Paul extended a hand toward Wendy. "Come on, girl. Are you ready for this?"

The Wendy he remembered from high school would have shrunk back. That wasn't this Wendy. She put her hand in Paul's.

"Sweet." Paul skipped off, dragging her after him.

The Widows Club huddled together. This was Booker's chance. Not just to communicate without words to Kimmy but to confess what he'd done. Beg forgiveness. Offer money. And perhaps salvage their friendship.

"Kimmy," Booker said sharply, staring at her with mind-meld intensity.

She stared back. And then understanding dawned in her eyes as she seemed to receive his message.

"I've got this." Kimmy tapped Mims on the shoulder. "Can you excuse us, ladies? Booker paid a lot for a date with me, and I'd like to give him his money's worth."

CHAPTER FIVE

It's official. We're being targeted for wedding dates," Booker told Kimmy as soon as the Widows Club set off to rescue Wendy or collect their two hundred dollars. It wasn't clear which.

"Why are you panicking?" Kimmy sipped her champagne. "You never used to freak around the Widows Club."

"They brought me Wendy Adams." He'd have preferred they brought him Kimmy. Instead, he'd had to buy her outright. Nothing was going right tonight. "They've never flaunted a date in front of me before."

"You're older now. And still single." Kimmy glanced toward the dance floor, where Wendy was doing the mom dance and Paul was bouncing around her like a pogo stick. "Besides, Wendy's got a smidge more personality now."

Was that a smile twitching at the corner of her mouth?

Kimmy faced him squarely, not a hint of a smile on her face. "Besides, I should be the one who's nervous. Clarice mentioned Iggy. My last resort."

They stared at each other for a moment and then burst out laughing.

Kimmy drank more champagne, mischief in her eyes. "You know what this means?"

Booker shook his head.

"You'll have to be my wedding date." She said it with a straight face.

Booker sucked in a breath, afraid if he blew it out, he might just break his cheeks by giving her the biggest smile on record. "You're asking me..."

She nodded.

Booker's heart swelled. He'd hidden his feelings for Kimmy for two decades. But he had to hide them a while longer. She was asking him out at the worst possible moment—right as he was about to confess to basing his sandwiches off her concoctions.

He blew out a breath. "No." It pained him to refuse her.

"Hang on." She laid her palms on the table and narrowed her eyes. "*No?* Is this about prom?"

Prom. She'd debuted her dance style there. And he, as her let's-go-as-friends date, had been unwilling to step out on the floor and join her.

Stupid, fragile teenage ego.

Paul tossed bills at the widows and then ran to the bar. He scrambled onto a stool and then onto the bar itself. A swing of his arms and his button-down sailed into the crowd, which was clapping and egging him on. A twist and a shimmy and his T-shirt followed. And then he boot-scooted toward the far end of the bar.

"Booker. Book." Kimmy waved a hand in front of his face and glanced Paul's way. "This is about how I dance, isn't it? Wedding dates are obligated to dance."

"This has nothing to do with your dance moves." And everything to do with his obligations to his family.

"I'm not asking you to promise to have and to hold until death do us part." Her shoulders were bunched around her ears.

"It's one date between friends. Don't make such a big deal out of it."

Booker ran a hand over his face. It was hard to present logical arguments with Paul dancing a few feet away. The town exterminator reached the end of the bar and boogied along the short end, not caring that the bartender was on the phone, most likely with the sheriff.

And then something Kimmy said sank in. "Hold the phone. Did you just say *promise*?" Booker stilled, trapping Kimmy's gaze with his own. "You know how I feel about promises." And he knew how she felt about hers.

"Promises to you always come with conditions." She studied him carefully, shoulders lowering. "Name yours."

This is your chance, his inner voice whispered.

Yes, his chance to clear the air about sandwiches and the past. But maybe a chance to win her heart as well.

"If you don't agree," she said impatiently, "the widows will try and set me up with all kinds of men for the wedding. And you...Wendy Adams was just the start for you."

Booker shook his head. "You know how they get." The widows. They were like a bouncy Labrador who kept bringing his owner a different toy to play with until..."I need more than a wedding date this week. I need a girlfriend to avoid more permanent matchmaking."

The words dropped between them, drowning out the music and the crowd noise and the approaching siren.

"So..." Kimmy was looking at him as if he were a box of spices that was unlabeled, one she couldn't believe she was considering purchasing. "You're saying we date for real?" Her head was shaking before she'd finished her sentence.

"I'm saying we *pretend* to have fallen for each other." Easy enough on his part. "We show up at the wedding events. There's a family-and-friends barbecue Monday, the wedding party celebration on Wednesday, a rehearsal dinner on Friday, and then the actual wedding on Saturday."

"You do remember prom," Kimmy said, staring at her hands and grimacing. "I want to dance."

"It'll get you out of the bake sale." One less Widows Club event to worry about. "And I'll get out on the dance floor. I promise."

Her barriers were coming down. Kimmy was no longer looking like she'd swallowed vinegar. "Still..."

"You've got nothing to lose." Whereas he...This could definitely boomerang. In fact, it would as soon as he told her about the contract.

Kimmy reached across the table for his hand, rubbing her thumb over his knuckles. "We're putting years of friendship on the line."

Sometimes you had to fish or cut bait. "We'll be fine." Booker came around to Kimmy's side of the booth, sliding in next to her. "We'll hold hands, like this." He took one of her hands in his, noting the way her eyes widened. "And occasionally, we'll brush the hair from each other's eyes." He smoothed her hair back from her forehead, noting the way her breath hitched. "And every so often—just to sell it, of course—we'll kiss." She held herself very still as he leaned in and pressed a kiss to her cheek. "You can do that, can't you?"

He wasn't sure anymore that he could. He wanted to sweep her into his arms and kiss her somewhere besides her cheek.

"Promise me you'll be my pretend girlfriend all week long." This was important, perhaps more important than him proving that she wouldn't reject his touch. "Kim. Promise me."

"I promise," she said begrudgingly.

"Say the rest." Luckily, a waitress delivered their food— two blue cheese burgers with two sides of sweet potato fries— just in time.

Kimmy's eyes flashed to her fries and then back to Booker's face. "Did you plan this?"

"Nope." He shook his head. "Do you want me to go first?"

Eye roll. Huff. Kimmy put her hand a few inches over her fries. "I promise on an order of hot fries to be your wedding date for a week so you won't be harassed by the matchmaking Widows Club." She took a fry. "And you?"

He put his hand over his fries. "I promise on an order of hot fries to make sure Ariana knows you're no threat." The bride knew that anyway. He picked up a fry.

They both took a bite and then grinned at each other.

That's when the guilt set in, heavy on his shoulders. He knew Kimmy wouldn't renege on their deal no matter how mad she was at him.

"This is such a bad idea." Kimmy lifted the top of her burger and sliced it open to check the inside. "Medium rare. Love."

"Jeffrey's cooking in the back. My dad taught him everything he knows." Booker checked his burger. Also medium rare. "I've always admired how you keep a promise." He wrapped his fingers around his burger.

Kimmy was ahead of him. She took a bite and then made a sound of approval.

"You know my college grill?" he asked.

She nodded, snagging another fry. "Needs more garlic."

"I never told you what I put on the menu." Booker was coming up on her slowly, carefully. "And you never asked."

She'd teased him instead. "*What's on your menu, Booker? Plain burgers? Doubles? Extra-large patties on an extra-large bun?*"

And when she'd finished her teasing, he'd always nod and say, "*Something like that.*"

"It was your business," Kimmy said now, nodding her head slightly.

Guilt pressed down on him harder. Not just on his shoulders.

It closed around his throat, trying to halt his words. He pushed them out anyway. "The reason I was so successful...The reason I had loyal customers...It was because I used your sandwich recipes." Not at first. But that didn't matter.

For just a moment, Kimmy's head continued to nod. She continued to chew a fry.

And then her brow furrowed. Her head stilled, and she swallowed. The corners of her mouth turned down. "You what?"

"I—"

"You jerk." She shoved him out of the booth and ran.

"You're on his side?" Kimmy stopped digging through a box of kitchen utensils her aunt Mitzy had purchased at a garage sale for her, and straightened in the food truck. She clutched a metal spatula. "Booker's?"

She'd been dumping the events of last night in her father's lap while he installed her stove.

"Do you know how lucky you are?" Her dad slid the stove into place and rubbed his palms on his coveralls. "You have a large extended family supporting you. And he—"

"He stole from me." Kimmy shook the spatula in the air. She hadn't been able to sleep last night, not with betrayal burning her heart worse than too much four-alarm chili.

"Haven't you always told me the Belmontes give everything to Dante and nothing to Booker?" Her father laid a hand on her shoulder.

"So that makes it right?" Every time he'd asked her what was in a sandwich, she'd been filled with pride that he'd enjoyed her creation enough to ask. And all along, he'd been pilfering her work.

"I know this hurts." Her dad's gaze was soft. "Do you remember when you took my set of screwdrivers to Emory's to fix the loose storage lockers?"

"Don't try to say that's the same." Kimmy couldn't believe they were having this conversation.

I should have told Mom. She'd understand.

"I didn't begrudge you the use of my tools." He was in dad mode, words slow and deliberate, as if he knew her mind was circling around the possibility that she'd been betrayed. "I did ask you after a month to bring them back when I knew I was going to need them."

"Tools are not sandwiches."

"But you borrowed my tools without asking," her dad continued.

Kimmy swallowed a groan of frustration.

"You don't have to admit I'm right." His hand fell away. "But you know I am. Ninety-nine percent of the time."

Kimmy stared at the freshly painted ceiling.

Her mother climbed onto the lower step of the truck. "Are you almost ready to go? I promised Haywood I'd be there soon. He left us a key under the mat."

"Yes, Mom, but can you weigh in on this?" Because Kimmy would like to have someone on her side.

"Sure." The pleasant smile on her mother's face hinted at expectations of a food truck opinion. She had no idea there were much heavier issues at hand.

Kimmy explained what Booker had done.

Her mother didn't hop up and down in anger. "You're saying Booker used your sandwiches to finance his way through college?"

"Yes." Maybe her mother was doing a slow burn on this.

"Don't you create new sandwiches every week?" She was in mom mode, calmly presenting her arguments. "Do you even remember what sandwiches you were making ten years ago?"

No. "That's not the point."

A truck pulled up outside. It was a new truck, and Booker was driving.

Kimmy's pulse kicked up a notch.

"Family goes the extra mile, honey." Her mom hopped down and waved to Booker on her way back inside the house.

"Family." Kimmy watched Booker approach. She had on her grubbies: jeans and a T-shirt she didn't mind getting dirty. He wore pressed khakis and a black Burger Shack polo. "He's not family."

"Isn't he?" Her dad waved Booker inside. "For years, you would've argued he is."

She hated that her parents' arguments made sense. Scowling, Kimmy set her hands on her hips.

"Hey." Booker bounded up the steps and looked around. "What's all this?"

"Kimmy's future." Her dad excused himself and left them alone.

"Family's got your back," Kimmy muttered. "Not."

"What's that?" Booker ran a hand over the countertop the same way Kimmy did when she came in, a greeting of sorts to the kitchen. He glanced around and then faced her. His gaze was soft, forgivable.

Do not forgive.

"This is my big move forward," Kimmy said instead, planting her feet. "When we were kids, we always talked about having businesses of our own. This is mine." She plastered a smile on her face and shored up her defenses for his criticism. "I know it's not brick-and-mortar or white tablecloth but it's a start."

"What a great idea." Booker began opening cupboards, checking out her space.

My baby.

"Low overhead. Freedom to change locations if the grass is greener elsewhere." He poked around the box of utensils from Aunt Mitzy, muscles flexing as he moved things around. Every hair in place except that cowlick. His voice familiar, comforting, approving. "You can make your own hours. Work the catering circuit."

"You stole from me." There was no escaping that fact.

"Yes." He leaned against the counter, not running from anything.

"You operated an illegal grill from your dorm room. No health inspections. No business license." At the time, she'd thought he was daring for doing so.

"Yes."

"And because you cheated the system, you thought you could cheat me." Her words were roughened by hurt. "You didn't ask. I would've been okay if you would've asked." Because what her parents had said was true. He was like family to her.

Booker's gaze didn't drop from hers. "My dad gave me an indoor grill as a graduation present. I used it to cook meals. And then my college friends wanted me to grill for them. They were willing to pay." He scratched at his cowlick. "My roommate was a business major. Somehow, it went from this little thing to a big thing overnight. Except...people got bored with burgers."

"So you turned to sandwiches." Hers.

"It was weird," Booker said slowly, nodding. "When I prepared your sauces and put them on the grill, it was as if you were next to me, helping me, working with me." His gaze was so dark and sorrowful she knew she'd forgive him. "I miss us working side by side, bumping elbows and scooting around each other." His gaze took in the food truck's kitchen. It was just the right size for bumping elbows and scooting.

But he's not going to be cooking in here with me.

"I'm sorry I didn't ask permission." Booker's eyes were filled with regret. "I'm sorry I waited so long to tell you the truth."

The air between them seemed thick with significance.

Kimmy could forgive him, and their friendship would carry on. Or she could hold on to the hurt, letting it sit like the taint of rotten eggs. She wasn't the grudge-holding type. But she wasn't the brush-it-off-and-everything-is-hunky-dory type either.

Kimmy sighed. She'd forgive him and hope time would heal the wound he'd made. "You should have asked or at least told me sooner. But you always were a procrastinator." That wasn't true but a truce sometimes required levity. And there was the promise she'd made about the week ahead.

Booker gave her a rueful smile. He knew he was still on shaky ground. "There's something else. I—"

"Kimmy!" Her mom banged out the front door. "Time to go."

"I have to help my mom with a client." Kimmy moved toward the door. "Can we talk tomorrow?"

"Sure." Booker had a bewildered expression on his face. "What time?"

"What time?" Kimmy paused on the top step. "What time are you picking me up for Hay's party?"

CHAPTER SIX

Kimmy took Monday off to drive into Greeley.

She needed dresses, a pedicure, and a stylish haircut if she was going to spend the week pretending to be Booker's girlfriend on the wealthy side of town.

What I need is my head examined.

This was the one time she should've broken a promise. Her hesitation wasn't just because she was still in the process of forgiving Booker. Growing up, she'd never felt as if she fit with the kids who wore expensive tennis shoes and name-brand blue jeans. For heaven's sake, she'd cleaned Haywood's house yesterday for the party she was attending tonight. If that wasn't proof she was out of her element, she didn't know what was.

At the mall in Greeley, Kimmy ventured deep into foreign territory—a department store dress department.

"May I help you?" The woman who stepped between the racks had a style Kimmy envied. She wore a figure-flattering dress and a pair of attractive heels that didn't look torturous.

"I'll have one of those." Kimmy's gesture encompassed the woman. "I need three dresses to wear to wedding events and one to a wedding. Plus shoes. And…" She sighed. Might as well just admit all her failings. "This is what I normally wear to work." She gestured to her blue jeans and red T-shirt. "Your mission, should you choose to accept it, is to make me look like I know what I'm doing in the dress department."

The sales clerk—Lydia, her name tag said—took Kimmy by the arm. "I've been dreaming of you my entire life. Come on."

An hour later, Kimmy was armed with four dresses she'd never wear after this week, a pair of heels she could stand to wear for a few hours, and a referral to the spa in the mall.

At the spa, the hairstylist wasn't as excited to see Kimmy as Lydia had been. "What kind of product do you use on your hair?"

"Shampoo." By the woman's frown, she could tell that was the wrong answer. "I have to wear my hair back for work every day. I don't need product."

The hairstylist tried to run her fingers through Kimmy's frizzy hair but her hands moved slowly through the thick mass. "You need product. Good product."

Kimmy took that to mean *expensive*. She couldn't afford expensive. That was why she didn't go to Prestige Salon in Sunshine. With all her credit card spending today, she was setting her food truck timeline back a week.

The hairstylist ran a comb carefully through Kimmy's hair. "And you need bangs."

"I don't want bangs."

"You need bangs."

"No bangs."

"I'll change your mind."

"No, you won't," Kimmy said as politely as she could.

"You're tense." The woman continued combing Kimmy's hair.

"I'm tense because you keep talking about bangs."

"You need a complete spa treatment. Massage. Facial. Wax.

Mani-pedi. Hair. Afterward, you'll feel like a new woman." Her recommendations sounded convincing. Her hair, skin, and nails were flawless. Not to mention she styled hair while wearing high heels. She looked like she belonged at Hay's party more than Kimmy ever would.

"Okay, fine." Her credit card balance was going to be huge. "As long as you promise me no bangs."

The woman didn't promise.

Hours later, Kimmy left the mall with her purchases, muscles aching from a deep tissue massage, upper lip red from waxing, and bangs falling in a straight line across her forehead.

If it hadn't been for her promise to Booker, friend and sandwich thief, she might not have opened the door when he came to pick her up for the barbecue.

"Whoa." Booker took a step back. "Somebody's been out shopping and..."

"You hate them." Kimmy tried to pull her bangs down, hoping to help them grow out quicker. Like in the next ten minutes. "I don't blame you. I hate them."

"I wasn't looking at your bangs." He swooped in and ruffled them up. "That's better."

Kimmy doubted it.

Skippy sauntered out to rub against Booker's legs.

"I recognize you from your pictures." He leaned down to scratch her behind the ears. "Tell Kim she looks awesome, Skippy."

On cue, Kimmy's cat blinked up at her and meowed.

Kimmy took a moment to stare in disbelief. "Okay, let's get this show on the road." She grabbed a sweater and then locked her apartment door behind them, hurried down the stairs, and headed toward Booker's truck. When she noticed Booker wasn't with her, she stopped and turned. "What is it now? Did I leave a tag on?" She turned this way and that, tugging at her skirt.

"You have curves," Booker said, almost in awe. "And legs."

Kimmy sent her gaze skyward. "How many years have you known me?"

"Twenty-seven." He approached, circled, and smiled. The really good smile. The one that practically lifted her spirits along with her lips. "I can't remember ever seeing your knees after the sixth grade."

"That can't be. We went to prom..." She hadn't wanted to bring that up again.

"Everyone has an unfortunate event in their past." Booker caught her hand and led her to his truck. "So you ordered a prom dress online."

"It wasn't anything like the picture." Or anything that flattered her teenage shape in any way. "No big deal. I just wore my coat all night." And sweat like she'd taken hot yoga until one of the chaperones forced her to remove her coat in case she was harboring everyone's alcohol. And then Booker and Hay had dared her to dance. And she'd gotten out there—horrid dress, horrid dance moves, and all.

Booker opened her door and helped her into the seat. "If you want to feel better, I could tell you about my preteen acne, which required a prescription and a nightly treatment from my grandmother—who made a sickly-smelling poultice."

"Enough said."

When Booker was behind the wheel, he slipped her another smile. "I know I'm going to say this wrong but you look beautiful."

Kimmy's cheeks heated. "Which is another way of saying that normally I don't."

"That's enough whining." He brought the truck to a stop at an intersection and then brushed his knuckles gently over her cheek.

The air went out of her lungs.

"I've only recently learned about penalties for whining. Per the retirement home rules, you owe me a nickel." He drew his hand back and then made a right turn. "However, I'm willing to waive that fee since I owe you for the use of your sandwiches. I'll pay for that dress you're wearing. I'm sure you wouldn't have bought it if not for our pact."

Kimmy indignantly sucked in air. "You're not paying for my clothes."

"Then I'll get you something for your food truck."

"No thank you." She sat stiffly in the seat, fully cognizant that she could use the money. "You don't need to offer me money to make yourself feel better."

"Kimmy, I want to pay you. I want to make this right. I—"

"If you offer me money again, I'm going to have to break my promise." Her words tumbled out too quickly and at too high a pitch. Her cheeks began to heat again.

Booker glanced at her as he neared the town square. Her sister, Rosalie, was walking with her fiancé and their dogs. She waved.

Kimmy raised a limp hand. "If we both think this dating ruse is a bad idea, we can stop this now." She'd return the other dresses and ask Paul to be her wedding date. She was sure he'd dance with her.

"This isn't a bad idea," Booker said firmly. "And I should know. I'm the king of bad ideas."

"That you are." At least he was fessing up to it.

Booker took Kimmy's hand, and when she gave him an incredulous look, he said, "We need the practice."

And then her cheeks were heating for an entirely different reason.

They reached Haywood's place and went around to the backyard.

Kimmy stopped just inside the gate. She'd cleaned the inside yesterday but that had been before the decorators and caterers had come. "So pretty."

"Yes," Booker murmured next to her.

"Just look at all this." She dragged him forward. "It's wonderful."

"It is." His voice was gruff. His gaze intent. But he wasn't staring at the backyard. He was staring at her.

Attraction fluttered in her chest. She swallowed. "You're not even looking." She turned and pointed, focusing on her surroundings rather than on Booker.

There were Chinese lanterns in orange and blue. Twinkle lights were strung from the trees, their warm glow just beginning to challenge the dusky sky. Places were set on white tablecloths with bouquets of spring flowers. Cushy blue chairs and couches sat around a stone fireplace with a roaring fire. Perfect for a chilly outdoor mountain evening.

It was everything the magazines depicted for garden parties, everything Kimmy longed to have someday if she could earn enough money. It made her sad that she'd be turning into a pumpkin at the end of the evening and going back to her two-room apartment with its outdated, cat-clawed furniture and plain white walls.

"Booker!" Haywood set down his beer and strode across the lawn to greet them. "You brought my favorite coworker in the whole wide world, Miss Kimmy Easley." He hugged them each in turn.

Once released, Booker took Kimmy's hand and gave her a look that seemed to say *Here we go*.

"Book, you haven't seen the house since I bought it." Hay gestured around. "What do you think? Kim, Ariana, or I can give you a tour tonight." Hay winked at Kimmy.

Booker raised his brows.

"I'll explain later," Kimmy said quickly, because Ariana was drifting across the lawn in an exquisite green dress and a delicate pair of taupe sandals with a mane of blond hair that had never been tortured with bangs.

"Booker. Kimmy." Ariana noted their joined hands, and her smile broadened. "I was wondering when this would happen."

"What?" Kimmy's mouth dropped open. She wouldn't have noticed if Booker hadn't lifted her chin to close it.

"The chemistry between you two has been off the charts for years." Ariana clapped her hands. "Come on. Hay's been grilling but everybody knows he can't hold a candle to you two in that department." She hooked her arm through Kimmy's and led her to a bar setup. "How about a glass of wine?"

"Sure."

"Cabernet? Sauv blanc? Pinot noir?" Ariana tilted the bottles as she read the varieties.

The last time Kimmy had wine, it had been strawberry moscato and sweeter than soda pop. "I'll have whatever you're drinking." Because she had no idea what kind of taste to expect from the wines before her. But she was determined to fit in and finish whatever was in her glass.

"Sauv blanc. This one's from South Africa." Ariana poured white wine into a glass and handed it to Kimmy. She paused, staring at Kimmy's forehead. "Those bangs..."

"I know, right? Huge mistake." Kimmy tugged at them.

Ariana gently moved Kimmy's hand aside. "They should have blended them, whoever it was. Bangs are the right idea with the shape of your face, but not blunt cut. What was your hairstylist thinking?"

"I don't know."

"Come into the salon tomorrow at eight."

"Oh, I couldn't impose." No matter how awesome it felt to be asked.

"It'll take five minutes. Ten tops." Ariana fluffed Kimmy's bangs again. "And you'll feel ten times better."

"Okay." Who could argue with ten times better?

"What are we talking about?" A long, heavy arm came to rest over Kimmy's shoulders.

Kimmy would never admit Booker's touch sent her heart fluttering or that she edged closer to him.

"I was just about to say that you two are needed at the grill." Ariana smiled at Booker. "But you're so cute together."

Kimmy stopped a reflexive disbelieving eye roll. Booker being gorgeous and Kimmy being bang-challenged—a cute couple they didn't make.

"We are, aren't we?" Booker drew Kimmy closer, next to his firm chest and his body heat.

Instinctually, Kimmy wanted to turn into him, to snuggle closer, to lift her face for a kiss.

But this is Booker.

"Whew." Kimmy skirted out from under his arm on unsteady feet, balancing her wineglass with one hand. "It's getting hot out here. Come on, grillmaster. Let's see what's for dinner."

For a moment, there was a look in Booker's eyes that Kimmy didn't recognize, a gleam that left her feeling breathless.

This isn't my Booker.

But then Booker fluffed her bangs and glanced away.

Kimmy stared at him, trying to reconcile this Booker with the Booker she'd known most of her life and failing.

"Go mingle," Booker told Kimmy in a gruff voice. "I've got this covered."

"Are you sure?" Kimmy cradled the bowl of her wineglass between them.

"Yep." He went over to join Hay at the grill.

Leaving, Kimmy feeling oddly bereft.

"Well, aren't you a surprise?" Haywood poked a steak with a fork, releasing some of its juice.

"Did you learn nothing while working at the Burger Shack?" Booker took possession of the fork, leaving Hay to pick up his beer.

"How long have you and Kimmy been dating?"

"Long enough."

"Best-kept secret in Sunshine," Hay teased. "That is, if it's been longer than a day."

Booker jabbed the meat harder than Haywood had. "You don't have to go telling everybody." In case things crashed and burned sooner than the wedding.

"Are you kidding?" Hay moved closer, lowering his voice. "Let's tell everybody. This is what you've wanted for years."

"You always did gossip like a girl." But Booker smiled. "Don't jinx it."

Hay sipped his beer and stared toward the outdoor fireplace, where his guests were congregating. "Don't break her heart."

"I won't." Booker knew he couldn't have Kimmy's heart *and* her sandwiches. "This is just a friend helping out a friend."

"Who's helping who?" Hay turned serious. "Hurt her and I'll have to give you a pounding."

"I told you, I won't." But Booker's shoulders were as stiff as steel.

Kimmy laughed at something Ariana said. The sound of her laughter was magnetic. Who was he kidding? Kimmy was magnetic. Smart, attractive. And she was gutsy. That food truck…He'd looked into the business once. It took hustle to make those profitable. If anyone could succeed at it, she could.

Hay raised his beer bottle toward her in salute, cheery on the outside, threatening with his words. "Have you told her?"

"I told her about college." He'd been interrupted trying to tell her about the menu at the Burger Shack.

"She must have taken the college part of your story well." Hay studied Booker's expression. "Or not."

"You never should've taught her how to give a charley horse." He rolled his arm where she'd shoved him at Shaw's and then turned the steaks.

"Good for her." Hay grinned. "You know, I had a late lunch at the Burger Shack today, hoping to see you. Got a glimpse of Dante. He looked like working there was punishment."

He'd whined like it too. Booker needed to get a whining jar for the Shack. "He'll get over it. I did."

Hay shook his head. "Your dad started you there when you were ten. Dante is seventeen. He's not going to get over it."

"Hard work has a way of changing people."

"It changed us," Hay agreed. "But that's because we had to work—you so Dante could get well and me because my family needed food on the table." And now Hay was a successful real estate agent. Maybe not selling million-dollar homes the way he'd dreamed as a kid, but he did okay.

"Whatever's being said here is way too serious." Kimmy came to stand between the two men. She had no idea how beautiful and sexy she looked. Kimmy stared at the steaks and breathed deeply. "There is nothing like the smell of grilled meat."

Booker put his hand on Kimmy's waist and tucked her to his side. He was nearly overcome with a sense of rightness, a need to pull her close and keep her there.

She gently pinched his waist. "I said, there's nothing like the smell of grilled meat."

"Ah, the sensory game," Hay said, draining his beer. "I haven't missed playing that at the Shack."

Booker knew from his friend's wry grin that wasn't true. Hay liked mental challenges, and the sensory game was full of them—sights, sounds, tastes, touches, smells. "We're doing good aromas? I'm partial to the *smell* of buttered popcorn."

"Coffee, first thing in the morning." Hay set his empty bottle down on the grill's side table. "Too easy."

"It's only too easy if you win the game," Kimmy insisted. "Mention a smell we both dislike and you lose. I like the smell of chocolate chip cookies."

"Oh, man. We haven't played this game in forever. I'm rusty." Booker curled his fingers around her hip, trying to think of an answer. "There's nothing like the smell of..." He drew in a deep breath.

There's nothing like the smell of Kimmy's hair.

Hay and Kimmy were staring at him, waiting.

His gaze caught on the flowers on the table. "There's nothing like the smell of roses on a hot summer day."

That earned him dual groans.

Barbara Hadley approached. She was the town queen bee, the owner of Prestige Salon, where Ariana worked, and the mayor's wife. She was too thin, too put together, too brittle. Although she was smiling, she looked as if she knew something they didn't. "Well, well, well. Booker and Kimmy. What a surprise." She tossed her blond hair artfully.

Next to him, Kimmy stiffened.

Barb sidled closer, a spider looking for a fly. "How long have you guys been seeing each other?"

"Not long." Booker pressed a kiss to Kimmy's bangs.

"But long enough." Kimmy slipped her arms around Booker's waist and stared up at him. She was smiling broadly, and if he fuzzed his vision, he couldn't see the hint of worry in her eyes.

The queen bee could be cruel. And if Barb sensed their relationship was a sham, not only would she expose them but she'd never let them forget they couldn't fool her.

"Long enough?" Booker murmured, dipping his head. "Long past due, you mean."

And then he kissed her.

CHAPTER SEVEN

H*oly moly. The man could kiss.*

Kimmy nestled closer, drawn to the warmth, drawn to the intensity, drawn to the combination of strength and softness. Drawn to...Booker.

Hot. Dog.

"Nothing to see here." Hay's words drifted to her through the fog of desire.

Booker pulled away enough to stare into her eyes. It was the same face she'd grown up with. Handsome, strong. Dark eyes that gave away only the secrets he wanted you to know. This time she recognized the look in them. Booker wanted her. He wanted to kiss her again.

She stiffened because...

Holy moly. I want him to kiss me again too.

This was wrong. All wrong. They were friends. They'd always been friends.

And yet it felt right. So right.

She half expected Booker to pull back farther and laugh, that deep chuckle he released when he'd pulled one over on some-body, as if that kiss had been a joke. And if he did that, she'd have to laugh, force air through her lungs and make a light-hearted sound that said she knew what he'd done was all in fun, and she approved of the kissing charade.

Booker and Kimmy and Hay. The trio used to be a team. Working together like a well-oiled machine at the Burger Shack for years. Ribbing each other and the world at large good-naturedly.

Booker and Kimmy and Hay. They were friends. Regardless of her childhood crush, they had had fun together.

But that kiss... That kiss had been Booker and Kimmy. Friend zone breached. No fun intended.

Her knees were weak, and it wasn't just because of the way Booker's kiss had affected her. It was because it was a surprise.

Booker and Kimmy, no Haywood. The dynamic wasn't exactly wrong but it was different. New.

She'd felt attraction for Booker before he'd returned but she'd never picked up on his want, his need. She didn't know how to react or what to say.

Without moving away, Kimmy slid her gaze toward Hay, seeking out the familiar connection of the three musketeers.

Immediately, Booker released her. "Meat's about to burn."

"I'll get it." Kimmy reached for the fork.

Booker held it away. "I've got it." The chill in those words. She got the message. He thought she cared about Hay's reaction to their kiss.

She didn't. She stepped back, taking in Hay's beautiful backyard. The guests' upbeat chatter. Barb's melodious laughter. Ariana's delicate beauty. The twinkle lights. The Chinese lanterns. The breeze swaying the branches.

Kimmy stared at Booker's broad back and remembered...

Summers when she helped her mother clean Ariana's house or Barb's. Watching Barb and Ariana sun themselves in the backyard while she dusted their pretty, expensive things. Every visit making her realize the differences between them.

She remembered winters when they couldn't keep the heat on higher than fifty in the house at night because they couldn't afford their electricity bill. Sleeping in two layers of clothes and beneath two blankets and a sleeping bag to stay warm.

She remembered high school bells ringing. Kids running to after-school activities—sports, clubs, causes. And Kimmy running to work at the Burger Shack. She was a member of the family at the Shack. Never cold. Checked on by Mrs. Belmonte if she called in sick.

And then there were Booker and Hay.

For three years, the teens had done the heavy lifting at the Shack while little Dante battled for his life. They'd signed up for the most shifts and worked the most hours.

Oh, they hadn't been complete angels. There'd been food fights and grill-offs. And competitions. Man, the competitions. Who could eat the most burger patties in five minutes (Hay). Who could clean the dining room the fastest (Kimmy). Who could prep and slice the most potatoes for French fries before Mrs. Belmonte came back from the dentist (Booker).

Three teens who enjoyed each other's company and shared the value of hard work.

And now?

It was as if they shared nothing.

The only time Kimmy saw Haywood was when he stopped in for a sandwich. She hadn't seen Booker in years. What kind of friendship was that?

Kimmy knew the answer. It wasn't a friendship. She didn't belong here.

She took another step back.

She could leave. No one would miss her.

She could walk home a mile or so in heels. She'd suffered through worse. She was suffering now.

Another step and...

"I'm glad you came." Hay took her hand and gave it a squeeze.

"Don't go." Booker took her other hand and gave it a squeeze.

She felt their gazes upon her but couldn't look at them. If she had, she might have done something stupid, like shed a tear, grateful as she was for their past friendship.

But here in the present, Booker had kissed her.

And she was afraid nothing was ever going to be the same again.

"Did I hear right?" Booker's mom came through the back door into the Burger Shack, dressed for work in black slacks and the Shack's black polo shirt. The thick streaks of gray in her hair glimmered under the fluorescents. "Are you dating Kimmy Easley? Can I say I heartily approve? It's about time you took a moment to think about your future."

"Mom." Booker jumped into the void when his mother took a breath. He'd been prepping potatoes, and he dried his hands on a towel. "Don't start planning my wedding. Kimmy and I have always been good friends."

"And she always had that crush on Haywood." His mother tsk-tsked. "Patience really paid off for you, didn't it?"

Patience? He'd kissed Kimmy at the first opportunity. And when it was done, she'd looked at him in just the way he'd imagined. Slightly breathless, slightly dazed, completely blissful.

And then she'd looked at Hay. *Shades of summers past.*

Booker gritted his teeth.

And then Hay had taken her hand, sensing—much as Booker had—that Kimmy wanted to bolt.

Booker's jaw clenched so hard that it popped. He'd driven her home but the ride had been quiet.

"Can you imagine the two of you together?" His mom opened the supply cabinet and grabbed a bag of napkins. She was like a savant, sensing the staff who'd closed last night hadn't refilled the dining room's napkin holders. "Dark-haired babies with your smile and her smarts."

"Mom." Seriously, the woman needed a hobby. "Shouldn't you be home? Gardening or knitting or something?"

"Knitting?" His mom rushed to his side, dark eyes wide and hopeful. "Baby booties?"

"No. No babies." Booker put his hands on her shoulders. "I meant you shouldn't come in the Shack every day. I bought it from you so you'd be able to enjoy life. You've given so much to Dante and me. It's time you focused on you. Book a massage at Prestige Salon." If she didn't, he'd make the appointment for her. "Join the gym."

"But..." She crushed the napkins to her chest. "This is my life. And when Dante leaves for college..."

"You'll have Dad," Booker was quick to say. He drew her back toward the office. "You can travel, like you always talked about."

His mother sat down in a chair by the door, still embracing the napkins. "Your father doesn't want to travel. All he's interested in is the television remote. He discovered he can record shows last night. And this morning, he's watching all the shows he recorded."

Booker frowned.

"So you see, Booker"—his mother turned puppy-dog eyes his way—"unless you're going to give me a grandchild, the Shack is all I have."

"Your bangs bothered me all last night." Ariana shook out a black polka-dot cape and fastened it around Kimmy's neck. "I even dreamed about them."

"I'm sorry?" Kimmy was still unsure of her footing where Ariana was concerned. Add to that the fact that she'd helped her mother clean the salon a time or ten and it felt odd to sit in a client chair. "I didn't know hairstylists were bothered by the botched work of other hairstylists."

"All the time." Ariana picked up Kimmy's bangs and let them fall. Repeatedly. "So." Her gaze met Kimmy's. "What was it that finally got you and Booker together? Hay and I have talked about the chemistry between you guys for years."

"Years?" That couldn't be.

Ariana chuckled. "Were you the last to know?"

"Apparently." It was hard to believe that others had noticed an attraction and she hadn't. Booker was just…Booker.

Caring. Considerate. Smart. Handsome. Sandwich thief. Booker.

Ariana lightly sprayed Kimmy's bangs with water and took thinning scissors to her hair. "To think we were all in high school together. It's funny, isn't it? I was such a dork back then. Trying so hard to fit in."

"You did fit in." Ariana had hung out with Barb and the in-crowd.

She shook her head. "I felt like I was one wrong shoe decision away from expulsion. If it hadn't been for Haywood…" Ariana fluffed Kimmy's bangs. "He's so grounded. And funny about money. I wanted to get engaged way back. You know, when we had that little break."

Oh, I know.

Kimmy pretended the silence wasn't awkward as she waited for Ariana to continue.

Haywood's bride-to-be worked some mousse into Kimmy's hair. "There was a reason Hay didn't want to get married when we were younger. He wanted to make sure we were financially stable. His parents never have been."

Kimmy kept silent.

Hay's parents, like Kimmy's, were blue-collar workers. But Hay's sports ability had earned him a place on the popularity ladder, which Kimmy had been unable to climb. But she wasn't about to admit any weakness while in Prestige Salon—the hub of town gossip.

"So I waited because he's so totally worth it."

Booker might be worth it too.

A dangerous thought. So Kimmy chose silence again.

"And then at the town's tree-lighting ceremony, he proposed with the choir singing Christmas carols and the lights sparkling in the trees. It was perfect." Ariana grabbed a hair dryer and blew Kimmy's bangs dry, raising her voice to be heard. "I hope Booker is as romantic as Hay is."

Kimmy wanted to say, *That man is not going to propose to me.*

Kimmy should say, *I hope so too.* If only to keep up the ruse that she and Booker were indeed infatuated with each other, which would give the impression that Kimmy was no threat to Ariana's special day.

But Kimmy managed only a meek "Yep."

Who was she kidding? Booker was going to be gone in a week, managing his growing restaurant empire from Denver. He'd probably forget about that kiss before he returned home. If he was thinking about settling down, he certainly wasn't thinking about settling down with Kimmy, chemistry or not.

Ariana returned her hair dryer to its place near the rest of her tools and picked up a flat iron. After a few passes over Kimmy's bangs, it was time for hair spray and a final fluff. "There." She whipped off the drape as dramatically as a stage magician. "Booker is going to love this. Parted to the side, it gives interest to your face and makes your eyes look huge."

The face that stared into the mirror looked the same to Kimmy. She was the woman behind Emory's lunch counter. The woman who'd stood in the crowd in the town square when Hay had proposed to Ariana.

Kimmy stared at her reflection and nodded. Bangs made no difference whether blunt cut or fluffed to one side. Same woman.

She'd best remember that.

CHAPTER EIGHT

Sʜee you tomorrow, Emory." Kimmy shut off the lights behind the deli counter. She had to hurry home and get ready for another wedding-related event.

She hadn't seen Booker since the dinner at Haywood's house two nights ago. She wouldn't be surprised if he texted and gave her an out for the evening, regardless of whether he'd noticed chemistry between them for years or not.

Emory walked into her path, blocking her exit. His bow tie today was a solid blue. "I hear they're testing their new menu at the Burger Shack this Friday at lunch." His tone had the quality of Eeyore's doom and gloom. "I don't expect much business that day. And you shouldn't either."

Kimmy resisted the urge to check the time on her cell phone. "We'll be fine." Of course, she experienced a niggle of doubt as she said it. She was just the lunch-counter clerk, not the store manager. "People are loyal to us."

Emory considered her words, pursing his lips until he came to a judgment. "You and Booker…"

Oh, not Emory too. Customers in her line today had asked Kimmy about her relationship with Booker.

"Booker is loyal to you," Emory was saying. "He'd show you their new menu if you asked. And if you saw it, you could design something better for us."

"That seems kind of low, doesn't it?" Besides, she'd declined to review it twice. How would it look if she asked now?

"It's called survival." Emory shook his head. "You know, Kimmy, there's a push to turn that abandoned mill down by the interstate into a distribution center. If that happens, every-thing's going to change. New homes will go up out there. New businesses too. And we'll be left here to wither away."

"No." Regardless of her short-term-employee mentality, Kimmy refused to believe Emory's prediction.

"Mark my words." Her boss eyed her. "Unless you come up with something new and slam-bang, something that keeps cus-tomers here, the Burger Shack will ruin things for this store."

Then Emory was paged to the front of the store, leaving Kimmy to ponder his opinion and whether they applied to food trucks too.

"I was just about to call you." Kimmy stood in the open doorway of her apartment, trapped between the hot late-afternoon air and Booker climbing her stairs and the cool air-conditioning and the safety of her normal life inside.

Should she kiss his cheek hello? Drag him inside for a lip-lock? Or ask about his menu?

Booker hurried toward the door in a dark suit and tie, check-ing his cell phone and looking like a businessman from Denver, not her childhood friend.

"I thought you might cancel." She'd give him an out. After all, Booker still hadn't looked at her. That kiss. Every second that passed made it more awkward to bring up.

He drew his brows together, released them, and then pocketed his phone. "I'm late, that's all. Dante was out at the old mill with some friends and somehow got left behind." He stopped on her welcome mat and looked at her. A slow smile built on his face. "Now that"—he gestured toward her from head to toe—"all works together, bangs included."

Booker's attention was building her confidence. Her dress this evening was a sapphire-blue sheath. Kimmy was getting used to the new haircut and dressing like an adult. She could get used to Booker's compliments too. And yet she felt deflated. The fact that they hadn't talked about that kiss had to mean something.

"What's wrong?" His smile fell, and he hustled her inside, closing the door behind them.

"This." Why beat around the bush? She gestured from him to her. "Us pretending. Me holding your hand. Being in your space. Kissing you."

Booker tilted his head and studied her face, saying nothing as the heat built in her cheeks.

"Say something," she whispered.

"I'm just putting everything in context." He came forward slowly until he was close enough to brush the bangs from her eyes, although he didn't touch her. "You're taking responsibility for a deal we both agreed to. It isn't you deciding to hold my hand. As far as I recall, I've always reached for your hand first."

So true. Her cheeks burned with embarrassment. "We don't have to do this."

"Oh, but we do." His hands came to rest on her shoulders, sliding slowly down her arms until his fingers closed around hers. "You haven't been moving into my space. I've been dragging you into it. And that kiss the other night? *I* kissed *you*, not the other way around."

"I didn't just stand there," Kimmy mumbled.

"No." He broke out that infectious smile. "You didn't."

"But…" How to say this? "Everyone's been telling me

this…" She held on tight to his hands and shook them. "That this was bound to happen. That all the signs were there."

Booker stared at her tenderly. "And you didn't see these signs?"

"No."

"Does that mean you want to call things off?" There was a wary note to his voice that hadn't been there before. "Like you suggested the other night?"

"And go back on my word?" *Yes. No.* She didn't know which would be worse.

"I know you'd never break a promise." He leaned closer and pressed a kiss to her forehead.

"I can tough it out," Kimmy said, unsteady in her heels. She risked looking at Booker, so close she could have leaned forward and kissed him again. "If you can."

His trademark smile returned as his arms came around her. "Like it's a hardship." Before she could ask him what he meant, he'd released her, grabbed her purse and her keys, and ushered her out the door.

The dinner for the wedding party was being hosted by Ariana's parents. Another home Kimmy used to help her mother clean.

"We need a set of tongs." Ariana's mother glanced around.

"I'll get them." Kimmy hurried from the patio into the kitchen.

Booker followed her, although not as quickly. "I thought you might need help rifling through Camilla's drawers." He slowed to a stop at the large kitchen island, where Kimmy stood holding the tongs she'd dug out of a drawer. "How did you…"

"Mom and I used to clean this house." She'd never told him that. Back in the day, it'd been too embarrassing. "Come on." Kimmy retraced her steps. "Don't look at me like that. This is my Cinderella moment. As soon as the wedding reception is over, I'm turning into a pumpkin."

He fell into line behind her. "Besides the fact that Cindy

doesn't turn into a pumpkin at midnight, you were never Cindy. You were Sleeping Beauty, and I'm sorry it took me so long to show up and give you a kiss."

Kimmy's breath caught. That was without a doubt the most romantic thing a man had ever said to her. And he'd spoken the words when she was wearing a beautiful dress, standing in a beautiful home, and having a good hair day. Could life get any better?

Booker caught Kimmy's arm, bringing her around to face him. "In fact, I'd like to give you another."

Kimmy stared at him through her lashes. If he was going to kiss her, she wasn't going to object. "Camilla needs her tongs."

"Camilla can wait." Booker's arms came around Kimmy. He tilted her chin up and gathered her close, hesitating, lips practically touching hers. "You want another kiss, don't you, Sleeping Beauty?"

Kimmy's heart pounded out an answer he couldn't hear so she had to say, "Sometimes the magic takes more than once to work."

His eyes sparkled, and he was smiling when his mouth came down on hers.

Their last kiss had been soft and surprising. A first-date kiss stolen on a whim.

There was nothing soft or whimsical about this kiss. There were heat and hunger, demand and declaration.

This. Him.

Her heart pounded harder, emboldening her to kiss deeper, to hold on tighter.

The floodgates opened in her head, and she put together pieces of memories she hadn't allowed herself to previously. The flutter in her chest when Booker's shoulder brushed hers in the school library as they worked through a complex equation. The weakness in her knees when his smile connected with hers in the school hallway. The tremble in her fingers when he asked her to scratch his nose while he was elbow-deep in dirty dishwater.

Yes, she'd been attracted to Booker as a girl. But he was going places, and everyone knew it. Kimmy was the daughter of an auto worker and a maid. She might have talked big dreams about going to college with Booker but she'd known the truth. She wasn't going anywhere. Haywood came from her side of town. He was the more logical choice.

But now...

But this...

She was falling in love.

"Wow," Booker whispered.

"Ditto." Dizzy, Kimmy had to lean against the wall.

"Hey," Camilla called, "do you need help finding those tongs?"

"Found them." Kimmy drew a deep breath and pushed Booker back, gaining much-needed space.

Booker followed her out to the patio. "I think we found more than tongs."

"Kimmy looks happy." Haywood nudged Booker and gestured with his beer to the cluster of women sitting on the enclosed patio.

"She makes me happy." But for how long? Once Kimmy knew the whole truth... The grilled oyster appetizers he'd eaten squirmed in his stomach. Booker should have told her the rest of the truth at Shaw's or in her food truck or tonight before he kissed her.

The two men stood at the outdoor bar. Haywood was opening beer bottles. Booker was mixing another pitcher of margaritas.

"You told her though, right?" Hay asked, counting beers and then comparing his number to a head count. "About the menu?"

"Not yet." Booker doled out ice cubes in tall bar glasses. "But she'll understand." He held on to a sliver of hope.

Hay stopped double-checking his beer order and began giving Booker the stink eye. "She won't. I wouldn't. It's one thing to use her sammies to work your way through college." He lowered his voice. "It's another thing entirely to use her to make your fortune."

Booker kept his voice just as low. "You know how Kimmy is. She'd give you the shoes off her feet if she thought you needed it." Those oysters banked and rolled in his gut.

"And what would you give her if she needed it? A share of the profits? Part ownership in the Burger Shack?" Hay waited for an answer. When he got none, he gathered beer necks between his fingers. "You know, I showed her a lot of empty buildings to buy or rent when she was considering opening her own sandwich shop here in town. She couldn't afford any of them. And yet you…"

"I'm going to give her a fair offer, Hay." Booker sucked down some water, hoping to drown the oysters who'd taken on the role of his conscience. "She'll get paid. I promise."

"I understand you wanting to protect the family business but…" Haywood nudged Booker's chest with a handful of beer bottles. "But Dante…" He bit back whatever he'd been about to say.

"Dante what?" Booker pushed the beer aside.

"Dante doesn't deserve a free ride." Hay's voice was hard and unforgiving. "Yeah, I know he had cancer back in the day. But what has he done with his life since then besides being a mama's boy?"

"Don't you remember what he went through?" Outrage shook Booker's voice. "Pale. Sunken eyes. Tubes coming out of him." Half-dead before he was even four.

"I remember what he looked like *when he was a toddler.*"

Hay blew out a breath. "Has it ever occurred to you that we turned out so well because it was either sink or swim? Adversity builds character. Let it build Dante's."

"So you'd have me stop everything? Change the menu back to burgers only?"

"Yes. And do you know why?" Haywood leaned closer. "Because you love Kimmy."

The oysters hardened. Booker rubbed his chest, trying to relieve the heartburn, unable to deny Hay's statement.

He loved Kimmy. He'd always loved Kimmy.

But he didn't deserve her.

CHAPTER NINE

After that hot kiss in the kitchen, Kimmy had expected a hot good-night kiss.

She'd received a very chaste peck on the cheek at her door.

But she was nothing if not optimistic and fully expected Booker to call or text or swing by Thursday after work.

That was a big nada.

She made excuses for Booker: he was busy preparing for a relaunch; he was busy with ownership responsibilities for two businesses. But it wasn't until she remembered that Haywood's bachelor party was tonight that she stopped making excuses and relaxed.

He'd call. He'd call tomorrow.

Friday dawned clear and bright, belying the forecast of overcast skies and afternoon thunderstorms.

Kimmy went to work and prepped the lunch counter for the day's special sandwich—bacon, zucchini, and spicy mozzarella paninis. Her sauce was divine. The grill was hot. And she had a date with Booker tonight. Who cared if a storm was on the horizon?

At eleven thirty, Emory came up to the counter, wearing a

dark expression and a black bow tie. "I haven't seen any of our regulars. Today's the Burger Shack test run with their new menu. All proceeds go to charity. If I wasn't so nervous, I'd appreciate how brilliant Booker's strategy is."

"The bell hasn't tolled on us yet." But Kimmy smoothed her clean, already smooth apron. "You'll see."

By noon, she'd served five customers instead of ten and was getting nervous.

Emory walked past slowly, raising his brows at her one customer.

By one thirty, Kimmy was ready for an early lunch break. With Janet behind the counter and no line, Kimmy removed her apron and walked the two blocks to the Burger Shack under gathering clouds.

Thunder rumbled over Saddle Horn Mountain. Trepidation rumbled inside her.

Kimmy went around to the back.

"Kimmy!" Mrs. Belmonte sat at the outdoor employee table, the same one where Booker, Haywood, and Kimmy had taken breaks on summer days. She closed a travel magazine and scurried over to give her a hug. "Seems like I haven't seen you in ages." She held Kimmy a little too long. And her smile was a little too big. "I'm so glad you and Booker are finally dating."

Kimmy made a noncommittal noise and entered the Burger Shack, looking for Booker.

She'd worked at the Shack on some popular burger holidays— Memorial Day weekend, Fourth of July, Labor Day. It had never been this chaotic before. What kind of menu change had Booker made that had created such a feeding frenzy?

The chill hand of suspicion grazed the back of her neck.

Seven people were working in the kitchen. They had the fryer crackling and the grill sizzling. There was a crew working the assembly row, nervously checking the posted ingredient lists as they put together sandwiches and then placed them on a panini press.

Sandwiches.

She moved deeper into the kitchen, peering over Agnes Hempstead's shoulder to see what she was making.

Monte Cristo Waffle Sammy.

The bottom dropped out of Kimmy's world. It was one of the first few sandwiches she'd created in this very kitchen. For Booker and Hay.

She stepped to the left, looking over Joyce Jamison's shoulder.

Mac and Cheese and Pepper Panini.

Again, it was a sandwich she'd created for Booker and Hay. Her heart flattened as if someone had put it in a hot panini maker.

She circled around the assembly stations, finding more familiar recipes. Somewhere along the way, she found her anger. It flamed hot, burning romantic hopes to ash.

"Hey." Booker, standing tall but maybe not so proud. A man who knew he had some explaining to do.

Thunder rolled across the valley—*boom boom boom boom*.

A voice in her head echoed its cadence—*fool fool fool fool*.

"Outside," Kimmy told Booker. "Now." She didn't look to see whether he'd follow. She was too busy trying to make sure her legs didn't give out.

She pushed through the back door and stomped out from under the cover of the portico.

"Is something wrong, honey?" Mrs. Belmonte asked from her place at the table.

"You need to go inside, Mrs. B." Kimmy worked hard to keep from shouting. "There's a storm coming."

On cue, thunder cracked overhead. Lightning sparked through her.

Mrs. Belmonte went through the door, passing Booker on his way out.

They stared at each other. Kimmy, feeling empty and betrayed, standing unprotected from the elements. Booker, looking handsome and unreadable, standing beneath the portico.

"You said you used my recipes while you were in college." Her words were as jagged as the lightning flashing overhead.

"Yes." His answer was disappointing.

She'd expected him to apologize, maybe grovel a little. It might have been a fantasy but hearing him beg would've been good for her heartbroken soul. But no. He'd gone for taciturn. He was going to make her dig out every transgression.

Kimmy wasn't going to play that game. "I need to hire a lawyer."

His eyes widened. He probably hadn't counted on her cutting right to the chase.

Thunder shook the buildings around them. It shook the legs beneath her.

"I..." He faltered then, gaze sliding toward the Burger Shack.

She knew the family business had always been his top priority, overriding everything. Apparently even what little honor she'd ascribed to his character.

Booker swallowed. "I drew up a contract to pay for your recipes. I was waiting for the right time to show it to you."

"Now. Now would be the right time. Or last weekend before the auction. Or before that first time we kissed." *Before I fell in love with you.*

She felt so empty. There was nothing inside left for him to hurt.

Big, fat drops began to fall, striking the pavement angrily. They were like her tears, those drops. The tears she didn't want to fall.

Booker held out a hand. "Come inside. We'll talk in my office."

The pace of the drops increased, along with the pounding of her heart.

"You had your chance to talk." She was being pelted by drops but it was a good thing because tears were rolling down her face nonstop, and she didn't want Booker to realize she was crying. "You had days of chances to talk."

Her chest was folding in on itself, brought down by heartache and betrayal. And the rain was dumping on her, harder and faster, the way life was dumping on her. The way life always dumped on hardworking people reaching for the elusive American dream.

"Your lunch business is going to shut down Emory's lunch counter." She knew that for certain now. "I'll be out of a job."

Just six more weeks.

She didn't think Emory would keep her on the payroll that long.

"I'll hire you." Oh, how he was quick to speak now.

She hated him for that speed. And the hate rose up inside her like too much fiery kimchi. "I'm not going to work for you on the assembly line. Those are my sandwiches. *Mine!* And you stole them the same way you've stolen..." *My heart.*

Her breath hitched, and she could no longer speak. He'd betrayed her trust. He'd sabotaged her dreams.

She had to go. She had to run.

Into the heart of the storm.

And away from him.

Booker sank into his chair in the office and put his head in his hands.

"Everything okay, honey?" His mother closed the door behind her. "Was it safe for Kimmy to leave in this storm?"

"No, Mom. No." But he'd been unable to stop her, because every word she'd thrown at him had been true.

"If it wasn't safe, why did you let her go?" His mother came around behind the desk and put her arm around his shoulders.

"Because I've always put you and Dad and Dante first." Only

this time, he'd gone too far. He hadn't listened to Hay's warnings, even though he'd known in his heart he should have.

"I love her." The words sounded raw and lost.

"I know, honey." His mother rubbed his arm consolingly. "You've always loved her. Such a good, sensible choice."

"Love isn't sensible." If it were, he'd have done everything differently. He'd have asked Kimmy's permission. He wouldn't have stayed away while building the business, burdened with guilt. He'd have stopped trying to prove to his family that he could solve all their problems and ease all their worries. "Love isn't sensible," he said again. "Especially not in this case."

"You're selling her sandwiches, honey. Without her permission, I imagine."

He nodded.

She slapped him upside the head, not hard but with enough verve to get his attention. "What were you thinking?"

"You hit me." He stared up at his mother in amazement. She wasn't one to discipline with more than stern words. He'd never even been spanked.

"Well, someone's got to knock some sense into you." She crossed her arms over her chest. "We've never given you the credit you deserve for holding this family together. But you can't just make a mistake this humongous and then wallow in self-pity. You've got to own up to those boo-boos and set things to rights."

Booker rubbed his head. Not because it was sore but because he knew it would annoy his mother. "So my humongous mistake is just a boo-boo, eh?"

"Has Dante's experience taught you nothing about life being too short?" She began to pace. "I've been thinking about life a lot lately. About your father. About you. About Dante."

"If this is your midlife crisis, all I can do is beg you not to leave Dad." His old man would never recover.

"If it is my midlife hurrah, then I'll do as I please." She tossed up her hands. "And if I needed to divorce your father, I would. But he's having a little crisis all his own." Judging by her tone, her patience with his dad was at an end. "Why do you think I come here every day? Your father has been trying to come to terms with this new life stage. It's...It's pitiful." She shook her finger at Booker. "And if you tell him I said that, I'll deny it."

The fire in her eyes went out, and she dropped into a chair. "We can't sell Kimmy's sandwiches."

"Not without her permission, I know." He would have talked to her about it if he hadn't kissed her Monday night. Or Wednesday night. "I was afraid that I'd lose her when she found out." And now he had.

"You were blinded by the dollar signs, I suppose." His mother sighed. "Before you were born, your father tried selling pizza. Burgers and pizza. The way he talked about it, you would've thought it was the second coming." She huffed.

"What happened?"

"Our good friend Jerry over at Sunshine Pizza paid him a visit." His mom wore her I-told-you-so smirk. "He told your father he'd blanket the town with coupons and deals so great that no one would ever order pizza here again, much less burgers. And your father—valuing Jerry's friendship, of course—returned the pizza oven he'd purchased and stuck to burgers."

"You're saying I should honor the original menu of the Burger Shack." Booker stared at his hands. Burgers wouldn't finance Dante's college education.

"I'm saying it's your business." His mother stood, back straight, chin high. "Do what you will. But make it right with Kimmy. You love her. And you'd make such beautiful children together."

CHAPTER TEN

I hear you need a wedding date." Clarice stood on Kimmy's doorstep, leaning on the doorframe and shouting. "May I come in? I brought my hearing aids." She dug a small container from her raincoat pocket and rattled it gently. "Didn't want them to get wet."

If it hadn't been raining, if Kimmy hadn't been crying, she'd have politely declined. But it was raining and she had been crying. In a moment of weakness, she opened the door wider.

She ushered Clarice inside, took her coat, and found her a seat that wasn't covered in cat hair.

Skippy lumbered out, sniffing at her visitor.

"You have a three-legged cat." Clarice was putting her hearing aids in. Already, her volume was below shouting range.

"I got her from that rescue Eileen Taylor runs." Kimmy brought Clarice a glass of water and a small bowl of almonds. "I don't have much else in the house to offer you." Today was payday, and under normal circumstances, she would have done her grocery shopping after her shift ended but she'd been too drained emotionally to push a cart through the store.

"Now, let's get down to business." Clarice fiddled with her ear before patting the couch next to her, waiting for Kimmy to sit before continuing. "I'm breaking the rules here but it had to be done. I wanted you to have the perfect wedding date for Hay's wedding, someone who'd make it a most glorious evening, one you'd never forget."

"Never fear. I'm not going to go to the wedding." Kimmy couldn't bring herself to attend, not when Booker was the best man.

Skippy wound her way around Clarice's rain boots.

"That seems rather cowardly." Clarice bent to pet the cat. "And you don't strike me as a coward."

"It's more complicated than me breaking a date with Booker." And she'd given him her word, sworn over French fries. But he'd honored nothing, not even their childhood friendship. "He stole from me. And he wasn't going to tell me." That much was clear. "I went to see Rupert Harper today. He's going to represent me in this case."

According to Rupert, it was going to be drawn out and messy and cost her a small fortune. There went the money she needed to pay for her transmission.

Damn you, Booker.

"Well"—Clarice slapped her palms on her pink polyester pants—"you've picked up the pieces of your life rather quickly. More quickly than Booker, who—from what I hear—hasn't come out of his office since you stormed away from the Burger Shack."

"You mean the Burger & Sammie Shack." Apparently, a broken heart made Kimmy snarky.

"It will always be the Burger Shack to me." Clarice waved a thin hand. "Just like your memories of Booker will always be tied to your grill."

Kimmy tried to speak but she didn't know what to say, so only a strangled noise came out of her mouth.

"Anyway..." Clarice petted the cat in long strokes, head to tail. "I don't think you should hide from the wedding tomorrow with Spanky."

"Skippy."

"That's why I came here with a solution to your problems." Clarice drew herself up. "I want you to go to the wedding, and I'd like to be your plus-one."

Booker was waiting for Dante in the kitchen when he got home on Friday night.

His little brother carried his skateboard and a teenage smirk.

Where Booker took after their father, with his broad face and shoulders, Dante took after their mother, with her lean frame and delicate features. But the family value for hard work...That seemed to have shot past the mark in Dante's case.

"Come on over here, little brother." Booker pulled out a chair for him. "I made empanadas at the Shack."

"Cool. Those are my favorite." Dante sat down, dumping his stuff on the floor next to him. He grabbed the largest empanada on the plate and took a big bite, wiping at his face with his fingers and then licking his fingers clean.

Booker handed his brother a napkin. "I've been thinking about your summer," he said, being careful to sound upbeat. "I talked to Mom and Dad."

"Cool." There was less enthusiasm to Dante's response this time. He practically inhaled the next empanada.

"I got you an early graduation gift." Booker gestured toward an electric grill in an unopened box in the corner. An indoor model that was large and smokeless. "It's the same gift Dad gave me when I graduated high school. Do you remember?"

Dante shook his head, giving the grill a sideways glance. He picked up his third empanada.

"I know I told you I'd pay your college tuition and living

expenses, but something's come up, and I don't have the cash flow I'd expected to have."

Kim's drenched, tear-streaked face came to mind as powerfully as a punch to the gut.

"Wait." Dante nearly dropped his empanada. "What?"

Booker nodded, continuing to keep his tone light. "I can't keep my promise to you. You're going to have to pay part of your way through college." He gestured toward his graduation gift. "By working."

"Mom." Scowling, Dante pushed his chair back. "*Mom!*"

Booker tsk-tsked. "I wouldn't wake her. She and I already discussed this. She's one hundred percent on board, same as Dad."

"Nuh-uh." Dante may have been in honors English but he wasn't showing any of that vocabulary.

"Yuh-huh, little brother." Booker gestured toward the grill once more. "I suggest you pick up some shifts at the Burger Shack this summer. You'll need to know how to grill if you want to supplement what I give you."

"But…but…" Dante swallowed hard and said almost rebelliously, "I have cancer."

"No, you don't. You've been clear for almost twelve years." Booker clapped a hand on Dante's shoulder. "Let's look at the positives. You're healthy. You're smart. You're good at sports. And you've got a great scar to impress the girls. That and a good grill will get you far."

He left Dante sputtering.

Phase one of his plan was complete.

He wouldn't sleep a wink tonight, wondering whether everything would go well with phase two tomorrow.

CHAPTER ELEVEN

The church was decorated with white ribbons and pink roses.

Organ music, brightly dressed guests, and murmured voices filled the sanctuary proper.

Kimmy sat in the back of the church, surrounded by the board of the Widows Club—Clarice next to her near the aisle, Mims and Bitsy on her other side. She fanned herself with the wedding program.

"It's lovely," Clarice said in a loud whisper. She had her hearing aids in but Kimmy suspected she didn't have an indoor voice in her vocal arsenal. "And look, Mary Margaret is wearing a fascinator."

The redhead passed by with her fancy hat on.

"I hear the reception has a fairy-garden theme." Clarice hugged herself.

Kimmy raised her eyebrows and told her date, "I'm beginning to think you offered to be my plus-one because you needed an invitation to Sunshine's biggest event of the year."

Clarice's leathery cheeks turned rosy as Mims and Bitsy laughed.

A tuxedoed man walked behind Kimmy and around her pew and sat down in front of her.

"Hay, what are you doing out here?" Kimmy touched his arm. "Is everything okay?"

"Do you have cold feet?" Clarice asked breathlessly.

Bitsy and Mims shushed her.

"Not even a cold toe." Hay winked at Clarice. "I'm showing my face and drawing all kinds of attention..." He pointed to the assembled, who were turned to get a good look at him. He waved. "Because I thought it was important to tell you about Booker."

Kimmy crossed her arms over her chest. "This isn't middle school. I don't accept apologies by proxy."

"Good one." Clarice elbowed Kimmy.

Hay's expression sobered. "He's been in love with you longer than I've been in love with Ariana. But you've been strong-arming him into the friend zone for decades."

"True, but that doesn't excuse what he did." Kimmy waved Haywood off. "This isn't a conversation we should be having on your wedding day. This is between Booker and me."

"You're right." Booker came around from behind them and stood at the end of the pew, looking like he should wear a tuxedo every day of the year.

The entire church seemed to have turned and was watching them. No one was talking. Even the organist had stopped playing.

"Which part is she right about?" Clarice demanded.

It was a good thing she asked. Kimmy couldn't speak. Booker was supposed to be in the bowels of the church, telling Haywood what a great day this was turning out to be.

"Kimberly Anne Easley has been right about everything she's ever told me." Booker paused, stared at Clarice, and raised his brows. "*Everything.*"

"That's my cue." Clarice stood and edged toward Booker and the aisle.

Her cue? What did that mean?

"Where are you going?" Kimmy latched on to Clarice's arm, nearly dragging the old woman into her lap. "You're my plus-one."

"I...I...I have to go to the bathroom." Clarice lifted her chin and extricated herself from Kimmy's hold, leaving no buffer between Kimmy and Booker.

"Your cue?" Kimmy said, understanding dawning. A quick glance around those sitting close to her confirmed Kimmy's suspicions.

Mims and Bitsy gave her encouraging smiles. Hay winked at her. Clarice hesitated at her back.

Kimmy glared at Booker. "This was all part of your evil plan." And he'd recruited Haywood and the Widows Club board.

"Yes," Booker said unapologetically.

Kimmy's head hurt, right behind her eyes. And her heart felt as if it were withering in her chest. All the pain, all the sadness, all over her body. But she wasn't backing down. She wasn't running away. Not today.

"Hay's right too." Booker's dark gaze captured hers. "I should have told you I liked you when we were thirteen and lab partners. But it didn't strike me as romantic when you were making moon eyes at Hay while we dissected our frog."

"For the record..." Hay turned to his wedding guests. "While this was going on, I was making moon eyes at Ariana."

Booker ignored Hay and stared at Kimmy. "I should have told you I liked you when we had ice cream during freshman orientation. But you were making moon eyes at Hay."

"I sense a theme," Clarice said loudly in Kimmy's ear.

Kimmy batted at her as if Clarice were a pesky fly.

Booker ignored Clarice. His gaze never left Kimmy's face.

"I should have told you when I picked you up for prom that I loved you."

The wedding guests were quiet but at that statement, a hush fell over the room as if everyone was holding their breath. He'd gone public and declared he loved her. Kimmy wasn't holding her breath with the rest of them. She was huffing like Emory during the Thanksgiving shopping rush when they ran out of turkeys.

Booker wasn't quiet. He wasn't huffing. Hay's best man was unflappable. He kept right on talking. "I should have told you the day I drove off to college that I loved you. Or when I was away at college and missing you. I should have told you when I called. I love you, Kimmy Anne Easley."

"I sense a theme," Clarice piped up.

"I do too." Kimmy turned in her seat, facing Booker squarely. "You love me. Great."

He loves me.

Kimmy wanted to curl up into a ball and die.

"Yes. I love you." His calm was finally broken. His voice rose. "I love how you check your ego at the door. I love how you help your mom in her job and your dad in his. I love that you're restoring a food truck so you'll have a business of your own. I love how you talk. I love how you walk. I love how you dance. It's unconventional and the sweetest thing ever."

Kimmy rolled her eyes.

But Booker wasn't done. He ran a hand through his black hair, upsetting that cowlick. "I love how you don't take any guff from me. You call me out, even if it means I'll call you out in return. But mostly, I love how you love me. There were days this week when we knew we were meant for each other. It scares me how much I love you."

She waved off his fears and declarations of love. "That doesn't excuse what you did to me."

"Just so we're clear"—Booker's eyes narrowed—"and so everyone knows... We're talking about my using your sandwich recipes."

Oh, that was low. He was admitting all his sins to the town.

"Stealing." Kimmy nodded.

There were gasps from the crowd.

Kimmy played to their audience. It was obvious she was going to need them. "I forgave him for using them in college. Although it was still a betrayal of trust, but—"

"I was wrong," Booker said loud and clear. "All my life I've tried to do the right thing. I tried to be part of the team that made it possible for Dante to beat cancer. I tried to plan for the future so that I could fund my parents' retirement and my brother's college years. And in the process, I cut corners, and I leaned on you because deep down I hoped—*no, I believed*—that'd you'd forgive me. Which is why, four weeks ago, I had my lawyer draw up a contract, giving you ten thousand dollars for the right to use your recipes."

Hay's wedding guests had opinions about that. Their voices rose up and gave Booker and Kimmy a small measure of privacy.

"That's not enough, Booker." Kimmy didn't know where she got the guts to say it. She didn't believe it was true. Ten thousand dollars was a lot of money. She could pay for the food truck's transmission. She could stock the cupboards with food and fill the gas tank. She could hit the road with confidence about what was ahead.

Even as she left everything she loved behind.

"You're right about the money." Booker pulled a folded sheaf of paper from his inner pocket and ripped it up. "It's not enough."

The room went still. The pages didn't flutter to the ground. They flopped. Along with Kimmy's dreams.

"I don't understand." Reeling, Kimmy leaned back against Mims, who sat next to her in the pew.

"I'm here to offer you a better deal." Booker raised his voice so that everyone could hear his proposition. "Half ownership in the Burger & Sammie Shack."

Kimmy couldn't breathe. Not one breath. She clutched the neck of her dress and stared up at Booker in disbelief.

"Say something." Clarice whacked Kimmy on the back. "She's in shock."

Kimmy slurped in air and wheezed. "Thanks, Clarice." She shook her head at Booker. "You need a better business manager." One who'd caution him against making such bad business deals. "I'm just a sandwich maker."

"Kim." Booker dropped to one knee and took her cold hands in his. "You're more than a sandwich maker. You're the love of my life. You make me smile." His gaze shifted to Hay and then back to her. "Oh, how you make me smile."

Kimmy was horrified to discover her eyes were filling with tears.

"What good is having a business if I'm not having fun with it?" Booker ran his thumbs over the backs of her hands. "You and I...we were meant to be together. To bump elbows as we cook and to laugh when you can't convince someone to add garlic to their burger. We're meant to prep food at the same station and sneak sandwiches together on our breaks."

Was this...Was he...proposing?

Kimmy couldn't breathe. She couldn't swallow. She couldn't move.

His parents stood in the corner behind him, beaming at him. Her parents stood next to them, beaming at her. And there was Hay, of course, beaming like he'd helped plan it all. Which he probably had.

They'd known. They'd all known.

They should have known she couldn't say yes.

"Say something." Clarice whacked Kimmy on the back again.

"Shock," she said again by way of explanation when people turned frowny faces her way.

Kimmy looked at them all—the wedding guests, her family, and her friends—and still she couldn't speak.

She stared at Booker, taking in his warm gaze, his tender smile, his gentle touch. He loved her. The sincerity of his words was sinking in, having snuffed out some of the hurt and anger at what he'd done.

"I don't want to be your business partner," Kimmy said softly.

"What did she say?" someone at the front of the church asked.

"She said she doesn't want to go into business with him," Clarice shouted.

Mims and Bitsy shushed her.

"I just want to be your wife," Kimmy said in a small voice. "I knew back in the science lab that you were special. I knew at freshman orientation that I loved you. And...And...And all those times afterward. I know the difference between a crush and love." She freed one hand and cupped his cheek. "But I valued your friendship too much to step up and risk telling you how I felt." Her throat threatened to close. "In case you didn't feel the same way. Because we come from different places and we've always been going different directions."

"I can't hear," someone at the front of the church complained.

"She said..." Clarice tossed up her hands. "Ah, someone will tell you later."

"Do you know what I think?" Booker placed a kiss on her palm. "I think we've always been headed in the same direction, just on different paths. Let's meet somewhere in the middle. I think we have a lot of time to make up, you and I. And I promise you—"

"On an order of fries." Hay lifted a small paper basket of fries he'd had on the pew next to him. "Sorry, no longer hot."

Kimmy's chest constricted around her heart. These two men,

her friends, she loved them both but she was in love with only one.

"And I promise you," Booker said again, holding their hands over the fry basket, "to tell you I love you every morning, noon, and night. No more holding it in. No more holding it back."

The wedding guests heaved a collective sigh. Both sets of parents beamed. And Kimmy struggled not to cry. It was the most beautiful moment in the history of beautiful moments. And it involved food, which made it even better.

Booker drew her closer. "Kimberly Anne Easley, will you make me the happiest man alive by agreeing to be my wife?"

"Yes," Kimmy said thickly, blinking back tears. "Yes."

"I take offense to the happiest-man-alive comment," Hay said, munching on a cold French fry. "Seeing as how it's my wedding day."

"Kiss her," Clarice said, a sentiment echoed by the assembled.

And Booker did.

He made Kimmy's heart full.

He made it fuller at the wedding reception, after the bride and groom had their special dance.

Booker showed up at Kimmy's table while Clarice was admiring the reception's Bohemian decorations. He drew her to her feet. "Honey, I think I owe you a dance."

"You certainly do." Kimmy couldn't wait. She practically led Booker to the dance floor.

The DJ spun "It's Raining Men."

The dance floor filled, and after a bit of sidestepping, Kimmy let the music move her. She had her own version of the Dougie, while Booker was more of a Carlton man. It didn't matter that his dance moves were from the generation before hers. He had better rhythm than she did.

Paul danced over to Kimmy, and they did the floss and the cobra. And then he bounded over to the bride and groom.

After a few fun songs, the DJ put on a slow dance.

Booker drew her into his arms, which was exactly where she wanted to be. "Your dance moves have improved."

"Paul and I took lessons." At the junior college. "Only Paul got so good they asked him to teach." Whereas Kimmy had learned just enough steps to dance better than she had in high school.

Booker laughed. "How was your dinner?"

"My steak was grilled to perfection." She swayed closer because a man who'd ask her about food deserved an extra cuddle. "It even had enough garlic."

"I'll tell you a secret." Booker's smile morphed into a mischievous grin. "I had the chef prepare a steak specifically for you."

"I knew there was a reason I loved you." That deserved a kiss. And then another.

They might have kissed all night if the DJ hadn't spun "Can't Stop the Feeling!" That brought out more wedding guests and more dance moves than anyone could put a name to.

Everyone was outdanced by Paul but no one seemed to care. It was a wedding. And for two couples, it was one of the happiest days on earth.

EPILOGUE

How's the stock of paninis?" Kimmy ran a finger down the supply list.

Booker opened a cupboard with a Vanna White flourish. "I bought enough to feed a small army."

Kimmy scoffed. She'd go through that in one day. "What about chicken? You know I don't like the frozen stuff."

"It's all fresh." Booker opened the refrigerator. More flourishes occurred.

"What about fresh garlic?" Kimmy scanned the counter. "Did you buy enough garlic?"

"Yes." Booker produced a mesh bag large enough to hold a basketball. It was full of garlic cloves. "Can we go now?"

"No." Kimmy set down her list of supplies, wrapped her arms around Booker's neck, and kissed him thoroughly. "I don't think you've met your promised quotas of *I love you*s for the day."

"I love you, honey." Booker framed her face with his hands. "But if we don't get this food truck down to Greeley, we won't get a good spot for the festival."

"You're right." But Kimmy kissed him one more time anyway.

She loved being able to show him her love whenever she wanted. She headed toward the front of the truck and then stopped. "Wait. Who's running the Shack today?"

"Dante." Booker's younger brother was becoming skilled at the grill. "My parents went to Denver to check on our location there."

His parents had decided they wanted to be semiretired. They were part of the Burger & Sammie Shack management team.

"You think of everything." Kimmy wound her arms around his neck again.

"Not everything," Booker admitted, drawing her closer. "Just you."

ABOUT THE AUTHOR

Melinda Curtis is the *USA Today* bestselling author of light-hearted contemporary romance. In addition to her Sunshine Valley series from Forever, she's published books independently and with Harlequin Heartwarming, including her novel *Dandelion Wishes*, which is currently being made into a TV movie. She lives in California's hot Central Valley with her hot husband—her basketball-playing college sweetheart. While raising three kids, the couple did the soccer thing, the karate thing, the dance thing, the Little League thing, and, of course, the basketball thing. Between books, Melinda spends time remodeling her home by swinging a hammer, grouting tile, and wielding a paintbrush with her husband and other family members.

Learn more at:
  melindacurtis.net
  Twitter @MelCurtisAuthor
  Facebook.com/MelindaCurtisAuthor

Looking for more Western romance?
Take the reins with these cowboys from Forever!

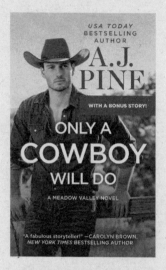

ONLY A COWBOY WILL DO
by A.J. Pine

After a lifetime of helping others, Jenna Owens is finally putting herself first, starting with her vacation at the Meadow Valley Guest Ranch to celebrate her fortieth birthday. Colt Morgan, part-owner of the ranch, is happy to help her have all the fun she deserves, especially her wish for a vacation fling. But will their two weeks of fantasy lead to a shot in the real world, or will their final destination be two broken hearts? Includes a bonus story from Melinda Curtis!

Discover bonus content and more on read-forever.com

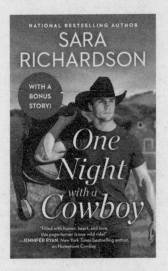

ONE NIGHT WITH A COWBOY
by Sara Richardson

Wes Harding is known as a devil-may-care bull rider—but now, with his sister's pregnancy at risk, Wes promises to put aside his wild ways and take the reins on their ranch's big charity event. Only he didn't count on his co-hostess—and little sister's best friend—being so darn distracting. One kiss with Thea Davis throws his world off-balance. But with her husband gone, Thea's focused only on raising her two rambunctious children. Can Wes convince her that he's the man on whom she can rely? Includes a bonus story by Carly Bloom!

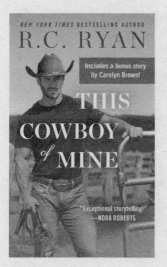

THIS COWBOY OF MINE
by R.C. Ryan

Kirby Regan just quit her career in Washington, D.C., to buy her family's Wyoming ranch. But when a snowstorm hits while she's out hiking in the Tetons, her only option for shelter is a nearby cave. She didn't realize it was already occupied...by a ruggedly handsome cowboy. Casey Merrick doesn't mind sharing his space with a gorgeous stranger, as long as they can both keep their distance—a task that begins to seem impossible as the attraction between them heats up. Includes a bonus story from Carolyn Brown!

BLACKLISTED
by Jay Crownover

In the small Texas town of Loveless, Palmer "Shot" Caldwell lives on the edge of the law. But this ruthlessly hot outlaw follows his own code of honor, and that includes repaying his debts. Which is exactly why icy, brilliant Dr. Presley Baskin is calling in a favor. She once saved Shot's life. Now she needs his help—and his protection.

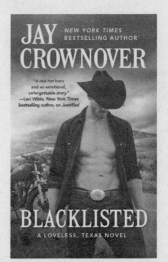

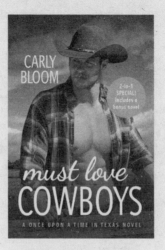

MUST LOVE COWBOYS
by Carly Bloom

Alice Martin doesn't regret putting her career as a librarian above personal relationships—but when cowboy Beau Montgomery comes to her for help, Alice decides to see what she's been missing. She agrees to help Beau improve his reading skills if he'll be her date to an upcoming wedding. But when the town's gossip mill gets going, they're forced into a fake romance to keep their deal a secret. And soon Alice is seeing Beau in a whole new way...Includes the bonus novel *Big Bad Cowboy*!